D0521998

05/17

CUNARD

❖❖

Library

Out of respect for your fellow guests, please return all books as soon as possible. We would also request that books are not taken off the ship as they can easily be damaged by the sun, sea and sand.

Please ensure that books are returned the day before you disembark, failure to do so will incur a charge to your on board account, the same will happen to any damaged books.

www.oceanbooks.com

A Distant
JOURNEY

Di
MORRISSEY

A Distant
JOURNEY

MACMILLAN
Pan Macmillan Australia

First published 2016 in Macmillan by Pan Macmillan Australia Pty Ltd
1 Market Street, Sydney, New South Wales, Australia, 2000

Cataloguing-in-Publication entry is available
from the National Library of Australia
http://catalogue.nla.gov.au

Internal images:
Chapter illustrations and endpapers by iStock.

Typeset in 12.5/15 pt Sabon by Post Pre-press Group
Printed by McPherson's Printing Group

With love to my family in Nevada and California –
especially in Palm Desert.

Acknowledgements

Love and thanks to . . .

Boris, my stalwart, who creates the space for me to write and share a happy life.

My children, Nick and Gabrielle, for your thoughts and suggestions which are welcome and insightful. It's a joy being with you both and my four beautiful grandchildren, Sonoma, Everton, Bodhi and Ulani.

Liz Adams: fun, feisty, a dear friend and as always, a forensically brilliant editor.

Samantha Sainsbury (and her dear little Ayrton): always a cool, calm and efficient coordinating editor.

Bri Collins for her kind words and eagle-eyed copy editing.

Ian Robertson, for many years of sage advice and friendship.

After twenty-five years, a big thank you to those who were there at my start at Pan Macmillan and carry on still! Ross Gibb, Tracey Cheetham, Siv Toigo, Sally Devenish, Roxarne Burns, the legendary Joybelle Macintosh, Leanne Cramond, Jeff Reeves and Robin Clark.

And, added to the originals, many thanks also to: Katie Crawford, Cate Paterson, Kirsty Noffke, Danielle Walker and Rebecca Hamilton. Plus all the sales team, and not forgetting Lisa Eady from Post Pre-Press Group for heading up the typesetting of my books and Debbie Davies from McPherson's Printing Group for the beautiful printing of all my books.

Thank you all!

For further reading on the wool industry, see *Breaking the Sheep's Back* by Charles Massey, Penguin, 2011.

Prologue

SHE COULD SMELL IT coming. Taste it. Feel it.

The rasping dryness in her nostrils and throat, the thick stickiness of the air, the burning behind her eyeballs. Her skin felt like old paper. She strained her reddened eyes at the horizon, dreading the changing colour of the sky, fearful of a golden puff, a sliver, curling above the skyline.

The stillness was all around, broken only by edgy horses, silent birds, dogs lying under the house on their bellies, ears flattened. Sheep in the paddocks, huddled together in fear.

They knew it was coming towards them. Their fate would depend on the turn of the wind. There was nowhere to go.

It was the waiting that was hardest. Men and women stood poised with whatever they had to hand, no matter how ineffectual, ready to fight their worst nightmare – an Australian bushfire.

The pregnant woman was alone, pressed to her mattress. The oppressive heat and air pressure had exhausted her, drained her of energy, of hope. They'd soaked the walls outside, even the verandah, with precious water. Containers of dam water waited, as well as blankets, towels and hessian sacks ready to soak and use as weapons against the flames.

She heard the fire truck scream uphill from the muddy dam, the weight of water in its belly challenging its tyres to grip the hot, dry grass. It made her feel less isolated, if only for a moment. She climbed off the bed and went out onto the verandah.

The heat of the day had not diminished. Across the parched brown paddocks, ominous colours had begun to bleed into the searing sky: oily red, evil orange.

The surreal sunset only confirmed her fears. As she stood gripping the rail, night closed in around her. The smell of smoke was stronger now, the air temperature and pressure changing, as though some yawning mouth was sucking the air upwards before spitting it back as specks of ash that drifted through the charred sky.

She heard rumbles in the distance as vehicles sped off to where the sneaky advances of orange tongues had begun to lick through paddocks, shrubs and trees.

Now it was real.

She pictured the crouching and rising beast, marshalling hordes of fiery sparks. The fire would form a front that stretched for miles, pushed ever forward by the howling wind behind. A single guerrilla spark could ignite trees, forests, hillsides. The relentless surge would spare nothing; growth, creature or person. Irascible, mercurial, leaping roads and rivers, it would race across the land, changing direction in a breath, allowing no escape.

She knew that the men would spread out through the paddocks, damp towels turbanned on their heads, wet cloths knotted at their throats, alert to any lick of flame, any glowing ember. They would swiftly pound at the fire with their primitive equipment, snuffing out its red heart, until another fire came to life somewhere else and threatened to race away beyond their control. Sometimes there was no help for it; the sparks would catch and a new fire would flare up to form a snapping, crackling, searing wall of flames, forcing the men to retreat as best they could before being encircled.

The smell of smoke menaced the air now. She gasped for breath and stumbled back inside. She made her way to her bed and lay down, her eyes stinging.

Not long afterwards, she heard the wind rattle against the window. Did this signal a change in its direction? Was she in the fire's path, or had it turned away?

She was so alone. She went to the bathroom and looked down at the bathtub, which was partially filled with water. *Do not leave. Keep low to the ground where the last breath of fresh air might be. If the fire comes, lie low in the water with a wet blanket over you*, she'd been told. She'd been drilled and warned. But now she was consumed by fear. Surely someone would come for her?

Time passed. Conditions deteriorated. She waited. The noise of the wind outside grew and grew, snarling and roaring like an animal released from its cage. The smoke in her eyes and throat grew worse and despair crept inside her like a shadow.

She prayed for herself. Prayed for her child. Prayed that someone, anyone, would come and find her before it was too late.

I

As THE TAXICAB STOPPED in front of the small apartment complex of Hacienda Hideaway, Babs Mason brushed her fair curls from her face and craned forward. She was immediately captivated by the pueblo-style building with its wide balconies, stucco walls and shingled roof. She turned to the small blond boy sitting next to her and forced a smile onto her tired face.

'Well, Joey, we made it. This is Palm Desert,' she said.

Though they had been on a long bus ride, the boy bounced on his seat in anticipation. At first Joey had been skittish and shy, but their fellow passengers had been kind to him, sharing candy and crackers. The changing scenery had kept him entertained, as had the occasional commentary from the Greyhound driver. But in spite of his excitement, he reached now for Babs's hand.

4

'Is this our new home, Mommy?' he asked as they climbed out of the cab.

'Sure is. C'mon, let's go explore.' Babs opened her handbag and carefully counted out the change for the cab driver, who'd driven them from the Palm Springs bus station some thirty minutes away. She glanced at the carefully folded notes in her purse. The money would have to last for some time. A taxi was a luxury, but she'd felt it was worth it for the final leg of their journey. She snapped her purse shut. The driver took her bags and a portable sewing machine from the trunk and left them beside the front door. He wished her luck, and then walked briskly back to his cab.

'Mommy, can we see the pool now?' Joey hopped impatiently from one leg to the other. Babs smiled at his enthusiasm. He'd endured such a long journey to see this much-promised pool, so Babs left their things by the entryway as the two of them went to search for it.

Hand in hand, mother and son strolled across the neatly clipped green lawns around the complex of six apartments. In the centre was a kidney-shaped swimming pool and several sun lounges. Joey raced to the edge and dipped his hand in the blue water.

'What do you think, Joey?' Babs asked.

Joey grinned. 'Can I get in now?'

'I think we should get settled first, don't you?'

Joey frowned and seemed about to argue, but one glance at Babs's face and he reluctantly nodded his head. Walking back towards their apartment, Babs saw the communal laundry, complete with modern washing machines, dryers and ironing boards. 'Goodness, you'd think with all this sun, you wouldn't need a clothes dryer,' she murmured to Joey.

'Oh, you're not allowed to hang anything outdoors,' said an older woman who was walking past them, carrying a basket of dirty washing. 'And you can't hang towels over the railings, either. They're strict about it, but it keeps standards up.' She stopped for a moment and gave Babs a welcoming smile. 'Are you going to be staying here?' she asked.

Joey hid himself behind Babs as the woman leaned down to greet him. 'Hi there,' she said. 'My name is Deidre Kramer. My husband, Sol, and I are in number two.'

Babs gave a small smile. 'I'm Barbara Mason, though everyone calls me Babs, and this is Joey, my son. We've just arrived from Portland, Oregon.'

'Well, welcome to Palm Desert,' said Deidre with a wide smile. 'That's a big trip for a little guy. I bet you and your mother are both tired after such a trip. Say, why don't you come up and have a cold drink with me. I'm sure you'd like a cookie, wouldn't you, little man?' Joey nodded shyly. Deidre dumped the basket inside the laundry. 'I can always do this later. Come on.'

Babs felt a bit hesitant about taking up Deidre's offer. She would really have preferred just to settle into the place quietly and without fuss, but the woman seemed so nice and welcoming that she thought it churlish to refuse. Besides, Babs thought, she might need a friend in the future, and Deidre might turn out to be that person.

'Thank you very much for your offer. That would be lovely.'

As Joey sat quietly eating his cookie and sipping his lemonade through a plastic straw, his mother looked admiringly around Deidre's apartment. The living area was small, but Babs thought it very stylish. The plush red lounge with its wooden legs was teamed beautifully with a low wooden buffet which sat next to the television set in its polished wooden cabinet on the far side of the room. A small but very modern dining table setting was just outside the kitchen. There was a small drinks bar in the corner of the living room, its red vinyl-covered stools matching the lounge. *How chic*, Babs thought. Several framed paintings of the surrounding desert hung on the walls.

'Deidre, you have a really lovely home. I love the way you've decorated it,' she said. 'Those paintings are beautiful.'

'Well, thank you, Babs. My husband did them,' said Deidre, plumping a pillow next to her on the couch. 'Palm Desert might not be as ritzy as Palm Springs, but it's a handy place, quiet, and not at all pricey like Palm Springs, which is going crazy with those new houses they're building. Have you heard about those?' She rolled her eyes. 'They call them "Alexanders" after the construction company that's making them. Very smart, compact and a simple design. They're also building a development they've called Twin Palms Estates. Every apartment has its own swimming pool and I can tell you, you won't get much change from twenty thousand if you want to buy one.'

Babs's jaw dropped. 'Heavens, who has that sort of money?' she exclaimed. 'Anyway, like you said, it seems quiet and clean here. I'm sure we'll be just fine.'

'Certainly the peace and quiet and the convenience here suits me and Sol, and Palm Springs is only twenty-five minutes away by bus. But don't get me wrong, Palm Desert is a go-ahead place, too. This land used to be where General Patton's tank repair facility was during the war, but after the war Edgar Bergen and some of his buddies got together and developed it. Now look at us,' Deidre said proudly.

'You mean *the* Edgar Bergen, the ventriloquist?' asked Babs, her face lighting up. 'How exciting.'

Deidre smiled. 'Is that what brought you here? The film stars?'

'Sort of,' replied Babs vaguely, looking away. 'I'd seen a lot of magazines that featured Palm Springs and I thought it looked like a very glamorous place.'

'Long way from Portland, though,' said Deidre, eyeing her guest speculatively.

Babs gazed out the window at the sunny view and shrugged her shoulders. 'Portland's not very nice in winter. It's cold and wet, and I wanted to raise my son someplace pleasant and sunny.'

'Joey seems a very nice little boy,' said Deidre, looking at the lad, whose blond head was bent intently over his drink. 'How old is he?'

'Six.' Babs glanced fondly at her son.

'He seems tall for six. Takes after his father, does he?' Deidre shot Babs a curious look.

Babs had no intention of discussing Joey's father with Deidre on such a short acquaintance, so she cleared her throat and returned to the subject of Portland.

'Yes, I wanted to live someplace where the sun shines all the time. Besides, Portland isn't always a very safe city to live in. There's a lot of crime.'

Deidre nodded. 'Well, you'll get a lot of sun here, all right. It gets up over a hundred degrees in summer. But don't worry, you'll get used to it. It's a dry heat, but you can't go running around in the middle of the day, young man,' Deidre said, turning to Joey. 'Still, I expect you'll enjoy using the pool. Can he have another cookie, Babs?'

Joey gravely accepted another cookie from Deidre.

'Joey, say thank you to Mrs Kramer,' prompted Babs. Joey nodded but didn't speak. He slouched down in his chair and nibbled on the cookie despondently. He looked tired. Babs gathered her handbag and stood up. 'Well, Deidre, it's been so nice chatting to you. I'd better get our bags up to our apartment. Can you tell me if there's a diner close by? I simply couldn't cook this evening after our trip.' Babs took Joey by the hand and helped him up.

'Oh, there sure is. Betsy Morgan has a cute little place half a block down called Betsy's,' Deidre said as she walked them to the door. 'Not a very adventurous name, but she does good food. It's all decked out in red and white, you can't miss it. Can I help you with your bags?'

'That's kind of you, but I'll manage. I haven't got very much.'

'So it's just the two of you, then?' asked Deidre as Joey finished the last of the cookie.

'Yes, that's right. Just Joey and me,' said Babs as she steered Joey out the front door. 'What do you say to Mrs Kramer, Joey?'

Joey murmured a thank you as Deidre patted his head and waved them off. 'You and I will be friends, Joey. You'll see.' She turned to smile at Babs. 'Just holler if there's anything you need, Babs. It's a nice bunch of folk around here, you'll soon fit in.'

*

As soon as Babs opened the door of their apartment, she smiled. It had exactly the same layout as the Kramers' and was wonderfully light and airy, although the furniture that came with it was not nearly as smart as Deidre's. In one corner of the living area was a brown sofa. There was no buffet or television set, although there was a small book-case and an incongruously large dining table surrounded by four solid, if unfashionable, chairs.

Just the perfect place for my sewing machine, Babs thought to herself.

Putting her bags and sewing machine down, she and Joey explored the bedrooms. There was a large main bedroom and a smaller one off to one side. She was pleased to see that there was an air-conditioning unit as well as large built-in closets. *How modern*, she thought. Next to the bedrooms was a good-sized bathroom.

Although the furnishings in the apartment were basic, everything seemed clean and functional. She hoped they would do well here. She had taken such a big gamble with their lives. She took a deep breath and closed her eyes for a moment. She tried to quell the anxious knot in her stomach. She just had to trust that she had made the right decision.

After supper at Betsy's Diner, Babs and Joey walked hand in hand in the late afternoon light along the dusty road at the edge of town. Joey was subdued and Babs peered at him. He was often anxious and she was worried about how he would handle the move. She hoped this fresh start was the right thing for him. They paused and stood on the edge of the road. Behind them lay the small village of Palm Desert with its neat rows of houses and apartments, the carefully planned streets coupled with well-watered emerald green grass verges. In front of them the desert valley stretched out towards the base of the mountains.

'Joey, will you just look at that view. So much space.' She pointed to a distant mountain topped with white snow. 'That mountain looks like an ice-cream cone, doesn't it?'

A small grin appeared on Joey's pinched face. 'Can we make snowballs, Mom?'

'The snow's too far away to walk to, honey, but maybe one day we'll go up there.'

Joey grew serious again. 'Mom, when am I going to see Dad? Is he coming to Palm Desert, too?' he asked anxiously.

Babs inhaled sharply. She had been dreading this question. She knelt down in front of Joey. 'Darling, I think it might be better if we don't see Daddy for a while,' she said gently. 'But you're going to love it here. It's so beautiful. We're going to have a marvellous new life, a better one, you'll see.' Joey nodded and Babs put her arms around him and hugged him briefly. Releasing Joey, Babs straightened up and looked across to the serene mountains. She thought about her plans for the future. She wondered if she had been too optimistic about them. What if she failed? She couldn't go back to Portland. She felt fear rise in her chest.

'Mom, look at the horse!' said Joey. He tugged at her hand and pointed down the road. A horse was trotting towards them, whinnying loudly. Sacks of what looked like corn hung behind the saddle, and in front of the rider sat a small boy, younger than Joey. The man was dressed in leather chaps and a faded blue shirt, while the boy had straight dark hair, cut below his ears. Joey stared at them, fascinated.

'Indians,' said Babs quietly. 'That's something you don't see in Portland.'

As she stood there with Joey, watching the Indians, a car drove by, slowing as it passed, its occupants giving her a curious look, then a nod and a smile. The graceful woman with sad blue eyes smiled back, then, swinging her son's arm, she turned and they walked back to their apartment. In the distance glittered the glamorous town of Palm Springs, waiting there for them to discover.

*

The next day, after Babs had unpacked their belongings, she and Joey made their first foray into the swimming pool. Joey was beside himself with excitement and Babs spent quite some time with him, splashing and playing. When she saw Deidre Kramer coming over to the pool, Babs stepped from the water, still keeping a watchful eye on Joey, who was under strict instructions to stay at the shallow end.

Deidre greeted Babs warmly. 'I see you've made it into the pool.'

Babs shyly returned her smile. 'It's wonderful. I never thought I'd be able to swim in a private pool like this. Joey is in seventh heaven. I hope he learns to swim properly quickly.'

11

'I'm sure he will, if you bring him here every day.' The two women settled themselves on the plastic sun lounges and Babs mentioned the Indians she and Joey had seen the previous evening.

'They're the local Agua Calientes,' Deidre explained. 'They tend to keep to themselves on their missions, even though they pretty much own the joint.'

'What do you mean by that?' Babs asked, keeping Joey in sight as she glanced at Deidre.

'The Indians own all the land around these parts. They just lease it to us whitefaces.' Deidre laughed and adjusted her sunglasses. 'Say, did you hear that the Rat Pack have moved into Palm Springs? Frank Sinatra has built a beautiful home over there. I'm told his pool is shaped like a piano!' Babs sensed that Deidre liked nothing better than to talk about the film stars who lived and stayed in Palm Springs. She was somewhat relieved not to have to talk about her own situation.

'Imagine that. I just love him, and Dean Martin, too. Deano is so funny with Jerry Lewis,' said Babs. 'I can't wait to see Palm Springs properly. We're getting settled in today, but we might go over there tomorrow and look around and maybe have a little lunch.' She said it lightly, but going out to lunch was not something she would be doing very often. She thought again of her limited funds, but decided it would be worth the expense to see Palm Springs. Besides, she knew she needed to bite the bullet and start looking for work, which would more than justify the bus fare.

'You do that, Babs. There's a whole bunch of new stores in the plaza: I. Magnin, Bullock's, and so many other pretty places for shopping. Beats LA and San Francisco, if you ask me.'

Babs nodded. She wouldn't be buying anything for herself there. She had spent a year saving hard for this move to California, carefully squirrelling money away until she had enough to afford the Greyhound bus fare as well as three months' rent on the apartment in Palm Desert, which she had quietly been able to secure with the help of a trusted realtor friend back in Portland. She had sworn her friend to secrecy about her plans and she could only hope that he kept his word to stay silent. She fidgeted on the lounge chair and pushed away the scary thought that she and Joey might be found here in Palm Desert. She tried to focus on the here and now. She was eager to catch the bus into Palm Springs not just because it was famous as a playground for the stars, but because she yearned to see the place she had dreamed of for so long. The idea of Palm Springs had kept her going. She needed to see it with her own eyes.

*

The following day Babs was agog as she walked down Palm Canyon Drive holding Joey's hand. She walked slowly so Joey could keep up and to give her time to take in everything: the stores, the sights, the people strolling in the sunshine. She noticed that the teenage girls mostly dressed in a uniform of colourful tops and tapered pants, some capri length, although she saw one or two in dungarees, carefully folded up at the hem. The boys wore shirts with tightly rolled-up sleeves, their hairdos slick and shiny. She noticed that a lot of older men sported checked shirts enhanced with embroidery, their outfits complemented by shoestring ties and fancy cowboy boots. It seemed to Babs that almost anything went in desert attire.

'Mom, look at those cars!' Joey pointed to the shiny cars of all colours with gleaming chrome grilles, elaborate trims and enormous tailfins that were parked on either side of the street. Then he stopped and stared in fascination as a convertible cruised down the block.

'The car roof slides down so you can be in the sunshine,' Babs explained. 'It must be nice to have the wind in your face,' she added, looking at a passenger wearing a scarf knotted under her chin and sunglasses that turned up at the corners like cats' eyes.

Babs was awed by the fancy stores they passed. Taking a deep breath, she squeezed Joey's hand and steered him into a clothing shop. The saleswomen in the store were heavily made-up and expensively dressed, with lots of jangly gold jewellery, and looked rather unfriendly. Suddenly Babs felt self-conscious. She knew she must look out of place in a store like this, wearing just sandals and a simple cotton sundress she'd made herself. *Maybe they are allowed to wear clothes from their shops*, Babs told herself.

Politely she asked if they needed a shop assistant. When she said that she'd had no experience at all in retail, she was given a withering look and her inquiry was dismissed out of hand. She tried a few more stores and received the same treatment. She and Joey continued to wander along the main street for a while, but by lunch-time Joey was tired, hot and hungry, and Babs was feeling dispirited.

'These restaurants look too expensive. Let's get a soda at that drugstore over there,' she suggested. The pair sat in silence as they slowly drank their sodas, making them last. Eventually Babs spoke, trying to inject some light-heartedness into her voice.

'So, do you think you're going to like living in the desert, Joey?' She forced a smile.

Her son dragged his straw around the bottom of his glass, trying to suck up the last of the creamy bubbles. He nodded. 'I guess.'

'That's good, honey, so do I. Shh, don't slurp, that's not nice.' Joey stopped and then sat silently flicking his straw. Babs smoothed her son's hair and gently turned down the collar on his shirt. She'd spent a couple of evenings embroidering the red and yellow train, which

14

she'd copied from one of his picture books, on the pocket, and then she'd trimmed around the collar, the buttonholes and the edge of the short sleeves with the same red thread. His shorts were made from material the same dark red as the trim on the shirt. Babs loved sewing and she knew that she had a talent for it. Her grandmother had taught her as well as her sisters, and they rarely bought ready-made clothes. Grandma French had been a wonderful seamstress. She had made Grandad's suits as well as overcoats and jackets for all of them. Babs smiled to herself when she thought of the formal portrait her grandparents had always proudly displayed, a picture of herself with her teenaged sisters, Alice and Deborah, all wearing pretty dresses lovingly made by their grandmother. In the portrait Deborah had a serious expression while their older sister Alice looked poised and beautiful, as usual. But Babs, very much the baby of the family, wore a big fat bow in her hair and shiny Mary Jane shoes, and had one of her socks sliding down her calf. Babs had never been quite as elegant or as self-assured as her sisters, but she'd taken to sewing as if she'd been born to it, and was very grateful to her late grandmother for passing on her skills.

Thinking of the well-dressed young people she'd seen out on the street, Babs recalled the way young women dating local boys and going to parties and dances hated wearing the same dress more than twice, and Babs was no exception. For very little money she could buy attractive fabric and create pretty outfits for all occasions. She had developed an eye for quality early on and had begun experimenting with her own ideas and patterns. She always felt confident with her skills. She sighed. That all seemed a long time ago now. She counted out some money from her purse to pay the bill and frowned at the number of notes and coins left. She was trying to be as frugal as possible, but her money wouldn't last forever. She needed to find a job quickly. Taking Joey by the hand, she led him to the bus stop. Finding work would have to begin in earnest very soon.

*

A few days later, Babs enrolled Joey in the local elementary school. He was clingy and anxious about starting at a new school but his teacher seemed kind and distracted him with the promise of a cuddle with the class pet, a guinea pig, while Babs snuck out. She decided to go into Palm Springs and try again for a job, this time unencumbered by a small boy. She took the bus and began where she'd left off on Palm Canyon Drive, asking in several shops if there were any positions for shop assistants. No one was willing to employ an unskilled shop assistant. As she went from store to store, she became increasingly distressed. She had really thought that she would have no trouble finding a job, but no one seemed interested in her. She was not prepared to give up, however, so for the next week she continued to take the bus into Palm Springs while Joey was at school. But when asking for work, the answer was always the same. Finally, in one very up-market shop, where the response to her request was also negative, Babs asked pleadingly, 'But how can I get experience if no one gives me a chance?'

The woman shrugged. 'I see your point. I'm sorry that I can't be of more help.'

'So am I,' said Babs. She turned and began to walk towards the door. Passing a rack of children's clothes, she picked up a little girl's smocked dress and looked at the price. 'Heavens, you could almost buy a car for that,' she exclaimed.

'People around here have plenty of money. They are quite prepared to pay for the best, and they do,' said the sales assistant.

Babs stood looking at the little dress and then said slowly, 'How does the shop go about getting the best clothes?'

The assistant sniffed. 'Mrs Bourke is the buyer for our children's range. She sources them through the big stores and manufacturers, but sometimes buys handmade one-offs. People bring her samples and she decides what to take. She's a bit of a dragon, but she has excellent taste, and this place is well known for its exclusive babywear, although it's only a very small part of our stock.'

Babs looked closely at the children's clothes and an idea bloomed in her mind. 'I'm sure I can make clothes as good as these,' said Babs as confidently as she could. 'Can anyone bring in samples?'

The assistant shrugged. 'I don't see why not.'

'Great,' said Babs, smiling broadly. How silly she had been. She would do something that she was good at, not something about which she knew nothing. She told the shop assistant that she would be back sometime soon to see Mrs Bourke, and, her head filled with ideas, she caught the bus back to Palm Desert. As soon as Joey went to bed that night, she began writing lists of what she would need to start her sewing enterprise.

The next day, after Joey had gone to school, Deidre asked Babs in for a morning coffee and the younger woman shyly revealed her plans for making children's clothes. 'But the thing is, Deidre, I have no idea where to buy what I need. I hope you can help.'

'That's a wonderful scheme,' said Deidre. 'I noticed Joey was dressed beautifully, but I hadn't realised you'd made the outfits. And your clothes . . . now I understand how you had the right kind of wardrobe for the desert after living in Portland! Clever you. Now, what do you need?'

'I brought my grandmother's sewing machine with me, but I had to leave most of my materials behind in

Portland. I'll need to source fabrics and threads and that sort of thing,' Babs explained.

'Sol can take you tomorrow. He knows everyone and everything around here, so you'll be able to find what you need, I'm sure.'

Sol was almost as round as he was tall, always cheerful and utterly in love with Palm Springs. Babs sometimes thought that the city had been founded just to make him happy. The following afternoon he drove her to places like Cathedral City, Bermuda Dunes, Indian Wells and Indio, where Babs bought fabrics, trims, needles and threads and a couple of new attachments for her old machine. In one of the shops, she was excited to find a small smocking pleater.

'Wow, having one of these will save me so much time!' Babs exclaimed. 'It will be a wonderful investment. I'll have to finish the smocking by hand, but having this will sure speed things up.'

Although it was obvious that Sol didn't understand a thing about the art of smocking, he smiled indulgently at her excitement.

Babs was delighted to find that shopping with Sol meant that no one expected her to pay retail prices so, later that night, when she added up what she'd spent, she realised to her relief that, thanks to her kind neighbour, she had saved quite a bit.

For the next three weeks, as soon as Joey had left for school, Babs set up her sewing machine on the dining room table and established a working routine. She drafted patterns, sewed and smocked and embroidered. Her dainty baby dresses were decorated with little animals and delicate flowers in lazy daisy, bullion and fly stitches, as well as neat French knots. She enjoyed the work and thought the outfits she'd created were adorable. She just hoped the buyer at the boutique liked them too. She didn't want to think about what would happen if no one bought her stock.

Then, just before Joey was due to arrive home from school, she would pack everything up and be ready to take her son for a swim in the kidney-shaped swimming pool. Joey was thriving in his new environment, no longer withdrawn and anxious, so Babs was reassured that she had done the right thing in moving them both to California. At night sometimes she still felt frightened, afraid that at any moment they would be dragged home, but as the weeks passed, her fear dimmed and she too began to enjoy their sunny new home.

Most afternoons they were joined by Deidre and Sol. Sol had owned a string of laundromats in Sacramento and Santa Barbara, but had sold them when he retired. In his new-found free time he'd taken up painting as a hobby and, much to Deidre's surprise, he was actually quite good. Sol had offered to teach Joey to paint. So one afternoon Babs and Joey went to Sol and Deidre's apartment for Joey's first lesson. Sol had somehow found a small easel and had set up a little canvas with several cans of bright paint and a paintbrush sitting on a stool nearby. He began patiently showing the boy a few painting techniques, encouraging Joey to try painting the desert scenery, while Deidre and Babs watched.

'What else do you do now that you've retired, Sol?' Babs asked, sipping some lemonade that Deidre had made for the four of them.

'Oh, he's quite the big cheese at the Historical Society,' said Deidre, before Sol could speak. 'Can't stop him talking about the history of Palm Springs. He gives talks and tours, you know.'

'We'll have to do a tour with you sometime then,' said Babs. She glanced at Joey's canvas. He had painted a bright blue sky and a large sun, and was now attempting to add a four-legged blob that Babs guessed might be a horse.

'You're doing so well, Joey,' she said. He beamed.

'You know, Joey, many famous artists have been inspired by the desert and its beautiful landscape,' said Sol. He disappeared into the back of the house and returned with a print. 'This one is by one of my favourites, Carl Eytel.' The artist had captured the dry, scrubby plains perfectly. Babs glanced around the room and her gaze fell upon a pile of large canvases leaning against a chair. She got up and went over to the paintings, tilting one forward to glance at the canvas behind.

'These paintings are beautiful,' said Babs. 'Are they yours, Sol?'

'Yes,' said Sol, looking pleased. 'Actually, those paintings are a series about the founding of Palm Springs.' He turned to Joey. 'They tell a story. Would you like to hear it?'

'Yes, please,' said Joey, putting down his paintbrush.

Sol pulled out the first painting and gestured at three figures, two larger and one smaller, travelling with a horse and burro through boulders, dunes, cacti, clumps of agave, mesquite trees and the tough, thorny plants growing amongst rocks and sand. 'About seventy years ago, an Indian agent, that's a man who's supposed to look after the Indians, his son and a guide were travelling through the hot, dry desert. The boy was sick and Pablo, their Indian guide, had promised to show them some magic springs that would make the boy well again.'

'What was wrong with the boy?' asked Joey, frowning.

'He had an illness called tuberculosis,' said Sol. He pulled the second painting forward. 'One evening, they made camp.' He showed Joey a picture of the horse and the sturdy little burro tethered in the shade of an ancient fig tree. Beside them stood a buckboard and a wagon, both covered with a film of sand and desert dust. Everything was dwarfed by the arrow-straight palms that rose majestically overhead.

Sol gestured to another figure on horseback in a corner of the painting. 'On a nearby rise, Pablo halted his horse as he surveyed the valley below.'

Joey was looking at the painting with interest. He pointed to the shadowy mountain ranges circled by sand dunes in the background.

'I've seen these mountains,' he said.

'I'm sure you have,' said Sol, smiling at the boy. He turned back to the painting. 'To the south-east was an ancient lake and directly to the south rose the Santa Rosa ranges. In the south-west were canyons lined with palms, and towering eleven thousand feet above it all were the San Jacinto Mountains.' Babs spied the jagged peaks of the mountain range ringing the edge of the picture.

'Wow,' said Joey.

Sol pulled another painting from the pile. It depicted the ranges in a soft lavender colour, their outlines etched against the late afternoon sky. In the picture, the man and his son had removed their boots and clothes and were standing in a bubbling pool of water, while their guide was watching nearby. Babs could almost imagine what it would be like to be there: the air dry and fresh, a little breeze rustling the palms. Looking closely, she noticed the detail of the painting. The man was stocky but the boy, though smiling, looked frail and thin. The guide was squatting by the pool, smoking a roughly made cigar.

Sol returned to his story. 'Finally, after their long trip, they reached the magic springs and the boy laughed as he paddled in the water.

'"It's warmer than a bath, Papa!" he said.

'"These are healing waters, son. They will make you well and strong," said his father.'

Sol pulled out another painting of the valley with the magic pool. Water coursed down from the mountain peaks.

Simple thatched huts nestled close to the hot springs, and Babs could see Indians painted in the foreground.

'The man and his son stayed with Pablo in his village and Pablo's wife served them mushy beans and baked hearts of agave on flat roasted breads cooked over the small fire outside the huts. Each day the three of them would return to the springs in the lingering light of the afternoon to soak their bodies in the healing waters.

'Now, the man's name was John Guthrie McCallum, and he thought that the only way his son would get better would be if he moved his family away from the damp and cold climate of San Francisco to start a new life where the weather was warmer and drier. So he purchased some land to build a home for himself.' Sol paused and pulled out the final painting. It showed the same man, his wife, more children and more Indians in front of a simple adobe home surrounded by planted fruit trees. 'He called the place Palm Springs,' said Sol.

'So that's how the place started,' said Babs.

'Did the little boy get better?' Joey asked.

Sol paused and answered slowly. 'Yes, the little boy was fine.'

Babs and Sol exchanged a glance. Babs appreciated Sol telling Joey a white lie. Joey would have had night-mares for weeks if he'd realised that the boy had died.

'Poor old John McCallum,' said Sol. 'Things didn't go well for him at all. He and a friend devised a scheme to irrigate Palm Springs, and spent a lot of money trying to make the desert bloom, but he sold the land to the wrong people. Most of them were sick, so they couldn't make a go of it and went back to the coast without paying for their land. As a result, old John almost went broke.'

'Then why did Palm Springs keep growing?' asked Babs.

Deidre took up the story. 'McCallum had several children, but it was his youngest, Pearl, who carried on his legacy. She married Austin McManus, who was a property developer, and she utilised her father's land much more successfully,' she said.

'She built the Oasis Hotel in the twenties. You know, that's the tower you can see on Palm Canyon Drive,' said Sol. 'All the movie stars used to stay in the rooms in that tower.'

'Which movie stars?' asked Babs.

'Oh, Clark Gable, John Wayne, Loretta Young, even Shirley Temple,' said Deidre, returning to her favourite subject. 'Pearl also developed some estates, as well as establishing the tennis club.'

'I wish I could see some of the famous stars,' said Babs wistfully.

'You will,' Deidre assured her.

'Mom, what do you think of my painting?' Joey asked. Babs glanced at the canvas, which was now covered in bright splodges.

'It's marvellous, darling, well done.' Babs hugged Joey. 'Now say thank you to Sol for teaching you.'

'Thank you, Sol,' said Joey, smiling brightly.

'Come back and paint any time, little man,' said Sol.

*

Working all day and every day, Babs had eventually managed to design and make a dozen little outfits for babies and toddlers. One morning, after Joey left for school, she made her way into Palm Springs carrying her small suitcase of clothes carefully folded in tissue paper. Her money was now all but gone and she was feeling very anxious. What if no one wanted to buy her clothes? What would she do for money? How would she pay the rent? She tried to steady her nerves as she headed along North

23

Palm Canyon Drive to the shop where she'd seen the expensive baby clothes. As soon as she walked in, she saw the same shop assistant she'd spoken to on the previous occasion and went over to greet her.

'I don't know if you remember me,' said Babs nervously, 'but I was talking with you a few weeks ago about children's clothes.'

The assistant peered at her. 'Yes, I do. How can I help you now?'

'You told me that your buyer Mrs Bourke might be interested in handmade clothes. I've spent the last few weeks designing and hand-making baby clothes and I was hoping that she would consider stocking them here.'

The assistant pursed her lips. 'I can't guarantee that she will without an appointment.'

Babs's heart sank. 'I see. I didn't understand. I haven't done this before,' she said despondently. She felt completely out of her depth in this unknown commercial world. But then she thought of Joey, who was being so brave in this new place, and tried to pluck up some courage. She'd gone to a lot of trouble, and she knew her clothes were pretty and well made. She couldn't just give up. Taking a deep breath, she took one of her designs out of her suitcase. 'It would just take a moment.'

The assistant studied the sample. 'Wait a moment, I'll go and have a talk with her. It can't do any harm.'

As the woman hurried away, Babs looked around the store. She had to admit that the clothes in the shop were beautiful. There were silk, lace and embroidered cocktail dresses, stylish capri pants, fashionable halter-neck tops, as well as the glitziest sandals she had ever seen. It was certainly a world away from the clothes stores in Portland. And the prices! She couldn't believe that anyone in the world would be prepared to pay so much for a pair of shoes.

'So you want to see me, do you?' said a voice behind her.

Babs turned around to be met by an elegantly dressed woman who she guessed was in her mid-fifties.

'I'm Mrs Bourke, and I believe you have some items you want to show me. Please come to my office and I'll take a look. I understand you've been quite persistent.' She was brisk but not unfriendly.

As soon as they arrived in Mrs Bourke's wood-panelled office, Babs introduced herself and opened her suitcase. She began to lay out little girls' dresses, boys' shirts and baby clothes on the office desk.

Silently Mrs Bourke picked up the clothes and examined them. Finally she said, 'I take it that you made these yourself? I think that some are quite saleable.'

Babs almost collapsed with relief.

'I think I can take this,' said Mrs Bourke, lifting up a daintily smocked baby's dress. 'And this little boy's outfit with the yellow ducks is quite charming. Perhaps I'll have this little frock in white as well. Now, I'll need them in a variety of sizes. Do you think I could have them by next week? If the standard remains as good as this, we have a deal.'

On a piece of paper, Mrs Bourke wrote down the sizes and quantities of the clothes she wanted Babs to make and the price she would pay, so that there would be no mistakes. Babs's elation was tempered only slightly by the fact that not all her handmade clothes were wanted, but when she saw the price Mrs Bourke was offering, she felt her face flushing with outrage. It was a pittance in comparison with what the store would charge for them. Nevertheless, Babs thought she had no choice other than to agree. She needed the money. And she figured she had to start somewhere, so she nodded and thanked Mrs Bourke for her time, promising to get the order to the shop by the end of the following week, although she wondered how she would ever be able to accomplish it.

'By the way,' said Mrs Bourke, 'what age range do your designs intend to cover?'

'From newborn up until six or seven,' replied Babs. She didn't want to limit herself just to baby clothes.

'And what is the name of your label, or shall I put my store name on them?'

Babs was about to say that she didn't have a design label, but suddenly an idea popped into her head.

'I'm sorry I didn't have time to do the labels. It's "Heaven to Seven", Mrs Bourke. I'll have my labels on the clothes when I bring them in next week.'

After she left the shop, she felt her knees go weak. She sat down on a nearby bench and took a deep breath. She'd done it. She'd made a sale. She and Joey would be able to stay in Palm Desert. Gathering her things, she smiled to herself as she walked down the street, but as she swung the suitcase, she realised that her bag was still full of unwanted samples. Maybe she should show them to other stores? But which ones? Over the road she saw the tower of the El Mirador Hotel. They must have a shop in there, she thought, as she hurried across to the spacious porte-cochère. From the luxurious foyer she looked out at lawns and cabanas as she made her way across to the hotel shop. She could see right away that it would be unlikely to sell baby clothes, but now that she was here, she thought there was no harm in asking. Fortunately, the young man behind the counter turned out to be a mine of information.

'You're right. We don't sell baby clothes. This is more gifts for the ladies,' he said. 'Flowers, chocolates and jewellery, that sort of thing, but you could try I. Magnin. And if you keep going in that direction,' he pointed, 'you'll come to a store that sells nothing but kids' clothes. I bet you could do well in there.'

Babs thanked him for his suggestions and said, 'It must be great working here. I bet you see lots of film stars all the time.'

'Sure do.' Suddenly the young man lowered his voice and in a conspiratorial tone said, 'Say, if you want to see some now, just wander out to the pool. No one will stop you, and if they do, just say you're a friend of Mac's. That's me.'

Thanking him, Babs quietly made her way towards the hotel pool. She walked outside and there, sitting on sun lounges, were Tony Curtis and his wife, Janet Leigh, talking to Robert Wagner and Natalie Wood. She tried not to stare, but she found it almost impossible to believe that she was so close to some of her favourite film stars. Babs retreated into the hotel lobby before anyone asked any awkward questions, and headed out into the sun again.

Taking the young man's advice, she found the store which specialised in baby clothes and they were pleased to give her an order, although what they were willing to pay her was only marginally better than Mrs Bourke's offer. The saleslady at I. Magnin was enthusiastic about her clothes, but said they'd want them exclusively and that their buyer was in Los Angeles. Still, on the whole, Babs felt pleased with the way things had gone. She felt that she had a toe in the water and was sure that if she could maintain a supply of clothes to these stores, things could only get better. At least she'd be able to pay the rent, and maybe even save enough to buy a television set. Things were finally looking up.

*

That night, after she'd tucked Joey into bed, Babs gazed at the view from her bedroom window. For the first time in a long time, she felt positive about her future. It had been a hard road. Unbidden, memories of the past she'd fought to escape washed over her. Howard's face flashed into her mind and she shivered. She went to the front door and checked it was locked. Satisfied, she returned to her bedroom. She hoped she would never have to see Howard again. She sighed as she lay down on her bed and gazed out at the darkened sky. She'd been so young, so naïve, when she'd met Howard. He was older than her and had seemed so dashing. He'd impressed her with his stories about the war, where he'd won a Purple Heart. He had seemed so sophisticated compared to her high school friends. He'd pursued her and Babs had been smitten by him. One evening, in the back of his roomy old Buick, Howard had persuaded her to make love. It was painful and rough and, when it was finally all over, Babs had felt confused, disillusioned and frightened. Not long afterwards, she had discovered she was pregnant. Howard was reluctant to get married, but her father insisted. The wedding had been simple and rushed. The trousseau, beautiful wedding gown and blissful entry into marriage that Babs had always dreamed about hadn't eventuated. Her father had been tight-lipped, sad and stoic, and Babs had felt ashamed that she'd let him down.

At first the marriage had worked just fine, but gradually their relationship deteriorated and rows became commonplace. Then one night Howard had hit her. Babs was shocked and horrified. Howard apologised and promised it would never happen again. Babs forgave him, and for the sake of their marriage and Joey, she vowed to try harder. But it had happened again and again. Her efforts to tiptoe around him, trying to please him, only seemed to make him more furious. On and on went the cycle of blows, tears and apologies. Babs had felt desperate and trapped. She'd tried to speak to her father about her situation, but he'd just told her to stop making Howard angry

28

and urged her to stay with her husband for the sake of their child. His lack of empathy had made Babs wish, not for the first time, that her beautiful mother had not died when she was a child, so that she was still around to help her find a solution. Her sisters had not been a lot of help either. Deborah, the sibling with whom she'd had the closest relationship, had moved to Spokane, in Washington, nearly four hundred miles away, and Alice was too bound up in her own life to be of much use. When Babs had tried to bring it up, neither of them quite understood what was happening, and Babs just hadn't been able to bring herself to explain in detail. She felt too ashamed about her disastrous marriage to really tell them what was going on. When her father had died suddenly of a heart attack, Babs had been devastated. She had always felt that, if things between herself and Howard became too bad, her father would be there as a refuge and now even that safe haven had been taken from her.

Then one day, in a rage, Howard had slapped Babs in front of Joey. The little boy cried. Howard had stormed out of the house, shouting that he was sick of the sight of both of them. Babs had taken Joey in her arms and soothed him. Holding her son, she'd decided that the only way she could give him a happy future was by running away. The prospect of leaving home had terrified her. She had never held a proper job and never travelled far. Still, she'd known that she had to get out, so for a year she'd saved every cent she could and she hadn't given Howard any clue of her plans, hoping that before he knew what had happened, they'd be long gone. She'd heard from Alice that Howard had asked around after he'd discovered them gone, but hadn't been able to locate them. Babs feverishly hoped her luck would hold and Howard would stay away. She had longed to live in Palm Springs, a place where, she had been sure, dreams came true; a place where she and Joey could start over. And here they were. She raised her chin as her eyes drank in the skyline. A new home. A new life. She'd done it.

*

Over the next week, Babs worked hard to meet the orders she had taken. Deidre and Sol were always there to look after Joey when the need arose, but gradually, as she got into a routine, Babs was usually able to pack up her sewing and clear the dining room table just before Joey got home, so that the two of them could spend time together before she prepared dinner.

All the shops were pleased with Babs's work and they continued to give her orders. Babs and Joey settled into the pleasant life of the village and Babs even joined the tennis club, playing at night under lights when it was cool, which she thought was a wonderful novelty. Joey grew more confident as he became accustomed to life in Palm Desert. He loved his school, his new friends and swimming. He asked about his father less and less as the weeks went by, and Babs heard nothing from Howard. Gradually, she relaxed, letting go of the anxiety that had gripped her for so long. Seeing Joey flourish, Babs knew the decision to leave Portland had been the right one.

With her work, a growing son and new friends, Babs's life was full, and one day she was astonished to realise that two years had passed since she and Joey had arrived in Palm Desert. But then a small cloud appeared on the horizon in the form of her eldest sister, Alice, who had written to announce she was coming to visit. *And maybe if I like it, I'll stay.* Alice could be so overbearing and bossy. As fond as she was of her sister, Babs was also fond of her new-found independence and feared that Alice would try to undermine it.

*

The morning of her sister's arrival, Babs was nervous. She stood in front of the mirror and smoothed her hair, which she'd had straightened at the beauty salon. She'd painted her nails in the coral shade that everyone was wearing lately. Babs thought about the relationships she'd had with her two sisters. Deb had been gentle and easy to get along with, but she had married a furniture salesman and moved to Washington state when Babs was still young, so Babs had seen less and less of her over the years. Deb had one child, Cynthia, who was always called Cindy. Although Babs didn't see a lot of her niece, she loved sending her pretty little dresses to wear. In spite of the distance between them, Babs had always loved Deb and was shocked when she learned that her sister had been diagnosed with cancer, just as their mother had been. When she died, leaving her husband to raise their teenage daughter alone, Babs had carried on making an effort to keep in touch with her niece, writing her letters, ringing occasionally, and continuing to sew special clothes for her.

Her other sister, Alice, had married rather well, but Mitchell, who had been an attorney and quite a few years older than Alice, had died a year ago. Babs was in no doubt that he had left her sister a tidy sum. Not that Alice was any slouch at making money herself. She had a real head for business. When Alice had announced her impending arrival, Babs had told her that she was welcome to use her bedroom and volunteered to sleep on the sofa until her sister decided what her plans were to be.

When Babs told Deidre the news, the older woman had remarked tartly, 'Well, I wouldn't be giving up my bed for anyone! But it will be nice for you both to have some family around. Does your sister have any children to keep Joey company?'

'No, Mitchell and Alice never had any, so Alice dabbled in business instead. She's very clever at that sort of thing. If she decides to stay in Palm Springs, she'll find something to do right away, I bet.'

'Well, so did you, Babs. You're making quite a name for yourself with your Heaven to Seven clothes.'

'Alice is clever with her hands, too. Our grandmother taught us all to sew, and she makes her own clothes sometimes. She copies them out of the smart magazines. Very haute couture.'

Deidre snorted. 'The desert isn't very haute!'

'Alice is very striking,' explained Babs. 'She'll make her mark, I'm sure.'

'Babs, if you ask me, it sounds like you have a bit of an inferiority complex as far as your sister is concerned,' said Deidre, with an eyebrow arched.

Babs shook her head. 'Deidre, you'll understand when you meet Alice. She's always so clever, so in control. At school she was always bandbox smart and perfectly turned out, while I always seemed to be untidy. My hair used to escape my ribbons and my dresses got crushed. Mom used to call Alice "Little Miss Perfect". Deb never cared, but I did.'

'Well, you shouldn't be intimidated by your sister. I've seen what you can create and I would call your children's clothes just about perfect,' said Deidre staunchly.

All the same, when Babs heard a car pull into the courtyard parking lot her heart started to beat faster.

'It's a grey Oldsmobile, Mom,' Joey called out as he leaned over the balcony.

'That will be your Aunt Alice. Let's go down and meet her.'

As they came through the front door, Alice Collins got out from behind the steering wheel and straightened up, looking over at the apartment complex. She was immaculately dressed. Her wide-legged cream linen slacks were barely creased. The red and cream striped knit top was tucked into her slacks and a wide red and silver leather belt showed off her narrow waist. Her hair was short and smartly styled into a smooth bob and she wore red and black high heels. Her wrists and throat were heavy with silver jewellery.

'I thought I was driving to the end of the earth!' she exclaimed as she stretched her back. 'What have you done to your hair?' she asked as Babs came forward to greet her and give her a kiss on the cheek.

'Oh, I had it straightened at the beauty shop, it's a new thing they do,' said Babs, touching her hair self-consciously. 'Joey, give Aunt Alice a kiss.'

'Well, if you ask me, it was a waste of money. It doesn't suit you, and besides, those curls of yours will bounce back in no time. Nothing could ever keep them under control.' She leaned down so Joey could peck at her cheek. 'Heavens, he's not a baby any more, that's for sure,' said his aunt.

Babs sighed inwardly. She was the same old Alice, then. 'Come on inside and have a cool drink. We'll get your bags later,' she suggested, as Alice reached for her smart leather handbag.

Alice pursed her perfectly painted lips. 'Why does this place look like something Mexicans live in? I saw some very smart places when I drove through Palm Springs.'

'It's all we can afford at present, but I like it. We might move later,' Babs replied defensively.

'If you can't afford anything else, then I suppose you can't move,' said Alice crushingly.

Babs tried to smile. 'It suits us just fine, and the neighbours are lovely. I've given you my bedroom, Alice, and Joey drew you a welcome picture.'

Alice sniffed. 'I hope the room has AC. This weather will take some getting used to and it's not even summer.' She strode towards the front door.

Babs sighed and followed her sister inside and up to the apartment. Alice stepped through the doorway and glanced around, examining the room but being careful not to touch anything. She turned to Babs. 'What are the plans for this evening?'

Babs moved towards the kitchen to prepare their drinks. 'Ah, I hadn't actually planned anything, Alice,' she stammered. 'I thought you might like to rest a bit after your long drive and spend a little time with Joey and me. I made some chili con carne and we recently bought a little TV . . .'

'I'm not so ancient that I need to be rested!' said Alice forcefully. 'And I don't eat spicy food. I have a whole new food regime, as I'm determined to live healthily. You'll feel much better if you do that, too. Five vegetables, five fruits a day. No bread or sugar. No meat or very little. Meat killed Mitchell, you know. You should try it, maybe you could lose a few of those unwanted pounds.' She eyed Babs's curves.

Babs placed her hands on her hips. 'I'm still the same size as I was in Portland, Alice.' She called out to Joey. 'Joey, please show your aunt to the bedroom while I get the lemonade. It's homemade.' Babs escaped into the kitchen before she said something she would regret.

'Thank you, Joey, although it's not as though you could get lost in this apartment,' tinkled Alice as she followed Joey to the main bedroom.

After Alice had unpacked and tried some of Babs's lemonade, which she pronounced too sweet, she agreed to spend some time at the pool so Joey could show her how well he swam. Babs wasn't sure if Alice was actually watching him. Her sister's sunglasses had impenetrable black lenses and a large floppy hat shaded her face. Babs sensed that her eyes were closed. Although Alice wore a swimsuit under a short sarong-style pair of shorts, she refused to get wet. 'You don't know who's been in that water,' she announced.

'It's only for residents and their guests,' said Babs.

'When you wrote you said that you'd been to the pool at the Desert Inn.'

'Not very often. It's too far away without a car.'

Alice pushed her sunglasses up her nose. 'I think you need to make new friends who'll take you to interesting places. My, when I think of the devoted friends I have back at home. They were all so devastated at the idea of my moving away. I can't tell you the parties they all gave me to send me off.'

'Don't you think that moving away from all your friends is a big step? I hope you don't feel you have to come and help me. We're managing just fine. Please don't change your life on account of us,' said Babs.

'Of course I'm not! I wouldn't do that.' Alice shook her head vigorously in exasperation. Babs felt irritated when Alice's hair fell neatly back into place.

'It was so unfair that Mitchell went first and left me,' said Alice in a tone which intimated that Mitchell had chosen to die just to inconvenience her.

'Yes, it was very sad. Mitchell was a lovely man,' said Babs. 'I wasn't so lucky in my choice of husband.'

'Luck has nothing to do with choosing a husband, Babs. You can't get too emotional and rush into things. You don't buy any pair of shoes or piece of fruit without checking them out, do you? The same goes for a husband, as far as I'm concerned.'

Babs burst out laughing. 'Alice, that's ridiculous! You fall in love or you don't.'

'Nonsense. Anyway, it wasn't as though you really had a choice about getting married, did you?'

Babs refused to dignify that remark with a response.

Alice sailed on. 'No, my mind is made up. I really didn't think I could go on living in Portland without dear Mitchell, and you made Palm Springs sound quite interesting in your letters – although, of course, what you and I find interesting might be quite different things. Anyway, you know how organised I am. And I've had the very best advice from my dear friends – they're lawyers and financial advisers, you know. They look after me. Everyone thinks I'm so adventurous. They just know I'll be a success here.'

Babs felt that she too had been very brave in taking the risk of leaving her husband and striking out for California, but she held her tongue. There wasn't much point making a fuss; Alice never changed.

'I'm sure you'll find something to do,' Babs replied. 'Palm Springs is full of tourists and retired people, so there must be something to interest you. I'm sorry I can't help much, but between Joey's school hours and my sewing workload I don't have a lot of spare time. It's fortunate I can work from home.'

'I think what you're doing is ridiculous! A production line on your dining room table, whirring away into the night. Your neighbours must be sick of the sound of Grandma's sewing machine!'

'I wouldn't dream of disturbing them. I never use it in the evening, I just hand-sew or cut out,' Babs retorted.

Alice held up a perfectly manicured hand. 'No, no, we have to move your cottage industry into a proper business, with our own outlet. I bet you get paid a pittance for the work you do. I know all about the mark-ups in those fancy stores, and I bet you didn't bother negotiating a reasonable price for your work. I'm right, aren't I? Well, I have a million ideas,' she continued. 'And as I'll be bank-rolling this next step, we'll have to come to a business arrangement . . .'

Babs felt herself beginning to shrivel. Here was Alice steamrolling over her, yet again. Her delight in her new life began to fade before her eyes. Alice had stopped speaking and was staring at her as Babs began fanning herself, struggling to find the right words.

'Good gracious, what's the matter with you? Has the heat got to you? Do you want me to get you some water?' asked Alice, making no attempt to do so.

Babs tried to regain her composure, but rather than shout, *Go away, Alice! Let me live my life!* she only managed to mutter, 'I don't want to put you out . . . you do whatever you'd like to do, Alice . . .'

'Of course I will. You've gone about it all wrong, but for once you have hit on an idea with a bit of potential. You need me to put it right and see to it that it really works. I think I've come at just the right time.'

'But I was enjoying doing my designs and sewing them,' Babs said faintly, but Alice airily waved a hand.

'You might be all right at that, but you're no good at selling, and that's the important part of any business. You need to leave that to me.'

'So what exactly are you thinking?' Babs wondered how Alice could arrive on the scene and work out a way to take over her entire business in the space of a few hours. Then again, maybe she shouldn't be so surprised. Alice was Alice.

'Let me lay it all out for you later. I need to do a bit more research first. You know, soak up the local atmosphere, get the lay of the land, get a feel for this place. Have you been to any clubs in Palm Springs?'

'What sort of clubs?'

'The smart ones. The nightclubs and the tennis and golf clubs and private clubs.'

Babs frowned. 'I belong to our local tennis club, but the private clubs, like the Thunderbird Club or the Racquet Club, cost a fortune to join – not that I know anyone who would put me up for membership in the first place.'

Alice smirked. 'Honey, what have you been doing all this time? Just leave things to me.'

She leaned back, lifting her face to the sun, and closed her eyes. Babs pursed her lips and walked over to Joey, who was climbing out of the pool. She sat on the edge of the pool and dangled her feet in the water as Joey prepared to dive in. She glanced over at her sister, stretched languidly on the lounge, seemingly without a care in the world, until Joey's bellyflop splashed cold water all over her precious-not-to-get-wet outfit. Babs stifled a laugh as Alice stalked back to the apartment. Alice hadn't changed. Still, it might be nice for Joey to have some family around, even if Alice could be overbearing at times. Besides, knowing her sister, it wouldn't be long before Alice had her own circle of friends, and Babs thought that her sister's enthusiasm for the baby clothes business might then begin to wane.

Within two weeks, Alice had rented a house in Twin Palms, a new estate in Palm Springs, and had already met some acquaintances from Portland who'd promised to nominate her for membership to the Thunderbird Club. Alice also joined the Racquet Club, though she rarely played tennis or golf, and took to lunching at all the smart clubs and restaurants in the plush hotels with her new-found friends, who also included her in their visits to nightclubs and supper dances.

Babs was never included in these occasions, not that she wanted to go – she was much too busy and had Joey to consider – but, as Alice explained, it was all about business, making the right connections with the right people, and Babs would be quite out of her depth in such company. So Babs kept quietly stitching and embroidering and smocking little dresses and pinafores, packing up her work when Alice came around to avoid facing her 'helpful' criticism.

But then one morning, Alice's voice cut in over the whirring of her sewing machine.

'Babs! Bar-ba-ra!'

'What is it? What's happened? Is everything all right?'

Alice swept into the apartment. 'It's all settled. We have a shop!' She waved a sheet of paper. 'And you'll never guess where!'

'What do you mean? We can't afford a shop!'

'It's small, I'll grant you that, but I know just how to make it work for us. It's inside the Desert Inn! Close your mouth, you look like a goldfish. Aren't you pleased?'

'How? I mean, I didn't know. This is all a bit of a surprise.' Babs was flabbergasted. She was not at all sure that she wanted to sell her baby clothes in a hotel. Did she really want to get into the retail side of things? 'How did you manage it, Alice?' she asked weakly.

'I'm doing some design work for the hotel. The place needs freshening up in some areas; I have to find the right people to do the work and oversee them, make sure that it's all being done properly. I mean, you really can't trust contractors. Anyway, there's a space available in the lobby. It's only small and the hotel management was not entirely sure how to make the best use of it, so I suggested that I could turn it into a kiddies' boutique. I thought I'd dress the window with a western desert theme for children. Good for our business and it will attract business for the hotel, too.'

In spite of her resentment that Alice had taken such a step without consulting her, Babs found her sister's excitement contagious. 'Oh my gosh, I can't believe it! A store for Heaven to Seven, that's so thrilling. What about stock . . . How long before it opens?'

'Well, you can't do everything yourself, Babs. We'll never keep up with demand with your little output. We can buy some things and you can design some of the outfits and we'll get other people to make them. And we

39

need a name for the shop. I thought "The Little Folk's Cottage" sounded cute. The interior designer can help with the signage . . .'

'Oh. Well, I guess it is kinda cute. But I insist the clothes I make and design still carry my label,' said Babs, finally finding some courage.

'Sure, sure,' said Alice, waving her hand, 'although I think we might want to change it to "Heaven to Eleven" so that we can cover a wider range of children's wear. Why limit ourselves?'

Babs swallowed. She supposed she could live with that. 'I don't know how you did all this,' she said.

'I got lucky,' Alice replied with false modesty. But Babs knew there was nothing lucky about it. Alice always knew what she was about and nothing in her life ever seemed to happen by luck or accident. 'You have to believe in yourself,' was one of her favourite aphorisms.

And so The Little Folk's Cottage opened and *The Desert Sun* newspaper took a photograph of the two sisters and Joey at the entrance to the shop. The window displayed a child mannequin dressed in a Heaven to Eleven cowboy outfit standing beside a large patchwork burro that Alice had made. The toy donkey was a big hit. The shop started quietly – so quietly in fact that Babs wondered if Alice had made the right decision to open a store – until one day Alice rang her.

'Babs, we're made. You will never guess who came in and bought three different cowboy outfits – Gene Autry! So if we now have the singing cowboy's seal of approval, the sky's the limit.'

And Alice was right. With a photograph of the famous cowboy star shopping at The Little Folk's Cottage displayed in the window, business started to take off. Other film stars began to buy children's clothes there as well, both for their own families and their friends.

Now Babs was working long hours at home as well as supervising the other seamstresses whom she managed to hire with Sol's help. Since they all worked from their own homes as well, she seemed to be forever travelling around the Palm Springs area, in the cheap secondhand car she'd bought on hire purchase.

'I know we're able to make more clothes for the store, but honestly, the work they do can be pretty rough. Look at this,' said Babs, holding up a little girl's dress. 'This work is far from perfect. It worries me that we're selling inferior clothes.'

'You need to keep a better eye on things,' replied Alice tartly. 'Make them unpick the shoddy work and don't pay them until it's fixed. You need to make more of an effort, Babs. I can't do it all myself.'

The shop became even more successful and Babs found herself working even longer and harder. She hardly ever got to work in the little shop and she missed the quiet evenings when she and Joey used to watch television while she cut out patterns and he sorted and rolled up threads and ribbons and bits of trimming and put them in the right boxes.

Alice, on the other hand, had carved a niche for herself in desert life with gusto. As she'd promised, she'd really got things happening. She was making plans for another store where she could sell expensive women's fashions aimed at the top end of the market. She'd bought a house in Palm Springs and traded in her Oldsmobile for a Cadillac coupe, and was dating an attorney called Spencer.

One evening, after Joey had gone to bed, Babs flopped on the sofa and put her feet up. She'd spent the day driving around, chasing up orders and wondering how she would ever keep the store stocked with clothes that matched her exacting standards. Still, when she reflected

41

on how much she had achieved in the last few years – a growing, popular children's clothing brand and a shop, whose success admittedly was due in no small part to the work of her sister – Babs felt that she could take some pride in her own efforts.

She was just about to get herself a glass of iced tea when there was a frantic knock at the door. Alarmed by the urgent rapping, Babs hurried to open it, thinking it might be Alice, impatient to float some new idea.

Instead, on the doorstep was a small, bedraggled young woman. Even though she hadn't seen her for years, Babs recognised her at once.

'Cindy?'

'Auntie Babs, can I come in? I've run away.'

2

CINDY STOOD IN THE doorway of the Palm Desert apartment in the cool evening air, tears rolling down her cheeks.

She was relieved now that she was here, but what if her Aunt Babs wouldn't let her come in? Maybe she'd insist that Cindy return home right away. What if her aunt rang her father? She felt a wave of panic surge through her as she tried to read Babs's expression. Maybe running away had not been such a good idea after all.

'Good heavens, run away?' Babs exclaimed. But then she put her arms around Cindy and held her close. 'Come in and tell me what's happened,' she added kindly.

When Cindy heard the gentleness in her aunt's voice, she put her hands to her face and started to sob afresh. Babs patted her back and held her until she felt calmer. With a rush of relief, Cindy knew she'd made the right decision in turning up unannounced, even though it had been years since she had seen Babs and cousin Joey.

Babs picked up Cindy's small bag, led her into the living room and sat her on the couch. Cindy looked around the little room. It was neatly but sparsely furnished, with an old sofa against one wall and a bookcase full of books on the other, next to a new-looking television set which clearly had pride of place in the room. The dining room table was covered in fabrics, and patterns sat beside a portable sewing machine.

'You look exhausted. Before you tell me anything, Cindy, how about I get you some food and something to drink? Would a sandwich and an iced tea be all right?' asked Babs.

Cindy sniffed and nodded. She was relieved to find that her favourite aunt was exactly as she remembered her, so calm and caring.

'Thank you, Aunt Babs. I'm sorry that I turned up like this, but I just had to get away from home. Where's Joey?'

'He's asleep. He'll be thrilled to see you in the morning.' Babs went into the kitchen, leaving the anxious girl twisting her handkerchief in her hands. 'Cindy, come and keep me company.'

Babs smiled at her niece as the teenager pulled up a stool at the breakfast bar. 'I don't know what's wrong, but I'm so glad that you could come to me with your troubles. I'm sure we'll be able to sort them out, whatever they are. Do you want to tell me what's happened?' she asked gently.

Cindy sat for a moment in silence as Babs made her a pastrami sandwich, then took a breath and raced head-long into an explanation.

'I know it's going to sound silly, but I just hate Spokane. It is the most boring place on earth!' Cindy shuddered. 'Dad and Lisa are making me go to secretarial college! I don't want to be a secretary! I want to get out and travel and *live*!' She flung her arms out as if to embrace the wide world. 'Dad and Lisa want me to get a boring steady job. Lisa's not my real mom anyway.' She frowned at the thought of her father's second wife. 'The idea of another day in Spokane made me feel so miserable, I just couldn't stay there anymore. Then I thought of you, and we all know how you took the plunge and came here to Palm Springs and then how Aunt Alice followed you, and I thought, why don't I do that as well? And so I have, and I couldn't bear it if you sent me back.' Her eyes filled with tears again as she looked imploringly at her aunt.

Babs handed Cindy a tissue and patted her hand. 'There, there now. There's no need to be quite so dramatic. I'm not going to send you home.' She paused a moment as Cindy blew her nose. 'You've just finished high school, haven't you?'

Cindy nodded. 'Yes, and that's why I thought it was time to leave. Nothing ever happens at home and I thought of all the fun you must have in a place like this, what with all the film stars and celebrities.'

'And a lot of hard work, too,' said Babs grimly. 'So how did you get here?'

'My girlfriend was going to visit her grandparents in San Francisco and her parents said I could go with her. I told Dad that's what I was doing, but when I got to San Francisco, I'd already made up my mind that I wanted to see you. I explained everything to my friend, then caught a bus to Los Angeles and another to Palm Springs.'

Babs shook her head. 'So your father still thinks you're in San Francisco, does he? Cindy, I know you might object, but I must ring him to tell him you're staying here for a while. What if he calls your friend's parents or grandparents and discovers you aren't there? We certainly don't

45

want him contacting the police or anything like that, do we? I'll just tell him you're having a bit of a vacation with us.'

Cindy leaned over and hugged her aunt.

'I knew you wouldn't send me back, Aunt Babs,' she exclaimed. 'I can't thank you enough.'

In the small apartment, it was impossible not to hear her aunt's conversation with her father. It was handled diplomatically and, in less than fifteen minutes, Aunt Babs had persuaded him to let Cindy stay for the summer vacation. She heard Babs add calmly, 'Yes, Deborah was such a dear sister to me; having Cindy stay is no imposition at all.'

After Cindy had eaten her sandwich, she helped her aunt make up a bed on the sofa.

'Try to get a good night's sleep, sweetie,' said Babs. 'You've had a very long and stressful day.' She kissed her niece good night.

Before she fell into a deep sleep, Cindy lay in the dark thinking how lucky she was that Aunt Babs was such an understanding person. Finally she was going to experience the sort of exciting life that had seemed impossible only a few days ago.

*

She woke the next morning to find a young boy with blond hair and a serious face looking down at her.

'I'm Joey,' he announced as soon as her eyes had opened properly.

Cindy smiled at him. 'I know you are. You've certainly grown since last time I saw you! How old are you now, seven?'

'*Eight*,' said Joey in a tone which suggested that Cindy should have been aware of that fact. 'Mom explained you came in the night. It'll be fun to have you stay with us. I'm

46

having a tennis lesson, but when I get back, I'll show you our pool. You can come swimming too, if you want.'

'Thank you, Joey, that sounds great,' said Cindy.

'See ya, I've got to go.' With that, Joey grabbed his tennis racquet and bolted out the door.

'Morning, Cindy,' said Babs as she came into the room. 'I hope you slept okay? It's not the best of beds, but I think I have a solution to that. Now, would you like some breakfast? I've rung your Aunt Alice and she's on the way over. She can't believe you're here either, and she's dying to see you.'

Half an hour later, Alice arrived in an efficient and energetic flurry. She looked Cindy up and down and then said to Babs, as if Cindy wasn't actually present, 'You're telling me she ran away from home? Why would she do that? Still, I have to say that she's become a very pretty girl, don't you think, Babs? I can see Deb in her, that's for sure.' Cindy had her mother's creamy skin and lovely red-gold hair. Alice carried on brusquely, addressing Cindy this time, 'I hope you won't be bored here. And I hope there'll be no hijinks. I know what teenagers get up to.'

Cindy noticed Babs raise an eyebrow, as though to question Alice's knowledge of teenagers, and Cindy wondered if Alice had ever come into contact with that age group at all.

'I'm so anxious to see your little shop, Aunt Alice,' Cindy said politely.

'It's not so little,' said Alice tartly. 'Are you keen on fashion? I have plans to open a dress shop of my own.'

Cindy nodded. 'I like clothes, of course. I just can't afford to buy them very often.'

'You look very pretty in that,' said Babs, admiring Cindy's full skirt, puffed out with stiffened petticoats. Tucked into its narrow waistband was a white short-sleeved blouse with a scalloped lace Peter Pan collar. Cindy had added white ankle socks and flat red shoes to complete the outfit.

'Do you make your own clothes?' asked Alice.

Cindy shook her head. 'I have no idea how to sew.'

'Can you cook?' asked Alice.

'No, I can't do that either. Lisa is always telling me I'm hopeless around the house.'

'You'll never land a husband if you can't do something practical,' said Alice, throwing up her hands. 'I can't believe you can't sew! What did they teach you at high school, for goodness sake?'

Cindy stifled a groan. 'Just because I can't sew, doesn't meant that I don't want to learn about fashion, Aunt Alice,' she said. 'I'm interested in proper fashion, made by famous designers, and what musicians and film stars like Grace Kelly wear.'

'Princess Grace has wonderful style,' agreed Alice. 'But unfortunately, the same cannot be said for a lot of rock and roll singers, whose influence on teenagers can only be described as unfortunate.'

'But Aunt Alice, nowadays teenagers are setting their own style. Hey, why don't you open a teenagers' clothing store? That'd be sensational,' suggested Cindy.

'I hardly think so,' said Alice, looking like she'd bitten a lemon. 'I would not like my name associated with anything so tasteless. And who would pay for these clothes? Teenagers don't have money.'

'Some do,' answered Cindy. 'If they have rich parents. And lots of my friends have part-time jobs, although that's also to help pay for college.'

'And which college are you planning on going to?' asked Alice.

'Dad wants me to go to *secretarial* college,' Cindy answered mournfully. 'Can't I go to a real college out here?'

'Of course,' said Alice briskly. 'You won't find a good husband in a college filled with other women!'

'What do you want to study?' asked Babs, turning to Cindy.

Cindy shrugged. 'I don't really know. I don't have a burning passion for any one particular career, I'm afraid. Maybe I could become a journalist? I love math, so maybe I could do something with that.' She cocked her head to one side. 'I know I would like to travel, so I'd like to do something that would take me anywhere in the world.'

'Then perhaps you should wait another year or so before you make up your mind,' said Babs. 'Wait until your ambition is a little clearer.'

'Good heavens, Babs, Cindy can't wait. Everyone goes to college these days and she needs to go right away,' said Alice emphatically.

'But we didn't go to college,' protested Babs. 'And you've never shown much interest in higher education before.'

'Different times,' said Alice briskly. 'I am now fully aware of the fact that the best way to get a good husband is to meet one at college. They say that if you haven't got a ring on your finger by the time you graduate, you've wasted time and money. If Cindy waits about before actually going, she will be the oldest girl in her class and that will severely limit her chances.' She held up her hand when she saw Babs trying to interject. 'No, she must go to a proper college. That's something she can do over summer: start applying to colleges. Of course, her father will have to pay, but I'll talk to him and I think we can also help by letting Cindy work for us during the break. All the college kids are mad to find work in summer.'

Cindy beamed at her aunt. Alice was certainly forceful. Cindy could see there was no point arguing with her. Instead she imagined meeting new people and experiencing a different, more exciting lifestyle in college. She would enjoy her summer break in Palm Springs and then head off to her new life. Then something else occurred to her.

'My father won't be too pleased,' she said quietly.

'We'll cross that bridge when we come to it. We can't always get what we want, your father included. We have to make decisions that are best in the long run,' said Alice.

'You've always got what you wanted, Alice,' murmured Babs.

Alice ignored the comment and continued, 'I don't think you can stay here with Babs while you're waiting to get into college, Cindy. There simply isn't the room.'

'I don't mind sleeping on the couch,' said Cindy hastily.

'No, Alice is right,' said Babs regretfully. 'As much as I would love you to stay with Joey and me, you'd have no privacy, and I get up very early to start work and I'd disturb you. Alice has more space in her place. It's not so far away, so you can visit, and Cindy, you will always be welcome here. I'll even give you a key, so you can let yourself in any time you like.'

Cindy thanked her aunt, thinking again how kind Babs was, and how thoughtful. She always seemed to know the right thing to say. Joey was so lucky to have such a wonderful mother. It was times like these she missed her own mother very much.

*

Alice's place was small but cleverly designed and sported lots of white, gilt, glass and mirrored décor. There were ornaments and photo frames everywhere and, as Cindy found out, these were never to be moved from their precise positions. The bathroom displayed a lot of cosmetics, including many free samples, and one shelf by the window was filled with Alice's collection of elaborate perfume bottles, backlit by the sunlight but never used. In the kitchen, leopard-print giftware paper had been glued to every surface, including the floor, and Alice had painted over it in layers of clear lacquer to make a hard, shiny surface. The kitchen was small and compact, which suited Alice as she rarely cooked, preferring raw foods like fruit and salads. On the kitchen bench stood several large glass jars holding raw cashews, peanuts, dried apricots and the fresh dates she constantly nibbled on. Her freezer contained organic ice-cream, yoghurt and frozen berries. Hidden in the back of the refrigerator (behind bowls of leftovers she kept till they were too awful to eat, but which seemed to imply that she wasted nothing), she kept a supply of dark chocolate, which, she explained to Cindy, was specifically for her blood and could not be shared. On her small patio a glass-topped table and white metal chairs were surrounded by pots of decorative cacti.

'I hope you'll be comfortable here,' said Alice. 'But no shenanigans, all right?'

Cindy loved staying in Palm Springs and working with her aunts in the little shop in the hotel lobby. As time passed she managed to curtail her excitement whenever a famous film star walked into the store, and instead was able to point proudly to the beautiful work on the handmade pieces. But she couldn't help but admire Alice's brilliant strategy of selling an outfit to just about anyone. She waged psychological warfare on every customer. Nor was Alice averse to a little set dressing. On the desk beside the cash register in full view of her customers, she kept a beautifully wrapped package with a note that she changed every few days. For example, she might write, *Hold for Dolores Hope*, implying that Bob and Dolores Hope were stalwarts of The Little Folk's Cottage.

Alice was as good as her word when it came to finding a suitable college for Cindy and talking Cindy's father into paying. One day she announced, 'My friend Spencer has suggested that you enrol in the University of California at the Santa Barbara campus, and I agree that it's an excellent choice. I'll speak with your father about the fees, and you can keep working for us over the summer to help cover the costs. However, you might have to look for a part-time job in Santa Barbara as well.' Cindy was only too happy to agree.

Alice made no secret of the fact that she was now committed to going full-steam ahead with her fashionable dress shop and had begun to look for suitable stock.

'I've found just the place for the store. Spencer has helped me so much. Being an attorney here, he knows what's what. Evidently, the man who originally leased the premises is in some financial trouble, so I can take over his lease at a good price,' she told Cindy one evening. Then, after a buying trip to Los Angeles, she decided to get Cindy to model the samples she'd brought back. Cindy smiled with pleasure and disappeared into the bedroom to change.

'Just be very careful putting them on. I don't want you doing any damage.'

There was a knock at the door and Babs let herself in to Alice's apartment as Cindy walked gracefully into the living room modelling a shantung sheath dress.

'Cindy, you look beautiful!' cried Babs.

Alice studied Cindy closely. 'I think I might put on a fashion luncheon at the Racquet Club. I know so many people there, and they always admire what I'm wearing, so I'll have no difficulty in arranging it. I think a fashion parade would be an excellent way of bringing my business to people's attention. And Spencer will know all the right people to ask. He has wonderful contacts, not just here, but in LA as well.'

'Spencer has certainly been a help. Very attentive to you,' said Babs with a raised eyebrow and a slight smile, both of which Alice ignored.

'What are you going to call the shop?' asked Cindy.

'It will be "The Sun Garden",' said Alice emphatically. 'The place has a little courtyard in the front, so I thought I'd put in a pretty garden setting with just a few tables, some umbrellas and wrought-iron chairs, then we can serve cream teas, sandwiches and coffees as well as cold drinks. Homemade food, of course.'

'How cute!' said Cindy.

'Sounds like a lot of work,' said Babs. 'Is that necessary in a dress shop?'

Alice threw her hands in the air dramatically. 'Of course it is. Haven't you noticed how people browse and try things on then go away for lunch to "think about it" and never come back? If they can eat on the spot, they'll buy at the same time. I just know it.'

Cindy looked at Babs, who gave her a wry smile. Alice certainly was formidable. Although The Sun Garden was exclusively Alice's venture, the two sisters talked about the new shop together: which suppliers to contact, how to get the best deals. Cindy returned to the bedroom and changed into her regular clothes. Listening to her aunts talk, she felt her mind wander. She loved her aunts and was enjoying her time with them, but sometimes she still felt a sense of restlessness. She would never say that to her aunts, because she didn't want to appear ungrateful, and it wasn't as though she wasn't having a good time. She wasn't trapped in Spokane any more, but at this time of year there were few visitors to Palm Springs, and Cindy had begun to feel bored. She found that she was counting down the days to the start of the college year.

*

Cindy found a welcome distraction in talking to her aunt's neighbours, Deidre and Sol, who could be very interesting company. It was Deidre who introduced her to Adsila, an

Agua Caliente Indian who came in once a week to do the ironing and help clean the Kramers's apartment.

Adsila lived on Section 14 on the edge of the town with her quiet and gentle husband Francis, who brought his alfalfa, dates and figs into town to sell each week at the market.

When she had the opportunity, Cindy loved to talk to the Indian woman as she ironed, although Adsila was usually quite reticent. One day, when they were talking, Adsila mentioned that she would have to catch the bus home that evening as her husband had to remain in town longer than usual and she didn't want to stay back. Deidre, who was obviously fond of the woman, immediately offered to drive her, and Cindy asked if she could come too.

Deidre drove out to Section 14, which wasn't far from the centre of Palm Springs, but the contrast between the two places was startling. The dwellings in Section 14 were made of bark and mud brick and it was clear that most of the living took place outside, by the open cooking fires. Most of the buildings had been erected before the building codes of Palm Springs had even existed, and Cindy was shocked to see that they were not much better than shanties.

Adsila got out of the car and asked the others to follow her, ushering them over to her little house with its dirt floor. They sat outside on stools as Adsila brought out some baked corn chips on a woven tray, and dates in a bowl.

When Cindy admired the beautiful woven baskets and painted clay cooking pots outside the door, Adsila looked pleased. 'I make these,' she said in her softly spoken way.

Cindy thought that the fine workmanship and intricate patterns, so tightly and smoothly woven together, made the baskets more like works of art than merely functional pieces. After they'd eaten, Adsila took them into a thatched granary where her food supplies were kept and showed them the dried grasses she used for weaving. When Cindy saw the huge storage baskets there, she was enthralled. She could see Adsila was also working on other baskets, their tightly bound coils kept in water so the grass stayed flaccid and soft and easier to weave.

'What do these patterns mean, Adsila?' asked Cindy as they sat down beside her on the beaten-earth floor.

In her careful, deliberate manner, Adsila explained that they were symbols for what she saw around her, the jagged yucca plants, delicate desert flowers, lightning in the sky, bird feathers and the whorls of a dust storm.

'Some patterns are traditional, but some I created myself,' she explained modestly. 'After white people came here many years ago, our people began to use metal and stopped making baskets. But I think weaving is important to maintain our culture, so I continue to make them. There are some white people who value what we do and like to collect our work.'

Cindy was fascinated as she watched Adsila's brown leathery hands demonstrate how she twisted the grass coils so smoothly and expertly. Smiling, Adsila handed the work to Cindy and slowly guided her hands, showing her the weaving technique the Indian woman had made look so simple and fluid.

'It's quite hard. I feel so clumsy.' Cindy laughed. 'What patience you need for this. Thank you so much for showing me.'

The women got to their feet, brushing the dust from their skirts, and, farewelling Adsila, made their way back to the car. Suddenly Adsila ran back into the hut. 'Please wait,' she called. A minute later she appeared at Cindy's window and pushed a small woven bowl towards her.

'From me,' she said simply.

'That's so generous. Thank you so much!' exclaimed Cindy. She clasped Adsila's hands in thanks as Deidre started the engine. As the dust whirled under their wheels, Cindy waved to Adsila.

'It's a shame their crafts aren't more appreciated,' Cindy commented to Deidre on the way home. 'Aunt Alice should buy some. They would make a lovely decoration for her new shop. She could even sell them.'

But when Cindy showed Alice the woven basket, her aunt dismissed the idea.

'Good heavens, Cindy. Whatever are you thinking? I'm starting a fashionable dress shop, not opening an Indian trading store.'

So Cindy put the woven bowl with its beautiful pattern in her room and treasured it.

*

Finally, the launch day of The Sun Garden arrived. Although the weather was still very hot and Palm Springs was bereft of tourists, Alice had decided to go ahead anyway.

'Not much point in paying rent and not opening. There are enough locals to make it work, at least until the crowds start arriving again.'

True to her word, Alice had organised a fashion parade at the Racquet Club. She had plenty of volunteer models, including Cindy, and considering that the event was out of season, a large crowd of women turned up. The guests sat under shady umbrellas that were set around the pool and Alice took centre stage with the microphone, describing each dress in detail. As the models made their way around the club's pool and through the appreciative audience, the outfits were much admired. By the end of the parade, when everyone was milling around with cool drinks, it was clear that there had been enough interest and orders taken for the event to be declared a success.

Although Cindy preferred to work in The Little Folk's Cottage, Alice demanded that she also work at The Sun Garden once it had opened.

'You need to expand your horizons,' she said. 'Selling baby clothes is too limiting.'

Cindy had to admit that Aunt Alice certainly knew how to sell fashionable dresses.

'Now listen to me, Cindy,' Alice instructed her niece on her first day in the store. 'When a woman shows an interest in something, don't rush at her. Always check out the stock first. Know what sizes and colours we have and if we don't have a bigger size, tell her the dress is the new hug-the-hip look, and it makes her look slim. If we don't have the frock in green, casually mention that this season's most fashionable colour is orange.'

And Cindy had seen Alice in action. When one customer had managed to squeeze her rolls of fat into a sequinned cocktail dress and then asked seriously, 'So, how do I look in this?' Alice had clapped her hands to her face. 'Madame, really . . . words fail me. Simply fail me.' And proceeded to kiss her fingertips and gesture like a chef recommending the day's special. Naturally, a sale was made. Cindy enjoyed working in the shop, although she never seemed to reach her aunt's exacting standards.

A short time after the shop opened, Cindy was thrilled when Deidre invited all the family, including Alice and Spencer to a big charity fundraiser at the Thunderbird Club. Pearl McCallum-McManus had a table and Bob Hope was to be the MC. Babs declined the invitation, even after Cindy had offered to babysit Joey, saying that it really wasn't her sort of thing. Cindy really wished that Babs would go out a bit more. It seemed a shame that such a lovely and attractive woman did not have a chance to socialise more.

Wearing a full-skirted, pleated chiffon cocktail dress, and with her hair up in a French roll, Cindy looked older than her eighteen years. The young waiters, who'd returned home from college or had taken summer jobs, were clearly impressed. But Cindy took little notice of them; she was far too excited watching the celebrities as they moved around the room, chatting to each other or dancing to the band music.

The round tables were covered with starched cloths and decorated with elaborate centrepieces of fresh flowers. The laughter and chatter, the band and the popular singer made the room noisy but exciting. There were raffles with fabulous prizes and the silent charity auction produced bids of dizzying sums. Most people danced the quickstep and slower-paced dances, but when the band played rock and roll numbers there were plenty of participants. For Cindy the whole atmosphere was like she imagined champagne to be: bubbles and light-headedness.

She was sitting by herself at the table, as Sol and Deidre were on the dance floor and Alice had taken herself to the bathroom to freshen up, when Spencer came over to her with a friend.

'What, no Alice? I wanted to introduce her to one of my favourite clients,' he said to Cindy. Turning to his friend, he added, 'This is Alice's niece, Kirk. This is Cindy.'

Cindy turned around and found herself looking at one of Hollywood's biggest stars, Kirk Douglas.

'How are you, Cindy?' he asked. 'Enjoying your night?'

Cindy, completely starstruck, could only manage a faint, 'Yes, Mr Douglas.' He was so tanned, such blue eyes, such white teeth.

'I suppose you're on your college break,' Kirk said.

'I haven't actually started yet. I go next week, Mr Douglas.'

'Where are you enrolled?'

'UC Santa Barbara. I'm so excited. Nervous too, though.'

'For heaven's sake, that's where my son Michael wants to go next year. I'll have to tell him I've met one very pretty gal who goes there already. Do you think you could manage a dance with someone who has a son nearly your age?'

'Of course! Thank you.' Cindy couldn't stop smiling, and for the next few minutes she could hardly believe she was twirling around the dance floor with one of Hollywood's biggest film stars. After the dance, Kirk Douglas returned her to the table and wished her luck. When Alice came back, Cindy told her what had happened.

'You were lucky,' said her aunt. 'Had I not been in the bathroom, he would have danced with me instead.'

During the next week, Cindy couldn't stop talking about the wonderful time she'd had, the people she'd seen and the sheer glamour and fun of it all. This was why she had left Spokane! And she was looking forward to going to college as well. With only days remaining till she left for Santa Barbara, she packed and repacked a dozen times in nervous anticipation. She pictured her dorm, her class-mates, the teachers and campus, and she was filled with excitement.

Before she left for college, Babs asked Cindy and Alice over for a farewell dinner. After the meal, Joey announced that he was in the middle of a very exciting Hardy Boys book and that he couldn't wait to find out what would happen next, so he went to his room to read, leaving the three women talking around the table.

'Cindy, I hope you enjoy yourself at college,' said Babs. 'I wish I'd had the chance to go. If you want my advice, you should play the field. Get to know lots of boys, so that when the right one comes along you'll know he's

Mr Right.' Babs sighed and looked down at her hands. 'I never got the chance to enjoy just being carefree and doing things with my friends. I met and married Howard so young and suddenly all other doors were closed to me. Joey is the only good thing to have come from my marriage.'

'I have to disagree,' said Alice, predictably, 'though Babs is half right. I think you should meet lots of young men, but don't wait too long before settling on someone suitable. If you hold back, someone else will get there first. Those boys from good families get snapped up fast.'

'The rich boys won't be interested in a girl like me. I bet they stick to their own kind,' said Cindy bashfully.

'I'm sure you'll meet someone wonderful,' said Babs, patting Cindy's hand.

'I hope so,' said Cindy. 'But I hope I get the chance to travel too.' She looked wistful. 'There's a big world out there and I'm just itching to find out all about it.'

Two days later, Cindy set off for college in the little second-hand car she'd bought for herself with some of the money she'd earned over the summer break. As soon as she arrived on campus at Santa Barbara, she fell in love with the school. Set dramatically on cliffs above the Pacific Ocean, UCSB boasted its own beach. With the Californian climate, much use was made of the outdoor settings for social and class events. Fraternities and sororities flourished, most established in boarding houses and shared homes in the surrounding district. Cindy was unsure which of the seven sororities she should join, but after attending the sorority teas and meeting members and being assessed in turn, she was thrilled when what she considered to be one of the best sororities invited her to be a member.

She shared a large room with a girl from La Jolla named Chrissie Simmons, who had a huge poster of John F. Kennedy on the wall.

'Isn't he the most gorgeous man you've ever seen? Way better than Tricky Dicky Nixon, don't you think?' she asked Cindy. 'I just love JFK. You are happy to have him on the wall, aren't you?'

Cindy looked at the picture of the handsome young candidate. 'He can stay, as far as I'm concerned,' she said. 'I think that Jackie Kennedy is one lucky woman.'

Chrissie was sports mad and spent most of her time playing softball, volleyball, or tennis. Cindy was less keen on sport, but she loved going to the beach with her sorority sisters. Here they would often meet the 'frats' from the men's fraternity houses, and swim together and then cook marshmallows over a fire on the sand after the sun had gone down. Some of the boys played guitars and they all sang along. Cindy found that, while others were home-sick, she thrived on being in a new place and meeting new people. She loved the novelty of college and being able to be independent and make her own decisions, while others struggled to find themselves and fit in. She was consci-entious about her work; her grades were always above average, and she excelled at math.

Her father paid her semester tuition, but she was responsible for paying for her food, rent, books and everything else, and Cindy quickly realised that the money she'd earned in Palm Springs would not be enough to last all year. So once she'd settled in she applied for a job as a sales assistant in a women's clothing store in downtown Santa Barbara. After a ten-minute interview, she had the job. Cindy mentally thanked Alice for the crash course she'd received in selling fashion. Even working some hours in the shop and attending classes, she still had plenty of time for an active social life. She was regularly asked out on dates by eligible young men, but none of them seemed quite what she was looking for. Then one day her sorority decided to have an open house and asked the college football team and cheerleaders over for a party. It was at this party that Cindy met star quarterback Robbie Wilson.

As soon as she met him, she was bowled over. He was unbelievably good-looking. At just over six feet tall and with thick blond hair and a laugh that made people stop to look at him with a smile, he turned heads everywhere he went. He arrived at the party smartly dressed in a preppy striped Brooks Brothers shirt with a button-down collar, a neat pair of sand-coloured chinos and tan brogues. Cindy noticed him as soon as he entered the room and they seemed drawn to one another. Cindy approached him, welcoming him to the sorority open house, and their conversation flowed effortlessly. Robbie told her that he was from Sacramento, where his family had lived for more than a hundred years. Cindy explained how she'd moved from Washington state to Palm Springs.

'The desert, huh?' said Robbie, flashing his movie-star smile. 'Cool place. Well, really it's not. It's hot.' They both laughed. Sitting on a sofa, a bowl of popcorn between them, they talked, laughed a lot and even flirted a little. Cindy felt interesting and attractive. Robbie was disarmingly modest, even though every other girl in the room had her eyes on him. At the end of the evening, he asked if he could visit Cindy at the sorority house. Cindy was ecstatic.

'Wow,' said Chrissie, when Cindy told her what had happened. 'That guy is a serious jock. Everyone will be so envious when he comes over. Just about every woman on campus has tried to get Robbie Wilson to show an interest, and he's never bothered with any other girl.'

It wasn't long before Cindy and Robbie became an item. Robbie was two years older than Cindy and more than halfway through his degree. He planned to go to law school when he finished at UCSB, but, as he pointed out, that was still some way off. In the meantime, they met regularly, though Robbie's training and games took up a lot of his time. Cindy went to the games, revelling in being his girl.

Despite having a very full calendar, Cindy liked to get back to Palm Springs to see her aunts when she had the chance, even at Thanksgiving and Christmas, when there was not enough time to drive back to Spokane to see her father. However, she was bitterly disappointed that she could not get away for the weekend of Alice's wedding to Spencer. Babs told her afterwards that it was a surprisingly low-key affair, very intimate and chic. Alice and Spencer were now busy building a house for themselves and were up to their elbows in plans, landscaping and décor. With The Little Folk's Cottage doing well, Babs had decided to rent a slightly bigger house not far from Hacienda Hideaway and Deidre and Sol. It was not much larger than her old apartment, but as it had three bedrooms, Cindy slept in Babs's sewing room cum guest room each time she visited and she found the new arrangements much more comfortable than staying with Alice.

When she was in Palm Springs, Cindy talked constantly about Robbie. 'I can't wait for you to meet him. He's promised to come here some time. I've told him all about you and Joey.'

'You seem very pleased with Robbie,' said Babs. 'But I still think you should look around. Don't get tied down with one person. Play the field.'

Alice shook her head impatiently and ignored Babs's comment. 'When he comes to visit, I'll get Spencer to talk to him about law schools. Spencer will be able to point him in the right direction. And you're not letting him take any liberties, are you?' she added bluntly. 'We don't want you ending up with an unwanted pregnancy.'

Cindy was shocked that Alice could be so tactless in front of Babs.

'Aunt Alice!' she said. 'No, Robbie is a perfect gentleman.' Cindy's sorority sisters frequently complained about fending off their overfamiliar boyfriends, but, much to Cindy's relief, Robbie respected Cindy's determination to save herself for her wedding night. She frowned at Alice and brusquely changed the subject. 'A group of us are thinking about taking a trip to Mexico during the spring break. Would you be upset if I went, rather than coming back here?'

'No, of course not. You just have a good time, but Cindy, do be careful,' said Babs.

'Personally, I don't think it's safe,' said Alice emphatically. 'Mexico is full of drugs and bandits and villains. Terrible place. Why would you want to go there?'

'We'll be fine, Aunt Alice. It's not like I'm going by myself. I'll be in a group. Please don't worry.'

*

Several weeks later, Cindy, Chrissie and a group of their sorority and fraternity friends headed south. Cindy and Robbie went separately, as they both took their cars. It took two days for them all to reach the beachside township where they planned to stay. The queues of cars and inspections at the border in Tijuana were slightly intimidating, but once they were through that, they all felt they were south of the border in more ways than one.

They stayed in a very basic hotel, which Chrissie described as being minus one star. Thin mattresses, no hot water and certainly no air conditioning, but its location was amazing. Cindy was stunned by the brilliant blue warm water, miles of sandy beaches, and rustic cafés and bars. The boys quickly flung themselves into the waves while the girls organised the rooms: the women in the ones nearest the beach, the men in the row behind. Several of the boys who were short on cash planned to sleep on the beach. Everyone quickly got into the spirit of Mexico and began ordering local long-necked beers with lime wedges jammed in the top and fresh shrimps in tall cocktail glasses soaked in tequila and tomato juice.

The food was spicy, the days hot and languid, and the stories and jokes they told each other became more and more outlandish. Everyone was drinking far too much of the cheap and plentiful alcohol. Cindy found out for herself that tequila really was potent stuff and once, after a big night, she woke up the next morning with a splitting headache. She was a bit more circumspect after that. But most of the boys continued to drink heavily, and after a while Cindy found their behaviour boorish, and it seemed to get worse when a group from Fresno joined them. She was glad that Robbie, who was a little older than the others, was not inclined to show off by getting drunk. And they both quickly found that they liked to get away from the others now and then by wandering into the little town behind the beach to look around and sample the Mexican food.

The night before they were due to leave, Cindy and Robbie walked hand in hand along the beach. They talked about the future and planned many more trips abroad.

'Have you had a good time on this trip, Cindy?' Robbie asked.

'It's been wonderful,' Cindy replied. 'But I can't help but notice how poor the people around here are. It makes me feel a bit uncomfortable when it's clear that we have so much and they have so little. They seem happy, though.'

'Maybe that's because they are perfectly content with their lives,' suggested Robbie.

Cindy considered this. 'Or maybe it's because they don't know any other way to live. Maybe they don't think there are any alternatives.'

'Perhaps for some people there *are* no alternatives,' said Robbie quietly.

'I think there are always alternatives,' said Cindy brightly, though as she spoke she wondered if she really believed this.

'I hope you're right,' Robbie murmured, then he bent over and kissed her, and she returned his kiss with passion, but Robbie seemed distracted.

'Robbie, are you okay?' she asked softly.

Robbie looked away. 'I'm sorry. I'm spoiling our last night. Let's have a swim in the moonlight while we still have the chance.'

As Cindy swam in the warm waters of the Pacific Ocean, she felt her heart overflow with emotion. She hoped she would have the chance to travel again soon. Seeing new places, meeting different types of people and experiencing new cultures fulfilled a deep need inside her, as though it was something that was meant to be. And as she glanced at Robbie, Cindy sighed with happiness. It had been a perfect trip.

As she drove back to Palm Springs at the end of her freshman year, Cindy thought about how happy she was with the way things had gone for her at UCSB. Although she had not topped any of her classes, she felt that she had done well enough academically. She had some great friends amongst her sorority sisters, and then there was Robbie. He seemed so much more mature than the other boys and she was pleased that he was single-minded about wanting to pursue a legal career and wasn't just attending college to have a good time. Robbie was so nice and so much fun to be with and all the other sorority sisters envied her good luck in finding such a wonderful boyfriend. In fact, Cindy hoped that soon he would be more than her boyfriend. She didn't want to jinx it, but she felt sure he would propose soon. When he put his arm around her, she felt a warm glow that went right down to her toes. Robbie had promised to visit her over the summer vacation and she desperately hoped he would keep his promise.

'You certainly seem infatuated with this Robbie,' said Alice, when Cindy went over to see her. 'But be careful, don't throw yourself away on the first boy who comes along.'

'But you said not to wait too long, or someone else would grab the good ones!' Cindy spluttered.

'Nonsense, Cindy, you can do better, I have no doubt. Besides, you need to make a good career for yourself. You can't just rely on a man to look after you. Your mother was far too wishy-washy. You need to be more like me. Independent.'

As much as Cindy loved her aunt, Alice always swung with the wind, so it was difficult to know just where things really stood with her. 'You haven't even met him yet. When he comes to visit, you'll see just how great he is,' she retorted.

Luckily Cindy didn't have long to wait. Only two weeks into the vacation, Robbie called to ask if it would be convenient for him to come and stay a few days. He had landed a summer job in a law firm in Sacramento, he said, and wanted to see Cindy before he started there. 'I'll just be an office boy, really, but it's going to be so exciting being part of a busy law firm. One more year and then I'll be in law school. I'm sorry that I can't visit for long, but I really can't let this opportunity go.' The enthusiasm was clear in his voice and Cindy hoped she was part of the future he was building towards.

As Robbie's arrival approached she found she was beside herself with excitement, and when Robbie pulled up outside Aunt Babs's house and climbed out of his car looking so handsome and so nicely dressed and present-able, Cindy felt as if her heart would burst. Even Alice couldn't find a critical comment to make.

Alice invited them all around to her new house for dinner the next evening, and all the men dressed in a jacket and tie, even Joey. Robbie, who had not expected to be attending such a formal event, had to go and buy a tie.

'It's such a shame Spencer is in Beverly Hills seeing a client this evening,' said Alice. 'But let me show you round. A little *tour de la maison*. This place is the latest in desert chic. One of the magazines is coming to take photos.'

Alice, in new sandals made of Perspex with plastic flowers trapped in the clear high heels, click-clacked her way across the patio. The house had a large open-plan living room, where the focal point was an enormous fireplace set in a wall made entirely of slabs of local stones. The furniture was sleek ultra-modern Danish. The kitchen had all the latest appliances, which amused Cindy as she knew her aunt was not at all interested in cooking. *Maybe Spencer cooks*, she thought. But then they were shown the barbecue and bar, which Alice told them was Spencer's domain. The roof of the house was flat, so anyone in the vast swimming pool had uninterrupted views of the mountains that rose in the distance behind the house. The living room had a plate-glass, floor-to-ceiling window that looked across the green lawn with its geometrically placed potted plants towards the desert and snow-capped mountains.

'Cindy tells me that you'll be working in a law firm over the summer vacation. My first husband was an attorney and Spencer is, too,' said Alice. 'I think it is the only real profession.'

'Alice, there are lots of real professions,' retorted Babs. 'What about doctors, or accountants, or dentists, for that matter?'

'I suppose you're right about doctors, but they tend to keep very long hours, which would spoil one's social life. And I think that all the other professions are not really on a par with attorneys. No, young man, you've made the right choice for a career. Money and prestige, that's what it's all about.'

'I'm quite interested in the law, too,' Robbie pointed out.

'Oh, that,' said Alice blithely. 'Well, I suppose Spencer is too, sometimes.'

'What law school do you want to get into?' asked Babs.

'I've applied for both Stanford and Harvard, but I would really love to get into Harvard. It's the best school in the States, and I would make such great contacts there, as well.'

Cindy gulped. Robbie had never mentioned Harvard to her. What would happen to their relationship if he got in there? Stanford was bad enough, but at least it was in California. Harvard was on the other side of the country! It didn't bear thinking about. Still, he might not get the marks. As soon as that thought occurred to Cindy, she felt mean. Of course she wanted Robbie to get into the best law school he could.

Dinner turned out to be a bit of a disaster. It started well enough when Alice presented everyone with a salad that she had made herself. It was beautifully decorated and only marred by the fact that the ranch-style dressing had sat in the refrigerator too long and had set. Then she brought a pie to the table.

'It's chicken pot pie,' she said. 'Now I hope that everyone is up for a big serve. Of course I shan't have any, I've had plenty of salad. As my family knows, Robbie, I don't think that cooked foods are very healthy. I try only to eat food that is in its raw state.'

So saying, Alice served up enormous slices of pie to everyone else. Unfortunately, she had bought a frozen pie from the supermarket and had not bothered to defrost it properly before putting it in the oven and then had not given it enough time to cook all the way through. Cindy realised straight away that the pie was only cooked at the edges and still frozen in the centre. Everyone dutifully tried to eat the edible bits, but Alice noticed how much they all left on their plates.

'Perhaps I shouldn't have commented on my dislike for unhealthy cooked food, because it seems to have put you all off your chicken pie. Never mind, I have a lovely Key lime pie for dessert.'

The Key lime pie certainly looked splendid and was piled high with meringue and thick cream on top, the whole confection standing at least eight inches high on the plate.

'This is lovely,' Robbie said politely. 'Did you make it yourself?'

'Why, thank you, Robbie. Actually, it's a Sara Lee, but I added all the extra cream myself.'

Cindy couldn't look at Robbie in case she started giggling.

*

In many ways, Cindy's sophomore year proved to be even better than her freshman year. She did not try for another part-time job because she thought that if she budgeted carefully enough, her summer earnings from working for her aunts plus babysitting for a wealthy client of Spencer's would be enough to see her through. She performed well academically, excelling in math as always.

Her relationship with Robbie was her one disappointment. She saw a good deal less of him that year than she had in her freshman year. He still seemed to delight in her company and was as affectionate as ever, and she was sure that there was no one else, but he didn't come around to the sorority house as he had the previous year, nor did he want to come out with their friends as often. When Cindy said something about hardly ever seeing him, Robbie said that everything was fine and he was just studying as hard as he could to get into law school.

Cindy told Babs that she was worried about him.

'Sometimes I think he puts way too much pressure on himself so he can get into one of the Ivy League law schools. Did I tell you he's decided not to play football this year because it will take too much of his time?'

'He sounds like a sensible young man looking out for his future,' said Babs. 'I hope that Joey is as single-minded when it comes to his future, too. You have to admire him.'

But Cindy didn't feel reassured. 'Auntie Babs, what if he gets into Harvard? That's all the way on the other side of the country. I'll never see him.'

'Well, then we just have to hope that he gets into Stanford,' replied Babs.

Robbie continued to reassure Cindy that, as far as he was concerned, their relationship hadn't changed, but Cindy wasn't so sure. At Christmas, instead of the engagement ring she had been hoping for, he gave her a single pearl pendant instead. Though she was a bit disappointed, the necklace was so lovely that Cindy decided to think of it as a sign of things to come. She vowed she would never take it off.

'That's just beautiful,' said Babs, as she admired the gleaming trinket.

'It looks to me like one of those Japanese cultured pearls,' said Alice. 'Still, I suppose it's the thought that counts.'

On the day of Robbie's commencement ceremony, she was almost as excited as Robbie himself. She sat proudly near his parents, pleased that his hard work had paid off, as he'd not only come third in his year, he had been chosen to give the valedictory speech on behalf of all the graduating students. Cindy felt very tenderly towards him as he leaned into the microphone and began to talk about the promise of tomorrow.

Afterwards, she posed for lots of photographs with Robbie and his parents. As he left with them to return to Sacramento, he assured her he would ring her regularly. 'Nothing is going to change between us, I promise you, Cindy,' he said as he kissed her goodbye.

Cindy returned to Palm Springs for the summer after briefly visiting her father in Spokane. Seeing her old town again confirmed that the move to California had been the right thing to do.

Robbie rang her as promised for the first couple of weeks. No, he hadn't heard back from the law schools where he'd applied, but as soon as he got any news, he'd let her know.

Then the phone calls became irregular. Robbie often sounded distracted and sometimes they struggled to talk at length. Cindy was upset, but she knew he was working again in the law office in Sacramento, and that he was probably busy, as indeed she was, working between her aunts' two shops.

Then a letter arrived from Robbie.

His excitement was clear in the opening line: *Wonderful news! I've been accepted into Harvard Law School!* But she had to reread again and again the next lines: *So I think it best if we break up our friendship now. You are so lovely, but if we try to keep the relationship going, I'll never be able to concentrate fully on my studies. I know this may seem unfair, as you've done nothing but support me and my ambitions in all the time I've known you, but in the end I feel that I must put my career first. I've struggled to make this decision as I truly had feelings for you, but now I must move on. I hope one day you find someone who is really deserving of your love. I wish you all the best for the future and I will never stop caring for you, and hope we will continue to be friends. Love, Robbie.*

Friends! Cindy burst into tears. She tore off her pearl pendant and flung it to the other side of the room, where it hit the wall and then slid down behind the bookcase. How dare Robbie break it off! Everything he'd said about nothing changing between them had been a lie. How cruel and selfish he was!

She read the letter through several times, trying to make sense of it. 'What is he saying? He loves me so much that I'll ruin his career?' she asked the empty room. But she didn't want him to leave her. She loved him and she knew that she would never be able to love anyone as much again. She was convinced that Robbie was the only man who could make her happy. All her wedding day dreams disintegrated before her eyes.

When Babs got home later that evening, she found Cindy on the sofa, her eyes red and swollen from crying.

'Oh, you poor girl,' she said, when Cindy had choked out what had happened. 'What a terrible, self-serving letter. You might not realise it now, but if that is the sort of person Robbie is, then you're well rid of him. I know you don't believe me, but you'll find out that I'm right.'

'But I love him,' sobbed Cindy, burying her face in her aunt's lap. 'I thought he was going to propose!'

Babs stroked her hair. 'I know, sweetheart. It's your first great love. We all get our hearts broken at some stage. I know that's no consolation.'

'I told you he wasn't up to par,' said Alice bluntly, when she heard about the letter. 'Move on. You can do a lot better. Personally, I think he has piggy, calculating eyes. You can tell so much about a person by their eyes. I had my doubts right from the start.'

'Oh, Alice. He does not have piggy eyes,' Cindy protested. 'They're a lovely blue, and sort of haunting.' Then she burst into tears again.

For the next few weeks, Cindy moped. She refused to talk to her girlfriends, not even Chrissie. She felt she could never again trust any man not to lie to her and besides, she just knew that none of them could ever compare to Robbie.

'What will I tell my friends back at college? Everyone thought that Robbie and I were the perfect couple. What will they think when I tell them that he dumped me?' she said to Babs.

'They'll think he made a very silly decision,' said Babs.

'Say *you* dumped *him*,' advised Alice. 'Many more fish in the sea, Cindy, but you won't catch them if you don't go fishing. You'd better get back out there soon! Besides, your mopey face isn't good for business. Who wants to buy an expensive dress from someone who looks so doomed?'

The thought of having to smile, chat brightly and put on her happy face for the rest of the summer seemed too hard. Cindy felt bruised and sad. She lay down on her bed and hugged her pillow to her chest. She caught a glimpse of the pearl necklace lying under the bookcase, the sunlight making its polished surface gleam. The sight of it caused her to burst into fresh tears. It was no use. Her heart was broken, her future in tatters, and she wondered how she would ever heal.

3

CINDY CAME QUIETLY INTO the room and studied Babs as her aunt stood before the long mirror.

The concerned gaze on Babs's face softened as she ran her hands over her hips, smoothing the silk cocktail dress she wore, finally allowing herself a small satisfied smile.

'You look gorgeous,' said Cindy. And she was right. Her aunt was shapely and tanned and looked years younger than she was.

Babs touched her fashionable new pageboy hairstyle. 'I feel good, too, especially in this dress. I think the tulle stole softens the outfit really nicely. Thank you for lending it to me. And wasn't it nice of Alice to let me borrow some of her costume jewellery from the shop? Most of her stuff is a bit too showy for me, but I have to say I like this little shell bracelet.' She fingered the matching earrings. 'It would have been nice to have a string of real pearls to wear, but I certainly couldn't afford anything like that. Maybe one day. I feel a bit nervous, though. I really don't think I'll have anything interesting to say to Spencer's friend.'

'That's silly, Babs,' said Cindy. 'You look so lovely, you won't have to say a thing. Men will just stare at you in admiration.'

Babs laughed. 'Thank you, though I very much doubt that. It's just that it's been such a long time since I socialised like this.'

Cindy felt a rush of love for her aunt. 'Now that Joey is getting older, you should take advantage of Aunt Alice's invitations. I mean, she and Spencer go to all the best places in town and I can't see why you shouldn't go with them from time to time. You ought to get out and meet more people.'

A frown creased Babs's lovely face. 'Don't you think I might be a bit old to start that now?'

'Don't be silly!' Cindy exclaimed. 'Live a little, I say!'

Babs arched a brow. 'I could say the same to you, Cindy. It's high time you got over Robbie and started to live a bit yourself,' Babs said firmly but kindly.

'I guess,' said Cindy quietly. 'But not right away.'

It was late when Babs arrived home that night. She popped her head into Joey's room and checked he was sound asleep. Cindy was curled up like a kitten on the sofa in her polka dot pyjamas, dozing. She sat up when she heard Babs come in.

'How was the night? Did you have a good time?' Cindy asked sleepily.

'Sorry I disturbed you. I had a wonderful night,' said Babs, smiling. 'I can't remember the last time I had such fun.' She dropped down next to Cindy on the sofa.

'What was Spencer's friend like?' asked Cindy curiously.

'His name is George, and he's about Spencer's age, I guess,' answered Babs. 'He seemed very nice. He had a friend with him, a man called Murray from Australia! George was in the war with Murray's father. Murray's in California on vacation and George brought him to Palm Springs to show him the desert sights. I've never met an Australian before.'

'Neither have I,' said Cindy. 'What was he like?'

'Pleasant enough. He speaks with a very odd accent, not that I couldn't understand him, but he certainly doesn't sound like an American. His father owns a big ranch. Thousands of acres where they raise sheep, not cattle. They have thousands of them.'

Cindy was intrigued. 'That's a lot. Wouldn't cattle be better? More money?'

Babs began to take off her jewellery. 'Not in Australia, it seems. According to George, big-time sheep farmers like Murray's father are quite wealthy. Evidently there is a lot of money to be made in wool. And they're not called ranches, it's a sheep station,' she said.

'What, like a train station?' Cindy laughed. 'Well, it's good you met someone so interesting. Do you think this evening might entice you to go out more?' Cindy asked.

'Yes, it just might,' said Babs with a smile.

Cindy made to get up but then turned back to Babs. 'Oh, I nearly forgot. Deidre came by while you were out. She's so kind. She knows how unhappy I've been since Robbie sent me that letter.' A pained expression crossed Cindy's face. 'She asked if I might like to go with her and Sol to Lake Tahoe for a few days, leaving tomorrow lunchtime. They've booked a cabin and there's room for me, if I want to come.' She paused a moment. 'Joey wants to come too. What do you think? The four of us would be there for a week. I don't really want to go, but I don't want to let Joey down,' said Cindy, almost defensively.

Babs hesitated for a moment. 'Joey's never been away from home before . . .' She stopped and shook her head. 'But he's old enough now and this will be the perfect opportunity to get away from his mother for a while! Besides, you two get along very well together.'

'He's my favourite tennis partner,' said Cindy.

Babs laughed. 'And I think that you and Joey have seen every musical that's come out at the movies this summer. All right, both of you go with Deidre and Sol. I expect a change of scenery will do you good.'

The cabin was at Meeks Bay on the lake's western shore in a quiet cove with a sandy beach and small marina. Sol took them to a classic wooden boat club and, to Cindy's surprise, she discovered he was a keen and skilful yachtsman. Over the next few days he taught Joey and herself the basics of sailing, and Joey learned to paddle a kayak as well. It was an idyllic time and sometimes almost an entire day could go by without Cindy thinking about Robbie.

It was a long drive back. Babs was happy to see them, especially Joey. She hugged him and asked him how he'd enjoyed himself, and Joey bubbled over with enthusiasm about the lake and all its activities. 'We went fishing, too. I caught two small ones, but I couldn't bring them back, so we ate them. The best thing of all is we went to the Ponderosa Ranch where they filmed *Bonanza*. That was so cool!'

'How fabulous!' said Babs, smiling fondly at Joey.

As they chatted, Cindy thought Babs seemed very happy and light-hearted. Cindy couldn't help thinking of her own mother and wishing she was still around to share things with her the way Babs and Joey did.

The next day, Cindy reported for work at Alice's dress shop.

'So you had a good vacation? I wouldn't let my skin

get tanned like that if I were you. It's ageing,' said Alice, by way of a greeting.

Before Cindy could go into detail about everything she'd seen and done, Alice was all business.

'Cindy, these dresses aren't hanging neatly. Space the hangers more evenly apart, would you?' Alice walked to the counter, where she smoothed the wrapping tissue next to the carry bags with their 'The Sun Garden' lettering entwined across a date palm and a snow-capped Mount Jacinto. She was just about to return to the back of the shop when Spencer came in, accompanied by two other men.

'Hello, Spencer, George,' said Alice, smiling. She turned to a tall, tanned man standing behind her husband. 'And it's so nice to see you again, Murray. May I introduce my niece? This is Cindy,' said Alice, beckoning Cindy over.

'Pleased to meet you both,' said Cindy, coming over to them. She reached out her hand to Murray and he shook it in a firm grip. 'My Aunt Babs told me she met you at dinner. You're from Australia, Murray?'

'I certainly am,' said Murray, smiling at her, the edges of his eyes crinkling in his lean and slightly weather-beaten face. He looked like a man who worked outdoors. He was at least six feet tall but slimly built.

'Aunt Babs says you have a sheep ranch – no, it's not a ranch, is it?' said Cindy with an apologetic smile.

'It's called a sheep station,' Murray responded, his blue eyes twinkling. He spoke slowly and his accent was charming and unlike any Cindy had ever heard before.

'It doesn't matter what you call it. There are a hell of a lot of sheep on it,' said George with a laugh.

'Honey,' said Spencer, turning to Alice. 'George and I have to make a quick run up to LA. We'll be back by tonight, but I'm not too sure when.'

'Then maybe we should eat out tonight,' said Alice.

'Good idea,' said Spencer. He turned to his Australian friend. 'Now, what are you going to do today, Murray? Play a bit more golf? You seem to have been on a golf course just about every day.'

'Well, this is the home of golf. We don't have anything quite like the courses you have here,' Murray said, rubbing his hand over his stubbled jaw. 'But I thought I'd like to see a bit more of Palm Springs. I might drive around and do a bit of sightseeing.'

'Say, I've got an idea,' said Spencer. 'If it's okay with Alice, why doesn't Cindy show you some of the sights? Would that be okay with you, honey?'

Cindy was trying to think of a way to decline politely when Alice said, 'I guess so.' She glanced at her watch. 'I've got Lucy coming into work in about thirty minutes. She's one of my better sales assistants, so I'll manage perfectly. Would you mind being a tour guide for a bit, Cindy?'

Cindy felt annoyed about being volunteered without prior consultation but then Murray gave her a slow, wide grin and she found herself agreeing. 'Sure,' she said, returning his smile. 'That sounds fun.'

'Why don't you go to Tahquitz Falls? It's not far and you could take a picnic and have a swim,' Alice suggested. 'It's a very popular spot with the locals, Murray. I've been myself.'

'Sounds good to me,' said Murray. 'I could go for a swim in this hot weather. Is that okay with you, Cindy?'

Cindy nodded. 'I'll round up some things for a picnic and I'll pick you up at your hotel in about an hour.'

Food and water loaded in a bag in the backseat, Cindy pulled up outside Murray's hotel to find the handsome Australian chatting with the doorman. *He's certainly very friendly,* Cindy thought to herself as she honked the horn. Murray waved to the doorman and hopped into the car. It was less than a fifteen-minute drive to Tahquitz Canyon, and Cindy found Murray easy to talk to and interested in everything she had to say. Glancing at him from behind her sunglasses, she noticed small flecks of red in his dark sandy hair.

Murray turned to her and Cindy realised he'd asked her a question.

'What was that?' she asked, looking at the road to hide her embarrassment.

'Is the hike far?' he asked again.

'No,' she said. 'Less than a mile – and there's a lovely waterfall at the end of it. But we'll need to get started right away, before the day gets too much hotter.'

'I'm in your hands,' said Murray with a grin. 'I'm not concerned by the heat. The summers at home can be as hot as the summers you have here.' He explained about the changeable weather and climate where he was from, amusing Cindy with funny anecdotes.

When they parked the car, Murray politely walked around and held the door for Cindy and insisted on carrying the picnic bag. They set off down a well-marked trail, stepping over large rocks as scrubby bushes scratched at their legs. Cindy had been up here with Sol and Deidre on a couple of occasions and so she was able to tell Murray something about the area.

'This is all managed by the Agua Caliente Indians. This rock,' she pointed out a large boulder as they passed, 'is called the Sacred Site. My friend Adsila told me that artefacts have been found around here that are sixteen hundred years old.'

They chatted easily as they hiked, commenting on their surroundings and sharing stories of their childhoods. Cindy found herself opening up to him in a way she rarely did with strangers. There was something disarming about his slow smile. He seemed genuinely interested in her and laughed at her jokes. They paused a moment to catch their breath and Murray passed Cindy a water bottle.

'Do your parents live in Palm Springs too?' Murray asked.

'No. I'm staying with my aunts,' Cindy said, taking a swig of water.

'I have an aunt, too, but I haven't seen her for years,' said Murray.

'My mother died of cancer when I was quite young. I still miss her. I guess you always miss your mother,' she said softly. 'Are you close to your mother?'

Murray was suddenly very still. 'No,' he said, not meeting her eye. 'My mother . . .' he trailed off and an expression of deep pain flashed across his face. Instinctively Cindy reached out and grasped his hand. Murray squeezed it tight.

'Did you lose your mother too?' she asked gently.

Murray nodded, still not looking at her.

'I'm so sorry,' Cindy said. 'How old were you?'

'Just a boy.' Murray's voice was barely a whisper. 'One day she was there, and the next she was . . . gone.'

Murray looked up and their eyes met. Cindy felt something passing between them, a recognition of a bond that they carried the same pain.

'We'd better keep moving,' said Murray, breaking the spell.

He replaced the water bottle in the bag and they continued hiking. By the time they reached the waterfall both of them were feeling the heat and were grateful to immerse themselves in the cool water. They swam idly and floated in the pool below the falls for a little while. Eventually they moved towards the edge of the pool, where they sat in the shallows and began talking again.

'Do you like college?' Murray asked, sitting on a rock near the edge of the pool. 'Not so many people go to university in Australia. I went to Agricultural College for a couple of years and then went back to work on our property.'

'I guess, if it's your family place, that would be the sensible thing to do. Where exactly is your sheep station?' Cindy asked. 'Not that I'll recognise the place! I don't know much about Australia.'

Murray grinned. 'The station is called Kingsley Downs, and it's near a little village called Yamboola, which is between the townships of Deniliquin and Hay, in western New South Wales, near the border with Victoria,' he said.

'I've never heard of any of those places,' said Cindy, with a laugh.

Murray's eyes twinkled. 'I'm not surprised. Yamboola is very small and the other two towns aren't much bigger. But the saltbush plains round the area make it great country for growing wool. It's dry and hot, a bit like around here, and it's very flat. You won't see any mountains where I live,' he added.

'I love the mountains here,' said Cindy. 'Even on the hottest summer's day, when you look at the snow on the peaks, at least you can think about being cool, even when you're not. Lots of people leave town when the weather starts to get really hot. Do they do that where you come from, too?'

Murray shook his head. 'No, you can't do that, not for any length of time, anyway. The sheep won't look after themselves. But you get used to the heat because it's always been there. You have to work in it, so there's not a lot of use complaining.' Murray splashed Cindy playfully and she laughed, splashing him back.

'Do sheep need a lot of looking after?' she asked.

Murray moved back into the water and floated onto his back, spreading his arms out wide. 'You'd be surprised. There's shearing, drenching and marking them, and we're forever checking the fences. We have a hundred miles of those and you always have to make sure that they are intact to keep the sheep in and the wild dogs out. It's a never-ending job.'

Cindy felt that, although her question had provided a lot of answers, she wasn't sure she understood those answers, so she changed the subject.

'With all that going on, you don't sound as though you have much spare time,' she said.

'Life on a station is hard work, but the social life in the country is rather fun,' said Murray. 'There's generally something going on, like a dance or a barbecue. There's also the annual show, and I play cricket in the summer and football in the winter with my mates.'

'Your mates?' said Cindy in a slightly puzzled voice.

'My friends,' Murray explained. 'You'd call them buddies. And then we're only a few hours' drive from Melbourne, so I go there a bit. Melbourne's a great city. And we go to Sydney for the wool sales, too.'

Cindy smiled. 'At last, two places I've heard of. The Olympic Games were on in Melbourne not so long ago, weren't they?'

Murray nodded. 'Correct. I went down with a couple of my mates to watch some of it. I like Melbourne. It's an easy place to get around and it has some good pubs.'

'Pubs?' asked Cindy. 'I know we're both speaking English, but sometimes you say words that I just don't understand!'

Murray laughed and turned back onto his stomach so he was facing her again. '"Pub" is short for public house, but you'd call it a bar. A hotel, somewhere to get a drink.'

'Oh, I see,' said Cindy.

'Speaking of which, how about I take you out for a drink when we get back?' said Murray, giving her his slow smile.

'Okay.' Cindy felt a tingle of excitement at the invitation. 'I can't actually have any alcohol, though. I'm underage.'

'How old are you?' Murray asked, peering at her.

'I'm twenty.'

Murray shook his head. 'What a crazy place. Back home it was legal for me to drink once I turned eighteen. Is there much underage drinking here?'

Cindy nodded and briefly told Murray about her trip to Mexico, without mentioning Robbie, but then she regretted calling Robbie to mind so she ducked under the water, as if to wash him away, then resurfaced, shaking her red-gold curls. 'How about we dry off and walk back to the car? I know a nice place to eat our picnic.'

Cindy pulled herself out of the water and made her way across the rocks to lie down in the sun for a few minutes. She had only gone a few steps over a large rock when Murray suddenly spoke.

'Cindy, don't take another step. Stay where you are,' he said calmly.

There was something in his voice that made her freeze on the spot. 'Why? What are you talking about?' said Cindy.

'Don't panic, Cindy. It's okay,' he said. 'There's a rattlesnake about three feet from where you are. Just don't move and don't make any noise.'

Cindy stood stock-still. She was so terrified that she couldn't have moved or made a sound even if she'd wanted to.

'I've found that if you leave snakes alone, they'll accord you the same courtesy,' said Murray gently. 'So I just want you to walk very slowly towards me. Don't look at the snake, just watch me. That's the girl, one very quiet, slow step at a time.'

Cindy looked at Murray, who was smiling at her encouragingly from the edge of the pool. Gingerly she started towards him. Suddenly she heard the snake's rattle and froze. 'Oh my God, it's going to strike,' she whimpered.

'No,' said Murray. 'It's just telling you to go away and that's exactly what you're doing. Just a couple more steps and I've got you.'

Cindy felt as though her legs were made of cement, but managed to move forward until Murray was able to reach out, put his hands around her waist and lift her off the rock, putting her safely down in the water beside him. Cindy couldn't stifle a frightened and relieved sob as he held her damp, trembling body close to his.

Finally she caught her breath. 'I thought I was going to die!'

Murray tightened his arms around her as if to further reassure her, and said, 'You handled it well. We have snakes at home. Best thing is to leave them alone.'

'You saved my life, Murray,' she said shakily, gazing up at him in gratitude.

'I don't know about that,' said Murray, giving her a lopsided grin. 'Even if you'd been bitten, we would have been close enough to town to get you quick medical attention. Still, it is nice to be thought of as a hero by such a pretty girl.' With that, he tilted Cindy's head up and kissed her.

Cindy's eyes flew open in shock. She was about to protest, but then she found that she was enjoying it, and started to kiss Murray back. It was the most delicious feeling. Her whole body seemed to tingle and for a moment she felt quite dizzy. In the back of her mind, she realised that Robbie had never kissed her like this.

Suddenly, a voice called out from the top of the waterfall.

'Hey, you two look as though you're having fun. How's the water, guys?'

Cindy pulled away from Murray, embarrassed that a group of hikers had come across them in a rather compromising position, but Murray was not at all concerned. Still with his arm around Cindy, he called back, 'Beautiful! Very refreshing. You can have it to yourselves, we're just about to leave. Oh, and by the way, we've seen a rattle-snake, so keep your eyes open.'

The hikers waved their thanks as Murray helped Cindy from the pool. 'I don't think we have to bother about drying off. It's so hot, by the time we walk back to the car, we'll be fine.'

Cindy took Murray to a shaded spot near where they'd parked and they ate their lunch quickly. They agreed it was really too hot to enjoy a picnic.

'I know Alice mentioned going out tonight for dinner with some of her friends, but really, I'd like a nice quiet dinner, just the two of us,' Murray said, taking her hand. 'What do you say I pick you up early, we go and watch the sunset and then have a nice meal somewhere that doesn't have a lot of people, or music – or rattlesnakes,' he said with his slow, engaging smile.

Cindy was flattered. Murray was so rugged, exotic and interesting. Perhaps her aunts were right and she needed to get back out there. Maybe that would show Robbie that she didn't care all that much about his leaving her.

'I'd love to,' she said, holding his gaze. He stroked her hand and she felt goosebumps rising on her skin at his touch.

'We should be getting back,' Cindy said.

'Sure,' said Murray. He let go of her hand and they packed up their things and headed back to the car.

After she'd dropped Murray at his hotel, she drove back to Palm Desert. She couldn't wait to tell Babs all about the day.

'And Babs, he was so calm about the rattlesnake,' she said breathlessly. 'I was scared, but he was so in control. Half the boys I know would probably just have thrown rocks at it and then I'd have been bitten. And did you know that he lost his mother too?'

'No, I didn't,' said Babs. She went on hemming a little dress.

'Well, I don't suppose that it's something you'd talk about at a dinner party,' said Cindy. 'Anyway, we're going out tonight.'

Babs gave her a curious look. 'So, you're over Robbie, then?'

Cindy sighed. 'I don't know, maybe. If I don't think about him, I'm fine, but some days he's all I can think of, and that makes me sad.' She paused a moment before rushing on. 'Murray is just so different!'

Babs paused. 'He's quite a bit older than you are, Cindy.'

'Murray is mature. I mean, some of the college guys are so juvenile. Not Robbie, which was one of the reasons I liked him so much. Maybe I just prefer older men,' said Cindy.

'Be careful, that's all. I don't want you getting your heart broken again,' said Babs, frowning. 'Murray is here for a vacation, so he obviously wants to have a good time. Just keep that in mind, won't you?'

*

Murray took her to the terrace lounge of his hotel, where he ordered her a creamy concoction decorated with a tiny umbrella and a cherry on a spear of pineapple.

'It's not alcoholic, but I think you'll like it.' Cindy did, and so Murray ordered her another as they sat and watched the sunset. After that, he took her to an Italian pizza place for dinner. They chatted as they shared a pizza and time seemed to melt away. Cindy found

Murray's stories about Kingsley Downs fascinating and so different from anything she'd ever heard before. His tanned face seemed to crinkle with pleasure as he spoke to her. Cindy felt sophisticated and worldly just being in his company.

When she got home, Babs was still up, engrossed in hand-sewing.

'I just wanted to get the last of this smocking done before bed. How was the date?' she asked casually.

Cindy beamed. 'Terrific. We went to a cute pizza place. Murray is so great. His home, Kingsley Downs, is thousands of square miles in size. Can you imagine anything that big? It would be like your own little country.'

'I think there are ranches that big in the States,' observed Babs.

'I suppose, but it seemed impressive to me. Anyway, Murray's asked me out again tomorrow,' said Cindy.

Babs looked up at her. 'Aren't you supposed to be working tomorrow?'

'Yes, but only in the morning. Murray says he wants to play golf then anyway,' said Cindy.

'Mmmm,' said Babs. She paused for a moment and caught Cindy's eye. 'Please remember what I said, Cindy; be careful about a holiday romance.'

Cindy shook her head. 'I'll be fine. Besides, when I'm with Murray, I hardly think of Robbie at all, so that's a good thing, isn't it?'

*

Over the next week, Cindy and Murray spent a lot of time together. To Cindy, Murray and his life seemed colourful and exciting and the remoteness of Kingsley Downs made him like a heroic pioneer.

Murray laughed at her romantic ideas of the sheep station. 'We're not all that primitive! The homestead has electricity and the phone works, although it's still a party line. I find it far more interesting around here. I can't believe the number of film stars and singers I've seen since I've been here.'

Murray seemed as fascinated by what she showed him in Palm Springs as she was by the stories he told her about Australia. They seemed to fit together like two pieces of a puzzle. Cindy was amazed at how quickly she developed strong feelings for him in such a short space of time. On the surface he seemed so relaxed and unhurried, but she knew from the incident of the rattlesnake that he could act decisively when he had to. He regaled her with funny stories about things that happened on his property that brought tears of laughter to her eyes, and he also shared tales of overcoming hardship and heartbreak that gave her pause for thought and admiration. But she knew he was going home in a few days and she had no illusions that her relationship with him was anything more than a fling, so when Murray pressed her for more than just a kiss and cuddle, she steadfastly refused. She wasn't going to ruin her future chances for the sake of a holiday romance.

Just the same, she was thrilled and surprised when one evening, as they enjoyed their ritual sunset drink by his hotel pool, he handed her a wrapped parcel.

'This is for you, Cindy. Call it a memento of a very pleasant holiday,' he told her. 'I'll miss you.'

'I'm going to miss you, too. I've had so much fun this last week. I have no idea what I'll do with myself when you've gone.' She carefully untied the ribbon of the box and opened it. Inside was an Indian bracelet made of chunks of turquoise set in highly polished silver.

Her face lit up with pleasure. 'Oh, Murray, thank you!'

'You know, Cindy,' said Murray, suddenly serious, taking her hand, 'I wish I could take you back home with me. I think we would make a very good team. You're so young and pretty and so full of enthusiasm and energy. I've never met anyone quite like you.' He stroked her hand.

Cindy didn't know what to say. Was Murray saying he wanted to marry her? No, you didn't propose to someone you'd known for barely a week and take them to a country thousands of miles away to start a new life. Murray couldn't be serious. What he'd said was flattering, but ridiculous.

She smiled. 'Murray, that is the nicest thing anyone has ever said to me, but I think we both know it's a pipe dream. Besides, I have to finish college.'

'Of course you do,' said Murray, releasing her hand. 'Why would you leave such a wonderful place as this to move to the other side of the world? Just a bit of wishful thinking on my part.' He gave her a crooked grin and looked away.

The two of them went to their favourite pizza place and the subject was not raised again. However, when Cindy got home and showed Babs the bangle and told her what Murray had said, Babs was horrified.

'Whatever is the man thinking? Murray must be nearly ten years older than you are, and Australia is so far away. It's ridiculous even to *suggest* that you leave your family and go and live on some isolated ranch!' she said furiously.

'It's a sheep station,' murmured Cindy. 'I don't know, I think I might like it there. It sounds wonderfully romantic, all those sheep and a huge lot of land and just the two of us fighting the elements!' She smiled dreamily.

'It's nonsense!' snapped Babs. 'You don't even know him properly. I'll be pleased when he leaves.'

Cindy was startled by her aunt's vehemence, but she supposed Babs was right. It was all too far-fetched. Moving to Australia would be the adventure of a lifetime, but living in Palm Springs was good enough for now, and she was looking forward to her junior year in college, even without Robbie.

'Don't worry, Babs. I'm sure he didn't mean me to take his suggestion seriously,' said Cindy, giving her aunt what she hoped was a reassuring smile. Going into the spare room, Cindy took the bangle and placed it in her jewellery box. It would be a reminder of the blissful week with Murray that she would never forget.

The following morning, Cindy was surprised by a phone call from her roommate Chrissie.

'I hope I haven't rung too early,' her friend said. 'I know you have to go to work and I've got to get to my vacation job as well, boring as it is. But I thought we should catch up. It seems like ages since we've spoken. How're things?'

'Terrific! I've had the best vacation ever,' Cindy answered.

'Oh good,' said Chrissie. 'I'm glad to hear you've got over that heel, Robbie.'

Cindy froze. She'd told none of her college friends that Robbie had dumped her, not even Chrissie. When she went back to school she'd planned for everyone to think that splitting up had been her idea.

'What do you mean, Chrissie?' Cindy asked cautiously.

'Honey, we all heard how he dumped you,' said Chrissie, sounding surprised. 'And in a letter too! It's just shocking. All the sorority girls think he's treated you really badly. I mean, he led you on for almost two years and then, *poof*, it's all over. Not even the suggestion of an engagement ring! It's just terrible! So humiliating and hurtful, you poor thing,' said Chrissie kindly.

'Well, I've found someone else now,' said Cindy defensively. 'He's an Australian and we've had a wonderful time together, only he has to go back to Australia soon.' And she briefly told Chrissie all about Murray.

'That's great, Cindy. I'm really glad he's helped you get over Robbie. Well, I've had a good vacation, too,' said Chrissie, her voice filled with excitement. 'That's what I wanted to tell you. I'm engaged!'

'Oh my goodness!' said Cindy, shocked by her friend's startling announcement. Chrissie didn't even have a boyfriend, as far as Cindy knew. 'Who to?'

'An old high school friend, Darren! We've known each other for years and this vacation we met up again and it was as though we've never been apart, and yesterday he popped the question. So now I'm going to be Mrs Darren Sinclair!' said Chrissie.

'That's wonderful news, Chrissie. Congratulations,' said Cindy warmly.

'Thank you,' said Chrissie. 'The wedding won't be for a while yet. I want to finish college. We're thinking of having the reception on Darren's family's ranch.'

Cindy was genuinely pleased for her friend, but as Chrissie prattled on about her fiancé and her wedding plans, Cindy couldn't help but feel all of her hurt and disappointment about Robbie come flooding back more painful than ever. All that time she had spent dreaming about getting married and now it couldn't be further away.

'I'm sorry that your Australian boyfriend is going back home,' Chrissie said, changing the subject. 'It seems a pity. I'm not sure who you'll go out with now that everyone is all coupled up, but who knows, you might still meet someone else at college . . .' Chrissie's tone was doubtful. 'But there'll be a lot of new freshman girls on campus this year. Much more fierce competition. Gosh,' Chrissie laughed. 'I'm so glad I'm engaged!'

Cindy drew in a breath sharply and Chrissie seemed to realise she'd overstepped the mark. She rushed on in a brighter tone. 'Sorry, Cindy, what am I saying? You're only twenty. You've got plenty of time. Gosh, if I can get engaged, so can you.'

But the damage was done. Cindy started to cry. She was all alone. Chrissie was right about the dwindling number of available partners. Robbie had been the best of them and even he didn't want her! She wouldn't meet anyone like him again. She wouldn't meet anyone at all, especially as Murray was going back to Australia as well. Tears coursed down her face.

Holding herself together so Chrissie wouldn't hear how upset she was, she said, 'Chrissie, thanks for ringing and congratulations again, but I have to go, I'm running late.' Cindy put down the phone. Her hands were shaking. Suddenly she had gone from the envied sorority sister to the odd one out. The unattached girl, the girl that no one wanted and now even Chrissie was engaged. Cindy was the only one left on the shelf. Her bright future was ruined; her hopes and dreams dashed. She went into her room and sat down on her bed. She reached for a hanky and her gaze fell upon the beautiful bracelet Murray had given her. Maybe it wasn't too late.

*

As soon as she got to work, Cindy rang Murray and arranged to meet him in the foyer of his hotel when she finished work at lunch time.

He was already sitting in one of the hotel's comfortable chairs when she arrived, drinking a cup of tea and reading a newspaper. As soon as he saw her, he rose to his feet.

'Hello, little Cindy,' he said with a smile. 'Can I order you a drink?' She shook her head and sat, pulling Murray down beside her. Then she took a very deep breath and plunged into what she wanted to say.

'Murray, you said that you wanted to take me back to Australia because we'd make a good team,' she said.

'Well, I think you're right. I love you and I would like to come to Kingsley Downs with you.'

For a moment, Murray didn't say a thing, and Cindy was horrified to think that maybe his suggestion had not been serious and that she was making a complete fool of herself. But then he smiled his funny smile that went all the way to the crinkled corners of his eyes.

'That's wonderful!' He leaned over and kissed her lightly. 'I love you too. And you're going to love it in Australia.' He unfurled her tightly clasped hands and held them gently. 'What brought on this sudden change of heart?'

Cindy swallowed. 'Well, I've always known deep down that I want to travel. Be adventurous. Australia just sounds so exciting. And I just didn't want to let you go.'

'That's my girl.' He lifted her hand and kissed it. 'But what about college?'

'I won't need a college education where you're taking me. You'll teach me what I need to know,' said Cindy, determined to let nothing stand in the way. Murray kissed her again, deeply this time. Cindy felt warmth spread throughout her body. Murray was the man for her.

She broke away. 'Murray, I wouldn't dream of leaving for Australia unless I was married,' she said emphatically. 'We'll have to get married right away.'

Murray nodded. 'Will your family let you marry me?' he said. 'Do you think they'll object?'

'Maybe Babs will,' admitted Cindy. 'She thinks you're too old for me and we haven't known each other very long. I don't know about Dad. I mean, you would have to go to Spokane and speak to him, and you might not want to do that. Aunt Alice? I have no idea. I have a lot of trouble working out what she's thinking. My friends will be surprised.'

Murray shook his head. 'Cindy, don't worry about what other people think. It doesn't matter.'

'Of course it matters!' said Cindy indignantly. 'One of my sorority sisters ran away to Las Vegas to marry her boyfriend so they could move into an apartment together while they were at college, because she didn't want people to think she had no morals.'

'Why Las Vegas?' Murray asked. 'Did they want to gamble on their honeymoon?'

'No, they went there because the legal age to marry in Nevada is only eighteen, no questions asked.' As soon as she said this, Cindy started to laugh. 'Why don't we do the same thing, and when I tell everyone we're married it will be too late for anyone to object!' She really hadn't thought about it, but now that she'd said it out loud, the idea didn't seem so preposterous.

Murray was grinning like a Cheshire cat. 'Why not? When do you want to go? Tomorrow?'

Cindy suddenly felt brave and reckless. An adult. She was in control of her life once more.

'Why wait? Vegas is only a bit over two hundred miles away. Let's do it now. We could be back by tomorrow. Unless you've had second thoughts?' Cindy asked. She desperately wanted to grasp this chance for happiness.

Murray shook his head. 'Me? No. I love you, Cindy. I can't wait to marry you. Which way to Las Vegas?'

'I'll race back home and grab a few things, and then we'll go,' she said, her voice filled with excitement. 'I'll be back in less than an hour, I promise.' With that, she hastily kissed Murray and jumped to her feet.

As she hurried away, he called after her, 'What's your favourite stone?'

Cindy spun around. 'What?'

'Your ring!'

'Oh. A diamond, of course! What else?' She giggled. This was going to be a great adventure.

As she drove home, her mind raced. For a moment,

she felt a bit sad that she wouldn't graduate, but she could see little need for a college education where she was going. She grinned madly when she thought of how impressed her friends would be by her ability to find a real man, and a wealthy one at that. Handsome and exotic, too, and here she was setting off with him on an adventure to remote Australia!

There was no one home when she reached Babs's house. Cindy hastily threw a couple of outfits into a bag, only briefly considering that she was choosing her wedding outfit. All those dreams of an elaborate wedding gown, a trousseau, the way Alice and Babs would have fussed over her, went out the window. Of course she felt guilty that she wasn't telling either of her aunts what she was planning, but she didn't want to risk them stopping her. Instead, she left Babs a note, telling her that she'd gone out with Murray and not to wait up. She knew her aunt would be worried when she realised that Cindy hadn't come home at all, but she wouldn't be away long. Cindy suddenly visualised herself and Murray driving back into the cool desert dawn as man and wife, and she grinned from ear to ear.

*

Arriving in Las Vegas in the daytime was disappointing. There were the casinos she'd heard about – the Golden Nugget, the Pioneer Club with its huge neon cowboy out the front and the Silver Slipper, complete with a giant silver shoe on top – but the town looked shabby, garishly artificial and a little on the seedy side.

'I thought it would look a lot more exciting than this,' she said to Murray.

'It probably looks better at night, when you can't see all the warts.'

After driving up and down the strip, Murray decided

to pull into the Sands Hotel. It looked sleek and modern, a hacienda-style building divided into four wings.

'This looks as good a place as any,' he said as he parked the car. Holding hands, they walked into the giant reception hall. The reception desk was in one corner, a Latin trio played in another, and along one wall was a row of slot machines. Scattered around the hall were roulette, craps and blackjack tables. Cindy had never seen anything like it.

'How the other half live,' commented Murray as he looked around him in amazement.

'You know they filmed *Ocean's 11* here,' Cindy whispered. 'I just loved that movie. It was so funny.'

'I didn't see it, I'm afraid. I don't get to the pictures all that much. Maybe I'll have to make more of an effort,' said Murray. He walked over to the young man at the reception desk and booked a room as Cindy waited shyly behind him. She was annoyed by the sly look the man at the reception gave her, but Murray seemed not to notice.

They were shown to their room in a mini tram. The pretty girl who accompanied them pointed out the pool and the restaurant and the famous Copa Room.

'Y'all have a nice day,' she drawled as she handed them the keys.

Once inside, Cindy glanced around the plush room with its veneer of opulence achieved with large satin cushions, brocade drapes and dim lights. A crystal bowl of fruit sat on an elegant small table. It dawned on her that she'd be sharing the canopied bed in the centre of the room with Murray, as his bride.

'Do you think we should get the wedding sorted right away?' she asked. 'There must be paperwork or something.'

'How about I ring reception and ask if they can recommend a place?' said Murray.

While he was on the phone, Cindy explored their suite, hung up her clothes and ironed her favourite silk dress.

Murray hung up. 'Well, it's all pretty easy. First we have to get a marriage licence, which I gather is just a formality, and then we take it to one of the numerous wedding chapels and someone will perform the ceremony. Done and dusted.'

'Really? Is that all?' Cindy swallowed anxiously, but Murray smiled and took her hand.

'Come on,' he said. 'Let's do it.'

A couple of hours later, they walked into a little chapel filled with white flowers. It was empty except for the celebrant and his wife, who acted as the witness. Cindy clung nervously to Murray's arm. Her simple rose silk sheath had an orchid corsage on the shoulder, which she'd bought from the florist in the hotel, and she'd added a mist of veiling to a tiny glittery cocktail hat no bigger than the palm of her hand, which she'd pinned amongst her curls. The ceremony seemed to take no time at all. Once she'd promised to love, honour and obey Murray for the rest of her life, he lifted the little veil and kissed her gently on her lips.

'G'day, Mrs Parnell,' he whispered.

Cindy felt a frisson of elation course through her, but there were other emotions too. Her elopement seemed exciting and dramatic, yet Cindy felt sad that she wasn't sharing her great moment with her family and friends. She wanted to call Babs straight away, but Murray was squeezing her hand and promising that champagne would be waiting for them back at the hotel. 'And of course, you're allowed some bubbles,' he said, winking at her.

'I don't really feel like Mrs Parnell, but I'm sure I'll get used to it,' said Cindy. She kept glancing down at the lovely diamond ring Murray had bought her. She looked at Murray, so handsome and sure of himself, and felt a rush of love for him. She was determined to prove that she was capable and open to any challenge life at Kingsley Downs would throw at her.

As soon as they got back to their hotel room, she kicked off her shoes, took off her veiled hat and curled in an armchair as Murray poured her a glass of champagne. They toasted each other.

Cindy sipped slowly, enjoying the sensation of the bubbles in the tart cold wine. Before she'd finished her glass, Murray put his down and came to her, picked her up and carried her to the bed. Slowly he began to unfasten the silk buttons down her back.

'Murray, wait. I've brought something to change into,' Cindy protested, thinking of the lovely nightdress she'd packed. It was a sample Alice had received, but the company had gone out of business, so Cindy had begged her aunt to sell it to her at a reduced price. Alice had raised an eyebrow, saying it was not the sort of garment most girls would wear around a college dorm, but she hated to lose a sale, so she'd agreed nonetheless.

Murray laughed. 'Sweetheart, I want to see you in nothing at all.'

Murray continued undressing her, then he sat back and looked at her as she lay on the bed. 'Believe me, Cindy, you are perfect just the way you are.'

Cindy suddenly felt very nervous, but he made love to her slowly and expertly. Later, curled in his arms, she looked at him in amazement. 'That was unbelievable. Is it always like that?'

Murray just smiled lazily at her, gently stroking her arm. 'What say we go and find something to eat?'

'Do we have to go right now?' asked Cindy, giving him a seductive look. 'Maybe I need some more practice.'

Murray laughed, but looked pleased. 'I've married a hussy. Well, I guess dinner can wait a bit longer.'

*

The restaurant overlooked the floodlit swimming pool. The place was busy, but they were given a table for two by the window. The waiter arrived and Murray waved the drinks menu away.

'My wife and I will have a bottle of champagne, French, not Californian, thanks.'

The waiter hesitated but saw Cindy admiring her ring as Murray reached for her hand.

'Newlyweds, huh? Champagne coming right up, sir.'

Cindy quickly found that she liked champagne. It was so easy to drink and she loved the way the creamy bubbles burst in her mouth.

'Oh, Murray. This is just marvellous. I won't drink anything but champagne for the rest of my life.' Unfortunately, drinking on an empty stomach had a soporific effect. Cindy could barely eat her lobster without feeling she was about to fall asleep.

'Come on, Mrs Parnell. I think it's time to call it a night. You've had a very busy day,' said Murray, his voice full of amusement. 'How about we leave dessert for another time?'

As she drifted off to sleep in the soft hotel bed, Cindy felt like she was in a dream. *Mrs Parnell,* she thought to herself, rubbing her wedding rings with her fingers.

The next morning, when Cindy woke up beside Murray, she could hardly believe that she had actually married him. Soon he would be taking her to Australia, a place that sounded fascinating and different. She could see herself on a horse, riding along the banks of a river with Murray. Proper cantering, not the plodding trail rides she'd done up to the canyons. The homestead at Kingsley Downs sounded quite grand, and visions of southern plantations popped into her head. *Perhaps there will be servants*, she thought.

Murray stirred beside her, then opened his eyes and smiled at her.

'Good morning, Mrs Parnell. Did you sleep well? And what would you like to do today?' he asked.

'Darling, we have to drive back to Palm Springs. Babs will be really worried about where I am,' Cindy said.

'Well, I was thinking that since we're here, we might as well stay another day,' he replied.

Cindy frowned. 'We can't do that, Murray. I haven't brought much at all in the way of clothes. I would really rather get back.'

'What I was thinking of doing requires very few clothes.' He tucked a stray curl behind her ear. 'Besides, I also want to try my hand at some of the games they have around here. I've never had the chance to play roulette before and I'd like to give it a go.'

Cindy rolled onto her back and gazed up at the ceiling. 'I think gambling is silly. We studied probability in math class and the gambling odds are always stacked against you in favour of the house. You'll lose money, nothing surer,' she told him.

Murray grinned at her. 'You're probably right,' he said. 'But, I'm still going to take my chances. I might never get to come back to Vegas again. If you want to stay here while I go and play roulette, that's fine by me.' He leant over and nuzzled her neck. Cindy batted him playfully.

'I suppose one more day won't make any difference, but I'll have to ring Babs and tell her where I am. I don't want her to worry.'

'What if we drive back after lunch?' he said. 'That gives me two or three hours to lose my money, and then we can be on our way.'

'Good idea,' said Cindy. 'Can we have breakfast first?'

Murray got out of bed. 'If we want to leave after lunch, I won't have time for any breakfast. You have some, though.'

He had a brief shower, threw on some clothes and kissed her quickly as he headed out the door for the gaming rooms. Cindy tried the novelty of ringing for room service, then reluctantly picked up the phone and called Babs.

'Cindy! Are you all right? I've been so worried. Where on earth are you?'

Cindy heard the anxiety in Babs's voice and felt guilt weigh heavily on her. 'It's okay, Babs. I'm with Murray.'

There was a short pause. 'You spent the night with Murray? Was that wise?'

'It was perfectly proper. We're married!' She couldn't keep the jubilation from her voice.

There was silence at the end of the phone for what seemed to Cindy to be an eternity. Then Babs spoke again in a shocked voice.

'What do you mean? Where are you? What's going on?'

'I'm in Vegas, of course!'

'Oh, Cindy!' Babs exclaimed. 'I can't believe you've done such a foolish thing! Oh my goodness. This is terrible!' Babs was clearly appalled. 'I suppose it can be annulled . . . We'll get Spencer to get you out of this –'

Cindy's heart sank. 'Babs! I wanted to marry Murray. He asked and I said yes. I hoped you would be pleased for me.' Cindy hadn't expected her aunt to be happy, exactly, but she hadn't expected her reaction to be this bad, either.

Babs's voice rose an octave. 'Cindy, you don't know a thing about him! This is complete lunacy! What are you thinking? That you'll go and live in *Australia*?' Babs sounded distraught. 'What will your father say? Alice and I are responsible for you. How can you do this to us? Words fail me.'

'Babs, I don't want to upset you and Alice. But this is what I really want: love and adventure. Murray is giving me such an exciting opportunity, can't you understand that?'

There was silence for a second, then Babs said, 'Cindy, I hope this rash decision has nothing to do with proving a point to Robbie.'

Cindy felt a pang of embarrassment, but then she shook herself. No, Murray was the one for her. He was a good man who loved her and would introduce her to a new and exhilarating life. She had done the right thing. Cindy ignored Babs's comment and said, 'We're coming home after lunch, so we'll see you tonight. I have to go now. I haven't had breakfast yet.'

'Put Murray on, I want to speak to him,' said Babs.

'He's not here, he's gone out for a bit,' said Cindy. 'We'll see you later, Babs. And please be happy for me.' She quickly replaced the receiver. The conversation had been so much worse than she'd imagined. *It's just shock*, she told herself. *Once we get home and she sees the ring and that we're properly married, she'll calm down.*

After breakfast, Cindy drove around Las Vegas, but without Murray she was soon bored and returned to the hotel, wishing she'd brought a swimsuit so she could at least have had a dip in the pool.

Murray was as good as his word, and after a late lunch they drove back to Palm Springs. As Cindy had predicted, Murray had lost his money on the gaming table, but he wasn't worried by it. They chatted amicably all the way back to Palm Springs, laughing and smiling, as happy as any other newly married couple. They arrived back at Palm Springs at Cindy's favourite time of day, the lingering afternoon. Cindy took it in with fresh eyes, knowing that soon she would be leaving Palm Springs behind, and maybe for a very long time.

'Do you want me to drive you to your hotel, or are you going to come with me to see Babs?' Cindy asked.

'How about you drop me in town, and then after you've spoken to your aunt, pick up some of your things and come and stay the night with me? We are married, after all,' said Murray, winking.

'Sure,' replied Cindy. She would have preferred it if Murray were with her when she faced her aunt, but on the other hand, it might be easier to talk to Babs without him. She was sure that if she could explain how she really felt about Murray, Babs would understand. But when Cindy finally pulled up at Babs's place, she was a bit disconcerted to find Alice's car in the driveway. She really didn't want to face both aunts together.

'I'm home,' she called out as she let herself in.

'Do I offer my congratulations?' said Alice, striding across the room. 'This is not exactly how I would have done things, Cindy. You've deprived yourself, and us, of the joys of a white wedding.'

Cindy crossed her arms. 'There was no time, Alice. We love each other and Murray has to go back to Australia.'

'You're not going straight away?' gasped Babs.

Alice turned to her sister. 'They're married, for goodness sake, Babs. Why would she stay here?' She turned back to Cindy. 'Murray is a good catch, if you ask me. Stable. Wealthy.'

Cindy felt a rush of relief. At least Alice was on her side.

'But Alice, it's all been so fast! And Cindy doesn't even really know him, and he's so much older than she is!' said Babs. She looked pale and wan. Cindy felt a stab of guilt at having upset her favourite aunt so much.

'Nonsense. The gap is less than ten years and you forget how much older Mitchell was than me. Marrying someone older means they're established in the world. Who wants to waste time having to start from scratch?' Alice turned to Cindy. 'While I don't condone the manner of your marriage, we must make sure this is recognised as a coup. I've already rung your father to tell him that.

You will have to speak to him yourself, of course, and explain that Murray is known and respected by Spencer.'

'Thank you, Aunt Alice,' said Cindy, feeling greatly pleased and reassured by her aunt's apparent enthusiasm.

'Cindy, you are so very young and this is a very big step. Not just getting married, but leaving all your family behind and going to live such a long way away,' said Babs, wringing her hands.

'There are airplanes and ships to Australia,' said Alice briskly. 'Cindy is young, she's adaptable. Just like I was when I married Mitchell.'

'Please, Babs, just be happy for me,' pleaded Cindy.

'This is such a shock. I feel I've let your mother down,' said Babs ruefully. She sat down on the couch.

'You haven't, not at all. You've both been wonderful to me. But I'm nearly twenty-one, and this was my decision and mine alone.' Both Babs and Alice opened their mouths to speak at once and Cindy suddenly felt the need to escape. 'Now, if you'll excuse me, I'm going to pack a few things and move into the hotel with Murray until I can get a visa to go to Australia.'

Babs looked stricken, but didn't say anything. She got up and began sorting through some stock samples. Cindy saw her wipe her eyes.

'Of course,' said Alice. 'And I'll get Spencer to pull some strings in Washington to get your visa sped up.'

'You'll have to tell Joey and Deidre and Sol that you're going to Australia,' said Babs, turning back around, her eyes filled with tears.

'For goodness sake, Babs, it's not as if we're telling everyone Cindy is *dead*. Australia may be at the ends of the earth, but she's married a rich man, so it's certainly not all that bad,' said Alice.

Telling Joey was almost as bad as telling her aunts. When he arrived home from school, Joey was elated to see her, but his joy soon turned to distress when he heard her news. 'I might never see you again,' he said.

'Nonsense,' said Cindy heartily. 'I'll be back for visits and vacations and, when you're a bit older, you can come to Australia to see me. It'll be a wonderful adventure for you.'

Joey looked at her mournfully and Cindy felt a twinge in her heart. Leaving behind her family was going to be hard.

*

They kept the farewells brief. Cindy wore an emerald-green going-away suit that looked striking against her red-gold hair. Sol put Cindy's bags in the car and shook Murray's hand as Cindy hugged Joey. Deidre put her arm around Babs.

Alice kissed her niece. 'Remember, you'll manage perfectly well in Australia if you think of my instructions and advice.'

'I'll have the things you've decided to take packed up and shipped to you as soon as I can,' said Babs. She leaned in and embraced Cindy, whispering, 'Cindy, I pray that this marriage works out as well as you want it to, but remember, if it doesn't, I'm always here for you.'

Cindy turned away. She didn't want Babs to see the tears welling up in her eyes as she realised just how much she was going to miss her. Instead, she said brightly, 'I'll write all the time and tell you all about my fantastic new life. I promise. Love you all!'

Murray keyed the ignition as Cindy blew kisses and everyone waved furiously. As they pulled away, Cindy saw the small huddle of her dearest friends and family watching her go, and she wondered if she would ever see them like that again. A cold feeling suddenly swept over her, the sort she imagined people meant when they said they'd felt someone walking over their grave. She shook her head. *No,* she thought. *I am doing exactly what I want to do. The best is yet to come.* With that, she turned to smile at Murray, and they left Palm Springs behind them.

4

CINDY WALKED ARM IN arm with Murray, the harbour breeze ruffling her hair. She couldn't believe how beautiful Sydney Harbour was, and that she was actually there. Murray had organised each day of their visit to show her the sights, and she was floating in his wake, still dazzled by the fact that she was married to this worldly and gorgeous man and about to start a new chapter of her life in this exotic country.

As they strolled back to their hotel along the quiet streets, bathed in the winter sun, she tried to soak it all in. She'd left behind her previous life, college, family and friends, and leapfrogged into another dimension. The idea made her tingle with anticipation.

In the lobby of the old-fashioned, slightly stuffy but expensive hotel they were staying in, they stood waiting in front of the elevators, or 'lifts', as Murray called them. Eventually the elderly metal doors clanked open and they were greeted by the uniformed operator, who closed the door behind them and started the lift rattling slowly upward.

'Fourth floor, Mr Parnell?' he asked.

'Thank you, John,' Murray responded with a nod.

Murray unlocked the door to their suite and went in, throwing his hat on the sideboard. He casually poured himself a tumbler of whisky and swallowed it before heading into the bedroom, where he changed his shirt and tie.

'I'm popping out for a few minutes,' he called to Cindy from the other room. 'I have to see a man about a dog, but I won't be long, sweetheart. Just make yourself beautiful – I want everyone at the restaurant to see how gorgeous my wife is!'

Puzzled as to why Murray wanted to worry about a dog, but with nothing else to do, Cindy decided to luxuriate in a hot bath. She went into the spacious bathroom and turned on the taps above the large enamel tub. She poured bath salts from the bottle provided, pinned up her hair and stepped in, sinking down until the water came up to her chin. Murray quietly came in and kissed her gently.

'I'll be back as soon as I can,' he said, his eyes lingering over her lean, shapely body. 'I can't stay away from you too long.'

Cindy shivered, though the water was warm. She still couldn't get used to Murray seeing her naked. Even brushing her teeth in front of him seemed unnatural. At college her sorority sisters had always respected each other's privacy in the bathroom, but with Murray there was no such thing. Still, she thought, they were husband and wife now, and she had to get over feeling self-conscious all the time. She leaned back in the bath and closed her eyes, remembering their lovemaking and how she was learning to please him, and a fleeting smile of satisfaction touched her lips. She had been very glad when Murray had told her they would be living separately from his father in a house of their own. She longed to make it a special place.

Babs was shipping a box out to Australia containing some of Cindy's clothes, books, favourite records and a few knick-knacks, but there had been no time for Cindy to buy anything. She thought about the décor she'd seen in some of the big homes in the desert. She'd once delivered a dress from Alice's store, still on its special hanger, to a customer who was renting a huge home. As Cindy was directed to the master bedroom with its walk-in closet, she'd passed glass walls with their views to the mountains and white rugs beside a turquoise-coloured leather lounge suite. Cindy had thought the furnishings breathtaking. She quite liked the way their hotel suite was decorated, too; pale coffee and dusty pink. Old-fashioned but tasteful. Cindy sighed. She didn't think Murray was a dusty pink or turquoise kind of guy. Besides, he'd said that the house they'd be living in already had everything they needed. For the first time, Cindy regretted the haste of her marriage. If she'd had the chance to indulge in a bridal shower or kitchen tea, she could have brought some of her own things to their home. Perhaps she would be able to add her own touches once she had seen the place, she thought.

Murray had already told her something about their house at Kingsley Downs. He said that it was miles not only from the main house, where his father lived, but also from other neighbours. Evidently the nearest shops were in a little township about thirty minutes' drive away. As Murray said, she couldn't forget something she needed for cooking and dash out and buy it, so she would have to buy everything in bulk. Cindy, who knew very little

111

about cooking, felt daunted by such a prospect, although Murray had suggested that Mrs Flowers, his father's housekeeper, might be able to help her. Cindy thought the idea of being alone on the land with Murray was just too romantic for words. She imagined greeting him at the door to their spotless house, a delicious meal sitting ready on the table. She conceded that the picture she had in her head of life at Kingsley Downs was a bit vague and woolly, but she knew she had some of the skills that would help her along. She was grateful that Aunt Alice had taught her to lay a table correctly and had emphasised the necessity of fresh flowers, so Cindy was determined to serve her husband romantic candlelit dinners, even if the meal might initially be a bit basic. She would learn to cook. How hard could it be?

Cindy stepped from the bath to dress for dinner. She loved dressing up, and tonight she took special delight in adding the pearl necklace and matching earrings Murray had bought her the day before in the jewellery shop next to the Hotel Australia. When Murray returned, they went to Romano's, one of Sydney's more fashionable restaurants for dinner. While she looked at the menu, Cindy listened intently as Murray told her more about life at Kingsley Downs.

'It all depends on where I'm working on the property,' he was saying. 'If I'm close by, I'll be leaving home early, but I'll be back for breakfast,' he said. 'I usually have lunch with Dad, but I might pop back later for "smoko".' When Cindy looked puzzled, Murray smiled at her indulgently and said, 'Just time for a cuppa and a bite to eat, although at shearing time it's a big thing. But during shearing there'll be a camp cook and Mrs Flowers, so you won't have to do much.'

'Oh, I see,' said Cindy, though it all sounded something of a mystery to her. A waiter appeared by their table to take their order. Cindy put her menu down and said, 'I think I'll have the lamb and a salad.'

Murray lifted his head from his menu and laughed.

'Darling, please order something else. You are going to have more than enough chance to eat lamb when we get home.'

Cindy glanced back at the menu. 'In that case I'll have a salad and steak.'

'Good choice,' Murray said. 'I'll have the same. And a bottle of champagne.' He winked at Cindy and then took her hand across the table. 'Cindy, times can be really tough on the land, especially when we need rain, but I think you'll be just fine once you've adjusted.' He squeezed her hand reassuringly.

Cindy hoped that was true. It all sounded so intriguing. Much as she was enjoying herself in Sydney, she longed to start her new life properly. However, she was constantly surprised by how different things were in Australia. When her steak and salad came together on the same plate, she looked at Murray in dismay.

'This isn't what I thought I was getting,' she said.

Murray just laughed. 'Sorry, Cindy. A salad in Australia is not served first as it is in the States! You'll get used to things.'

Cindy smiled. 'I'm sure I will.'

'Tomorrow night we'll be a world away from all this.' He lifted his glass and smiled. 'Let's make the most of this evening.'

*

The small aircraft began its descent. Cindy stared at the flat landscape around them, a melange of dusty paddocks, dirt roads, a winding, sepia-coloured river, and a dotting of scrubby trees. It sprawled below her with a wantonness of excess space. Coachella Valley, in which Palm Springs

113

was situated, was surrounded by the Santa Rosa mountains, which made the area seem contained and ordered. Here Cindy had the sense of a landscape running off at the edges into mysterious limbo.

They landed with a bump and taxied down the short runway at Deniliquin Airport. A blast of warm air ruffled Cindy's hair as she stepped out the door. Walking across the tarmac to the little box of a terminal, Cindy began to feel nervous. Murray's father was to meet them. Shading her eyes against the bright sun, she saw that quite a few people were waiting for the arrivals. Some of the men were dressed casually in shirts with rolled-up sleeves, but most wore tweed jackets over blue shirts and woollen ties. Women were dressed in skirts with knitted sweaters or bulky cardigans over their blouses. She could tell which women were travelling, as they wore smart suits and gloves. She wondered whether she would get to know these people and one day exchange friendly chatter with them as they were all doing now.

Murray was scanning the gathered crowd. 'There he is,' he said. He took Cindy's arm and hurried towards a tall man. Murray shook his father's hand and announced, 'Well, here she is, Dad, my wife! Cindy, this is my father, Lawrence.'

Lawrence Parnell had the same creases around his eyes as Murray, but he seemed to look past her and his face was cold and expressionless. He wore a tie, jacket, hat and shiny boots, and his pants were sharply creased. He removed his hat as he extended his hand, saying matter-of-factly, 'Welcome. I hope you'll be happy here in Australia.'

Cindy shook his hand and smiled nervously. 'I'm sure I will, Mr Parnell. I love Murray very much.'

'You have much gear with you, Murray?' asked Lawrence as he pushed his hat back on his head.

114

'Not really. Cindy's having a couple of boxes sent out.'

'Don't hold your breath for that, then. Ships are slow.' He nodded to a woman walking past, who smiled at him in return. 'Bit sudden all this, son,' he said, glancing at Murray.

Murray shrugged. 'Maybe it was, Dad, but if I hadn't married Cindy right away, she might have changed her mind!' Murray said jovially.

Lawrence did not seem amused. 'What did you say your name was?' Lawrence asked, turning to Cindy and looking at her properly for the first time.

'It's Cindy,' she answered in a puzzled voice.

'That's not a proper name,' Lawrence said scathingly, and Cindy was unsure if he was joking. 'What's your real name? What did your mother call you?'

'Oh, I see what you mean, Mr Parnell. It's Cynthia. She called me Cynthia Anne, but I've always been called Cindy. It's friendlier, don't you think?' She trotted to keep up with his long strides as he reached the baggage trolley.

'Cynthia's pretty enough,' Lawrence replied. 'Here, son. Give me that. You take Cynthia's suitcase out to the car.'

The car was a solid old Daimler that smelled of pipe tobacco and leather.

'Good trip, son?' asked Lawrence as they climbed in, Murray and his father in the front, and Cindy alone in the back seat with her hat box and beauty case beside her.

'It's a long haul from Los Angeles, so I'm glad we had the break in Sydney,' said Murray. 'How're things at home, Dad?'

As Lawrence drove out of the airport, the talk turned to wethers, ewes, crutching and boundary fences, a conversation that Cindy simply did not understand. There was no further mention of the sudden marriage. She leaned her head against the back of the seat, feeling weary and apprehensive. Lawrence ignored her for the entire trip except for

115

one moment when she caught his glance as he looked at her in the rear-vision mirror. But he said nothing. He obviously was in no rush to make her feel welcome. She dozed on and off, but each time she opened her eyes, the landscape outside seemed little changed. Flat country, stunted trees and shrubs, dry, cracked dams, a creek edged with dusty willows, stands of gums, and – a high point – the novelty of kangaroos bounding beside the road.

Murray leaned over and gently tapped her. 'Darling, wake up, we're here.'

Cindy jerked awake and craned forward, but could see nothing. They were bumping over a cattle grid that lay between two fence posts. Beside one of the posts sat a large covered box with *Kingsley Downs* painted along it.

'Welcome home, sweetheart,' Murray said, turning around and grinning at her.

'Where's the house?' Cindy asked, for she could only see a narrow dusty road running between two stands of eucalypts.

'Two miles ahead,' said Murray, facing forward again.

It was late afternoon. A golden light slanted through the tall straight trees, making their smooth white bark glow.

Shortly they passed a long raised wooden building surrounded by post and rail fences. Further along, Cindy could see other fenced paddocks containing several horses, then saw some farm machinery and another low corrugated-iron shed with several kennels outside, where chained dogs leaped and barked at the passing car.

'Kelpies good, Dad?'

'The bitch had another litter. Lizzie's a good mother, so the pups will make great working dogs.'

There was silence for a few moments.

'Damned dry,' muttered Murray.

Finally, Cindy could see some chimneys come into view and then a long rust-coloured roof, the rest of the building

116

momentarily screened by serried dark trees. Then, as the car drew closer, she saw that the house was large, with grey stone steps leading up to a wide verandah. The lawns of the garden were segregated from the scrubby grass beyond by a whitewashed fence, and were full of verdant shrubs and a rose arbour. As they pulled up at the front of the house, Cindy breathed a sigh of relief. The Kingsley Downs homestead was exactly as Murray had described it, a house reflecting taste, substance and breeding. She presumed Murray's house would be in a similar style.

In the vestibule, the men hung up their hats as a short woman with tightly permed hair hurried in to greet them. She was introduced as Mrs Flowers, the housekeeper, and as she shook Cindy's hand she flicked her gaze over the new Mrs Parnell and smiled warmly.

'Welcome to Kingsley Downs,' she said. 'You must be feeling tired after your trip.'

'Yes,' said Cindy, smiling back.

'Show her where she can freshen up, Mrs F. Can you make her a cup of tea or something? We'll be in Dad's office. Won't be long,' said Murray, as he and Lawrence walked away.

Cindy looked somewhat forlornly at Murray's retreating back before she followed Mrs Flowers to a guest bathroom, noticing the polished wooden floorboards and Persian carpet runner in the hallway, and the framed historic photographs on the walls, as well as photos of horses, dogs and prize-beribboned sheep. When she'd finished washing her hands and splashing water on her face, she looked for Mrs Flowers. Having no idea where to find her, Cindy wandered through the sitting room, the formal dining room with its long rosewood table surrounded by twelve chairs, till eventually she stepped through some French doors onto the verandah, which was a long, spaciously shady place dotted with well-worn leather furniture.

Vines twined around the verandah columns and in the distance, beyond the formal gardens, she could make out a clump of bare willows and a slight glint of water.

'Ah, there you are,' Mrs Flowers said, stepping out onto the verandah. 'Tea's ready. I'll bring it out here. Would you like a quick tour round the big house while it's brewing, dear?'

'Thank you, Mrs Flowers, if it's no trouble.'

Mrs Flowers showed her the kitchen and the well-stocked pantry. She pointed to some of the outbuildings and told Cindy they were for the staff, although she explained that she and her husband, Tom, who was the station manager, had their own cottage some distance away.

'How long have you been here, Mrs Flowers?' asked Cindy politely.

'Years now. Since Murray was a boy. Come on, I'll show you the rest of the house, if you like.'

Cindy followed the housekeeper down a long corridor to another part of the large house.

'This was Mr and Mrs Parnell's room,' said Mrs Flowers as they passed a set of inlaid double doors. 'It isn't much used any more, except when important guests come to stay. Mr Parnell uses the smaller third bedroom now because it's opposite his office.' Cindy lingered in the hall peering into the dim rooms. Though clean and neat, they felt abandoned and cold. She realised Mrs Flowers was waiting for her, so sped up to keep pace with the housekeeper. 'This bedroom is called the ladies' room and it's used for guests as well. There are two more bedrooms out the back. Any more guests and they have to make do with the verandah. But people don't mind sleeping out there, although it can be pretty cold at night, this time of year,' said Mrs Flowers cheerily.

Even so, Cindy wasn't surprised people preferred the verandah. The rooms were dim and heavy with old-fashioned furniture, and hung with sombre curtains. After the glass and light of the homes in Palm Springs, she felt she'd suffocate inside these rooms. If Murray's home had furniture and drapes like these, they'd be the first things she'd change, she thought.

'Of course, my dear, Kingsley Downs station is rather like a large family,' continued Mrs Flowers, as they walked back round to the front of the house. 'We're all thrown together, station hands and the like. You'll get used to it. Come on, let's have our cuppa.'

Over their tea, Mrs Flowers asked Cindy a lot of questions about her life in America, and when Cindy told her that she had once danced with Kirk Douglas, the housekeeper was enchanted.

'That's amazing,' said Mrs Flowers, beaming at Cindy. 'I've never known anyone who's even seen a Hollywood star, let alone danced with one. The most exciting thing that's happened here was when Mr Parnell danced with the Queen in '54. Wait till I tell Tom you've met film stars!'

For the first time since she'd set foot in tiny Deniliquin Airport, Cindy felt that someone was pleased that she was there. Though she didn't want to admit it, the rest of her arrival had been such a disappointment. She looked down into her teacup and felt a lump rising in her throat. The house was grand, but cold and empty. Her father-in-law had shown such disinterest in her, almost to the point of rudeness, and Murray had disappeared as soon as they'd set foot in the house. She'd thought she might have been greeted with some enthusiasm and acknowledgement. Instead she felt completely out of place, like the proverbial fish out of water. She felt alone and inexperienced and totally at sea in her new surroundings. It wasn't at all what she had expected.

As she cleared away the teacups, Mrs Flowers peered at her. 'Are you all right, dear?'

'Just tired,' Cindy said weakly. She excused herself and walked out into the garden and around the house. She took a few deep breaths and tried to steady herself as she looked around. There were several trees which she didn't recognise, and a rusty wrought-iron seat beneath one of them. She wondered if she should venture down to the creek, but as she got to the fence she couldn't see a path, and the ground looked too uneven for her high-heeled shoes. Besides, it was almost dark. As she turned back towards the house, Murray appeared on the verandah and called to her, 'Cindy, dinner is ready.'

*

The rosewood dining table was set formally with silver salt and pepper cruets, a silver gravy boat and crystal glasses. Mrs Flowers carried in a covered platter and set it in the centre of the table. 'You said not to do anything special for tonight, so I've just carved the roast, Mr Parnell, and there's potatoes, sprouts and carrots as well.'

'Thank you, Mrs Flowers.'

'Cindy, help yourself,' said Murray, pushing the platter of meat and vegetables towards her.

Lawrence was seated at the head of the table, with Cindy on his left and Murray on his right. There was desultory conversation, which mainly covered sheep and the working dogs. Cindy tried to be interested, but her ignorance on the subjects was clear. Once they had finished the main course, Mrs Flowers cleared the plates away before returning with a bowl of jelly and a dish of tinned pears in their juice. When they'd finished eating, Lawrence pushed back his chair.

'Do you want a port, Murray?'

'No, thanks. We'd better be off, Dad. I'll be back in the morning.'

'Right. Good night, then.' As they walked into the

hallway, Lawrence shook Murray's hand again and retreated into his office with barely a glance at Cindy.

A station wagon was parked in front of the house and their luggage had already been loaded into it. As Murray drove away into the darkness, Cindy breathed a sigh of relief that she didn't have to live with Murray's father. The man just didn't want to speak to her. In fact, he'd seemed to despise her on sight, she thought miserably. *Maybe he's furious about the marriage?* she thought. *Still, Lawrence doesn't seem to be upset with Murray.*

They had been driving for the best part of twenty minutes before Cindy saw the outline of a house. It was long and low and had a bull-nosed verandah. The bulky outlines of a nearby shed and circular water tank were just visible in the moonlight.

Murray pulled up outside the house. 'This is home. I thought Tom would get one of the boys to start the generator so we'd have some lights. Never mind, I can do it.' He turned to Cindy. 'Do you want me to carry you over the threshold?'

Cindy shook her head. 'No, it's okay.' She picked up her handbag and got out. She frowned. 'We need a generator?'

'No mains power out here, so it's the only source of power at night. The genny's going to be your best friend. Sit tight and I'll get her going. It's in a shed at the back.' Murray disappeared into the night.

Cindy stood in the silent blackness, shivering when she realised there was not a light to be seen except for those in the sky. She could be on another planet with all that nothingness out there. She felt overwhelmed. What had she come to? She'd always loved the space, the openness of the desert and its night sky, but in Palm Springs there were always the twinkling lights from cars and houses. Here it was just . . . emptiness.

Then, with a bang, a roaring animal seemed to come to life, hammering and reverberating inside its metal confines. Cindy jumped and gasped.

'Right, got that generator going. I'll turn the lights on as soon as we're inside,' said Murray, reappearing around the side of the house. He took her by the elbow and guided her up several steps and along the wooden verandah to the front door, which he pushed open. He reached inside and flicked a switch. A dim, sallow light brought to life a depressing tunnel of dark wood, spotted wallpaper and faded linoleum.

'The kitchen is at the end, turn right. See what you can find. Mrs Flowers said there was food and milk for our tea. I'll bring in the bags,' said Murray, heading back outside.

Cindy stepped gingerly into the house. There was a long central hallway with rooms off either side. Cindy slowly started working her way along it, walking into each room and flicking on old light switches to illuminate drab, barely furnished spaces which looked as though they hadn't been touched in twenty years. There was a strong, musty smell in the air. The lounge room was small and cramped with mismatched chairs, each with a little drinks table beside it. A dusty traymobile with upturned glasses and decanters stood in one corner. Cindy pulled the heavy curtains at the main windows to one side and sank into a chair, staring into the darkened garden in dismay.

'There's a kerosene fridge in the kitchen and it's going,' said Murray, coming into the room and sitting in the chair next to her. 'You can get the wood oven started in the morning. We won't worry about it tonight.' When she didn't answer, he said quietly, 'Look, Cindy, I know this place needs some work. There've only been station hands living here for the past few years, but you'll get it sorted.'

Cindy swallowed hard. 'Did you say there was a

wood stove?' she asked faintly. 'I . . . I don't know how to use a wood stove. I've only ever used an electric one. You know, you turn a knob and the thing works.'

'Of course the wood stove might be a bit of a challenge for you at first,' said Murray, as he leaned over and took her hand. 'But sweetheart, it's going to be all right. Once you get used to it, you'll love it. I'm sure Mrs Flowers will show you how to use it in no time.'

Cindy's eyes filled with tears and she put a hand over her mouth as she tried to stifle a sob.

'Don't get upset,' Murray said, gently taking her hands in his. 'What's important is that we're together. I love you, Cin.' He reached out a hand and wiped a tear from her face, smiling at her reassuringly.

Cindy felt a rush of love and she squeezed his hand. She brushed the tears from her eyes. 'I guess I'm tired. It's such a big move. I just feel so disoriented.'

Murray nodded sympathetically. 'Don't fret. Everyone will love you. Besides, you have spunk, Cindy. You came here with me, didn't you? It takes a certain type of person to live on the land, but I'm betting you're up for it.'

Cindy looked at Murray and all at once the spirit of adventure that had so attracted her to him in the first place reasserted itself.

'I know I am.' She gave him a watery smile. 'I saw some sheets in the bedroom. I'm guessing Mrs Flowers left them there, so I'll make up the bed, if you like.'

Murray gave her a cheeky grin. 'Good idea. I'll turn the generator off for the night and we can hit the sack. I've a big day tomorrow.'

*

Cindy woke in the not quite daylight as she heard Murray's boots clomp along the verandah and a car engine start. She lay there in the dim, unfamiliar room for a few moments, trying to adjust to where she was. Then it all came back to her in a rush; the flight, meeting Lawrence, the house . . . She felt a sense of doom wash over her and she squeezed her eyes tight. *No*, she thought resolutely. *I love my husband. I'm here for an adventure. I'm going to make the best of it.*

She sat up. It was so quiet. Nothing seemed to be moving, although she could hear some birds singing. She was longing for a cup of coffee. Cindy slid from the bed and pulled the curtains apart. Murray liked to sleep in a cave. She looked out, and stretching as far as she could see was a flat tawny grass plain, monotonous and parched. Bleached wooden fences and the glint of the shed's tin roof in the first sunrays caught her eye. Distant grey clusters of animals were dotted here and there, and she guessed they were sheep. There seemed to be no water or shelter for them save for a distant row of sturdy trees.

She took a short shower, not just because Murray had told her that water needed to be conserved, but also because the water was freezing. She dressed and walked into the kitchen, where she looked helplessly at the wood-fuelled oven and the refrigerator. Cindy shuddered and checked to see if by chance Murray had thought to get in coffee for her. Australians didn't seem to drink it, so she wasn't terribly surprised when she couldn't find any. Resignedly she looked for a teabag instead, but all she found was loose tea leaves in the caddy next to a large china teapot under a knitted cosy. The novelty of the knitted hat on the pot made her smile for a moment. In the kerosene refrigerator was a jug of milk, a bottle of lemonade and three large bottles of pilsener beer amongst the butter and jars and dishes of unrecognisable products. Cindy had no idea when Murray would be back, and with no way of cooking anything, or even boiling water, until she'd learned how to work the wood oven, she decided to go for a walk. She pulled her cardigan around her and stepped outside.

The air was crisp and fresh, though she expected the day would warm up. She trudged around the house, assessing its layout and hoping to find a woodpile from which to light the wood oven. But all she saw depressed her further. She could see there had once been an effort made to grow a kitchen garden, but it was now a patch of brown weeds. She found what she thought must be the laundry room, since strands of clothesline ran alongside it. The room contained two large tubs and a tap, and what she thought at first was a washing machine, but on closer inspection realised was only a freestanding metal tub. *How am I supposed to wash clothes out here?* she thought to herself in dismay.

She went back indoors, agitation rising in her chest as she walked from room to room. The large kitchen was sparsely furnished with a dining table and chairs, but there was no sign of any modern appliances. There were three bedrooms, the small lounge room she'd seen the previous evening and the very basic bathroom she had used that morning. The best part of the house seemed to be the long verandah that ran along the front, which was furnished with a few old cane chairs. She sat down on one of these and looked across the frosty brown paddocks, and wondered what on earth she was going to do next. It was so quiet and still. She was used to noise, movement, *people*. From somewhere in the house she heard a clock chime and then silence descended again. *Oh my goodness,* she thought. *Is this where I'm going to spend the rest of my life?*

Then, to her relief, she noticed a cloud of dust in the distance and realised that it was a car coming towards the house.

'There you are,' said Murray, as he got out of an old ute.

'Where did you think I'd be,' Cindy replied crossly. 'Where did you go? I had no idea when you'd be back.'

'I went to see Dad. Mrs F made me breakfast while I was there, so you won't have to worry about making me any at all.'

'Murray! All I've had is a glass of water. I have no idea how to work anything in that kitchen,' exclaimed Cindy in exasperation. 'I couldn't have made you breakfast even if you'd asked me to.'

'Keep your hair on, Cin.' He walked inside and Cindy followed him through to the kitchen. 'I'll get the stove started, so we can have a cuppa. The fridge runs on kerosene, by the way, so you can't let the kero run out.' He opened the cupboard doors. 'Not much in here,' he said. 'We'll have to do a run into town.'

'Today?' asked Cindy.

'I was thinking tomorrow,' Murray said casually.

Cindy stared at him. 'What about meals? What am I going to cook?'

'Don't worry, I'll let Mrs F know and we can eat with Dad.'

Having dinner with Murray's taciturn father was the last thing Cindy wanted. 'We're not going to be eating with your father every night, are we?' she asked. 'I'd like to look after you. After all, I am your wife.'

Murray gave her a lopsided grin. 'You said you couldn't cook. I thought you'd be happy going over to Dad's and letting Mrs F look after us.'

Cindy could think of nothing worse. She'd rather try her hand at cooking on that wood stove than sit through another dinner under Lawrence's unwelcoming gaze.

'Murray, I want us to start a life together. Just the two of us. You know, like the TV commercials. Husband comes home to a nice baked dinner and wife in a frilly apron.'

Murray laughed. 'Fair enough. All right, put your glad

rags on and we'll head off to town right now and stock up. Might grab a bite to eat while we're there. Save having to worry about lunch. We'll fire up the wood stove later.'

Happy to be getting out of the house and heading into town, Cindy selected grey pants, a silk shirt and a beaded pink cardigan, as well as a pair of grey leather flat shoes with cute bows on top. She slung a fine woollen scarf over her shoulders in case it was windy, adjusted her make-up and grabbed the good black leather shoulder bag Alice had given her.

Murray stared at her outfit. 'That might be a bit posh for Yamboola. Never mind. And where's your jacket? It'll be chilly on the way back. We'll have to take the ute. I've got to pick up some tractor parts as well as supplies.' Murray was wearing well-worn moleskin pants, a kangaroo-skin belt and a leather bomber jacket over a blue shirt. His favourite boots were covered in dust. As they left the house, he jammed his hat on his head. They climbed into the ute and Murray put on his sunglasses and shoved the ute into gear. 'Do you know how to drive a manual?' he asked Cindy.

'No,' she replied shortly. Murray glanced at her and she added quickly, 'But I can learn.'

Murray drove around the other side of the house by the machinery shed and Cindy pointed to a cluster of trees in the distance. 'What's over there?' she asked.

'That's Boomerang Creek. When it's full, there's a great swimming hole there where the willows are. A pretty spot. Good for picnics. When we have time, that is. Most of the trees by the river are red gums.'

The idea of a pretty spot on their station for a picnic pleased Cindy. It seemed to break up the uninspiring canvas of dry brown grass paddocks. 'Can we plan a picnic?' she asked.

'Of course.'

They seemed to drive for ages along a narrow dirt track before turning onto a wider dirt road, which Murray announced was the main road into Yamboola. Cindy didn't recognise it at all, then Murray explained that there were two roads in and out of the property, one which went to Deniliquin, which she'd been on yesterday, and the other that went to Yamboola. They only passed one other car, and Murray acknowledged the driver by lifting a finger off the steering wheel in greeting.

'You know him?'

'Yes, that's Roger, from Butterworth Station, but you always salute people on the road, whether you know them or not.'

After what seemed an age, they passed a pretty white wooden church surrounded by neatly tended grass, signalling their approach to Yamboola.

'Sweet little church. Do you go?' said Cindy.

'Sometimes. Dad goes a lot. That's the Anglican church; the Catholic church is further along.'

Cindy watched as they passed the weatherboard buildings that made up the school, tall gum trees shading its small playground, then they were in the centre of the little town. She could see a couple of banks, a newsagency, a general store, and a garage with a petrol pump out front. On the other side of the road was a large building with *School of Arts* written over the main entrance, as well as a shop with a sign reading *General Outfitters*, although it only had menswear displayed in its window, and on a corner was a hotel with a metal lace verandah upstairs proclaiming itself to be *The Majestic*.

Cindy sat for a moment in the ute and looked along the street. She could see where the houses stopped and the countryside resumed again. She drew a deep breath. The place was tiny.

'Coming, sweetheart?' asked Murray.

'Oh. Yes.' Cindy slid from the ute, which Murray had parked outside the cavernous machinery store.

'Pop over the road to the general store and get whatever you think we need. We have an account there, so don't worry about money.' With a wave, Murray headed into the machinery store.

Cindy looked at the general store. In Palm Springs, it would have fitted into a small corner of her favourite supermarket.

Walking in through the screen door, she was greeted by the man behind the counter, who went on serving two women, both of whom were wearing sensible tweed skirts, blouses and thick woollen cardigans. Suddenly, Cindy felt overdressed. She fingered her scarf awkwardly as she gazed at the packed shelves and the few items displayed around the counter, and then consulted her hastily scribbled note: *Bread, milk, bacon, eggs, fruit, ground coffee . . .*

Once the two customers in front of her had finished their business and stood gossiping by the entrance, the man behind the counter turned his attention to Cindy. She had barely said good morning before he pounced, asking if she was the new Mrs Parnell from America. *Heavens,* thought Cindy, *word certainly gets around in this part of the world.*

'I'm Greg Wilson. You've got a list?' He stretched out his hand with a smile.

Cindy gave it to him.

He glanced at it and then looked at her kindly. 'Not a lot of those things here, and you won't need much of what's on your list, either. You should be able to get milk from the Kingsley Downs house cow. They keep hens too, so, I think you won't need eggs. Bacon's from the butcher, and we don't stock ground coffee. I've got instant. Got plenty of fruit, but. Peaches, pears, apricots. Take your pick.' He pointed to the row of tinned fruit behind the counter.

Cindy felt rather at a loss. 'I'll take some potatoes,' she said finally. She realised she'd need to talk to Mrs Flowers to find out what she needed to keep in stock.

Greg Wilson smiled sympathetically at her. 'How about I let you have a few things, like flour and sugar and tea, and you come back later for whatever else you need when you're better settled?'

Cindy breathed a sigh of relief. 'Yes, that sounds like the best plan. And is there a butcher nearby?' she added.

'Certainly is. O'Brien's, down near the pub. How's Mr Parnell senior?'

'Very well, thank you.'

Carrying the box of groceries, Cindy headed down the street towards the butcher, but was relieved when Murray caught up to her.

'Hey, beautiful, going my way?' He took the box from her. 'Is this all?'

Cindy blushed. 'Oh, Murray, I got so flustered in there. I can't browse the shelves like I can in a supermarket. Everything is so different. Honestly, I have no idea what I should be buying. I'll have to talk to Mrs Flowers.'

The trays of raw meat in the butcher's didn't look very appealing to Cindy. The hygienic ready-to-cook packaged meats she'd plucked from misty chiller cabinets at home had seemed impersonal, not like meat at all. Here, confronted with soft oozing flesh, she wondered how on earth she'd manage to prepare it, let alone cook it.

Murray and the butcher plunged into a conversation about sheep prices and the hoped-for rain as Murray pointed to what he wanted. Lindsay O'Brien then wrapped steaks, sausages, bacon and a roast in large sheets of coarse white paper.

'Nice to meet you, Mrs Parnell.' The butcher gave her a friendly nod.

'Thank you,' answered Cindy.

'I'll pick up the parcel on our way out of town, Lindsay,' said Murray. 'Can't leave it sitting in the ute.'

'Righto,' Lindsay replied.

As Cindy and Murray made their way back down the street, Murray caught Cindy's arm.

'Your shoes aren't very sturdy, are they?' he said. 'You'll need something solid for around here. Might as well get you some decent boots while we're in town. Come on, let's go to Robinson's.'

The ladies' section was at the back of the rambling outfitters store, Robinson's, and would not have met with Alice's approval, thought Cindy. Nor did it bear any resemblance to the smart J. W. Robinson department store that had newly opened up in the plaza on North Canyon Drive. Here all the floor space was crowded with racks of flannel shirts, embroidered cottons and checked blouses, crammed together with cardigans and sweaters. On other racks were what Cindy could only describe as practical pants and woollen skirts.

Murray strode to the shelves along the walls where solid winter shoes, sandshoes and boots were lined up side by side.

'Here, this is what you need.' Murray picked up an elasticised ankle boot with a heavy sole and strong stitching. 'Last you a lifetime.'

Cindy wrinkled her nose in distaste, but said nothing. *When in Rome*, she told herself. Murray also persuaded her to buy a pair of moleskin pants and Cindy chose a dark brown plaid shirt to go with them.

'Please tell me I'm not going to wear one of those?' She sighed as Murray picked up a broad-brimmed hat.

''Course you are. Sun's a killer out here in summer.'

Murray paid for the items and they went back out onto the street. 'How about a drink and a quick bite before we head back?' he suggested.

Cindy nodded. Having missed breakfast, she was ravenous.

The hotel was dim, musty and old. Though she was trying not to be critical, Cindy still baulked at the odour of stale beer.

'Ladies Lounge through there, darling. What would you like? Maybe a shandy?'

'What's that?'

'Beer and lemonade.'

'I don't think so. Just a lemonade and something to eat.' She paused at the door on which *Ladies Lounge* was written in gold lettering.

'Tell me this isn't a women-only area, Murray,' said Cindy in a horrified voice.

'Don't worry, I'll join you. Women aren't allowed in the bar area,' Murray explained.

She pushed open the frosted glass door, thinking, *Is this so the men can't see in, or so the women can't see out into the bar?*

'Find a table and I'll bring in the drinks,' Murray called after her.

There were two men and a young woman at the only other occupied table in the room. They stared at Cindy briefly, before turning back to their conversation. Cindy looked around at the simple room furnished with framed photographs and a sideboard which sported a vase of dusty plastic flowers and some old magazines and pamphlets. After a moment, she got up and went over to study the black and white photographs of what she assumed were local scenes: a panorama taken from a plane showing scattered sheep entitled *The Great Rich Pastures of the Riverina*; another, showing a creek with tall trees, was called *Riverina Red Gums*, while *'Sir Stanley', Grand Prize Ram 1949* showed a man parting the thick heavy fleece of a beribboned ram.

Murray came in with their drinks and a menu and immediately greeted the other people.

'Hello, what are you lot doing here at lunchtime? Given the kids the flick, have you?' By way of explanation, he turned to Cindy and said, 'These are the local schoolies, Vince Walsh, Drew Edwards and – I'm sorry, I can't remember your name,' he said, turning to the attractive young woman.

'That's all right. I don't think we've met before. I'm Joanna, Jo, Bright. I've only been in town since the start of the year.' Jo had shoulder-length brown hair, little make-up, but strong, friendly features, a big smile and wide blue eyes.

'We're celebrating the half-day school holiday for the Hay Show,' said Vince Walsh, raising his glass.

Murray nodded. 'Of course. I forgot.'

'So you're Murray's new missus,' said Drew, eyeing Cindy. 'Congratulations. I heard he'd been swept off his feet in the USA. It's nice to meet you.' He glanced back at Murray. 'I'm glad we've run into you, actually, Murray. I think we might have a couple of problems with the footy team.' With that, the three men put their heads together and started talking about ruckmen and full forwards and terms that made no sense at all to Cindy. She looked helplessly at Jo, who laughed.

'I don't know what they're talking about either. It's Australian Rules football, which is the game played around here in winter, but I'm from Sydney, where it isn't played at all, so it's all gobbledegook to me.' She gave Cindy a kind smile. 'I suppose that it's silly to ask this when you've only just arrived, but how are you finding things, Cindy?'

'I've only been here a day, so it's all a bit overwhelming,' said Cindy, pleased that there was someone in town who was almost as new as she was.

Jo smiled sympathetically. 'I bet it is. I'm a city girl myself and I find this way of life very different from what I'm used to. I only graduated from Teachers College at the end of last year, and this is my first posting. But I'm getting to like it.'

'Are you living in town, Jo?' Cindy asked.

'Actually, I'm boarding with the Musgraves at Billadgery. It's a sheep property, too. It's only twenty minutes' drive to school and the Musgraves are very nice.'

'Have you decided on anything to eat yet, Cindy?' said Murray, pausing from his football conversation.

Cindy glanced at the menu. 'I'm not sure I'm quite up for the full eggs and bacon and all the extras.'

'The meals are huge here,' warned Jo.

'Maybe I'll just have a toasted sandwich.'

'Try a meat pie. It's an Aussie classic and they serve good ones here,' Murray suggested.

'Okay, I'll give it a try,' said Cindy with a smile, handing him back the menu before resuming her conversation with Jo.

The young teacher seemed very interested in Cindy and asked her where she had lived in the States and what she'd been doing.

'Wow,' she said, after Cindy had told her about Palm Springs and college. 'You've had an exciting life. Far more interesting than everyone else's around here, I can tell you.'

'Oh, I don't know,' said Cindy modestly. 'What I've seen so far of Australia has surprised me. Murray told me that you can drive for days here without seeing anyone or anything, and when we flew in to Deniliquin and I saw all that land, as far as the eye could see, I could believe it.'

'Here, get your teeth into that,' said Murray as one of the hotel staff put a plate in front of her. 'I'll just get another round of drinks.'

134

'What a cute little pie.' Cindy stared at the steaming pastry smeared in ketchup. *Tomato sauce*, she mentally corrected herself. She took a cautious bite. 'Oh my, this is delicious. It's kind of a stew in a pastry bag.'

Jo chuckled. 'So you're at Kingsley Downs,' she said. 'I've heard it's a wonderful old homestead.'

'The big house is very grand, I guess,' said Cindy carefully. 'But we have a place of our own, and lordy, it needs a lot of work. It'll give me something to do, fixing it up. I have no idea where to get what I need for it, though.'

'Deni, or Hay, or you could order what you need from the big city stores. They're used to sending things out to the country,' said Jo. 'I can certainly help you contact them, if you like.'

Cindy thanked Jo. As she finished her meat pie, she and Jo chatted amicably and Cindy felt grateful to have met a potential friend in a place that seemed to have so few inhabitants.

'Tell me, Jo, can you borrow books in Yamboola? Is there a library? I love reading.'

'So do I,' said Jo enthusiastically. 'Yes, there's a little library in the back of the CWA rooms. It runs out of Deniliquin and is only open two mornings a week, but the stock is changed regularly and the people who run it will order in books if you ask.'

'Sounds good,' said Cindy. 'What are the CWA rooms?'

'The Country Women's Association. Very important organisation in the country, you'll have to join. Even I have, although I hardly ever get the chance to go to a meeting.'

Cindy felt she was none the wiser after that explanation, and made a mental note to ask Murray about it later.

Finally Murray stood up and said, 'As nice as it's been talking to you blokes, it's time Cindy and I headed back. You ready, Mrs Parnell?'

Cindy scraped up the remainder of her pie and sauce and said goodbye to the others.

'We'll have to meet up again,' she said to Jo.

'Absolutely,' said Jo, smiling.

When they had collected their meat from the butcher's and were driving out of town, Cindy spotted a green oval with young men dashing about on it.

'Is that the football your friends were talking about?'

'Yep. That's Aussie Rules. I'll take you to a game as soon as I can.'

'I'd like that,' said Cindy, feeling buoyed after her enjoyable lunch. 'I want to learn all I can about what goes on here.'

*

Murray carried the groceries and meat into the kitchen. 'I have work to catch up on. See you at dinner.' He kissed her quickly and headed back out.

Left alone once more, Cindy began putting the food away and her thoughts turned to how to deal with dinner. She stared balefully at the crouching iron hulk of the oven. She realised she should have asked Murray how to light it before he left. *Oh well*, she thought, *I'll just have to work it out on my own.* She opened the metal door of the firebox, where a bed of silver-grey ashes lay. So she headed out into the garden, looking for wood. She managed to find a few twigs, which she put into the firebox along with some newspaper she'd found in one of the cupboards, and lit it. Holding her breath, she grabbed the lump of meat that was rolled up and tied with string and glared at it.

I can do this, she thought to herself. *Murray said he was a meat and potatoes man, so that's what he'll get. And tinned peaches.*

She pushed the meat into the oven, together with a few peeled potatoes. She found some household candles, which, in lieu of candleholders, she wedged into eggcups. She checked the firebox again only to find that it had nearly gone out, so she raced back into the garden to find some more wood.

After she had re-stoked the firebox, she returned to the garden to find something to put in the centre of the table. The garden had nothing in it at all except a very healthy-looking thistle. *Maybe a bunch of gumleaves might look nice*, she thought. She collected more twigs from under the trees next to the house as she broke off a small cluster of gumleaves with their fat dry gumnuts.

She washed the dusty plates from the sideboard and set the table with all the cutlery she could find, hoping the candlelight and floral arrangement would distract from the plainness of the food. In between, she kept going out to the garden to find more fuel for the insatiable firebox.

I can't spend the rest of my life cooking like this, she thought desperately. *I certainly hope the effort is worth it.*

It was not. The roast was virtually raw and the potatoes as hard as rocks. It was inedible. Murray quietly buttered chunks of bread and said little.

Cindy was distraught. 'Murray, I am so sorry, but I couldn't get the oven to stay alight no matter how many twigs I put into that firebox. It was impossible.'

Murray stood up. 'Cindy, follow me.'

He picked up a torch and led her outside. He pointed the torch towards a large pile of wood, stacked neatly under the house. 'Darling, this wood has all been neatly cut and split for you to use in the oven. You only use twigs to start the fire. They don't give enough heat to cook anything.'

Cindy burst into tears. She felt a complete failure.

'It's okay, sweetheart. You'll get the hang of it,' said Murray, putting his arm around her. 'Come on. Let's crack open that tin of peaches. And I have to say that I have never seen gumleaves used as a table centrepiece before. This has certainly been a very memorable meal. Wait till I tell the chaps at footy.' And he threw his head back and roared with laughter.

Trying not to cry or throw something, Cindy served the peaches and said nothing as Murray ate and chuckled to himself.

*

Despite the dinner disaster, the next morning Cindy felt more positive. Murray had already left, but she managed to relight the oven using the wood from under the house and make herself a cup of tea, wondering if she could ask Babs to send her over a large tin of her favourite coffee.

She guessed Murray wouldn't be back for a while, so she decided to explore past the fence that surrounded their house. It was still early and the morning mist hovered over the foggy paddocks. She put on her new boots, took down one of the stiff oilskin coats that was hanging on the coat rack by the kitchen door, and struggled into it. It was chilly outside, but she was determined to start to learn about Kingsley Downs and a morning walk seemed a good idea.

Cindy followed the track that ran alongside the paddock fence until it took a ninety-degree turn in the direction of the shed. She wished there was a rise some-where that she could climb to get her bearings; it was all so flat. The grass in one paddock had been cut, but in the adjoining one it was knee-high. There were no sheep in either of these paddocks, so Cindy decided to head towards the line of trees at Boomerang Creek to see what was there.

The rays of blurred sun were struggling through the mist, which clung like sticky candy floss to the paddocks, treetops and fences, and occasionally swirled around Cindy's feet, deadening all sound. She could just make out the smudged dark silhouettes of the river gums, so she kept heading towards them, carefully watching where she stepped. The uneven ground and low clumps of matted grass made a brisk pace all but impossible.

At first the thick air muffled sound, but then she heard the unmistakable sighing of weeping willows, as their naked branches knocked against each other in the light breeze. As she approached the creek, she could see the cluster of skeletal, bowing canes. Standing guard above the willows was a line of river gums. She picked her way closer to the bank and saw puddles of muddy water pooled along the creek. She imagined this could be a joyous swimming hole when there was more water in it. Certainly the rope hanging from a branch of one of the gum trees suggested this was a favoured spot for a dip.

It was eerie, here on the bank, with wisps of shadowy mist still wreathing through the trees. Suddenly a shriek made her jump. She froze and looked up, realising that the sound came from a type of parrot with emerald-green feathers splashed with red and yellow. It flew into a tree and was swallowed up by the mist. Cindy kept her eyes on the treetops, hoping the stunning parrot would reappear. There was an exchange of screeches with other birds and rustling leaves, but she couldn't see anything, so she gave up and continued to pick her way along the bank.

There was something a bit creepy about the place, and Cindy shivered, not from the cool of the morning but from the sudden sensation that she was not alone. She stopped and listened, but there was no sound now, not even from the willows. She took a few more steps, head cocked, listening, wondering if the feeling was just her imagination playing tricks on her. Yet she couldn't shake the sensation that this was like the calm before a storm.

Suddenly there was a blur, a shape that she sensed was out of place. She glanced across the creek and there, amongst the tall, dry grass, she saw movement. Then it was gone. She peered hard into the scrub, then took a few steps and stopped as she saw two large black pigs digging and snuffling under the roots of the trees on the opposite bank. Cindy didn't like the look of them and instinctively she began to back away. Then she heard a sound to one side of her and stopped abruptly. She spun around and gasped at what she saw. On her side of the creek, a hundred or so yards away, partly hidden by the bushes and disguised in the shifting mist, was another pig. It was far bigger than the other two. It lifted its snout and sniffed, but did not look in her direction. Cindy was stunned at the sight of its enormous, dangerous-looking curved tusks. What if it charged her? She doubted her ability to outrun it.

Shaking, she started to move back along the creek in the direction of the house. But suddenly the big boar swung its head around and Cindy could see its glinting, mean eyes fix on her. As it lowered its head, Cindy exploded into a run. She reached the gum tree with the rope that she'd noticed earlier and, grabbing it, she pushed off the bank and swung over the creek in a wide arc. The rope took her back to the tree, and she managed to hook her leg over a low fork in one of its branches. With an enormous effort, she hauled herself into it, holding on tight. She could hear the pounding of the pig getting closer, the ground tremors seeming to shake the tree. There was an angry grunt and a thud and, looking down, she saw that the boar was butting the trunk of the tree.

Cindy panicked. 'Go away!' she screamed. 'Murray, anyone, help!'

She was not very far above the enraged wild pig, and a quick glance upward told her she could climb no higher. With sweat pouring down her face, she shut her eyes and prayed. *Oh my God, where is Murray? Where is anyone?* She was going to die out here, gored and eaten by wild pigs. What hellish place was this? She was unable to stop the feeling of despair that coursed through her. She screamed again, but she knew her voice would be muffled by the fog that still clung to the land.

'Murray, Murray,' she sobbed. 'Please, you have to help me.' She stared hopelessly through the leaves at the solid black shape at the base of the tree. It was there. Waiting. 'MURRAY . . . ' she screamed once more, tears streaming down her face.

Then she heard a dull crack, and a second one, much closer. All at once the boar took off, loping along the creek bed.

Her voice breaking, she screamed again, 'Murray, is that you?'

'Cindy, where are you?'

Relief flooded through her at the sound of Murray's voice. 'Over here. In the tree with the rope.' Now she heard Murray coming nearer, and finally she could see him, running along the creek bank, carrying a rifle.

He let out an expletive.

'Shit, he's enormous – my shots are bouncing off his backside. Stay there, Cindy. You're all right now.'

Cindy had absolutely no intention of moving. She stayed rigid in the tree. She heard several more gunshots and finally Murray walked back towards her.

'It's over. They're gone, the bastards.' He stood under the tree as she peered anxiously through the leaves. 'I'll help you down.' He reached for her as she clambered down. She fell into his arms and clung to him.

'Thank God you came,' she sobbed. 'I thought it was going to kill me.' She couldn't seem to stop trembling.

'It's okay, it's all right now.' He rubbed her back as he held her.

'They were hideous, horrible-looking animals. There were some others further down.'

'Yeah. I hate pigs, razorbacks especially. They're dangerous, all right. They take out the lambs. Have feral pigs on your place and you have real problems with stock losses. The ewes don't know they're a threat. They must've smashed through a fence somewhere. We'll have to try and find where they're getting in. What were you doing out here anyway?'

Cindy couldn't speak. She suddenly felt that she had been very foolish. Eventually she said, 'I just thought I'd take a walk. That's the second time you've saved me, Murray. I'm so sorry I came down here. How did you find me?'

'I came back for breakfast. When you weren't at the house, I thought I'd best see where you'd got to. I grabbed the rifle just in case. And that's all there is to it. Sorry you got such a fright. Don't get a lot of pigs on Kingsley Downs, certainly not this close to the house, so I really didn't expect it.'

He held her hand as they trudged back to the house in the pale sunlight. 'I see you've got the stove going. Make a pot of tea. That'll fix you up. I can't stay. I'll grab Tom Flowers and see if we can spot any more of those mongrels before they get into the sheep, and I'll have to get the fences fixed.'

Inside, Cindy pushed the black iron kettle onto the stove hob, longing for a cup of coffee. When she heard the ute drive away, leaving her alone once more, she slumped onto a chair and buried her head in her arms on the kitchen table and sobbed. What on earth had she come to? This was not at all what she'd expected. It was some kind of nightmare.

Her shoulders shook as tears rolled down her face. All she wanted to do was to go back home.

5

CINDY LEANED AGAINST THE fence, studying her paint job on the verandah posts. Painting the decorative wooden fretwork trim around the posts in the few weeks since her arrival at Kingsley Downs had been a lot more work than she had anticipated. However, it had kept her mind occupied and given her something to do. She thought the 'old house', as everyone called it, an apt name for their home, and she found it rather a depressing place, but the steady rhythm of the slapping paintbrush had distracted her from the emotions that swept over if she allowed herself to stop and think about where she was and what she was doing here.

She certainly knew what she was not doing. She was not breathing the clear crisp desert air. She was not chatting with friends or sitting in Babs's kitchen sharing a pot of coffee, nor was she in the shop with Alice, admiring her aunt's latest buys. And she definitely was not strolling down a busy street, past bubbling fountains or elegant stores. When she lifted her eyes, she could not see the picture-perfect Santa Rosa Mountains towering in the distance. Instead, she was breathing the dry dustiness of the flat brown paddocks where dun-coloured sheep blended into the landscape, looking faintly ridiculous in their woollen overcoats, their only shade coming from a few scattered trees, survivors of the clear-felling axes of Murray's ancestors. When she looked out on all this desolation, sometimes Cindy felt she couldn't breathe for the weight of her homesickness.

As she watched the sun glint off the freshly washed windows – which, Murray had told her, would only become grimy again in the first dust storm – she felt a wave of sadness. In an effort to distract herself from the tears that threatened to come, she picked up her paint-brush and stood back to admire the main entrance of the house. She'd transplanted some roses that she'd found struggling beside a shed, and put them along the front verandah, hoping they would eventually climb their way up the verandah posts.

Once she'd washed her brush and jammed the lid back on the paint can, she went indoors. In the dimness of the house it was cooler, but her spirits sagged further, for while she had been able to make improvements to the garden, there seemed to be less she could do with the house. 'Money is better spent on stock improvements and fencing than tarting up that old place,' Lawrence had said pointedly during yet another awkward dinner at the big house, where Lawrence's word ruled. Cindy had waited for Murray to say that he would like to renovate and refurnish their home, since they had to live in it, but he'd said nothing.

Though she was disappointed not to have the chance to make great changes to the place, Cindy was determined to brighten up the house as best she could. She had asked Tom if there was any other paint and had pounced on a gallon of white gloss and repainted the old wicker chairs that sat in the enclosed verandah. The first time Murray had driven her into Deniliquin, she'd bought material and made bright cushions for them. The leather chairs in the lounge room were worn but comfortable and she made colourful cushions for those, too. She'd pulled up decades of dusty, peeling linoleum and layers of old newspapers, intending to set about restoring the floorboards, but Murray shook his head, muttering that his father wouldn't like it. When she'd mentioned to Mrs Flowers how disappointed she was, the housekeeper had told Cindy that there were some old rugs stored in a back room of the big house. Tom brought them over to the old house and Cindy had flung them over a fence and whacked years of dust from them before dragging them indoors.

When Murray had got back that evening, Cindy asked him what he thought of her efforts.

'Those rugs were in the big house when I was a child – I'd forgotten all about them. I think they look great there,' he said, smiling at her. So they stayed in place and Cindy continued to mop and polish around them each week, trying to bring some life into the old floorboards.

Now, walking into the kitchen, Cindy could not avoid the pots and pans she'd put off washing after last night's dinner, since they were still piled up in the old-fashioned sink. Life, she reflected as she put on the kettle to heat the water so she could wash them, was much different from what she'd expected when she'd initially visualised her home in Australia.

Another wave of homesickness and self-pity swept over her. She struggled again not to cry. As she filled the

145

sink with the hot water, she gazed at the view from the kitchen window. It was like a still life painting. Nothing moved, not even the leaves of the gum trees that hung limply in the breathless landscape. The quietness unnerved her. She'd always had people around her: her father and Lisa and her friends at high school, her sorority sisters at college, as well as Babs, Joey and Alice. Here at Kingsley Downs there was just endless emptiness. Sometimes she would go a whole day without speaking to anyone except Murray. Mrs Flowers was always busy and rarely came to the old house. Tom appeared on occasion, but was not one to chat. Cindy missed being able to talk to people whenever she wanted. There wasn't even a phone in their house. She could hardly believe it when she found out and had suggested that it would be nice to be connected, but Murray had explained that the cost of running a line miles from the big house to theirs was prohibitively expensive. Cindy could see his point, and it was not as if she had anyone to phone anyway, for she had not yet made any real friends. She felt disconnected in every sense.

Cindy plunged a frying pan into the soapy water and began to scrub. The water was already cooling, and without boiling the kettle again there was no way to top it up with hot. Washing up was just one of the many household chores that was made much harder and more time-consuming without proper electricity or modern appliances. Cindy felt the tears coming in earnest this time and paused to take a deep breath. She felt overwhelmed by the new life she had so blithely – so unthinkingly – said she wanted. How naïve she'd been, she thought. Each day she made the bed, did the dishes, mopped the floors and dusted, stoked the stove and struggled to get a fire burning steadily for the oven. In the evenings, when the generator was running, she would do the ironing. Then it was time for bed, and in the morning she would start the routine all over again, except for the days when she did the washing. Then she would do battle with the wood-fired copper in the laundry at the back of the house, putting the washing through the mangle to squeeze out the excess water before she hung it all out on the line. Cindy managed to find some time to wash her hair, but trying to factor in any other beauty ritual that she'd once enjoyed now seemed an impossible dream.

As she scrubbed at a persistent stain on the frying pan, she took off the rings Murray had given her. She smiled as they twinkled in the light. In spite of her bouts of home-sickness and her dismay about the reality of her new homelife, she certainly didn't regret marrying Murray. He was kinder and more thoughtful than she had realised. Most days he left at first light and often didn't return till evening, but sometimes if he was passing the house he'd walk in and surprise her.

'Just wanted to see you smile,' he'd say, kissing her, before heading back out.

At first Murray had been slow to appreciate the magnitude of the adjustment Cindy had to make to life at Kingsley Downs, but as soon as he did, he tried to offer practical solutions where possible. He was patient and kind as he explained the ins and outs of her new life. He was a good listener and when, late at night, Cindy's doubts plagued her most, he took her in his arms and kissed her until all her fears had gone.

He never mentioned the disaster of Cindy's first roast to anyone, although he would playfully threaten to do so. Instead he had taken her over to see Mrs Flowers, who'd given Cindy lessons in cooking in a wood-fired oven, as well as lending her a couple of cookbooks. Cindy quickly caught on to the basics and, although she could hardly claim that her meals were gourmet, they pleased Murray and she told herself that her efforts were a lot better than

Alice could manage. When she finally successfully cooked a big Sunday night roast lamb dinner, she was so proud she considered taking a photograph to send to Babs, but then abandoned the idea as being rather silly.

Cindy quite liked being in the kitchen, as it had big windows and was not as gloomy as the rest of the house. She'd occasionally sit at the kitchen table and treat herself to a coffee from the precious tin Babs had mailed to her. She'd then flip through the old cookbooks Mrs Flowers had lent her, wondering who had written the small annotations on some of the recipes or cut out a recipe from a magazine and left it between the pages.

But today she had no such inclination. Once the pots and pans were done, Cindy set about sweeping the kitchen floor and wiping down the countertop and kitchen table. She felt nothing but frustration at the never-ending repetitiveness of her tasks.

'It's only going to get dirty again,' she sighed. Suddenly she felt the urgent need to get out into some sort of civilisation.

Is it too late to drive into Deni? she wondered to herself.

Glancing at the clock, she decided that if she left right away, there was plenty of time to drive all the way into Deniliquin.

If I go now, I'll have time for a late lunch and a bit of a look around, she told herself.

*

Not long after her arrival, after having to drive Cindy into Yamboola when she'd forgotten things on her shopping list more than once, Murray had decided that she should learn to drive a manual car. So he had taken her out along the dirt road that connected the two houses until she'd got the hang of changing gears and using the clutch.

'Not bad, Cindy,' Murray had said, smiling with pleasure as she drove smoothly down the road. 'Next time we drive into Yamboola, I'll let you take the wheel. Once you've driven in there once, you'll be able to go in and out of town as you like.'

Now Cindy loved being able to drive. She felt less trapped and she had an escape route from the house when she became fed up with her solitary confinement.

Feeling confident about driving into Deniliquin alone, although she had not done it before, she quickly changed into a pencil skirt and a silk blouse. Gazing at herself in the mottled bathroom mirror, she swiftly applied some make-up and her favourite red lipstick. She hastily scribbled a note to Murray to tell him what she was doing, just in case he came past to see her, and propped it on the kitchen table under the Worcestershire sauce bottle he kept handy for each meal.

Climbing into the car, she started the engine and drove carefully along the dirt track that connected the two houses, then along the two-mile driveway until she came to the gate and the main road into town.

Cindy wound down the window and felt the breeze on her face. It was a warm day and smelled of eucalyptus leaves. She felt a sense of freedom as she drove along the empty road and her spirits lifted even further when she arrived in Deniliquin. It was not a big town, but it was a regional hub and it bustled. There were always people about, in the streets and the shops. Cindy parked the car and got out, smoothing her skirt and feeling rather pleased with herself.

She browsed through one or two shops and then stopped for a light lunch at a small café. She found the shops a great deal less exciting than those she was used to in Palm Springs and Santa Barbara, but she was pleased to be able to look at any merchandise at all. It was certainly preferable to doing housework.

Cindy decided there was just enough time for a quick visit to a nearby women's fashion boutique called Wattle I Wear before heading back home. Rifling through the clothes jammed onto the racks, she smiled to herself. *What on earth would Alice think of this?* she wondered, lifting up a heavy knit olive cardigan. It was practical, but certainly not glamorous. Cindy had noticed that everyone who came to town made an effort to be well dressed. The styles were conservative, but Deniliquin gave Cindy a reason to leave her boots and plaid shirt at home and put on some of the fashionable clothes she had worn in Palm Springs. Some of her very pointed shoes, especially the pink ones, and her tapered slacks, were not entirely appropriate for a country town and attracted a few stares, but at least she had the chance to wear them.

Putting the cardigan back onto the rack, Cindy called her thanks to the shopkeeper and left the shop. As she stepped outside, she saw her nearest neighbour, Shirley Jackson, crossing the road towards her, a bulky shopping basket looped over her arm, her purse sitting on top. For a moment Cindy considered turning back into the shop, but Shirley had spotted her and was sailing purposefully towards her.

'Good afternoon, Cindy!' Shirley chirped. 'And what are you up to in Deni? Murray with you?' Not bothering to wait for an answer, Shirley lowered her basket to the pavement and launched into a description of a series of harrowing events involving an accident Mr Jackson had had while fencing and how the bull had taken off when someone hadn't fastened the gate properly and they'd had the devil's own job getting him back into the paddock. 'And all the while we're after that damned bull, Perce is holding on to his finger that was hanging off by a thread. Doc Forde had to sew it back on. Perce is in the pub consoling himself and telling his mates what happened. The way he's going on, though, you'd think he'd hacked his arm off at the elbow. Men, they're sooks, aren't they?'

'I'm sorry to hear about that. Poor man. Do give him my best wishes,' said Cindy, relieved to see Shirley stoop and collect her basket.

'Thank you, dear. We must get together for a scone and a cuppa. I'd best go and drive him back home. Hates not being able to drive himself, poor old bloke. Nice to see you're getting out and about, Cindy. Toodle-loo.'

The Jacksons had a much smaller place than Kingsley Downs. Murray thought they struggled a bit, but he'd told Cindy they were good, reliable neighbours who were always willing to pitch in. Shirley Jackson, who liked to keep abreast of the local news, had been swift to pop in just a few days after Cindy had arrived, curious to discover just what Murray's American wife was like and determined to be the first to be able to spread an appraisal of Cindy around the district.

Cindy had taken no notice of the dust cloud spiralling along the road towards the house, thinking that it was just one of the jackaroos, so she'd been unprepared when a car pulled up in front of the house. She subsequently learned that the dust signal gave her enough time to race inside and tidy herself before having to greet visitors.

A tall, weather-beaten man and a stout, middle-aged woman had stepped out of the car and chorused hello as Cindy had put down her gardening shears.

'The missus and I thought we'd pop in and say g'day and welcome you to the district, Mrs Parnell,' said the man, climbing the steps of the verandah. 'I'm Percy Jackson and this is the missus, Shirley. Murray over with his father?'

'Lovely to meet you,' Cindy had stammered, desperately hoping she had some biscuits left in the cupboard and wishing that she'd had time to tidy herself up. 'No, Murray's in the shed working on a tractor. Do come in.'

'I'll go and see what he's up to.' Mr Jackson seemed to know his way about and Mrs Jackson showed no hesitancy in making her way into Cindy's house, either.

'So you're fixing the place up, are you?' commented Mrs Jackson, glancing about as Cindy led her into the kitchen. 'Has Murray hired someone, or has he got you working on it?' Shirley was dressed in a comfortable flannel skirt and a handmade knitted brown jumper and carried a wicker basket.

'I'm just pottering away by myself, brightening it up a bit,' said Cindy, blushing. She felt embarrassed that the house still looked so shabby. 'Can I make you some tea?'

'Never say no to a cuppa,' trilled Mrs Jackson. 'We've been so keen to meet you. Now, I've brought a sponge cake.'

'Oh, how kind of you. Shall I call Murray and Mr Jackson in?'

'They'll toddle in when they're ready,' said Shirley cheerfully. She put her large basket on the kitchen table and lifted out a tin cake container, followed by a jar of jam and a fat photo album.

'Some of my peach jam. Had a good crop this year. And I thought you might like to see some pictures of our place and the local sights. Perce got me a camera when we first moved here, twenty years ago now, and I've recorded just about everything we've done to the property. Really wonderful to look back on it all. It'll give you a good idea of the country. How it can change, like.'

Two hours later, Cindy was staring desperately at the door, willing Murray to appear. Shirley Jackson was worse than the Inquisition. Cindy had never been interrogated with such vigour. Each time Cindy had suggested freshening up the tea and calling in the men, Mrs Jackson had waved a hand and said brightly, 'Leave them to it, it's nice for them to have a catch-up and a bit of a yarn. They know where the kitchen is!'

Helping herself to another piece of cake, she then said, 'Now, Cindy, when are you thinking of having a baby? You mustn't leave it too long, you know. I was barely seventeen when I had Glenda! How old was your mother when she had you?'

When Murray finally brought Mr Jackson into the kitchen, Cindy exchanged a quick glance and saw that her husband looked slightly amused.

'Any cake left?' asked Mr Jackson. 'Think we've solved the riddle of the carbie on the tractor. Ah, good-o, plenty left. You want a piece, too, Murray?'

'I have never been known to turn down a piece of Shirley's sponge cake. Cindy, Shirley has won so many prizes for her cakes, she's a town legend,' said Murray.

Shirley glowed at Murray's compliment.

'Yes,' said Cindy faintly. 'It certainly was lovely.'

'Pleased you liked it. Cindy and I have had such a lovely getting-to-know-you chat, haven't we, dear?' Shirley beamed. 'Tell you what, I'll make another cake soon and bring it over. I'll bring the photos of my girls' deb ball, too. Everyone said they looked gorgeous. I'm sure you'll agree when I show you the piccies. Well, Perce, we can't hang around all day gasbagging. Time to be on our way.' With that, Shirley hauled herself to her feet and she and Percy drove off in a cloud of dust.

Despite her desperation for company, it had been the longest two hours Cindy could remember. When the Jacksons had left, Cindy told Murray that, while Shirley was clearly good-hearted, she had asked rather a lot of personal questions.

'And honestly, Murray, every photo in that album looked like the one before. I hope she won't inflict her daughters' deb ball on me, whatever that is. Do all the neighbours just drop in like that?'

Murray had just smiled and told her she'd get used to it.

Now, having escaped Shirley and driving triumphantly back from Deniliquin, Cindy slowed as she passed a paddock near the start of their property, hoping to catch a glimpse of Murray. She missed his company, and their long talks together. But these days he was usually gone for most of the day and when he arrived home for dinner he was tired, and either dozed off while they listened to the radio or was asleep even before Cindy came to bed. As much as Cindy would have liked to spend more time with him, she could not deny that her husband was an extremely hard worker. Moreover, she was beginning to realise how much people in the district respected him. She would often hover on the sidelines watching and listening when he dealt with people, and quickly saw that he always seemed to be straight and fair with them. Even when the shearers were difficult or the jackaroos lazy, he was firm, tough, but even-handed, and as she watched him in action she could not help but admire the easy rapport he had with them.

It was approaching sunset when she pulled up at the old house. Murray was not yet home, so she threw her note away and was about to make herself a cup of tea and organise the evening meal when a spiral of dirt on the horizon announced Murray's return. Cindy rushed to the bedroom and retouched her hair and lipstick before greeting her husband at the door with a kiss. Murray's eyes creased as he smiled.

'Now that's what I call a welcome. How was your day, sweetheart?'

'Great –' But before she could say more, Murray interrupted her.

'I hope you haven't started dinner. Dad wants us over at the big house for dinner. I'd better go wash up and change. You can tell me about your day in the car.'

Cindy was quiet on the drive over to Lawrence's house, dreading the uncomfortable meal to come. She was doing her best not to complain about the difficulties of the life that she now shared with Murray, but really it was her father-in-law who was her greatest irritant. Lawrence had made it clear to her right from the start that the Parnell family stood for something: they were graziers, landowners who represented not just a lifestyle but a productive part of a valuable industry, one on which the entire country relied. And wool was more than a means of income. It represented the struggle of pioneers, the adaptability and ingenuity of Australian sheep breeders who'd developed their wool to be the finest in the world. Kingsley Downs was modest in comparison to some of the much larger properties both in the Riverina and in other parts of the country, but Cindy was sure there must be wool growers who weren't as successful as Kingsley Downs, for it could not be denied that the Parnells had a fine reputation for producing quality wool. Unfortunately, Lawrence had also made it crystal clear that he did not want Cindy interfering in this world, his bailiwick. She wasn't sure why he so disapproved of her, was disdainful even, and Murray could supply no satisfactory explanation.

'Why is your father so cold to me? Why doesn't he like me?' she'd asked, close to tears after an earlier visit to the homestead when Lawrence had barely spoken to her for the entire evening. 'Is there someone else he wished you'd married? Someone he thought would have been a better choice? What is so wrong with me?'

'Cindy, stop saying things like that. Don't be silly. Of course there was no one else. Look, I can't explain

Dad . . . it's just how he is,' Murray had said. 'I know he's difficult to get on with, but eventually he'll grow to accept you, I'm sure he will. Just give it time.'

Cindy had tried hard to make friends with Lawrence, but her approaches were always rebuffed. Since Murray and his father worked so closely together, she wanted her relationship with her father-in-law to work, but no matter what she did Lawrence remained cold, and even contemptuous. She might have given up on him altogether had it not been for one night when, out of the blue, Murray had turned to her in bed. She'd thought he had been asleep and was startled when he'd reached for her and taken her in his arms, muttering softly into her hair, 'Please try, Cin. I know Dad can be hard, but just try to be nice to him. For me.'

It was a small voice, like the pleading of a little boy, and then, as if regretting the words that had tumbled from him, he'd stilled her mouth by kissing her hard and holding her tight, making love to her almost violently, as if to force away the weakness he had momentarily shown.

There was something about Murray's actions that had warned Cindy not to question him or mention the incident again. So she did try to swallow her annoyance, her hurt and her outrage at Lawrence's incessant rudeness and pointed barbs, and be as civil to her father-in-law as she could, for Murray's sake. For both their sakes. But she hated doing so.

Entering Lawrence's house after their silent drive over, Cindy smiled brightly at her father-in-law. 'Good evening, Lawrence, how was your day?'

As usual Lawrence barely acknowledged her presence, turning instead to Murray and beckoning him into his study as if she hadn't spoken. Did he know how rude he was? she wondered. Left standing awkwardly in the hall, Cindy sighed and went to find Mrs Flowers.

156

At dinner, she sat quietly as Murray and Lawrence discussed the events of the day and future plans. She fingered the lace edging of the tablecloth and picked at her food. She yawned a couple of times, feigning tiredness and hoping Murray would suggest they leave. Murray gave Cindy several sympathetic glances and smiles, but continued to talk to Lawrence. Cindy took a deep breath and tried to be patient. Murray was caught between a rock and a hard place, between his wife and his father. She wished he was more supportive of her, but she knew he was doing his best. She'd confided to Babs in one of her frequent letters to her aunt that she found Murray's father to be cold and stand-offish to the point of rudeness and that she had no idea how to handle the situation.

Babs had written back, *Well, at least you only have one in-law and not a whole tribe!*

Cindy didn't say anything more about Lawrence's chilly demeanour to Babs, so as not to upset her. Darling Babs, so warm, affectionate and outgoing. Always so caring and generous, she would be devastated if she knew how Lawrence was treating her niece.

As Murray and Lawrence talked on, she looked about the room. How austere it was, old-fashioned and cold-looking. It certainly lacked a woman's touch, Cindy thought. Indeed, there was nothing really personal in the décor of the house at all; no hint that a woman had ever lived here and made it her home. She had asked Murray once why there were no photos of his mother about and he'd replied tightly, 'It's too painful for my father to be reminded of her. Please don't ever say anything, will you?' And then he'd swiftly changed the subject, as he did whenever Cindy mentioned his mother.

Pushing her food around her plate, Cindy chewed over lots of scenarios in her mind, trying to explain Lawrence's attitude. Was he jealous that his close relationship with his son had been invaded by an outsider? Or did Cindy's loving presence in Murray's life remind Lawrence of what he had lost? Was he fearful that she might steal Murray away, back to the States, with emotional blackmail? Or was it that Lawrence thought that she was the wrong wife for Murray, an interloper who would never fit in? If only Lawrence would say how he felt, then there was a chance things could change. But, thought Cindy, maybe Lawrence had so adored his wife Rose that her loss had totally crippled him emotionally. The more she thought about the reasons that might explain Lawrence's attitude towards her, the more powerless Cindy felt.

Finally, Mrs Flowers appeared to clear their plates. She smiled at Cindy as she stacked them and Cindy asked after Tom. Cindy had quickly grown to like the Flowerses. She chatted with Tom when he came to the house, but he was a quiet bushman who spoke when spoken to, and never used four or five words when two would suffice. Cindy liked to talk to Mrs Flowers and tried to prise bits of information about the family from the housekeeper when she had the chance, especially about Murray and what he'd been like as a little boy. But, although Mrs Flowers was not as quiet as her husband, neither was she one to gossip, so when an occasional anecdote or small morsel of information was winkled out of her, Cindy savoured it.

After Mrs Flowers had departed with the dishes, Murray finally turned to Cindy and suggested they leave, as he had an early start. They rose from the table and made their way into the hall, where Lawrence shook his son's hand and, without a backwards glance at Cindy, stalked off to his study. Cindy repressed the urge to yell after him and instead meekly followed Murray to the car.

She watched Murray's face as he drove back to their place. Passing the fields between the two houses, she could see his mind turning over the work to be done. She'd learned that, whatever his interests might have been as a child, Murray's future had always been linked to Kingsley Downs. He would never join the navy and see the world, become a banker or a geologist. Cindy couldn't help wondering what it would be like to know your destiny from day one. As far as she knew, Murray had not entertained any ambition other than running Kingsley Downs. It seemed so different from her life, which had taken some unexpected twists and turns. When she was young, she would never have expected she would one day live in a place like Palm Springs with two aunts who had given her two very different perspectives on life. Or that she'd go to college at Santa Barbara, where she'd met girls intent on pursuing a variety of ambitions, from travelling the world to getting a job, but above all, finding a husband. And she'd never once entertained the idea that she would find herself married and living in Australia.

It had been so different for Murray, who'd lost his mother when he was so young and had only had Lawrence as a mentor, parent, guide and friend. Apart from his years at boarding school and his one trip abroad, her husband seemed to have had a very narrow existence. Perhaps, when he had fallen for Cindy, it was because she was such an exotic flower, so different from the girls he and his friends were expected to marry. Had marrying Cindy been an act of rebellion on Murray's part, and it was that which had made Lawrence resentful of her?

Arriving at their house, Murray retired to bed almost immediately, with Cindy following soon after. Folding down the thick flannel sheets, Cindy climbed into their bed and leaned over to smooth the hair off her husband's sun-beaten face. No matter what, Murray had chosen her. He loved her. He was doing his best to support her. She wouldn't let him down. And, while she didn't like Lawrence's behaviour, or condone it, Cindy decided Murray's father was a deeply wounded man, a bitter man, but there was nothing she could do to change him. As she lay down and felt sleep creep over her, she thought of what Alice would advise: 'If you can't change it, lump it or live with it, girl,' and she smiled. The least she could do was give her husband all the love and tenderness she could. That would be enough.

*

As the weeks passed, Cindy found, rather to her surprise, that she was beginning to accept the unpalatable and look forward to the things in her new life that she enjoyed. She relished her weekly drive into the little township of Yamboola. She had become a more than competent driver, the gears no longer crunching when she changed them and the days of kangaroo jump-starts gone. The roads were generally empty, which gave her the feeling that she had the world to herself. Sometimes, she sang as she drove, recalling some of the songs of the Palm Springs stars which Babs so liked. Slowly she found herself appreciating her surroundings. The different greens and browns of the bush, the ever-changing sky and the contrast of starkness and stillness gave the landscape its own kind of beauty.

Besides Lawrence, Cindy found her isolation the hardest thing to deal with, and she disliked being left alone for most of the day. After a few weeks, determined to do something about it, she asked Murray if he could vary his routine and come home for lunch.

Murray said he'd do his best. He still left at the crack of dawn, but now he returned a couple of hours later for breakfast, and if he could get back for lunch, he would. Sometimes Cindy would take his lunch and a thermos of tea out to where he was working and they'd sit and share the sandwiches he liked. But mostly he was busy with dogs, horses and sheep and she got the feeling he was anxious to get back to work and check that the jackaroo

160

wasn't slacking off or having a sly cigarette while Murray was occupied by lunch with Cindy.

'It's lovely of you to take the trouble to drive out this way and bring me some lunch, Cin. Mrs F could have made some and Tom could have brought it out, you know.'

'*I'm* your wife, not Mrs Flowers. It's my job to look after you.'

'And you do a great job,' said Murray cheerfully.

*

As much as she loved Murray, and even though she was feeling more positive about things, Cindy yearned for more companionship. As luck would have it, one Friday afternoon as she was leaving the general store in Yamboola, she heard a voice call out, 'Hi there, Cindy!'

Cindy turned around to see who it was who knew her, and saw Joanna, the schoolteacher she'd met on her first day in town when she'd been ushered into the Ladies Lounge at the hotel.

'Why hello, it's nice to see you again,' she said, walking over to Joanna.

'How are you settling in? Been shopping?'

Cindy smiled broadly. 'I always seem to forget something on the shopping list. Still getting used to not having a grocery store around the corner. But I enjoy the drive here. Gets me out of the house.'

'Do you have to hurry back? We could stop and have something to drink, if you like,' Joanna suggested.

Cindy nodded. 'Lovely.' She could think of nothing better than to spend some time with another woman close to her own age.

They settled at a table in the Ladies Lounge and ordered shandies. In no time, they'd shared brief histories and also found a lot of common interests, especially books and music.

'I really miss the TV shows I used to watch in the States,' said Cindy.

Jo nodded. 'I don't have TV where I live, either. But I like to listen to the radio. It can be good company and you learn a lot about what goes on around here, as well as in the rest of the country. Do you like the movies?'

'I sure do,' exclaimed Cindy. 'My young cousin and I went all the time back in Palm Springs. I haven't had the chance to go since I've been here.'

'Then maybe we could drive into Deni when there's a good film on.'

Cindy grinned. 'What a great idea. I'd love to. Maybe Murray could come as well, although I think he only likes action movies,' she added.

As they finished their drinks, they agreed to meet regularly on Friday afternoons after Joanna finished at the school. Suddenly having a friend made Cindy's life seem a lot more interesting.

*

After a while, the moments when Cindy felt over-whelmed, sad and homesick became fewer and fewer. She still felt lonely sometimes and looked forward more than anything to letters from home. Babs wrote regu-larly, but Cindy also enjoyed the less frequent letters from her father and her college friend Chrissie, as well as notes and funny cards from Joey and the very occasional letter from Alice, who only seemed to write when she had something to boast about. It was often Babs's latest news that engendered in Cindy a bittersweet longing for Palm Springs, and sometimes made her giggle, especially when there was a drama involving Alice. Most recently, it seemed that Alice had declared war against a developer who wanted to build 'yet another gross resort complex' near to her new home.

Babs always asked for photos of Kingsley Downs and the surrounding district, so that she and Joey could visualise where Cindy lived. So Cindy decided to put to use the camera Alice and Spencer had given her for her birthday, hoping that her photos might show what she meant when she wrote about the sweeping vistas and the creek, or their funny old house and its surrounds, as well as Yamboola and Deniliquin. She wondered if they'd see these scenes as she had come to: as beautiful and interesting, pretty and magical.

So Cindy spent a lot of time in the first six months of her marriage staring through the lens of her camera, taking photographs for her aunt, showing Babs what she was doing in the garden to make the house look more welcoming. And, even though she suspected Babs and Joey might be a bit nauseated by the idea, she'd snapped pictures of the little gauzed meat house where Tom butchered their fresh meat. To Cindy, the odour of the slaughterhouse always hung about the worn surface of the butcher's wooden block outlined through the flyscreen. It had taken Cindy time to adjust to the tub of butchered lamb that was delivered to her regularly, and while Murray saw nothing wrong with eating lamb three times a day, Cindy found it heavy going. Alice would have been appalled. Cindy began to think she should raise some chickens and put in a vegetable patch to vary their diet.

As much as she hated going over to the big house, in case she ran into Lawrence, Cindy knew that Babs and Joey should see photos of the big house too, not just because it was the house where Murray had grown up, but also because it was the hub of the Kingsley Downs operations.

When Lawrence and Murray had gone off to a sheep sale one day, Cindy drove over to take some photos.

She passed the paddocks near the house, then stopped to take a picture or two of Stan and Simpson, two old

163

stockhorses quietly grazing in their yard. She parked the car and started to take some pictures of the outside of the big house as well as the beautifully kept gardens, then she headed over to where the great woolshed squatted on its stumps, surrounded by holding pens. Dotted in the sheepyards were a couple of peppercorn trees, their trailing leaves casting a tracery of shade on the hard earth beneath them.

The woolshed loomed large, its massive iron hat of a roof stained red with rust. Decades of heat, rain and frost had weathered the building. She looked at the chutes, down which indignant shorn sheep had been shunted a few weeks before, their pink skin barely covered with a baby fuzz of white wool, their valuable fleece left splayed on the wool-classing table.

Inside the building it was dim and cool, with sunshine slanting in from the high louvred windows over the sheep stands. Cindy looked up at the shearing machinery sitting silent in each stand. The wooden floorboards were solid, stained shiny, the tables greased from generations of oily wool. Log pillars, which held up the roof, were so big you couldn't wrap your arms around them. And everywhere Cindy inhaled the gentle smell of lanoline, softening the lost echoes of rough and tumble, shouting, sweating men, bleating animals and the buzz of the shears. Her footsteps reverberated, dust motes rose and flickered in the rays of sunlight. Details leaped out at her; proud numbers shorn in a day, initials and a date scratched here and there into the old wooden walls.

From the woolshed she walked over to the shearers' quarters. Ten basic rooms stood in a long row. Through a dusty window she could see an iron bedstead, rolled mattress, a cupboard with a sticky door and several rattling hangers dangling from a wire. There was a small fly-spotted mirror on a wall, a peeling picture, a poster and an old calendar. A naked light bulb hung from the ceiling.

The amenities block was a shadowy cement box of showerheads and lavatories.

Near the shearers' quarters was a small tin shed that served as the kitchen, beside a roughly built mess hall. Inside, a faded oilcloth was tacked to the long table. Mesh screens on the cupboards shielded food, plates and cutlery from the dust and flies. An old refrigerator leaned tiredly against a wall, its door ajar. Outside, a tin awning sheltered a forty-four-gallon drum cut in half lengthways, which stood on small brick footings so that it served as a barbecue. And in the dirt, a ring of blackened stones and ash was testimony of cheerful evenings around the campfire.

It was a masculine space; even Mrs Flowers rarely ventured here. The camp cooks tended to be obsessive rulers of their domain, and the best shearers' cooks, mostly men, were in great demand. It was stressed to Cindy more than once that if the food was good and plentiful, it kept the men happy.

Cindy passed the old machinery shed, home to hay bales, a tractor and farm equipment, spare parts and diesel drums, where Mrs Flowers took warm biscuits and a billycan of tea to Murray and Tom for their smoko when they were repairing some kind of mechanical disaster.

Later, after she'd had the photos developed and was carefully placing them in an envelope for postage, Cindy wondered what Babs, Joey and Alice would make of the pictures. For Cindy found it was almost impossible to capture what she had slowly come to love about Kingsley Downs: the space, the beauty of the changing sky, and the creek with its lovely trees. Now that she had put the episode of the wild pig behind her, she found it an enchanting place. She loved the birdlife that surrounded her; the loping flocks of emus, heads stretched forward, legs a blur when they ran, the darting finches, the clouds of brilliant emerald-green budgerigars rising from bare trees like exploding flowers, and the bird she'd first glimpsed when she had just arrived, the glorious superb parrot.

She loved waking to the chortle and songs of the birds that lived close to the house, the currawongs and magpies, kookaburras and butcher birds, and during the night she would hear the screech of the owls, and occasionally other strange cries she was yet to identify.

At first the night noises had made her afraid, but now even the distant calls of wild dogs and foxes didn't worry her. And lying in bed with Murray's steady breathing beside her, she loved the sounds of their house – the creaks of the aged timber, the rattle of loose tin on the roof – all of which had now become comfortingly familiar.

She tried to recall having had any interest in any of the wildlife around Palm Springs. Except for the distant howl of a coyote, she'd never had a sense of sharing space with other creatures; not in the way she did at Kingsley Downs. The first time she had seen black swans, she was captivated, and the wild ducks, wallabies and a bumbling wombat had enthralled her. So, although Cindy was more conscious than she'd ever been of sharing the land with nature's creatures, she felt they had all come to a kind of understanding. Each had its place and attendant right to be there, even the deadly snakes. She'd come to accept the country around her as it had accepted her.

She was very pleased to discover that the locals had embraced her wholeheartedly as well. As time went on, she became less of a novelty to her neighbours and more of a friend; she was simply Mrs Parnell from Kingsley Downs. She felt increasingly at ease in the shops and the pub, though she sometimes liked to idly compare enjoying a shandy in the Ladies Lounge of the Majestic with Jo on a Friday afternoon with the fancy cocktails in the smart surrounds of the Thunderbird and Racquet Clubs.

She had also to dispel more than one of the daydreams she'd had about her new life before she had any idea what it was really like. Her romantic notions of life on a sheep station, for one, turned out to be very different from the reality. Although the stud's fortunes rested on the wool from thousands of sheep, Cindy found she had little interest in them and almost no contact with them except when they were rounded up at shearing time. Murray had brought a baby lamb to her to be bottle-fed as its mother had been killed by wild dogs, but the novelty had soon worn off with the endless feedings and the fact that, wherever she went, the gangly little animal seemed always to be underfoot, plaintively bleating. She was pleased when Murray found a ewe willing to take it.

She had also pictured herself riding the range with Murray, checking fences and moving stock, but in actuality this had never been possible, as the gentle trail rides around Palm Springs had ill equipped her for the serious horsemanship needed on a sheep station. She also learned that the station's working dogs were not household pets and were kept at a distance. Even the haughty old cat at the big house earned its keep hunting mice and rats and disdained her overtures of friendship.

But she loved to stop and occasionally watch Murray when he worked. This was not the suave well-dressed man she'd met and fallen in love with in Palm Springs. Now he had a different demeanour: strong, sure of himself, his skin bronzed, and beneath the battered felt hat pulled low over his face, his blue eyes were like sapphires, and the sleeves of his work shirt were rolled high up his tanned arms, which strained as he lifted a sheep into the back of his ute. Yet there was a tender and gentle side to him which showed when he stopped to fondle the ears of his favourite dog or lift an injured lamb, or fondly rubbed his hand along his horse's neck. Sometimes Cindy felt herself overwhelmed by the love and admiration she had for her husband. He was her protector and guide in the strange new land of marriage.

*

It was a morning that promised rain. Clouds were scudding and there was a sense of electricity in the air; the horses were kicking their heels and feisty, and an invisible oppressiveness that suggested a change in the weather made eyes turn skyward.

The previous evening, Murray and Lawrence had been studying the accounts. Now, with rain imminent, there was a flurry of preparations and Murray wanted to meet his father at one of the dams to check its pipes and pumps, so he asked Cindy to take an envelope of documents to the big house for his father.

When Cindy drove up to the main house and wandered in, she found Mrs Flowers up to her elbows in flour, baking bread.

'Oh, Cindy, would you mind putting that envelope on Mr Parnell's desk in his study? I'm covered in dough. This weather isn't helping the bread rise,' the housekeeper muttered.

Cindy dropped the envelope on Lawrence's tidy desk and glanced around the room. It had as much personality as Lawrence: it was austere, formal and lacked anything personal. There were leather-bound books on the shelves, a carriage clock on the mantelpiece, and a gold pen set on the desk. She returned to the kitchen, her curiosity piqued.

'Mrs Flowers, are there any personal things in Mr Lawrence's bedroom?' she asked cautiously.

'Good heavens, what a thing to ask!' Mrs Flowers exclaimed, looking up.

Cindy pressed on. She wanted to know. 'What I mean is, photographs, things from the past. I've never seen any in the rest of the house. Not even the study. Her name isn't even mentioned. There seems to be no reminder of Murray's mother, Rose at all. It's like she never existed.'

'Perhaps you should ask your husband,' replied Mrs Flowers quietly. 'It's not really my place to discuss it.'

Cindy stepped forward. 'Mrs Flowers, I wouldn't like to put you in an awkward situation, but Murray never mentions his mother, and if I raise the subject, he gives an evasive answer.' Cindy threw up her hands in frustration, but then she took a breath and lowered her voice. 'I'm just curious, that's all. I don't understand why the topic of Rose is taboo. Were you here when she died? What was she like? What was Lawrence like when she was alive? Was he a happier person? I know it must have been a tragic event, but even so, I can't understand why there is no trace of Rose in her own house. It's like Lawrence wants to pretend she was never even here! I just wonder why the topic is so sensitive for Murray that he won't even talk about it with me, his wife.'

Mrs Flowers was silent for a moment, punching the dough down into the bread pans. Then she looked intently at Cindy.

'There's a reason that no one wants to talk about Rose and why Mr Parnell wants no reminders of her in this house,' she said quietly. 'She didn't die. She ran away. She left her eleven-year-old son and husband and did a bunk. It devastated Mr Parnell and I'm not sure that Murray ever got over his mother's betrayal.'

Cindy gasped. 'But I thought . . .' She shook her head. 'How can that be? I mean, surely a woman wouldn't just run off and leave her son?' she said in a shocked voice. 'That's so terrible.'

Mrs Flowers' face was hidden as she bent over to open the door of the oven. 'They won't talk about it, of course, so please don't say –' She broke off at the sound of heavy footsteps outside on the verandah.

'Mrs Flowers!' Lawrence bellowed. 'Can you come out here for a moment?'

Mrs Flowers slammed the oven door shut with a bang. 'Coming!' she called, adding in a whisper to Cindy, 'Please don't tell Murray I've told you this! He and Mr Parnell, they wouldn't like it.' She turned and hurried out of the kitchen, leaving Cindy standing dumbfounded and astonished by Mrs Flowers's revelation.

As she walked through the corridor to the front door, Cindy saw the house in a different light. The absence of any pictures or trace of Rose Parnell now made sense. No wonder Lawrence had erased her from the house. No wonder Murray never wanted to talk about her. His mother had abandoned him. But how could a wife and mother just disappear from her family's life? This explained Lawrence's coldness, his pent-up anger. And poor Murray! Cindy could only imagine his pain. She longed to speak to him about it, to reach out and console him, but how could she without letting on that Mrs Flowers had broken the code of silence and told her the truth? The housekeeper had been so kind to her, Cindy didn't want to get her in trouble. Perhaps she should just let the past remain unquestioned. Would it do any good to open up the old wound? She and Murray were happy, and at last she had an explanation of sorts for Lawrence's behaviour.

Driving home, Cindy resolved to wait for the right moment to talk to Murray. But, as time went on, an opportunity never presented itself. Still, for a long while she couldn't stop thinking about Rose, who had disappeared from the life of her husband and son seemingly without a trace and was bitterly, if at all, remembered.

6

CINDY SMOOTHED THE SHEET of paper in front of her and put down her ballpoint pen. She really didn't have a lot to tell since she'd last written to Babs. Alice and Babs always had plenty of news with all the happenings in Palm Springs, but little seemed to change around Yamboola.

Cindy took a sip of her tea, which had gone cold. Murray had made her a pot before he'd headed out to check on some new lambs. He'd be back soon now that the sun was peeping over the horizon, ready for a hearty breakfast and full of plans for the day. Cindy had hoped her letter would be finished for him to add to the mail that Tom would take into town, but it didn't look likely now. Sighing, she folded it and put it to one side.

She sat and gazed out at the rising curtain of sunshine, melting the mist and shining on a new day. The early light revealed a small mob of kangaroos; motionless, tiny paws daintily poised at the chest, ears twitching, ever alert to danger. These were close to the house and would scatter, bounding away, once they heard Murray's truck heading their way. Today would be like so many before it.

Cindy loved this calm. She cherished the peaceful early mornings before the routine of jobs and unexpected small calamities and surprises filled the hours till sunset.

She was content. Yes, happy too, as she'd told Babs in many letters. Adjustment had come at a price in some respects. She thought of the snakeskin she'd picked up near a fencepost, where one year's life had been shed and a new one begun. If only it were so simple; to peel off one's skin and start anew. Her life at college and her experiences in Palm Springs seemed now to be those of another girl, a more carefree girl, one who hadn't waded into the conflicting emotions of deep love and a new life that couldn't have been more different from the old one. The girl she'd once been had not envisaged having to fit into a set of deeply rooted traditions and a foreign landscape half a world away from what she knew.

As happy as she was, sometimes Cindy still felt like an outsider. Was she destined always to feel that she didn't quite belong?

Sighing, she stood and carried the tea things to the sink. Cindy knew the one thing she could do that would irrevocably link her to this place was to have children.

It had been two years since she'd married Murray, but there had been no sign of a pregnancy. Dr Forde, their family doctor in Deniliquin, had assured her that there was nothing wrong with her. She was young and healthy and he advised her to be patient, that these things happened when they were meant to, which, though she knew it to be sound advice, was of little comfort. It continued to prey on her. As she stood by the kitchen window, tears filled her eyes. *Will I never be a mother?* she thought. At the sound of footsteps outside, she hastily dashed her tears from her face and turned to greet her husband.

'Cindy, what is it, darling?' Murray said, concern creasing his face as he stepped into the kitchen. His kindness was her undoing and tears coursed down her face.

'What's wrong with me? I'm never going to have a baby,' she said, sitting down and covering her face with her hands. 'I feel such a failure. I'm letting you down.'

Murray sat down next to her at the table and took her hand. 'Don't be ridiculous. Of course you haven't let me down. All in good time.' He wiped a tear from her face and kissed her cheek. He put his arm around her and Cindy laid her head on his shoulder. 'Look, Cindy, what say we get out of here for a while? Give ourselves a break. Let's go away on a holiday. And I don't mean to Melbourne.'

Cindy looked up, elated. 'Oh, Murray, that'd be wonderful!' She flung her arms around him. 'Where, where? Overseas?'

Murray shook his head, but grinned. 'No, here in Australia. You've hardly seen the place. We could go to the Mornington Peninsula like Dad and I usually do, but what I'd really like is to fly up to Queensland, to Surfers Paradise. Myles and Tanya are always telling us what a great time they had there. Maybe we should see if some of our friends want to come along, too?'

Cindy hesitated. While Murray's friends of long standing were very pleasant and polite to her, she somehow didn't feel she really fitted into their circle. They all had the same background, came from well-to-do stations, had been to the same schools, married each other in similar churches, and most had children. They all met at local sporting events, cricket or football, went to the same picnics, race meetings and balls, and attended the wool sales together in Sydney or Melbourne. Cindy had found their conversations about restocking, market prices, auctions, sales, breeding, feed, rain, droughts, follow-up rain and field days interesting at first, but now it had all become monotonous. The majority of Murray's friends had grand and long-established properties. Their homesteads ranged from solid Federation and late-Victorian houses to newer, more modern buildings. These families had ridden the wool boom for several generations and people still talked about the time when wool fetched a pound per pound. They longed for those boom days to return. Cindy still didn't feel relaxed and comfortable in their company and couldn't really relate to them.

'Let's just be together, just us,' she said. 'A proper honeymoon, not just a few days.' She leaned over and kissed him on the lips, to show exactly what she meant.

Lawrence was less than impressed with the idea when Murray told him about the proposed holiday as the three of them were sharing a Sunday night dinner at the big house a few days later. Whether it was the cost or the fact that Murray would be spending time away from the property – or both – Lawrence had pursed his lips and muttered to Murray about shirking his responsibilities. But Murray had stayed firm.

'You know not much happens at this time of year, Dad. You and Tom can manage things easily,' said Murray.

Cindy had the impression that Lawrence considered this inconvenience to be entirely her fault, but she smiled and remarked pointedly, 'I'm so thrilled. It was so lovely of Murray to surprise me with the idea of a break like this.'

'I suppose you'll like Surfers Paradise. Tawdry bright lights and questionable establishments, if you ask me,' said Lawrence tartly. 'I prefer the Mornington Peninsula myself. Don't stay away too long.' His sullen disapproval having been voiced, Lawrence turned his attention back to Mrs Flowers's baked custard and tinned pears.

*

And so it was arranged. They flew to Sydney and then due north towards Queensland. Peering from the window of the plane, Cindy was captivated by the endless coastline, the blue sea and the never-ending beaches, the lush landscape broken only by the occasional river making its way to the ocean. As they began their descent towards the coast, Cindy turned to Murray and kissed him.

'Thank you,' she said.

They spent their days in Surfers Paradise at the Chevron Hotel, enjoying its numerous swimming pools and tropical gardens. They had breakfast on their private balcony, swam in the surf and walked hand in hand along the beachfront. They enjoyed the novelty of eating in a different restaurant for lunch and dinner every day.

Sitting by one of their hotel's pools, Cindy could watch the glamorously dressed women as they paraded around the gardens and pools in glittery high-heeled sandals, flaunting their stylish beachwear: glitzy swimming costumes that never got wet, silk and chiffon cover-ups, some with matching turbans, and weighed down with heavy gold jewellery.

'Fancy hanging by the pool in diamonds and full make-up,' said Murray. 'These women take their fashion rather seriously, don't they?'

'They'd feel right at home in Palm Springs,' said Cindy, laughing.

They went to Stradbroke Island for a couple of days and lazed in the sun and swam in beautiful clear water. They read books, picked at the endless array of sweet tropical fruit, enjoyed cocktails at sunset and made love beneath a softly humming fan. To Cindy it was a true honeymoon, and she found she was even more in love than ever with the man she had fallen for in Palm Springs. Here in the laidback atmosphere of Queensland, Kingsley Downs and cold, hostile Lawrence were far away. A few times recently, she'd tried subtly to raise the issue of Rose's disappearance with Murray, but she did not want to betray Mrs Flowers's trust, so any conversations about Rose were vague and ultimately pointless, as Murray would immediately shut down and change the subject. She briefly considered trying to talk about Rose again while they were away from the property and Lawrence, but then decided against the idea, as she didn't want to spoil their perfect idyll. Why bring up a painful memory in such a beautiful setting? She was determined to enjoy every second of this heavenly break.

*

They returned home and, in a couple of weeks, Cindy felt their holiday had been a dream, for life at Kingsley Downs was as it had always been – until she discovered she was pregnant. She held on to her happy secret until she was sure, and then she told Murray, who whooped and laughed, scooping her up in an enormous hug before gently placing her on the ground again, as carefully as if she were made of china.

'So now we know what we have to do next time,' she said, laughing delightedly. 'Take a romantic holiday!'

Murray kissed her softly. 'This is wonderful news! What did Dr Forde say?'

'He says that there's nothing for me to worry about. I'm extremely healthy.'

'Wonderful,' said Murray. 'This is just wonderful.'

Excited as she was about starting a family, Cindy was not looking forward to caring for an infant in addition to the constant grind of her normal household jobs. It was a daunting prospect. The work was hard enough to keep up with now, let alone with a baby in tow.

As the days passed, she began to feel bloated and slow and more and more tired, finding herself nearly faint with fatigue by the end of the day. Suddenly she couldn't bear the smell of meat, and the mere sight of freshly butchered lamb turned her stomach. But she was grateful for the little life growing inside her and at night, when she lay in bed with Murray's arms around her, she stroked her stomach and fell asleep with a smile on her lips.

When her first trimester was up, Cindy persuaded Murray to let her phone Babs from the big house and break the news. She had already written to her father and had promised to call him as soon as his first grandchild arrived.

Babs was overjoyed. 'I'll start sewing right away. Your baby is going to be the best-dressed infant in Australia,' she said, her voice bubbling with excitement. 'Wait till I tell Joey. Are you going to ring Alice? She'll be so happy for you.'

'Calls to America are very expensive here, so I'll write to her and let her know, but you can tell her if you like.'

As she was about to say something to Murray about telling his father, Lawrence walked into the house. Beaming at his father, Murray told him the news.

For a moment there was no reaction, and then Lawrence stretched out his hand and took Murray's, shaking it enthusiastically.

'That's great, just great. Another boy for Kingsley Downs, no doubt. Why don't you come over tonight, son? We'll have a port or two to celebrate.' He nodded to Cindy and then briefly smiled at Murray and left.

'Well, he could have said something to me,' said Cindy. 'I'm the one doing all the work.'

'But you could see he was really pleased. I haven't seen him this excited for years. You don't mind if I have a drink with him tonight, do you?' asked Murray.

'No, you do that. I'll be going to bed early anyway. I'm too tired to stay up late these days.' She hesitated a moment, then said, 'Murray, I've been thinking, though, should I go to Melbourne to have the baby?'

'Some women do that, I suppose,' he said cautiously. 'If they have families in Melbourne, it makes it easier. But most women around here manage perfectly well at the local hospital in Deni. Besides, I don't want to be away from you when the time comes.'

'Of course, I'd rather you were around, too,' said Cindy hastily. 'Do you think that Mrs Flowers would mind if I took the washing over to her, so that it can go through the electric washer? It would be so much easier than boiling diapers in the old copper.'

'That sounds like a good idea and I bet Mrs F will be pleased to help.'

That's one problem solved, thought Cindy, although she just hated putting herself in Lawrence's path over at the big house. She couldn't believe that the man was still so dismissive of her, even when she was about to present him with his first grandchild.

'Murray, I'm going over to Yamboola to do the shopping straight after lunch, and I'm meeting up with Jo at the Majestic, just for a lemonade, mind. Is there anything I can get you while I'm out?'

Murray shook his head and gave his wife a kiss on the cheek. 'Drive carefully. We'd better fit one of those seatbelt things they've introduced. Sounds a sensible idea.'

'If such a thing will go round me, when I've really grown,' said Cindy with a laugh, patting her stomach.

*

178

As she drove towards town that afternoon, Cindy wound down the car window and let the breeze blow in.

The heat was searing. Driving down Yamboola's main street, she saw Joanna's car parked out the front of the Majestic.

Cindy was so grateful for Jo's friendship these past years, not least because, while they both enjoyed living in the country, they were city girls at heart. They'd found they had similar interests and a shared sense of humour and they had just clicked. Now all she wanted to do was talk to Jo about her baby news.

'How simply marvellous for you both!' Jo said, hugging her friend, when Cindy told her. 'I'm so pleased for you. How does Murray's dad feel about the baby? He's not exactly the grandfatherly type.'

'True! I still find him so difficult, Jo, even after three years,' confided Cindy as they sat in the relative coolness of the Ladies Lounge.

'Maybe he'll warm up after the baby comes,' said Jo. 'Have you started thinking about the nursery yet?'

'I want things for the baby, but Murray considers a lot of items to be frivolous and unnecessary,' replied Cindy.

'Or is that what Lawrence thinks?' Jo said, arching an eyebrow. 'Mind you, it's typical of most of the men around here. Property comes first, family second, even when they really love their wives and children. But of course you want things for your baby. Have you started knitting a layette?'

Cindy shook her head. 'Goodness, I don't knit. Babs taught me to sew, though.'

'I'd love to knit you something for the baby,' said Jo.

Cindy grinned. 'Thank you, that'd be lovely. It will be good for the cold winter nights and it would be a special keepsake.'

'We could go on a bit of a spree into Deni and buy some fun baby things,' suggested Joanna.

'That would be great! Then I can put anything I buy on our accounts.'

'Murray doesn't give you any cash?' asked Joanna.

'I don't need it. We have accounts everywhere. We always have a good time when we're at the wool sales. I can go into the big department stores and charge whatever I want. I bought a gorgeous outfit that I wore to the races when I was in Melbourne. I expect I'll be living in Murray's old shirts and maternity smocks soon, though. I should write to Aunt Alice and Babs to think about designing smart outfits for pregnant women!'

Joanna studied Cindy for a moment. 'You wouldn't prefer to have the baby back in America, would you?' she asked.

'Oh no! The baby will be Australian, and besides, I want Murray close by when the time comes.' She paused to take a sip of her drink. 'Jo, I wonder how I am ever going to manage after the baby arrives. I don't feel as capable as all the other women around here.'

'Nonsense, it's just that most of them have grown up on properties. They're doing what their mothers did,' said Joanna gently. 'You're a different kettle of fish. It's harder for you, as everything here is so different from what you've ever known. Really, I think it's amazing how well you've adapted to station life already. It can't have been easy for you, so take a bow and stop worrying.'

Cindy felt a rush of gratitude to her friend. 'You're so kind. Murray says that too.' She dabbed her mouth with a serviette. 'Sometimes I just can't help worrying about things. About the future. If it's a boy, Murray wants to book him into his old school in Melbourne, a boarding school. I don't want my child living most of his life away from home.'

Jo nodded. 'Cin, lots of graziers send their children to boarding school. Don't worry. You can cross that bridge when you come to it. I also think that whether your baby is a boy or a girl, Murray will love it to bits. Shall I come over to your place this weekend and help you paint the baby's room pink?'

Cindy laughed. 'It's being painted yellow, regardless of what the Parnells think. I think it's best to be practical – though I have a wallpaper frieze of pink roses tucked away just in case,' she admitted with a smile.

'Have you thought about names?'

'Not really. If it's a boy he'll have his great-grandfather's name and Lawrence as a middle name, I'm told.'

'And if it's a girl? What was Murray's mother's name?'

'It was Rose.' Cindy hesitated, then quickly added, 'But Murray suggested I call a girl Barbara Alice after my aunts. Anyway, I'd love you to come over on Saturday. Murray will be tied up with pre-season footy training.'

'All right, then. I'll bring some patterns and some wool samples, although it would be much nicer to knit something from Kingsley Downs wool sometime. Does Mrs Flowers spin?' asked Joanna.

'I have no idea. I'll ask her.'

Joanna reached across the table and touched Cindy's hand affectionately.

Cindy smiled. 'How is your family, by the way?'

'Doing well. I told you my sister's engaged, didn't I? Well, now she's asked me to be one of her bridesmaids. Mum's delighted. So I'll be off to that wedding in a few months and will be able to catch up with everyone.'

The two girls finished their drinks and walked back to their cars, and Cindy drove home to Kingsley Downs.

It was hard to ignore the deteriorating condition of the land. There'd been plenty of rain the previous winter, sending some of the roads boggy, but the water tanks had been replenished and there had been a wonderful rush of green grass, a welcome relief after the previous dry months. Now the hot summer had sucked all moisture from the dams and creeks. The grass in the paddocks was dry and brown and the weeks of relentless heat had worn everyone down. Murray became irritable at the sight of the dried paddocks and tired trees. Cindy's vegetable garden was dispiriting, as it was no more than a patch of dead, crisp leaves. The creek was just a string of smelly puddles of suppurating mud. The men had to patrol the gluey waterholes and dams, rescuing muddied and near-dead sheep which had strayed too close. Lawrence grumbled at the cost of having to hand-feed the valuable sheep if things did not improve soon. Nor was there any relief as night fell, when a hot wind would steal over the land, carrying an odour of smokiness from distant grass fires.

That night, Cindy lay on top of the sheets, tossing and turning, her body sticky from the unrelenting heat. How she longed for the air conditioning she'd had in Palm Springs, or even an electric fan to cool her down, but without constant electricity these things were not possible. Sometimes she could hear the rumble of distant thunder, but never a drop of rain followed.

*

A couple of days after Joanna had been to visit and they'd sat on the verandah, looked at knitting patterns and discussed ways of furnishing the baby's room, there was a shift in the weather pattern. The wind picked up and changed to the north. At night Cindy could see a dark smudge and a faint red glow in the sky which, Murray told her, was not the remnants of a summer sunset but distant fires.

'It's going to be a race, Cindy, between the weather breaking or the fires taking off,' Murray said, sitting at the table for dinner. 'We'll have to be ready.'

'What does that mean exactly?' Cindy asked, placing Murray's meal in front of him.

'I've spoken to Wally in Yamboola. He's in charge of the rural fire brigade and our one water tanker. It's ready, but one water tanker is not going to be all that effective if the fires really take hold.' Murray paused to squirt Worcestershire sauce onto his vegetables. 'Still, there are enough hoses for it and pumps to be able to access water from the dams – if the dams have any water left in them in the first place. Tom's going to start moving the sheep from the northern paddocks closer to the big house, away from the most likely direction of the fire. The young jackaroo can help him.'

'But the fire seems so far away. Are we really in any danger?' asked Cindy anxiously.

'If the wind gets up behind a grass fire, you have no idea how fast it can move. But the houses are much easier to protect than the paddocks or the sheep. You'll be fine if you stay here and don't go outside.'

'How do we know what's happening? Will someone phone the big house?'

'Yes, they'll let Dad know if the fire looks like it's reaching Kingsley Downs, but we'll do our best to stop it before it does. We all have two-way radios, so we can keep checking on each other, but in all honesty, I'd hate to have to rely on them entirely. They're not always the best of equipment,' said Murray, laying down his cutlery, suddenly sounding tired. He took her hand. 'Look, we've been through this before. We have to help our neighbours and they'll help us. If you want, you can drive to the big house and stay with Mrs Flowers. My guess is the fire won't come this way, so I think you'd be fine here, but if it seems that it might, I'll come back and get you.'

'Of course I'll stay. Just tell me what we have to do,' said Cindy.

During the course of the following day, preparations continued. The fire line was now visible, and a pall of inky smoke was suffocating the sun, turning it an eerie red. Tubs and containers of water were placed around the house, and discarded bathtubs and water troughs in the nearby paddocks were filled with water. Hessian sacks, blankets and mats were stacked by the water containers, to be used in fighting the fire in hand-to-hand combat, if it came to that.

'We need anything that we can wet and use to smother sparks,' explained Murray after breakfast. 'Look, I can't stay. You'll be right. The fire's not coming this way. If there's no change in the wind direction, it will miss the house.'

Cindy prayed he was right. She felt she had to stay with her home, although the light outside was eerie, and the smell all around her was suffocating.

Later in the day, Mrs Flowers drove over to see her.

'Are you sure you're all right here by yourself? Please come over to the big house. Better than being on your own at a time like this.'

Cindy was about to agree, but the thought of having to leave her home deterred her.

'No, thank you, I'll be fine. Murray said that the fire was unlikely to come this way, but if anything changes he'll come and get me. Really, I would prefer to stay in my own house. But if I get scared, I'll drive over in the ute, I promise.'

Mrs Flowers nodded. 'Of course. As you like. I have to get straight back to organise food for the firefighters. Lots of sandwiches to make for those hungry men. Now, you take care.'

As kindly Mrs Flowers drove away, Cindy felt guilty that she had not volunteered to help, but she was determined to stay put in her own home.

*

184

The afternoon simmered towards sundown. Cindy lay in her darkened bedroom, her hand on her stomach, a wet towel on her head, the oppressive heat from the scorching temperature making her feel faint and breathless. Maybe she should have gone to the big house for the night. It might have been nice to have Mrs Flowers's company at such a frightening time. Then she heard a truck rattle up to the house. She went outside and found four men, including Murray, dressed in long-sleeved shirts, boots and hats, their thick work gloves tucked into their cuffs. One even had a scarf around his neck.

'The maps of the area just aren't accurate enough,' she heard one of the men say as they went over to the garden hose, where they took great gulps of water and washed their faces.

Cindy tapped Murray's arm. 'Can I have a word? I've decided that I don't want to stay here by myself. I think I should drive over to the big house.'

Murray shook his head. 'I'm sorry, sweetheart, but it's too late for that now. We need all the vehicles we can lay our hands on. That's why we're here – to get the ute. The forecast is predicting even stronger winds. Things might get much worse. The wind is the devil.'

'What do you mean . . . too late? Are we in danger?' asked Cindy, suddenly really frightened. Why on earth had she been so stubborn and insisted on staying by herself?

'No, it's okay for now,' Murray said reassuringly. 'How are you feeling? Do you think you could go inside and start soaking those hessian bags in water? They're to smother spot fires.' Cindy looked at him, her eyes wide with alarm. 'I'll try to get back to check on you. It's going to be okay, Cin.'

Cindy moved around in a dream, trying to keep her fear at bay. Surely this was all precautionary. She felt like an extra in a movie in which the action was somewhere else. Then there was the waiting. She soaked the hessian sacks as Murray had asked, but wondered how she would use them.

Murray came back and briefly turned on the radio to hear the latest weather report, and then sat on the two-way radio talking for a few minutes.

'I want to get back over to the Jacksons's. Don't want them to lose their house,' Murray said, hanging up the radio and reaching for his hat.

How awful for Shirley, Cindy thought. *She loves that house.* She wondered if Shirley had all the photo albums in a safe place.

'Do we know any more?' she asked anxiously.

'No, the weather forecast wasn't helpful, so just pray that the wind doesn't pick up. Don't worry if I'm not back anytime soon. I'll leave you the two-way.' Kissing Cindy hastily, he was gone.

*

Cindy sat alone in the quiet house as the evening slipped by. She couldn't see the moon, let alone any stars, for smoke. She wondered whether she should go to bed, but didn't like to until Murray returned home.

Cindy paced about then sat down and distracted herself by picking up the baby's top she was embroidering. She lost track of time, but when her eyes started to smart from the smoke, she put her sewing aside. She walked to the side verandah and stared outside, and the view made her gasp. The horizon was illuminated by a dangerous glow, etched in red and orange beneath a long black cloud. For a moment she was puzzled by a smell, but then she recognised it as eucalyptus. Murray had once told her the eucalypt trees went up like firecrackers because of the volatile oil they extruded. She felt her skin prickle at the sight of the burning sky and hurried back inside. Trying to keep calm, she went to the two-way radio, glanced at the numbers on the bit of paper Murray had left, and made the transmit call. To her dismay, Lawrence answered.

'Well, what's happening at your end? Over,' he asked brusquely.

'It's me, Cindy,' she said. 'Lawrence, I can see the fire. It's to the north. But which way is it coming? Over.'

She could almost hear Lawrence bristle. 'We can all see it, Cynthia. The bloody sky is alight. Stay where you are. The wind is going to blow up. Over.'

'Where is Murray? And the others? I'm alone here!' she shouted, then quickly added, 'Over.'

'Out fighting the fire. What do you think, that your husband's at a party? Over.' Lawrence's tone was sarcastic.

'Of course,' replied Cindy quietly, feeling embarrassed and very foolish. 'Over.'

Crackling static answered her. She put the two-way radio down on the kitchen table and went outside to the front garden, which was drenched in a strange smoky light.

Cindy stopped suddenly and caught her breath, staring into the darkness in fright as she discerned the outline of some people coming towards her. 'Hello? Who are you? What are you doing here?' she demanded.

A small group of dark-skinned Aborigines was clustered beside the front gate, their bodies silhouetted against the sky. There were seven or eight of them and a couple of children, their figures motionless as they stared at her. Her immediate impression of them was of their straight stick-thinness and subdued demeanour, and the odd assortment of clothing they were all wearing. One woman was breast-feeding her baby, and a little boy had a dog on the end of a rope. All were barefoot. Even in the dark, Cindy could tell they were worried.

A man in a loose open shirt and tattered shorts stepped forward. "Ullo, missus. Our truck, it broke. Left it up the track and walked. Fire comin' through soon 'nuff.' He pointed vaguely.

'Isn't it still a long way off? Is it coming this way?' Cindy asked worriedly.

'Mebbe,' the man replied. 'Mebbe it all right.'

Cindy thought this was not a helpful answer, but she could hardly expect them to keep walking. What could she do?

Suddenly she felt energised and pleased to be doing something constructive to help people.

'There's an empty feed shed over there at the back of the house. Well, it has some stock feed in a corner. You can sleep in there if you want.'

'Your old man around, missus?' the man asked.

'No, but he'll be back soon,' said Cindy, now wondering if she had been wise to allow these natives to stay when she was by herself.

'Okay, missus, thank you, missus,' they all muttered, nodding at her.

Cindy looked at the small children and the woman with a baby. 'Do you need any . . . tucker?'

'Okay, missus. Little ones, they hungry. Mebbe big wind comin'. Thank you, missus.'

They all turned and shuffled to the water trough where they filled some canvas water bags and then straggled towards the distant feed shed.

Cindy went indoors feeling relieved that she was not totally alone, though she did have a niggling concern about letting the motley mob stay. What would Murray say? Perhaps they'd be gone before he found out.

Oh, blow it, she thought. *I can't let those kids go hungry*. And with that she rounded up some food and took it out to the shed. The Aborigines thanked her for her kindness and shared out the food among the little ones.

Walking back to the house, Cindy stared at the rim

of fire snaking across the distant landscape, but it was too far away to really know how bad it was. There was a sudden rising wind, rattling windows and guttering, and Cindy hurried inside, closing doors and windows to keep out the strange hot gusts. She lay down on the bed with the damp towel on her face, overcome with fatigue. She closed her eyes and prayed that Murray was all right.

*

Had she fallen asleep? What had awakened her? She sat up and realised the house was shaking, though certainly it shouldn't be. *It can't be an earthquake*, she thought. She'd experienced some of those in California. Then she quickly realised that there was no mistaking the roar of the wind that was whipping around the house.

She grabbed a torch and walked down the hallway. It was still pitch dark. As she got towards the front of the house, she was shocked by the violent rattle of the windows. She thought they might explode. She could hear the sound of crashing coming from outside and realised branches were being ripped from the trees and smashing to the ground. The howling wind filled her with dread. This was more than just a high wind. Things were beginning to be thrown about outside. She could hear pots breaking and furniture being hurled against the walls and verandah posts. Suddenly there was a splintering sound as the enclosed part of the verandah started to disintegrate.

Now thoroughly frightened, Cindy tried to think where she might be safe. In an earthquake, people hid under heavy tables. Or no, was it best to stand in a door-frame? She hurried from room to room, feeling as though the whole world was falling in on top of her. And the noise! Screaming, whipping and howling ferociously, the wind sounded like a mad beast.

Then, all at once, there was the sound of ripping metal. She looked up at blackness. Was that the *sky*? She was in a corner of the front room and she felt a powerful gust of wind, like a giant paw, reaching inside the house.

Screaming, Cindy pushed herself out the front door, which was instantly ripped from its hinges, and she glimpsed it spinning down the verandah, slamming into the posts she had lovingly painted, breaking them like matchsticks.

She ran blindly towards the front gate, her body being propelled sideways by the force of the wind. Unable to stand on her feet, she grabbed the sturdy front gateposts. The gate had gone, she realised. As she hugged the gate-post for dear life, she could hear the sound of ripping, rattling tin and the splintering of wood. Then she was blown onto the rough ground and felt herself sliding along it, her hands grasping for purchase, her cries for help blown away by the horrific wind.

The last thing she heard, before a piece of flying debris knocked her out, was the roof lifting and being spun in a windstorm of wreckage into the eastern paddock. She didn't hear the frightful sounds as the old house collapsed into a pile of rubble, more thoroughly demolished by the wind than by the work of any bomb.

*

They told her it was the Aborigines who'd found her and carried her to the feed shed, which had been spared the full force of the mini tornado. They had looked after her as the pain had gripped her stomach and the tiny life within her had slipped away. Murray had come as soon as he had heard and rushed her to hospital, but it was too late.

Now, her head swathed in bandages, her cuts and scratches treated, she was lying in the crypt-like stillness of a small room in Deniliquin Hospital behind stiff white curtains. She started to cry, not for herself, nor for Murray, or the house and everything in it, not for the dead sheep and the burned paddocks, but for her lost child.

She cried and cried. Her precious baby was gone.

They gave her something to help her sleep, but she woke on and off for the next few hours, and every time she opened her eyes she remembered anew the terrible loss she'd suffered. She felt her heart would never heal.

*

Jo sat by the hospital bed in silence, holding Cindy's hand.

'Do you want me to call your aunts in Palm Springs, or your father?' she asked anxiously.

'No. I don't want to worry them. There's nothing they can do,' said Cindy sadly. She felt hollow and exhausted. 'I'll tell them later.'

'When you're feeling stronger, you could go and visit them, perhaps?'

'I'd love that, but there'll be the cost of rebuilding the house. That's more important than anything else. I want my home again.'

'I brought you some books, if you're up to reading, but you should rest while you can.'

Cindy nodded but was quiet. Finally Jo said, 'The fire damage in the north was pretty horrendous but it's all out now, thanks to a wind change. The fire burned back on itself. The locals tell me that it was the worst fire in many years. Thank God it didn't head your way. That mini tornado you experienced was quite an isolated incident – you were the only one affected. It was such a bizarre thing to happen. I'm so sorry.'

Cindy turned her face to the pillow and tears slid down her face. 'None of this would have happened if I'd gone up to the big house. It's all my fault. Am I being punished for something?'

Jo reached out and stroked Cindy's hair as her body

shook with grief. 'Of course it's not your fault. How were you to know that there was going to be a freak tornado?' said Jo vehemently.

'I feel like I'm cursed,' sobbed Cindy.

'Well, if you really were cursed, those Aborigines wouldn't have been around to rescue you,' Jo said gently. 'You were damn lucky they turned up when they did. You were kind to them and they were grateful.'

'I didn't do anything special,' said Cindy, her tears easing. Jo handed her a tissue and she wiped her face.

'Maybe not, but some people around here wouldn't have let them stay, I can tell you,' replied Jo. She took Cindy's hand and held it. 'Listen, I have some news. Maybe it's not the time but, well, there's something I need you to know.'

Cindy stared at her serious face. 'Jo, what's wrong? Are you all right?'

'It's Mum. She has been diagnosed with a heart condition and I'm really worried about her, so I've decided to ask for a transfer to Sydney on compassionate grounds. I'm leaving Yamboola.'

Cindy stared at her dear friend. 'Oh no! You poor thing. That is terrible news. It's good that you'll be close to her.' A lump rose in her throat and once again tears sprang into her eyes. 'What am I going to do without you? You've helped me so much, Jo. I shouldn't be selfish when you're so concerned about your mother, but I am going to miss you so much.'

Jo smiled sadly. 'Cindy, I'll miss you, too. I thought I'd never find a kindred spirit out here. Look, we won't lose touch. You'll have to come and visit me. Be an excuse to come to Sydney. Think of the good times we'll have! I want you to meet all my family.'

'I'm really so sorry about your mother,' Cindy managed to say. The news was devastating for Jo, but it was bad news for her as well. They sat quietly for a while until Jo had to leave.

'I'll call in again tomorrow, okay?'

'Jo, don't be silly, it's miles to come to see me in Deni.'

'Nonsense, what are best friends for?'

Cindy watched Joanna turn at the door and give her a quick wave, then she shut her eyes. Coming on top of the loss of her baby and her home, the news that she was also losing her best friend was shattering. What had she done to deserve so much heartbreak?

*

Murray drove her home from the hospital two days later. He was sad and withdrawn. He'd been so excited at the prospect of finally becoming a father. She glanced at his profile and tight expression. He seemed to be in pain, but she could tell he was pushing it deep down inside himself, locking it in the secret place that was beyond her reach. Murray had told her that he'd been frantic with worry about her when he'd returned to the house to find nothing but a pile of rubble. Now he said little, as if there was nothing he could say that would lift their spirits or change their fate.

While she'd been in hospital, Cindy'd had time to think and she knew that she desperately wanted to mark the life she'd sheltered for three months. Murray refused to talk about it, only commenting that they had to put all this behind them. But Cindy did not want to deny the baby's existence. She wanted to grieve, to mark the little lost life. She needed a place to lay her grief, somewhere she could mourn and let her lost child know she hadn't forgotten the brief joy they'd shared.

And there was another matter she wanted to settle.

'Murray, I want to find the family group who rescued me. To say thank you.'

'Don't be silly. They've been thanked enough already. Besides, if you hadn't given them shelter, they might have all died. You've done enough for them.' Having dismissed that subject, Murray continued, 'Now, about the old house. Some of our stuff has been salvaged, but I have to warn you, it's not much. That tornado scattered our things far and wide. But we'll be perfectly comfortable at the big house. We'll have space to ourselves, and Mrs Flowers is looking forward to having you under the same roof. I think she gets a bit lonely for female company. She said she'd enjoy looking after you.'

'I won't need looking after, but that's nice of her.' Cindy paused. 'So, how long will it take to rebuild our house? How long before we can move back in?'

Murray gave her a quick glance, then shook his head.

'The place is a total wreck. It's completely flattened. Kaput. Dad hasn't assessed exactly what our losses are yet. The house was insured, but no matter what the payout, there won't be enough money to rebuild it.'

Cindy felt her stomach drop. 'But, surely . . . surely we have to have our *own* house, Murray . . .' She swallowed, hearing the rising panic in her voice.

'The main house is big enough for all of us. It's quite a substantial home. It has plenty of rooms,' Murray said reasonably.

'But your father . . . what does he think of the idea? He won't like having me underfoot one bit!' Never mind that she would hate to be living under the same roof as such an arrogant man who constantly snubbed her.

'His life isn't going to change if we're there,' Murray said matter-of-factly. 'And besides, you'll have Mrs F to work with you. You were always complaining about how difficult things were in the old place, what with limited electricity and having to use that old copper. Think how

194

much easier everything is going to be. And you have to admit that the old place was pretty run-down.'

'But it was *our* home,' said Cindy dejectedly, thinking of the work she had done to make it one.

'Cindy, I'd like us to have our own home too, but it's just not on the cards at present. Living with Dad in the main house is the only practical solution,' said Murray firmly, and Cindy knew she wasn't going to win the argument. He had already made up his mind. Lawrence had spoken. There would be no new house and they would have to adjust.

She bit her lip and stayed silent. They drove through the main entrance to Kingsley Downs and down the dirt road, where the gum trees had been scorched and the undergrowth charred as if a huge blowtorch had been waved across the land.

Cindy gasped. 'Everything is burned to a crisp! Did the fire come close to the big house?'

'No, we were lucky. This is all the damage to the place. We didn't lose much. The grass on a couple of the back paddocks went up, but the home paddocks were saved and Tom managed to move the sheep to safety. The old windmill got burned, as did those trees back there. Embers must have blown over. But everything else is fine. Could've been a lot worse.'

But it was, thought Cindy. *I lost my baby and my house. How much worse could it be?* She closed her eyes, suddenly tired and overwhelmed.

Murray drove them over to the remains of the old house and Cindy wandered around the flattened rubble that had once been their home, the ruined garden bringing painful tears to her eyes. She was shocked how little was salvageable from their old home; however, one of the things saved was the little Indian bowl that Adsila had made for her. She loved that bowl, because it connected her to Palm Springs. When she turned her back and they drove away, she vowed never to revisit the place where she'd spent the first years of her married life.

*

Over the next few days, Cindy tiptoed forlornly around the big house, keeping out of Lawrence's way and trying to make herself useful, but feeling that there was nowhere she could call her own. Then, several days later, she found a space that she could connect with, a retreat and a safety net, that would be hers and hers alone.

At the edge of a small gully where a few blackberry bushes grew was a grassy ravine, a few feet deep, and in it was a tree. She had glimpsed it from the front of the house on her previous visits and now she was drawn to it.

It was a peppercorn tree of immense girth, its branches gnarled with age and its delicate leaves shrivelled by the recent heat. But Cindy knew its roots went deep and that it had survived storms and fires for decades. The tree spoke to Cindy; of strength, of permanence, of fortitude and aged beauty.

So it was here she chose to come quietly, tearfully, to bury a few small objects that told of a life expected and a life lost. She brought a little rattle, a pair of booties that Jo had made and a beautifully embroidered little jacket and placed them into the only thing of value she had left: Adsila's bowl. Then she dug a shallow hole into the dry ground and placed the bowl carefully in it. When it was covered over, unseen by any eyes, she clung to the tree, burying her face in its scratchy bark, and howled, a wild and desperate sound, as though her deep pain was being torn from within her.

When she had no more tears, she slid to the ground and leaned against the tree, drawing strength and comfort from its substantial presence. She knew that in spring there would be a whisper of new greenery and fresh leaves would unfurl. And at that thought, a small shoot of hope and strength trembled in her heart.

Slowly Cindy pulled herself to her feet and walked back to Lawrence's house.

7

CINDY COULD NOT BELIEVE that she was about to celebrate her tenth Australian Christmas. Here they were again, gathered at sunset in early December, in front of the rose arbour by the steps of Kingsley Downs's big house for the annual Christmas photo.

Cindy and Murray sat on wicker chairs in the centre of the lawn. Their younger son Russell sat at his father's feet, while his older brother Gordon stood at his side and Gordon's twin sister, Sally, perched on the arm of Cindy's chair. The boys wore crisp white shirts and navy shorts, long socks and shoes. Sally had been wrangled out of her shorts by her mother and was dressed in a spotted voile dress. Sally had drawn the line at wearing a bow in her hair, but mother and daughter had compromised on a plastic clip to hold back her thick, red-gold curls.

The photographer urged them to smile as he began snapping this year's Christmas portrait.

Cindy looked at her little family with a mother's pride and reflected on just how lucky she'd been these past few years. After the anguish of the windstorm and losing her baby, a dark cloud had hovered over her life for a long time. Then, joyously, she had discovered that she was not only pregnant again but expecting twins. It was a happy surprise, but one which kept her anxious until two gloriously healthy, if small, babies arrived: a boy and a girl.

'A pigeon pair . . . you clever girl.' Murray had kissed her with delight.

Cindy had hardly dared to believe such happiness was possible.

Having two tiny babies had been a blur of worry and exhaustion that Cindy had felt utterly unprepared for. There seemed to be a never-ending need to feed them, settle them, soothe and comfort them. They were hungry all the time, and she found she would nurse and settle one baby only to have the other cry and wake up its twin again. Cindy felt she was sleepwalking through most days, the deep urge to care for her children the only thing keeping her going. She washed nappies and baby clothes until her hands were pruned and chapped. She could not believe that two such tiny babies could create so much work. Cindy had no idea how she would have managed without practical Mrs Flowers, who was always willing to help with the washing or keep an eye on the twins so Cindy could catch some sleep. Mrs Flowers had delighted in the babies and adopted a proprietary air with them. Occasionally she had pushed them in the pram around the garden, and if Tom Flowers was about he'd lean down and admire 'the wee ones', as he called them. Murray adored his children and took every opportunity to cuddle and care for them, but life on the land continued unabated and, while he did his best, the sheep and stock still needed his attention as always. The twins brought Cindy and Murray deep satisfaction and joy. Occasionally, if somewhat miraculously, Sally and Gordon would sleep through the night, which though very welcome, would also throw Cindy into a fresh bout of anxiety that something was awry. Despite Murray urging her to rest while she could, Cindy would tiptoe into their room to watch them sleep, leaning close to their little bodies to hear and feel their soft breath.

Lawrence, however, had taken very little interest in the twins. Cindy had wished they had been able to move into their own home with the children, but Lawrence had sternly rebuffed any suggestion of rebuilding. Over time, Cindy had let go of the idea of ever moving out again. Lawrence seemed to find the chaos and clutter of the children annoying and Cindy felt on constant alert to stop them crying and fussing when he was around.

'How can he not love his own grandchildren?' Cindy had asked Murray. 'He takes no notice of them at all.'

'Of course he loves them,' Murray had assured her. 'He's just not very interested in babies. You wait. When they get older, he'll want to do lots of things with them.' And as the twins grew, their formidable grandfather did show more interest in them, though Cindy could see he was never going to be a source of love and affection the way her own grandparents had been for her.

Despite having to share a house with Lawrence, life for Cindy was full, happy and busy. Every so often she caught herself watching the twins as they gurgled happily, or slept, curled together like plump puppies, and her throat would catch with the overwhelming love she felt for her children.

Less than three years later, Cindy had been overjoyed to find she was pregnant again. And, after an uneventful pregnancy and a rushed trip to Deniliquin hospital, Russell had arrived in a hasty but uncomplicated birth.

Joanna had come to see her in the hospital and admire the new arrival. Much to Cindy's delight, her friend had moved back to Yamboola. Cindy had been devastated by Jo's leaving at the time when she had been in such dark despair. In the years that followed, it had been a struggle to find her feet without a woman friend to share things with, and although she'd grown to like many of Murray's friends' wives, those friendships had not been able to replace the rapport she'd had with Jo.

But now Jo was back, having been assiduously courted by Donald Fraser, a local grazier she'd known when she first lived in Yamboola. Donald had been doing a three-month course in Sydney and had looked Jo up. They'd started dating, and when Jo's mother had been given the all-clear after an operation to relieve her heart condition, Jo was delighted to marry Donald and move back to the Riverina. Cindy and Murray had flown to Sydney for their wedding, and now that Jo was living on the Fraser property, the two women had picked up their friendship where they'd left off, and became even closer when Jo gave birth to a daughter a couple of months after the arrival of Russell.

'Murray is so thrilled it's another boy,' Cindy had confided to Jo. 'It's like he's got an heir and a spare. He's hinted that another boy wouldn't go astray to help run things.'

'Did you want a girl?' asked Joanna.

'Maybe next time.' Cindy smiled. 'Or maybe three is just right.'

The children grew into adventuresome toddlers and then, so quickly, into delightful and entertaining children who ruled Cindy's and Murray's lives. Once, watching them lark about in the garden, Murray looked at Cindy and with a catch in his voice whispered, 'I never believed this was possible.' And Cindy felt she would burst with love and pride in her family.

Gordon and Sally, though twins, were very different from each other, not just in looks but also in personality. Gordon was steady and serious, where Sally was gregarious and boisterous. Gordon didn't like being teased and took things to heart. Sally, if upset, would burst into a storm of tears, stamp her foot and shout, but within moments of being appeased she would be her sunny self again. In similar circumstances, her brother would continue to look pained for a long time, sending everyone wounded glances, even if he had been at fault.

Russell, however, was as even-tempered and calm as the day he was born, and was never any trouble. At four, he ignored Sally's teasing, tottered after Gordon to watch whatever his big brother was doing and accepted whatever came along.

Cindy loved telling Babs about the children, constantly writing long letters describing their doings, along with photos and some of their clumsy and colourful artwork and school efforts. Cindy still didn't mention Lawrence in her letters home. As always, she tried to put the dark cloud that was his presence out of her mind. Her happiness in her family outweighed Lawrence's continued ill-will towards her.

Looking at her children now, fidgeting as the photographer took some final photos, their fresh-pressed clothes moments away from dirt and ruin, she felt a wave of contentment.

The town photographer lowered his camera.

'That's it. I think we've got some pretty good shots. I should have them ready for you in about a week.'

'Why can't we have a picture with horses or something next year?' sighed Gordon. 'I hate wearing these stupid clothes.'

'This is how Daddy and Grandfather like you to look,' explained Cindy. 'Like gentlemen and a little lady, not a gang of tree-climbing ruffians.'

'Why doesn't Grandfather come and be in the photo, then?' said Gordon.

'No,' squealed Sally, who had very definite ideas and who liked to be the centre of attention.

'Because we have a photo with Grandfather on Christmas Day. And these are the pictures I want to put in our Christmas cards to send to Aunt Alice and Auntie Babs. I want to show everyone what nice children I have,' explained Cindy.

'Mummy fools everyone every year,' said Murray with a chuckle, as he picked up Russell and put him on his shoulders.

'No, she doesn't,' said Sally indignantly. 'We *are* nice.'

'You certainly are,' said Cindy, putting an arm around her daughter.

'Can we go and take these things off now?' asked Gordon, plucking at his shirt, after Cindy and Murray had farewelled the photographer and headed into the house.

'No, darling. There are important people coming to dinner tonight, so Daddy wants you to keep your good clothes on.'

'Awww, do I have to stay in my dress?' wailed Sally.

'You do, darling. Just for a short while. You look lovely. Now, let's get going.'

The children trailed into the big house, Cindy issuing dire threats about the consequences for them if they did not keep clean and tidy. They would not eat with the family and guests, but Lawrence liked them to be introduced and to spend a few moments speaking to the company. Sally would be expected to pass around to the visitors a plate of hors d'oeuvres Mrs Flowers had prepared, while Gordon would answer questions put to him about school, his future and Kingsley Downs, his hands clasped tightly behind his back and not in his pockets. Russell would hold Cindy's hand until he was given a biscuit and cheese and told to sit quietly. Eventually, the children would be excused and led away by Mrs Flowers.

Cindy headed down the hallway to freshen up before the guests arrived. She enjoyed having guests visit, especially when they were people she knew and liked, but Murray had told her the guest list that evening would include the Gregsons, whom Cindy had not previously met. They were old friends of Lawrence's and had not visited for years, as they owned a property in western Queensland. Evidently they would also be bringing another man with them who was important in the wool industry.

'Are Storry and Maisie coming?' Cindy had asked Murray. Their local stock and station agent and his wife were often visitors to Kingsley Downs.

'They're away in Sydney on business, remember?'

'Are they still away? I thought they would be back by now. Oh, that's a shame,' said Cindy.

'But Alistair is coming, so you'll have your old champion to talk to,' said Murray in a teasing voice.

Cindy was relieved that the dear old family solicitor would be there that night. He had impeccable manners and was always so kind and attentive to her. Alistair Campbell might be semi-retired but he kept tabs not only on local politics but on the rest of the world as well, and he often gave her news about the US that he thought she would be interested in hearing. His secretary, Ngaire Seymour, was also a close friend of the family.

Cindy sprayed herself with perfume and ran a brush through her hair before a squeal from Russell announced the visitors were approaching. With a smile on her face, Cindy went to the door to welcome her guests to her home.

*

204

As the evening wore on, the talk was all about reforming the wool industry. Cindy thought that Lawrence, Murray and even Alistair were impressed both by the guest who had come with the Gregsons and his views on what needed to be done to bring about change to their industry. Bill Gunn, who sat opposite Cindy, seemed rather rough around the edges, but the authority with which he spoke as he railed against the current prices of wool made her think that he might well be an influential person.

Cindy studied him. He was a large, shambling, bear-like man with a florid complexion, and his hair was parted in the middle, two tufts of streaked silver sticking out on either side. Important and clever he might be, but there was no doubting he was a country boy with rough bush manners who was used to getting his way.

'The wool industry's in even worse shape than it was in the late fifties. It's downright cataclysmic. We have to make sure the Prime Minister understands the crisis we are facing,' he boomed across the table.

'Don't the politicians realise that if they don't do something right away to make sure the graziers get a consistent return for their wool, the industry will be decimated?' thundered Lawrence. 'People will just walk away from their places. The government has an obligation to protect our way of life. The wool industry made this country great. They can't just ignore the wool grower.'

Gunn nodded and slapped his hand on the table in agreement with Lawrence. 'I've been going to a lot of meetings across the state and there is huge support for the idea of an authority which will not only buy up all of the Australian wool clip, but also set a reserve price for it. If those buyers from overseas want our wool, then they will have to pay the price we decide,' explained the big man.

'But what if they won't pay the price you set?' asked Alistair softly.

Gunn glared at the old solicitor. 'Then we'll just hang on to the wool until they do. The buyers will have to accept our asking price if they want our wool. It's very simple, Mr Campbell: an authority will buy up all the wool and set the price for it. The banks will fund the purchase and the government will back the whole initiative.'

Mr Gregson leaned forward, his enthusiasm clear on his face. 'This policy will be the making of the industry,' he said. 'No more ups and downs in price. No more boom and bust. The wool producer will know exactly what price he'll be getting, year by year. He'll be secure in this industry.'

'And you have plenty of support for this idea?' asked Alistair Campbell.

'Some wool producers don't like the idea that every-thing will be controlled by one authority, but there is strength in being a monopoly, so they'll have to come on board,' Gunn answered.

Alistair looked dubious, but before he could say anything further, Lawrence raised his glass.

'We are privileged to be party to . . . shall we say, a small revolution?'

'Small, be damned.' The big man threw back his head and roared with laughter.

As soon as Mrs Flowers, in a freshly ironed apron, had cleared away the dessert plates, Lawrence spoke. 'Excuse us, ladies. Murray, the port, will you please, son.'

Cindy rose from the table and, turning to Mrs Gregson, asked, 'Would you care for an after-dinner liqueur? Tea, or coffee?'

'I wouldn't mind another sherry. The one before dinner was very pleasant,' the older woman replied.

They settled themselves in the sitting room and made small talk for a short while, then Cindy asked, 'I suppose you know a lot about the wool industry, coming from the land. It's a very different world from what I've known.'

'I understand how you must feel,' said Mrs Gregson warmly. 'Actually, I was a city girl before I got married. I worked in an accountant's office in Brisbane and that's where I met Mr Gregson. He was a client of the firm. I moved to the land after we got married, and quickly discovered that sheep were regarded as almost *godlike* creatures there. Heavens, even the new two-dollar note celebrates the industry,' she said with a slight smile.

Cindy chuckled. 'I always thought Merino rams looked rather snooty and silly. A huge mound of compacted wool waddling on silly tiny feet and legs. Like a large lady in a big overcoat tottering on high heels.'

Mrs Gregson laughed. 'We shouldn't joke. In good times, those wool clips can make a lot of money, thousands of dollars.'

Cindy was thoughtful. Mrs Gregson had seemed very proper and a little dull at the dining table, saying little, but Cindy could see that she listened intently. Away from the dominating conversation of the men, Cindy was finding her interesting company.

'What do you think about this reserve price idea?' Cindy asked.

The older woman studied Cindy. 'Well, from what I can gather, since Bill Gunn came into the picture there's been quite a bit happening. Something had to be done – the wool clip price has been erratic for so long. By promising a reserve price, this new authority – and not the buyers – will be able to control the price of wool so that wool producers will get a fair return for their work and investment in the industry. Sounds good to me.'

'But what if people don't want to pay this reserve price? My aunt has a dress shop in Palm Springs in America and she says that women are already loving and asking for synthetic fabrics. Artificial silk drapes beautifully and is highly favoured. What if the whole world starts to feel that way?' asked Cindy.

Mrs Gregson raised an eyebrow. 'My dear, synthetics will be a passing fad. Nothing will ever replace wool.' She put down her glass and glanced at her marcasite watch. 'We really should be leaving soon.' She smiled at Cindy. 'You're a lovely hostess. It's nice to see a woman back at the helm of Kingsley Downs.'

'I wouldn't say I was anywhere near the helm,' said Cindy with a small smile. 'Lawrence is still very much the master of the ship.' She paused, seeing an opportunity. 'Did you know Murray's mother?'

Mrs Gregson nodded. 'I did. Not long after I was married, we visited Kingsley Downs. Rose Parnell was very charming and warm to me. She was always a bit on the quiet side, and I don't think that she socialised a lot, but I do remember that she was a very loving mother. Quite doted on Murray when he was a little chap. Shame what happened later. I don't know what made her act the way she did. Hard on Lawrence and Murray. Still, you never know what really goes on inside a marriage, do you?'

'I suppose not,' replied Cindy cautiously, unsure whether to ask more questions.

Footsteps and voices in the hall announced that the men had left the dining room, so Mrs Gregson rose and picked up her handbag and Cindy walked her out to join her husband.

'Thank you for a pleasant evening,' Mrs Gregson said, shaking Cindy's hand. 'I do hope our paths cross again.'

*

As she brushed her hair in front of the mirror later that night, Cindy turned to Murray as he drew back the sheets and fell onto the bed.

'What did you think of this evening?'

'It was fine, sweetie. The kids and the food were great and you kept Mrs G occupied. I think the night went off well.' He yawned.

'That friend of the Gregsons, Bill, was quite forceful in his views.'

'Yes, he was. Dad certainly supports his plan. Hopefully it will make us more secure financially, and if that happens, who knows, we might even be able to expand our business in the next few seasons.'

Cindy put her brush on the dressing table and turned back to face her husband, who was lying on his back, bare-chested, his pyjama bottoms tied at his waist, his eyes closed, his boots on the floor beside him in handy reach.

'I thought Mrs Gregson a bit starchy at dinner, but later in the sitting room, I found her to be quite interesting.' Cindy paused. 'She mentioned she'd met your mother when she was first married.'

Murray didn't move. 'Did she? I wouldn't know. I guess my parents gave a few dinner parties back in the day.'

'I see. Was your mom involved in other social events, besides dinner parties?'

Murray opened his eyes. 'Why are you asking? I don't know. It's late. I'm tired.'

Cindy walked over and sat on the edge of the bed. 'It's just that I know so little about your mom.'

'Cindy, when Mum left, I was away at school. She just packed a bag and went. I don't know more than that. Come to bed. It's late.' He closed his eyes.

Cindy climbed into bed and lay beside her husband, reaching for him and putting her arm across his chest. He muttered incoherently and turned on his side, sleep quickly claiming him. Cindy felt the gentle rise and fall of breathing and was comforted. It wasn't long before she too drifted off to sleep.

*

When the children woke Cindy and Murray very early on Christmas morning, the birds had barely started their dawn calls and the day promised to be hot.

Amidst squeals of excitement, the children found their stockings from Santa and pulled out all the little presents Cindy had enjoyed packing inside.

After everything had been examined and played with, they all trooped into the kitchen. Mrs Flowers never made breakfast on Christmas morning, as she was too busy organising the lunch and, knowing how big that would be, Cindy made just a light meal of fruit and cereal.

Breakfast was quickly eaten so they could gather around the Christmas tree in the lounge room to open family presents – except for those from Lawrence, who made the children wait till after Christmas dinner for his gifts.

As usual, Murray played Santa, and everyone watched as each child opened a gift in turn. They all had a beautiful piece of clothing from Babs and Joey that Babs had made. Cindy was not sure that her children really appreciated the workmanship that had gone into the clothes, but she certainly did, and she couldn't wait to see them all in their lovely outfits. The gifts from Alice were a good deal less interesting, being useful rather than fun.

Cindy smiled to herself as she remembered how she and Babs had always had a pact between them to open their gifts from Alice on Christmas Eve, so as not to spoil Christmas morning. There had been the year of silver raincoats with gold medallion buttons, a look that never took off, which had been discounted in the store and still hadn't sold and so had ended up as gifts. And then there was the mock Pucci handbag that had spent so long in the shop window that one side had faded. When Babs had pointed this out, Alice had cheerfully replied, 'If you hold the faded side against you, no one will ever notice.' And there was the year of the tennis bracelet of faux diamonds whose clasps never worked. But as Babs always said, it was the thought that counted.

'Why are you smiling, Mummy?' asked Gordon.

'I'm just pleased to see that you like the cricket set Daddy and I gave you.' She turned to help Sally unwrap a large doll and a little bracelet with a gold teddy bear charm and Russell his huge set of Lego, which the little boy immediately wanted to put together. Cindy had also given them games, puzzles and books. She was pleased they all liked to read, or be read to, and she encouraged their reading. Murray seemed happy with his crocodile belt and new shirts and Cindy loved the pretty gold locket set with a small diamond he had bought for her.

'I'll wear it at lunch,' she said, as she gave him a kiss.

After the children had had a chance to play with their toys and burn off some energy came the ritual of dressing for Christmas lunch.

Sally always wore a dress. The boys had to suffer in jackets until the meal was over and Lawrence allowed them to take them off.

'You'll be all right,' Cindy said when Gordon complained. 'It's only for a couple of hours and your grandfather likes to see you nicely dressed on these special occasions. Besides, you're going to have your photo taken.'

Before Christmas lunch was served, Mrs Flowers came out of the kitchen long enough to take a family photograph with Lawrence included, as she did every year. Everyone lined up stiffly in the drawing room in front of the fireplace. Cindy had decorated it with branches of gumleaves, while the children had added paper chains and paper snowflakes they'd made.

Then the family all sat down to Mrs Flowers's traditional Christmas dinner of baked ham and roast chicken, in spite of the heat of the day. Cindy had put Christmas bon bons on the table and there was a lot of noise and fun in pulling them, then wearing the paper hats and reading out the silly jokes they contained. Cindy was not at all sure that Lawrence approved of the noisy frivolity, but he said nothing. Cindy did notice that he was swift to remove his paper hat.

The main course was followed by Mrs Flowers's Christmas pudding eaten piping hot with custard. This was a tradition Cindy still hadn't come to terms with, but she did quite like to have a slice of cold pudding with a cup of tea the next day.

After the meal, they all went into the front room where Lawrence liked to exchange presents with the children. He always gave them each a cheque in an envelope to add to their bank accounts, seemingly oblivious to the fact that a bank account they couldn't access meant little to them. They would murmur their thanks, and in turn would give Lawrence something Cindy had bought on Murray's advice.

This year, however, Lawrence announced that the children's presents were outside. They followed their grandfather out onto the verandah and Sally immediately saw a large doll's house, painted pink and filled with miniature furniture. Next to it sat a very large, red toy truck. Cindy was amazed. This generosity was so out of character for Lawrence, perhaps he was starting to realise that his grandchildren would be more excited by gifts than by cheques.

'This is very kind of you,' she murmured.

Russell's eyes lit up when he saw the truck. 'Mine?' he asked. His grandfather nodded and Russell raced over to it and hugged it in delight. Momentarily, Gordon looked crestfallen.

'Go down to the house paddock, Gordon,' said his grandfather. 'You'll find your gift there.'

The three children took off for the house paddock, Russell staggering as he tried to pull his truck along with him, and there standing in the yard was a small Shetland pony.

Murray and Cindy exchanged an amazed expression. As soon as he saw it, Gordon was beside himself with excitement.

'Grandfather, this is the best present ever!' he cried, racing over to the little pony.

But as soon as Sally saw the pony, she was overcome with envy, demanding to know where her pony was, the doll's house quickly forgotten.

'Be quiet, Sally! You have your present,' Lawrence said brusquely. Sally's face reddened, but Cindy hushed her.

'Son, get the riding tack out of the barn if you want to saddle the pony up,' Lawrence told Murray.

In no time, Murray had the pony ready to ride and helped Gordon into the saddle. Then he led the pony around the yard until Gordon was ready to take the reins and walk it alone.

Murray and Cindy stood by the paddock's rails and watched Gordon, who was loving every moment of his wonderful present, while Sally also looked on, seething at what she thought was the unfairness of it.

'You've got a very expensive doll's house to play with,' said Lawrence, when Sally began to complain again. 'Just be grateful for that, or I won't buy you a present next Christmas.'

'How about you give your sister a go?' Murray suggested, trying to pacify his daughter.

Gordon shook his head. 'Like Grandfather said, this is my present. Sally can play with her doll's house.' He continued to ride around the yard looking pleased with himself.

That was the last straw for Sally, who stormed off in a temper, only to return from the kitchen with a carrot. She climbed through the rails and tried to feed it to the pony, but the little beast, startled by her efforts, suddenly tried to bite her. Sally promptly slapped it on the nose.

Before the drama could get too out of hand, Cindy grabbed Sally and Murray pulled Gordon from the pony.

'I think you might all need a swim to cool off,' Murray said calmly and loaded the children onto the tractor and took them for a ride down to the creek. Cindy waved them off, relieved that the confrontation had been defused, but then, turning back to the paddock, she saw Lawrence, his face contorted with fury and a whip in his hand, striding towards the little animal. Cindy was horrified to realise that he intended to take out his anger on the pony. Without thinking, she quickly climbed through the rails and ran towards Lawrence, shouting, 'Please, stop it. It's not the pony's fault. Don't hurt the animal . . .' Seeing that Lawrence was paying her no notice whatsoever, Cindy shrieked, 'Stop, Lawrence, stop!'

Cindy stopped running as she neared the furious man. He finally came to a halt, glared at her, then slammed the whip against the fencepost and dropped it to the ground, and strode from the yard without a word.

Cindy watched him go and, once he was out of sight, dropped to her knees shaking. What had she just witnessed? Lawrence had been out of control. She had never seen him like that before. Standing again, Cindy brushed the dirt from her clothes and slowly made her way back to the house. Murray and the children would be back soon and would need some refreshments. Cindy decided she wouldn't let this incident ruin Christmas and set about putting together some tea. But somewhere in the back of her mind, she was worried.

*

Shortly after Christmas, Cindy came into the sunroom where Murray was sipping his morning tea, thumbing through letters.

'You have some mail,' he said, handing her an envelope.

'Oh, good.' Cindy tore open the letter from Alice and skimmed it quickly. 'Oh, wow! Alice and Spencer are coming to visit us! Oh, I can't believe it!'

Murray looked up. 'Is Babs coming too?'

'No, just Alice and Spencer. I can't believe that Alice would come all this way. She hates travelling. She thinks there's no point leaving Palm Springs, but she says here that she won a cruise in a big charity auction at the country club and she's not going to waste it, so they're on a cruise to Australia.' Cindy sighed. 'Of course, Alice wouldn't dream of bringing Babs or giving her the trip. Anyway, she and Spencer are going to get off in Melbourne so they can come up to Kingsley Downs. How wonderful! We'll have to meet them and drive them up here.'

'Do you think visiting Kingsley Downs is their sort of thing?' asked Murray dubiously. 'Why don't we meet them and stay in Melbourne, do the sights and that sort of thing?'

'Murray! They want to see where I'm living and spend time with the children. See the real Australia!'

Murray raised an eyebrow. 'Alice? Hmm, I'm not so sure that she'll like the real Australia. I assume it will be a short visit.'

'Yes, I think so. She says here they'll go back to Melbourne after visiting us and then fly back to the US. The trip sounds amazing. They stop in Vancouver, Hawaii and Fiji, Auckland, Sydney and Melbourne. Babs is keeping an eye on everything and Alice has pretty good staff to look after the shop.' Cindy clutched the letter to her chest and laughed delightedly. 'I can't believe they'll be here by the end of next month. It is so long since I've seen anyone from my family, I can hardly wait.'

Murray chuckled. 'Well, you'll have plenty of time to think of what to do with them.'

'Yes. What shall we do to entertain them?' asked Cindy worriedly.

'Guess they won't be interested in watching sheep crutching,' said Murray with a wicked smile.

'No. Alice wouldn't want to see sheep having their bottoms shaved,' said Cindy primly. 'I must tell the children that she's coming. It's so exciting!'

Cindy wondered how Lawrence would react to her aunt's visit and hoped he'd be away. He had become very involved with the establishment of a new wool corporation and was often away on business or at meetings these days. She always felt that everything was so strained when he was around and she didn't want Alice or Babs to know about the difficult relationship she had with her father-in-law, a part of her life that, if she was honest with herself, she had rather sugar-coated in recent years.

After Cindy had shared the news with the children, who bounced up and down with excitement at the prospect of meeting this exotic-sounding great-aunt and uncle, Cindy rang Jo to tell her the news and to ask for some ideas on how to entertain Alice and Spencer. The old party line had been replaced by a modern exchange, so Cindy and her neighbours could say whatever they liked without having to worry about being overheard. Cindy was grateful when she remembered some of the very frank conversations she'd shared with Jo over the years.

'Oh, that's easy, we'll think of something!' said Joanna. 'How long are they staying?'

'Only a few days.'

'I think the Picnic Races will be on at Lockhart while they're here, and that's always huge fun. You can take a picnic, bottles of bubbly and have a great day out. It won't be like anything they've done in the States.'

'That's a very good idea. Alice would probably prefer mixing with the members at the Melbourne Cup, and seeing all those lovely roses at Flemington – and she'd be more than a match for the fashion stakes! But it's the wrong time of year for the Cup. Anyway, you're right, the Picnic Races will be something quite different for them.' Then Cindy hesitated. 'Actually, I'm a bit concerned about Lawrence during their visit. I hope he'll make an effort in front of Alice.'

'I wouldn't worry. Lawrence is a snob – he'll be nice to rich people.'

'I don't know how rich they are, but I'm sure Spencer is quite well off and Babs told me that Alice was doing a little investing, though I'm not sure in what.'

'They'll impress Lawrence. And you can fill in a day just driving around Kingsley Downs. Lawrence would approve of that!'

'I'm not sure that would be very exciting.'

'Then pop into town, though I have no idea what your aunt would think of Deni. I've seen your photos of Palm Springs and it's more than a different world. It's a different planet!' Joanna laughed.

'It is, in a way. You should see Alice's house there – it's the very definition of modern.'

'Even so, I'm sure she'll be impressed by the Kingsley Downs homestead.'

'Yes, it is gracious, if a bit dim and dark.'

'One day when Lawrence isn't around you can revamp the whole place,' Jo suggested with a laugh.

'Lawrence is as tough as old boots and in rude good health,' replied Cindy.

'Forget about him, Cin. Look forward to your visitors. I can't wait to meet your Aunt Alice. She sounds like a hoot.'

*

Cindy felt giddy with excitement as they arrived at the Melbourne docks to meet Alice and Spencer. The dazzling white ocean liner towered above them as they stood on the wharf, looking up, trying to catch a glimpse of their American relatives. The children were awestruck by the bustling crowd and the large vessel.

Cindy peered through the gap where Gordon was watching the arrivals.

'There she is! Oh, Lordy! No mistaking her.' Cindy squealed, laughing and bouncing on her high heels.

Murray looked over her shoulder. 'Yep. No mistaking Aunt Alice.'

Alice slowly sashayed down the gangplank, staring out at the crowd below on the dock as if she were not so much looking for someone but was rather someone who was expecting everyone else to be looking at her. Though ten years had passed since Cindy had seen her aunt, Alice didn't seem to have aged a day. With one hand she held on to an enormous straw sunhat decorated with flying red ribbons. She wore a red and white striped nautical top and bright red, flared slacks. Gold jewellery glinted in the sun. Enormous square sunglasses with red frames obscured half her face. Spencer, in a blue golf shirt and jaunty cap, followed in her wake as they disappeared into the customs hall.

Cindy was absurdly pleased to see her aunt and hugged her tearfully when they emerged.

'I've missed you so much!' Cindy said, drawing back from her aunt. 'Hello, Spencer. How has the sea voyage been?'

He rolled his eyes, but before he could speak, Alice demanded, 'Show me these children of yours! Oh, hello, Murray.'

She proffered a cheek to be pecked as Cindy moved the children forward, all three gawking at the brilliantly dressed person before them.

Russell stepped forward and wrapped his arms around Alice's knees.

She patted his head. 'Charming little boy. Russell, I take it. Now, you must be Gordon, and you're Sally,' she said to the twins.

There were awkward hugs as everyone tried to avoid knocking Alice's hat off. The excited crowd swirled around them, calling out to each other, looking for bags, friends, taxis. Alice beamed at Cindy and the children, uncurled Russell's arms, smoothed her top and slacks and adjusted her sunglasses.

'Lead on, Murray,' called Spencer. 'Let's get the heck out of this melee.'

Murray navigated the old Daimler away from the dock with the twins squeezed in the back with Alice and Spencer, while Russell sat on Cindy's lap in the front. Alice insisted on keeping her carryall traveller's case with her, plus her handbag, so there was little room to move in the back seat. Their suitcases were in the trunk, as Spencer called the boot, although Spencer told Murray that they had several more back on board. Arrangements had been made for this luggage to be sent to the airport to be collected by the two of them when they flew back to the States.

'Thankfully we had a suite and extra closet space, but we could have done with a whole extra stateroom just for Alice's outfits,' said Spencer.

'Did you want me to appear at the captain's table in the same outfit twice?' demanded Alice.

'Oh, my Lordy, no!' exclaimed Spencer, holding up his hands in mock horror.

'He doesn't understand. I'm a walking advertisement for my store,' sniffed Alice.

'But your shop is in Palm Springs,' said Murray.

'People who travel in style will end up in Palm Springs at some stage,' said Alice calmly.

'Quite right, too,' agreed Murray with a grin. 'Now, we thought we'd take in some sights, let the children have a bit of a run in the Botanic Gardens, then head out for a smart lunch before driving home to Kingsley Downs. It's about four hours away.' He glanced at Alice in the rear-vision mirror. 'You sure you're up for the country, Alice? Not a lot to see, just a heap of sheep.'

'I am under instructions from Babs to drink it all in, my dear,' Alice assured him. 'I'm sure Cindy's photographs don't do it justice. Though we love getting your photos, Cindy,' she added.

It was a glorious day and Alice had to admit the immaculate gardens sprawling along the Yarra River were very beautiful.

By the time they got to the restaurant, the children were ravenous, but sat quietly, awed by the silver service setting and having been drilled by their mother to watch their table manners and be on their best behaviour around Aunt Alice. Not that Cindy had to remind them. To the little ones, Aunt Alice had stepped from the pages of a fairytale where witches and queens did battle. They were not sure yet whose side Aunt Alice was on.

After lunch they piled once again into the groaning car and Murray drove them out of the city, paddocks replacing streets as they ventured further into the bushland.

'Good grief, Cindy, how much further?' sighed Alice from the back seat. 'Spencer is asleep.'

'Not far now, Alice. We'll be home in time for a sundowner.'

'What on earth is that?'

'Cocktails at sunset.'

'Did someone say cocktails?' Spencer yawned. 'This is quite a drive. I don't imagine you would want to do this too often. You should get yourself a little plane, Murray.'

Having been up since the crack of dawn, the children

were all asleep when Murray turned into the entrance to Kingsley Downs, but bumping over the cattle grid woke them up.

After a few minutes' drive along the track, Cindy waited for Alice or Spencer to comment on the lovely slanting late afternoon sunlight that fell between the gums lining the driveway, but instead Alice asked in a querulous tone, 'Did you say that was the entrance to the property back there? Where in heaven's name is the house?'

'Coming up,' Murray replied cheerfully. 'As one of your compatriots said, "Go west, young man." We're nearly there. Mind you, Kingsley Downs is quite a modest property by some standards. You should see the stations outback. Now, they really have long driveways.'

'Sounds like a lot to look after,' said Spencer.

'What's to look after?' commented Alice, waving a hand. 'It's empty.'

'We have thousands of sheep out there,' said Gordon proudly.

'Goodness. That's a lot of wool,' said Alice. 'Of course, it's a little out of vogue at home. I love the synthetics. So easy to care for. People all ask for polyester these days.'

'Oh, gosh, don't say that in front of Murray's father,' said Cindy quickly.

'And don't stand in front of an open fire if you're wearing synthetics,' said Murray darkly.

'There's the house!' said Spencer as the gracious old home came into view. 'Wow, it's quite a joint.'

'I hope you don't have to clean the house by yourself,' said Alice.

The children were excited to be home and anxious to get out of the car. A beaming Tom and Mrs Flowers came out to meet them.

'Tom will get your bags, Spencer,' said Murray as he climbed out. 'Come on in and meet my father.'

'Mrs Flowers, Mrs Flowers, we got you something . . .' The children ran towards her, waving a small gift Cindy had helped them choose in Melbourne.

'Alice, do you want to freshen up after the drive? Murray's father will be waiting for us on the verandah with cold drinks, but I'll take you to your room first. Now, kids, off you go. Mrs Flowers will give you your dinner in the kitchen,' called Cindy after them as the children hurtled into the house.

'I'm up for a belt if it's the cocktail hour,' said Spencer. 'Damned big place, Murray. You have a few horses, eh?'

'They're stockhorses, Spencer. No gallopers here. My grandfather had racehorses years back, but Dad and I aren't really interested. Having racehorses is just a great big hole to pump money into as far as we're concerned. Come this way.'

*

Alice had combed her hair and added fresh vermillion lipstick and a quick spray of Arpege, her favourite perfume, when Cindy poked her head around the door to see if she was ready.

'Yes, all set, Cindy. Now, how about you give me a little tour of the house? It's old, isn't it?'

Cindy nodded as she led Alice down the long dark hallway. 'Murray's great-grandfather had it built at the turn of the century. Why don't I take you out to the verandah for a drink and you can see the place as we go?'

Alice didn't say much as she took her time trailing Cindy through the sitting room, drawing room and dining room, pausing to study a painting or lift up a vase or dish on the sideboard to examine it.

'It's all so *old*. I don't mean heritage old, like an English castle, but just old-fashioned,' said Alice, wrinkling her nose. 'And dark. This house needs a lot more light. Light is so important in Palm Springs. You should introduce it here,' continued Alice, as she looked around the dingy dining room with its heavy, unfashionable furniture. 'It'd be a big job bringing this house up to scratch. It's all so last century.' She shook her head slowly before turning to Cindy. 'Okay, let's go meet your father-in-law.'

Cindy had been dreading this meeting, but Alice sailed onto the pretty verandah, where Spencer, Lawrence and Murray were ensconced in comfortable chairs with drinks in their hands, chatting amicably. The three men quickly rose to their feet as the women approached.

'Ah, the famous Alice,' said Lawrence genially, shaking Alice's hand and making her gold bracelets jangle. 'I am honoured to meet you. It's lovely to have both you and your husband as guests. Cynthia has so been looking forward to your arrival.'

Cindy excused herself, mumbling something about going to see if she could help Mrs Flowers. This was not strictly true, but she simply couldn't stay there and watch Lawrence putting on his charm act.

Cindy walked through the house and stepped outside into the back garden, where she drew several deep breaths. She felt emotional at seeing Alice, and knew it was because her aunt brought her close to the life that had once been so familiar to her and which now seemed so long ago. She suddenly realised how much she had missed her aunts, especially Babs, as well as her cousin Joey, and how much she'd longed to introduce her children to the people she loved so much.

The sun would set soon. Steeling herself, she drew another deep breath and turned back into the house.

Cindy rejoined the group and sat quietly as they all watched an especially magnificent sunset.

'We laid it on just for you, Alice,' said Lawrence.

'Well, there's nothing blocking the view, that's for sure,' said Alice.

'The wide open spaces. Like the desert back home. So this is good sheep-grazing country, Lawrence?' asked Spencer.

'Yes, it's tough country, not like the lush coastal land, but sheep thrive on the dry, coarse herbage. They're perverse creatures. Spoil them and they're done for.'

'Wool breeders are a bit that way too,' added Murray. 'It's a gamble each season whether you're rich or ruined, depending on the weather. One day you can't give 'em away, the next you get two inches of rain and you've got buyers lined up at the gate.'

'It sounds an unpredictable business,' agreed Spencer.

'What are our plans for tomorrow?' asked Alice, clearly bored by the sheep talk.

'Perhaps Cynthia can take you on a bit of a tour of the district. And tomorrow night I've had Cynthia invite some of our local VIPs in for dinner,' said Lawrence.

'They're just our friends. It won't be a civic reception, or anything like that,' interjected Cindy.

'We wanted them to meet you. They've heard all about you from Cindy,' added Murray quickly.

'Lovely. We can tell them about Palm Springs,' said Alice.

'I'm sure they'd love to hear about it,' said Murray tactfully. 'And then we thought the following day we could go to the Picnic Races. They may not be what you're used to in the States, but they're a lot of fun and it's a chance for you to see how we enjoy ourselves in the bush. May I freshen your drink, Alice?'

'Sounds like something I'd like to see,' said Spencer cheerfully.

'I'll see how Mrs Flowers is travelling with our dinner,' said Cindy, as she excused herself again. Lawrence glared at her as she left the verandah, though no one else seemed to notice.

'Thank you, Murray. But I think I'll go and change for dinner, if I may.' Alice rose and followed Cindy out.

The children were in the kitchen, finishing their dinner, and Cindy could tell they were tired after their long day. Cindy ruffled Russell's hair affectionately. Seeing the children always made her feel better.

'Go and get ready for bed, you three, I'll be along shortly.'

'Don't worry about them tonight,' said Mrs Flowers. 'You'll want to be with your aunt and I've got dinner well in hand, so I'll take care of them.'

Cindy thanked Mrs Flowers and headed back along the hallway, where she met Alice coming the other way.

'Oh good, I was hoping to catch you for a quick word,' said Alice conspiratorially. 'I want to tell you something that you may not want your husband to hear. You know that boy you used to be crazy about, Robbie Wilson? Well, Spencer has heard that he's doing very well for himself. He's a partner in a big law firm in San Francisco. I bet if you'd married him, you'd have a place of your own. Such a shame.'

Cindy felt a flush of annoyance. 'Aunt Alice, Murray is a good husband and I love him dearly. I cannot imagine being married to anyone else. And we have three children whom I adore. They're everything to me,' she protested quickly.

The mention of Robbie had startled her. She had believed herself so in love with him all those years ago, but she hadn't given him a thought in years. She was vaguely curious about what had happened to him, but certainly she had no regrets.

'Alice, when I first came here, I didn't think I'd ever like it out here, but this country gets to you. I couldn't imagine living anywhere else now, not even San Francisco.

Believe me when I say that I chose the right man when I married Murray.'

Alice shrugged. 'If you say so. Anyway, you should bring the children back to the desert sometime. They'll enjoy it, and it will expose them to another way of life; to taste and glamour. It would be exciting for them, and Babs so wants you to come over.'

'Hopefully we'll visit one day,' said Cindy vaguely, wondering how they would ever be able to round up five airfares.

Spencer wandered in, looking for his wife.

'I wondered where you'd gone, dear. You gals having a chat? I thought I'd put my feet up for ten minutes. You getting dolled up, sweetie?'

'What do you think? I've been in these clothes all day,' said Alice.

'Tell her she doesn't need the tiara tonight, Cindy.'

Cindy smiled at them. 'Relax. Dinner will be ready in about an hour. When you've changed, why don't you go back onto the verandah and help yourself to another drink? It's lovely out there on a summer's evening.'

*

Alice swept into the pre-dinner drinks in a bold geometric print jumpsuit with wide palazzo legs and a deep V neck-line. Lawrence couldn't take his eyes off Cindy's exotic aunt. She must certainly have seemed like a bird of paradise to him. Spencer, sartorially slightly more subdued in a pale green polo shirt and plaid slacks, trailed behind her.

Murray wore moleskin pants and a checked shirt and Lawrence a blue shirt, grey slacks and a red woollen tie. Cindy had dressed hurriedly and wished she'd taken a bit more trouble when she saw Alice's critical eye flick over her simple cotton shirtdress, though she had added Murray's strand of pearls, which had been one of the items rescued by some miracle from the demolished old house.

Lawrence, who seemed to be enjoying Spencer's company, was in an expansive mood. Spencer began to ask him and Murray about their prize rams.

'I've been looking at the photographs in the hall and I'm quite amazed at the size of those beasts. They look like they can hardly walk under all that wool.'

'The Merino sheep in this area are Peppins, named after the family who first bred a tougher sheep for this type of country. Saltbush plains were good for cattle, but the sheep had to walk for miles to feed, so the Peppin family started to breed a bigger, stronger beast. Suits this area perfectly,' said Lawrence.

'Their wool's better, too,' said Murray. 'It has longer, stronger fibres that can be combed out and spun using the new spinning machines that help keep wool competitive with cotton. Our Merinos carry a lot more wool than other sheep, too. Peppin rams are now sold all over the world.'

'So the wool industry is still good, then?' asked Spencer.

'Times are changing,' said Lawrence. 'The wool industry wants certainty and we're going to get it. The new Australian Wool Corporation is taking control of that and Australia will be dictating wool prices for the world.' Lawrence leaned back in his chair, a smug smile on his face.

Alice flicked her leg, bored with the conversation. 'Well, I'm wearing silk, although frankly all I sell these days are synthetics. Fashionable people so prefer them.'

Cindy was stung by her aunt's tactlessness, but Lawrence made no comment.

'It must be time for dinner,' he said mildly. 'I'm sure I can hear Mrs Flowers in the dining room. Shouldn't you go and check, Cynthia?' His tone was clipped, implying

Cindy was failing as a hostess. Cindy's cheeks burned as she stepped out of the room, though no one else seemed to notice the barb.

At dinner Alice looked a bit dismayed at the huge lamb roast.

'Is it one of your own? I mean, it didn't have a name, I hope? I can't say that I enjoy meat. Perhaps I'll just stick with a few vegetables.'

Lawrence gave her a sharp look, but returned his attention to Spencer.

The rest of the meal passed without incident and Alice and Spencer turned in early, claiming fatigue from the 'epic' drive, as Alice described it. The first day had been a success. Cindy wasn't sure what Alice thought of Kingsley Downs, but she had never felt prouder of her home.

*

The next day Cindy took the visitors on a tour of the district. They went into Yamboola, where Alice and Spencer paused for some photos outside the Majestic Hotel, which they decided was quaint, but were not prepared to stop inside for a drink. They drove back to Kingsley Downs for lunch and then Cindy took them into Deniliquin. Alice was clearly unimpressed, so their visit was somewhat cursory, although both insisted on having their photos taken standing near the black swans which were resting on the banks of the Edward River.

The dinner party that night went off smoothly enough, even though it was soon apparent that Alice and Spencer had little in common with the other guests. Alistair had no trouble charming Alice, who was clearly flattered by his gentlemanly manners, and Joanna paid attention to Spencer. Lawrence was still cool and gruff towards Cindy, but continued to be so unexpectedly pleasant to Alice that Jo kept looking at Cindy in bemused surprise. But, in spite of all the conviviality, Cindy could see that the interests of the Riverina and those of Palm Springs were very far apart. Nevertheless, it was a pleasant evening, especially as all of their friends made such an effort at making her relatives feel welcome and interesting.

The Picnic Races provided the opportunity for a more stimulating day. Mrs Flowers kindly volunteered to look after the children so that Cindy could concentrate her attentions on her aunt.

Alice fussed about an appropriate hat to go with her floaty chiffon floral dress.

'Alice, wear that sunhat you wore when you arrived,' said Cindy. 'If you take off the red ribbons, it'll be perfect.'

Alice thought a moment, then asked Sally to take her around the garden, and they picked a mass of roses, which she pinned around the wide brim.

The rural setting and basic amenities of the country race meeting initially surprised the visitors, but the ambience and the picnic lunches – lavish or simple, from car boots, spread out on rugs on the grass, or under the trees on tables set with linen and crystal, or with paper plates and mismatched cutlery – created a unique experience for them. There were several barbecues and the smell of cooking meat wafted through the air.

'It's like a country fair,' said Alice, looking around at the refreshment tent, chocolate wheel, and the bookmakers shouting their prices, their boards hastily chalked with horses' names and their odds. 'But I can't understand a word they're saying. Is there no grandstand? And that's the track? With just that small railing?'

'We've found a good spot under a tree. Follow me. There's benches and a bit of shade,' said Murray with a grin. As they made their way over to the tree, they nodded and smiled at the other racegoers, Cindy, Murray and

Lawrence pausing to chat with the people they knew. Alice could not take her eyes off the women, examining what they wore with an expert eye.

'Glad to see these women have made an effort, anyway,' she said. 'Hats and even gloves in this heat and dust. Good golly.' She coughed and waved her hands as a cloud of dust descended on them as the horses in race number two thundered past on their way to the finishing line.

They settled themselves on the chairs that Murray had retrieved from the boot of the car, as well as a thick plaid travelling rug, and Lawrence quickly opened a bottle of champagne.

Murray waved away the glass of bubbles. 'Think I'd rather have a beer in this heat, thanks, Dad. What about you, Spencer?'

Drinks in hand, they studied the racing programme and, after some quick analysis of the form of the runners, the men made their way to the bookies to place some bets. By some fluke, Alice's first selection managed to come in second, and after that there was no stopping her. She placed multiple bets on all the races and sometimes even managed to win some more money.

Later in the day Alice graciously accepted the prize for the best fashions on the field, as was her due. But nonetheless she was pleased, and posed for the local newspaper photographer.

'Cindy, make sure that you get the photos from the newspaper and copies of the paper itself. No one in Palm Springs will realise what a little event these races are if I put the photos into gorgeous frames.'

Spencer, with a loosened tie and slightly flushed face, had also bet on every race and celebrated his occasional wins as if he owned each horse. 'Heck, this beats the Kentucky Derby!'

He gave Cindy a hot tip for the next race, but she laughed and shook her head. 'I've done my dash, as they say around here.'

'But you've not bet on one race!' Alice frowned. 'Haven't you got any money? Spencer, give Cindy some cash. You've won enough.'

'I wouldn't bother, Spencer,' snorted Lawrence, his face curled into a sneer. 'Cindy wouldn't know one end of a horse from another. She'd be just throwing your money away.'

Cindy cringed at Lawrence's harsh comment, but didn't want to make a fuss in front of her aunt.

'It's fine, thank you. And I am hopeless at picking winners. If I bet on a horse, it's sure to run last. I do hope you and Spencer had fun. I know it's a bit different from what you're used to doing,' said Cindy.

Both of them assured her that they had never experienced anything to match this day.

By the time they reached Kingsley Downs, the sun had set and the children were well and truly asleep in their beds.

'They wanted to stay up to see you,' Mrs Flowers explained to Alice, 'but I didn't know when you'd be back.'

'I expect they did, but I'll see them tomorrow before we head off,' replied Alice. Then, turning to Cindy, she added, 'How about the two of us have a little tete-a-tete while the boys have a drink on the verandah?'

When they had both settled into the chintz-covered chairs outside Alice's room, Cindy was about to say how much she had enjoyed having her aunt visit, when Alice spoke first.

'I do not understand this at all,' said Alice vehemently.

Cindy was taken aback. 'Sorry, Alice. What are you talking about?'

'Your father-in-law. Why do you allow that man to treat you the way he does? Why does Murray allow him to speak to you like he does? I had no idea Murray was such a weak man.'

Cindy was stunned. She thought Alice had been impressed with Lawrence, as he had been nothing but courteous, and even charming, to her.

As if sensing Cindy's thoughts, Alice sniffed. 'I can spot a phoney, a fake, and a hypocrite a mile away. I'm not like Babs, who thinks everybody is lovely. I am much more discerning. That man is a hypocrite. Speaks to me as though butter wouldn't melt in his mouth, but is appalling to you. So, what's the story?'

Cindy was still reeling. She'd always thought Alice was so self-centred that she took no notice of anything in which she wasn't the centre of attention.

'Well? What's the story with this man?' Alice demanded.

'Lawrence? Well, it's very difficult. I'm not entirely sure that I know –'

'Difficult? I'd say sharing a house with that man would be purgatory. Having to live in his house and have him treat you like staff!'

'Alice, you've only been here a little while –'

'And he calls you Cynthia. No one has called you that since the day you were born. Lord, how obnoxious he is. I've watched you grow up and you've turned out quite well. You do not deserve to be treated like that. Why doesn't your husband stand up for you?'

'That's not fair. Murray does take my side, but I guess we both just want to keep the peace. And it's difficult, because Lawrence owns and runs everything.'

'If you ask me, Murray's under Lawrence's thumb, too.'

'It might look that way, but we are a bit stuck.'

Cindy explained that Lawrence held the purse strings and, though one day Murray would inherit the property, while Lawrence was in charge they did things his way.

'Of course, Murray feels an obligation to his father. As I've told you and Babs in my letters, Lawrence raised Murray after his mother left.'

'Personally, she seems to me to have been a woman of good sense,' said Alice emphatically. 'I wouldn't have stayed either. Neither would Babs.'

'Well, I'm not going anywhere. This is my home, Alice. I would never leave like Rose did.'

'Then you're trapped.'

'No, I am not. Let's not talk about it.' To Cindy's relief, Spencer came into the room and Alice turned to him.

'Spencer, I'm thinking that Cindy and the children should come for a visit. We will fly her and the kids back to the States, anytime she wants, won't we?'

Spencer was taken aback. 'Huh? Have I missed something? Of course we will. Is there a problem?'

'You haven't missed a thing,' said Cindy hastily.

'Cindy, listen to me. You're living with a man who treats you with contempt and disrespect. If he continues in this vein, your children will lose all respect for you, too. Murray is caught in the middle, but he will stick by his father,' said Alice firmly. 'I can always tell with this sort of thing.'

'Alice, don't upset Cindy,' said Spencer.

'Nonsense, she needs to hear some home truths. In short, you have a father-in-law who's a pain in the ass. 'Scuse my French,' said Alice caustically.

'Hey, Alice, cool it. Cindy is a grown woman now.' Spencer reached out and patted Cindy's shoulder. 'But just the same, if you need to, all you have to do is call us.'

'Thank you.' Cindy was close to tears. 'Please, don't say anything to Babs. I don't want to worry her and I will come to Palm Springs when the children are old enough to appreciate it, I promise.'

'Cindy, this is my final word on the subject,' said Alice crisply. 'And that is, you need to stand up to Lawrence, show some backbone. You have every right. Take control of your life and don't let anyone walk over you. He's a man who takes advantage of the weak. It will only get worse. If you don't stand your ground now, you will regret it. Do it for Murray, too. If he can't, you'll have to do it yourself.'

Cindy drew a shaky breath. She knew Alice was right.

*

Cindy wanted to spend as much time as she could with Alice and Spencer as their visit drew to a close. Having Alice around made her realise just how terribly she missed Babs as well.

'I'm coming to the airport with you,' she announced. 'Because I want to spend every second I can with you. I'll miss you both so much once you've gone. It's been very special having you here.'

'We'll describe it all to Babs, and show her our photos. She'll be longing to hear,' said Spencer.

Murray smiled when Cindy told him she was going to the airport too. 'Of course. I think we might leave the kids behind this time, if Mrs F is okay with that. Do you want to stay overnight, go to dinner in Melbourne, and come back the next day?'

Cindy was tempted, but she really didn't want to leave the children for too long, and in any case she didn't feel it was fair to impose on the housekeeper too much. Besides, she'd miss them if they stayed for the night.

'So sweet and thoughtful of you, darling. No, we'd best head back. Maybe we can plan something another time.'

Cindy was tearful at the airport saying her goodbyes, but as they drove back out of the city Murray let her talk, and she reminisced about Babs and Alice and her life in Palm Springs. Mostly they were stories he'd heard before, but he let her prattle on, as it seemed to be her way of dealing with the parting from Alice and Spencer.

After a while, Cindy sighed and said, 'It's just been so nice to have family visit. I do hope we can take the children to California someday.'

'Let's see how the next wool sales go. Now that the Wool Corporation is up and functioning we'll have a much better idea of what our income is,' said Murray.

Cindy laid her head back on the seat and shut her eyes, glad to relax after four days of visitors. She realised she was quite exhausted.

She dozed, but woke suddenly as Murray muttered aloud.

'What is it?' Cindy saw that they were almost at their gate and the sun had set.

'Lights in the paddocks.'

'Maybe Tom's out after the 'roos? Or rabbits? I don't see anything,' Cindy suggested.

'Maybe,' said Murray, but his voice was strained. They rattled over the cattle grid and Murray drove down the driveway with unusual speed.

'What do you think is up?' asked Cindy.

'It's starting to get dark, so someone has lights out there, looking for something. Might be a missing animal.'

Cindy's hand flew to her mouth. 'Oh no. The children! You don't think something has happened to one of them?'

'We'll know in a few minutes,' said Murray grimly, putting his foot down even further and making the vehicle slew on a corner of the dirt track.

As they skidded to a halt outside the house, Murray put his hand on the horn. Mrs Flowers appeared straight away and Cindy could tell from her expression that something was terribly wrong.

'What's going on? What's happened? Where are the children?' cried Cindy, stumbling towards her.

Before Mrs Flowers could answer, Sally came rushing from behind her and flung herself at her mother, weeping hysterically.

'Where are the boys?'

'Gordon's with Grandfather.'

'Mrs Parnell . . .' started Mrs Flowers, then broke down and put her hands to her face as she, too, burst into tears.

Murray put his arm around her shoulders. 'What has happened?' he asked hoarsely, shaking her gently.

Between choking sobs, Mrs Flowers managed to say, 'It's Russell . . . He's missing. Everyone is out looking.'

As Cindy gasped, Murray ran into the house.

'Oh my God! What happened? When did he disappear?' Cindy grasped Mrs Flowers's hand.

Tearfully, Mrs Flowers managed to speak. 'The children were on the verandah, we had lunch out there. Gordon and Sally carried the plates in when we'd finished, and I went into the kitchen to wash them up. And, I don't know, it must have been only fifteen or twenty minutes later when we realised Russell wasn't with us.'

'Lunchtime!' shrieked Cindy. 'He's been gone all afternoon! Oh, my poor boy. The creek! Oh God, he's not down there . . . ?'

Mrs Flowers took her arm. 'No. No. We checked the creek and the dams straight away. There's no sign of him there. We think he just wandered off and got lost. Come inside and leave it to the men. There's a whole lot of them out here. Perce Jackson, the fire brigade, some people from town, the football team . . . my Tom and the jackaroo.'

'That jackaroo couldn't find his own way out of a paper bag. Where's Mr Parnell?' snapped Cindy, trying to keep the hysteria she felt rising in her under control.

'He's out there –' started Mrs Flowers.

'He's out there *with Gordon*? What does he think he's doing? Getting his other grandson lost as well?' Cindy could barely get the words out.

Murray came running out of the house. 'I'll get someone to send Gordon back,' he said, as he raced over to the farm trucks. 'It'll be all right. I promise you.'

In a couple of seconds, the truck had raced away into the gathering gloom.

Holding Sally's hand tightly, Cindy followed Mrs Flowers indoors, casting anxious glances over her shoulder at the swiftly falling night. Mrs Flowers made a pot of tea as Cindy sat at the table, her head resting on her arms, her face buried, unable to avoid the horror of what might have befallen Russell.

But as Mrs Flowers put the cup in front of her and lightly touched her shoulder, Cindy lifted her head.

'It's so unlike him. He was on the verandah, you came inside, and suddenly he was just gone?' she said in a disbelieving voice.

'That boy can be a bit of a dreamer, off in a world of his own. But they'll find him,' said Mrs Flowers, trying to sound positive, but the anguish on her face tore at Cindy. 'I'm so sorry that I wasn't watching him closely enough.' Tears started to roll down her cheeks once again.

'I'm not blaming you, Mrs Flowers. I know you love my children, but I just want him home. I can't sit here any longer. I'm going out to look for him.' She jumped to her feet.

'Where are you going, Mummy?' asked Sally anxiously. 'Don't leave me.' The little girl started to cry.

Cindy hesitated. 'All right, you can come. I'll get some torches. Sally, why don't you go and get Russell's red truck? It's got a loud siren thing on it. We'll search along the creek again. He loves it down there. The men might have missed him.'

Cindy drove carefully with the headlights on high beam, pausing at the woolshed to call out as Sally turned on the shrill siren on Russell's toy truck.

Cindy headed around the paddock, past the big peppercorn tree and around the blackberry bushes. She parked the car by the willows that hung over the creek and she and Sally hopped out.

'Sally, don't move out of my sight. Shine the torches along the banks. God forbid he's here.' For once, the creek water looked dangerous, murky and sinister. The tree roots and rotting logs in the oozy mud looked like traps for a small boy. Cindy looked carefully in the watery torchlight. There was no sign of any disturbance that she could see.

'Doesn't look like he came this way,' said Cindy after she'd gone as far along the creek as she could while still keeping Sally in sight. 'Okay. Back to the car.'

'Where to now, Mummy?'

'I'm going to drive slowly back down the track to the old gate, past where the old house was, and towards the Yamboola road.'

Cindy had always avoided going near the old house, now a pile of rusty corrugated iron, rubble, bricks and wood amidst the broken fences and overgrown garden.

'Mummy, that's miles away.'

'Who knows how far he's walked in five or six hours?' As the car pulled up, the headlights spotlighted the dismal remains of the old house. She started the engine again, turned the wheel and bumped onto the track that was once so familiar to her.

It was now very dark. The moon had yet to rise. And her baby boy was out there, somewhere, all alone. She shuddered.

'Mummy, what's that?' asked Sally, pointing out into the darkness.

'What? Where?' Cindy braked, peering into the night which was pierced only by the twin beams of her headlights.

Sally craned forward. 'I thought I saw something moving . . . to the side of the track. Maybe just a kangaroo. Mum, it's further up.' The little girl leaned forward and started to roll down the window. 'I hear something . . . like singing, sort of.'

Cindy turned the car to the right, the lights sweeping across the track to trees and grass on the opposite side.

'There're some people over there!' she shouted.

'People! Who are they?' asked Sally.

'I think they're blackfellas, Aborigines,' said Cindy.

Cindy brought the car to a halt and sprinted out as soon as she'd flung open her door.

'Mummy, Mummy!' Sally climbed out too, as she saw her mother start to run towards the shadowy figures and, grabbing her torch, followed her mother across the paddock.

It took only a moment for Cindy to grasp what was happening. The small group of Aborigines had moved from the side of the road into the beam of the headlights illuminating the track, still singing, their chant now quite loud.

In the lead there was an old man wearing khaki shorts and a faded shirt, followed by a dog, and a younger man who was carrying a bush knife. Cindy could see an older woman wearing a knitted beanie on her greying head, and behind her were several other young people. One of the girls was piggybacking another child. As Cindy ran towards them, the girl leaned down and the child jumped from her back and ran forward on his short strong legs.

'Mummy!'

'Russell!' Cindy shrieked. As she reached him, she picked him up, grasping him to her chest as if to embed him in her heart. She sobbed with relief.

The old man stopped singing and they all stood back watching Sally and Cindy cuddle Russell.

'Where've you been, young man? You scared us all silly,' said Cindy.

She put Russell down, but held his hand tightly.

'Thank you,' she said, and reached out her other hand to the Aboriginal elder. 'I remember you. You saved my life when my house was blown away.'

The old man gave her a large grin. 'Young fella bin walkabout, missus. We find him sleepin' under big tree. He legs tired, so we carry him back. We know he belong to you.'

'How far away was he?'

'Long way, missus. Too far for little fella.'

Cindy glanced down at her son again. 'Are you okay, Russell? You didn't hurt yourself?'

The little boy shook his head. 'I'm hungry.'

'Where've you been?' demanded Sally.

'Sally, your brother is safe and well, that's the main thing for now. Goodness, we have to let Daddy know. Russell, say thank you to everyone for finding you and bringing you home,' said Cindy. 'Shake hands.'

Russell went to the old man and flung his arms around his waist. 'Thank you. Thank you for my song.'

Cindy looked at the group who were standing quietly, smiling. 'What song? The song you were singing just then?'

The old man nodded. 'We sing him his country. So he know his way and no get lost no more.'

Suddenly the quiet night was shattered by an ear-splitting wail.

'My truck!' Russell ran towards the car as his sister pressed the siren on the little boy's red truck.

Cindy pressed the old man's hand in hers. 'We will see you again.'

He nodded and smiled. 'He a good young fella.' And the group turned back the way they had come.

'Can we give you a ride in the car?' Cindy called, as

they filed silently away on thick-soled feet. But no one took any notice as they continued moving quietly into the night.

*

There were people everywhere, friends and neighbours, the police and even a reporter from the local newspaper. As soon as Cindy pulled up in the car with her son, there was a sensation. Everyone rushed over to the vehicle as Cindy struggled out of it, holding the little boy. Murray pushed his way through the small crowd and took Russell from Cindy's arms. He hugged his son and kissed his wife. The mood in the yard was jubilant.

Mrs Flowers quickly brewed a big pot of tea and whipped up sandwiches and biscuits, which the twins passed around while Murray opened bottles of beer. Lawrence thanked everyone quietly and disappeared into his office.

Russell was briefly the centre of attention before being scooped up by Cindy to be bathed and fed and cuddled with a bedtime story. Russell was quickly asleep, tightly holding his stuffed teddy bear. While Murray farewelled the crowd, Cindy found the twins and gave them a quick hug.

'Thank you both for helping. Daddy and I appreciate it. Now, finish your supper and get ready for bed.'

'Is Russell going to get into trouble?' asked Sally.

'I think he's had a big enough scare to learn his lesson,' said Cindy. 'So let's not talk about it again, okay?'

'Grandfather already went mad at him, when you were outside thanking everyone,' said Sally as she headed to her bedroom.

'Hang on, Sally, what did Grandfather say?' asked Cindy. Then she noticed Gordon poke Sally in the ribs for speaking out. Sally, however, took no notice of her brother.

'He shouted at him for running away and giving everyone a fright. And then he shook him. Russell was really frightened by Grandfather, so he won't run away again, Mummy.'

'I see,' said Cindy, trying to keep her tone neutral for the children. 'And did he say anything else?'

'Well,' said Gordon. 'He did say that you didn't know how to look after us properly.'

'Did he now?' said Cindy. 'Go and see if Mrs Flowers has something ready for your dinner. Well, we'll start a new day tomorrow and put all this behind us.' She turned away with a set mouth and tight expression.

She found Mrs Flowers in the kitchen. 'Do you know where Mr Parnell is, Mrs F?' she asked.

'In his study. I'm just about to make us a bit of dinner for the twins and then I'll find something for the rest of us. I bet you're all pretty hungry.'

Cindy nodded, but her face was grim and Mrs Flowers raised an eyebrow as she watched Cindy turn away. Cindy marched down the hallway, her anger rising with every step. How dare Lawrence say she was a bad mother – and to her children! She was a good mother and she knew it. How dare he undermine her! Alice was right. She had to take a stand right now.

Cindy knocked on the study door and pushed it open before waiting for a reply. Lawrence looked up from his desk, and frowned when he saw her.

'Is there something urgent, Cynthia?'

She stared at him. 'Why do you insist on calling me that? You know I prefer Cindy – it's all I've ever been called.'

'Cynthia is your given name.'

'I've heard you call Sally "Sal".'

'Excuse me,' said Lawrence coldly, 'did you come in here only for this nonsensical discussion?'

'No. I came in here to tell you that you are not to

discipline my son. Don't you dare lay a hand on him ever again,' snapped Cindy.

Lawrence remained impassive. 'You spoil those children. You are a frivolous mother. My grandsons have to be strong, not the spoiled brats that you want them to be.'

Cindy was incensed. She narrowed her eyes at Lawrence. 'How dare you! They're my sons. I will raise them as I see fit. You have no right to criticise me.'

'I have every right. Now, I'm busy.' He looked away, picking up a paper from his desk.

Cindy put both palms on Lawrence's desk and leaned towards him. 'Lawrence, you are a rude and arrogant man and I will not have you bullying my children.'

'They will live by my rules in my house if they know what's best for them,' he snapped back. 'Kingsley Downs is their inheritance, but only if they do as I say.'

'Is that what you tell Murray? How can you threaten your own son?' Cindy was shouting now. 'I will not have you intimidating my children.'

'You have NO say!' thundered Lawrence and he stood up, towering over Cindy. 'Who do you think you are? Seducing your way into my son's affections, rushing him into marriage and then you have the audacity to think you can fit in here with us? You never will. Those children will do what I know is best for them and you will have no say in it. Hear me? No say. No say at all!'

Cindy was so furious she couldn't speak for a moment, but then she found she knew exactly what she wanted to say. 'I am their mother. I will not have you interfering with their upbringing. You are a horrible old man,' she shouted, no longer able to contain her anger.

They both heard footsteps in the corridor before Murray rushed into the study.

'What the hell is going on? I could hear you all over the house,' he said. 'What's this all about?'

'I am telling your father that he is not, I repeat, NOT to interfere in the raising of our children.' Cindy turned to Murray, her voice shaking with fury.

'What are you talking about?'

'Why don't you ask your father what I mean, Murray?' said Cindy angrily. 'Your father shook Russell and berated him for "running away". He didn't run away, he wandered off and got lost. Your father has no right to discipline our son that way, especially as he's a little boy who is a bit of a dreamer, and only four years old.'

Murray stood as if frozen to the spot, and said nothing.

'Say something, Murray!' yelled Cindy. 'Your father *shook* our child!'

Finally Murray took Cindy's hand. 'Cin, calm down. I just want to hear what Dad has to say.' He looked at his father.

Lawrence stared hard at Murray. 'Son, those children have to learn to obey rules. She's too soft with them. They need to toughen up and listen to me.'

'Murray, these are our children, not your father's.' Cindy was close to tears.

Murray put his arm around Cindy and spoke to Lawrence.

'Dad, you must understand how Cindy feels. Please leave any child-rearing to us. They're good kids. This was a one-off incident.' He looked pointedly at his father, who glared back at him. 'Cindy is a great mother. I'm proud of her.'

'If those children want to inherit and run Kingsley Downs one day, they will do so on my terms,' Lawrence said, his voice icy.

Murray stared at his father, and Cindy saw something pass between them. To her surprise, it was Lawrence who first dropped his gaze.

'You will regret giving in to her,' Lawrence murmured.

'You're supposed to be the boss, son. Please yourself and do it your way. You've made your point, Cynthia.' He opened a folder, dismissing them.

Murray squeezed Cindy's hand and nudged her towards the door.

Cindy went ahead of Murray.

'I'll see you in our bedroom,' she said, watching as his face dissolved into relief. Murray walked down the hall in the direction of their bedroom.

Cindy went into the kitchen and poured herself a glass of wine. It had certainly been a momentous day. She sat quietly and raised her glass and whispered, 'Here's to you, Alice. Thanks for your blunt advice. I certainly took it and there's no looking back now.'

8

THE CHANGE OF SEASONS came softly, sneaking in during the night, so that when Cindy woke, the air had a different smell and the dawn colours were newly bright, a melting pot of splashed paint. Watching the streaming light, she wondered again at the miraculous melange of hues. In all the years she'd been at Kingsley Downs, the unveiling of the morning always awed her.

Cindy stepped outside with her cup of coffee, claiming a moment of calm before the children's calls and the routine of the day began. Looking at the vista, familiar now but never dull, she had an inkling of what people meant when they told her about feeling at one with a place. She wondered if it was this feeling that had made the original settlers choose this place to put down roots, to stay, battling through hard times and giving meaning to all their work, both their struggles and their joys.

She had seen the quiet pleasure and satisfied exhaustion of Murray and the other landowners when a drought broke, or floods receded, when the feed was lush and the wool clip fine and bountiful. Theirs was no nine-to-five, walk-away-at-sunset job, but a life chosen, and bequeathed, lived moment to moment, day after day, year after year, and the knowledge that this life of obligation would be inherited by her children gave Cindy a sense of belonging she had never known or ever anticipated.

But, while Kingsley Downs gave her a feeling of permanence, there was nonetheless a feeling of disruption that haunted her, just below the surface of her daily life, almost as though she were living on an earthquake fault line or beneath a dormant volcano: the ever-present Lawrence.

After the terrible row she'd had with him over Russell's disappearance, more than eight months ago now, he'd kept his distance by simply ignoring her. When conversation could not be avoided, his obvious coolness, which bordered on disdain, irked her. Cindy knew that there was now an even higher fence between them and, although Alice had given her the strength to stand up to her father-in-law, she felt that often the best way to deal with him was simply to turn away from his challenging stare. Long-term peace was doubtful.

Murray was supportive and loving and made it clear to his father that, although he would work with Lawrence on the property, Cindy was his wife and the mother of his children and it was to her that he owed his first loyalties. Cindy was touched by his outspokenness on the subject. Sometimes she glimpsed a swift, sad expression, close to pain, in Murray's eyes, which was never acknowledged and quickly extinguished if he realised she was looking. Occasionally she thought it might be better if they moved away and started from scratch somewhere else, but she never raised the idea with Murray as she knew it would be a difficult thing to do. She sipped the last drop of her coffee and then sighed. These peaceful moments were few and far between. She took a deep breath of morning air, raised her mug in salute to the rising sun, and turned back into the house.

*

Later that day, as Cindy walked from the Deniliquin post office after mailing her regular letter to Babs, a woman touched her arm.

'Hello, Cindy, how lovely to see you,' came a clipped but friendly voice.

'Ngaire,' Cindy exclaimed as she turned to greet Alistair Campbell's secretary, who was dressed as usual in a tailored skirt and jacket with a brooch on the lapel, her hair neatly coiffured. 'It's lovely to see you, too. I'm just running a few errands. Are you working today? How is Alistair? When you see him, please pass on my regards.'

Ngaire nodded, her perfect hair not moving an inch. 'I'm heading back to the office in a minute, and of course I'll tell Alistair you were asking after him. It has been a while since I've seen you. You must come over to Stonycroft again soon. The garden is looking a treat at the moment, I think you would enjoy it. Perhaps lunch next week? I don't work on Wednesdays.'

Cindy accepted the invitation quickly. 'I'd love to come. I love your garden, especially your roses. I've tried to keep the roses at Kingsley Downs going, although it isn't always easy when water is scarce.'

'I know,' Ngaire said sympathetically. 'The stock and land come first. How about midday, then?'

'Yes, of course.'

'Then I look forward to seeing you.'

*

On the following Wednesday, Cindy drove up the tree-lined driveway to Ngaire's Federation-style house, Stonycroft, which was surrounded by lawns and garden beds. To Cindy, the place always had a gracious old-world charm that seemed to suit Ngaire Seymour perfectly. She remembered the first time she had been introduced to her. Cindy had liked her at once. Ngaire had had a firm handshake and sharp blue eyes. Later, Murray had told her that Alistair Campbell trusted Ngaire with all the firm's most sensitive business.

'She has the dirt on everyone in the district,' Murray had said with a laugh. 'But she's very discreet.'

As Cindy parked the car and walked across the lawn, she passed several mature trees shading well-weathered furniture. Ngaire came out onto the verandah wearing a printed cotton dress and a large straw hat, smiling in delight at her visitor.

'Welcome, welcome. Come and have a cold drink and then we'll have a stroll in the garden before our lunch. I made some sandwiches. I hope that suits you.'

Cindy followed Ngaire indoors and was struck again by the difference between Stonycroft and the house at Kingsley Downs. This house was home to a woman who lived amongst the memorabilia of her well-lived life: the paraphernalia of parties and special events, photographs and personalised needlepoint cushions, doilies and crocheted throw rugs, and books and games stacked on shelves. Souvenirs and mementos such as shells collected with care on beach holidays were all on display, testimony to full and happy times. As Cindy walked through the house, sipping the iced water Ngaire had given her, she felt the echo of laughter and conversation lingering, as if her family had just left the room. Ngaire pointed out some of the photos, chatting about her parents and her memories of growing up here with her brother, who had died in a Japanese prisoner-of-war camp.

'I'm still very close to my nephew and nieces, but they all have their own careers and are full of their own ideas. I don't think that living on the land is for them, but who knows? Maybe they'll change their minds. Now, how about we head out here through the conservatory and look at the kitchen garden?'

They strolled through the kitchen garden, with its beds of herbs as well as vegetables. Each time Cindy exclaimed about a particular plant, Ngaire produced a pair of secateurs from her pocket and snipped off a cutting.

'We'll put these in some water for you to take home and strike,' she said.

Cindy was always entranced by the creativity that Ngaire had put into the delightful gardens. What Ngaire termed the formal gardens were a riot of English cottage garden pastels, where blossoms complemented the hardy local plants so well that it all looked spontaneous and yet had been carefully orchestrated.

'Ready for lunch?' said Ngaire with a smile as they left her stunning rosebushes, which were just about to burst into bloom. 'Those roses are my pride and joy. Some of them are quite old and they need some looking after, but they do well if they're given tender loving care.'

'You always lavish a lot of attention on them,' said Cindy. 'Mine are somewhat neglected.'

'But you have children to raise,' said Ngaire gently. 'So much better to look after them. The roses can wait until you have more time.'

The Minton tea set was laid out on a drawn thread linen tablecloth which Ngaire confessed had been a domestic science project from her school days.

Cindy sighed contentedly as the two women sat down.

Ngaire carefully poured the tea. 'Now tell me, how is your Aunt Alice?'

'Aunt Alice is fine. She loves talking about her visit here.

My Aunt Babs says she makes it sound as though she was one of the last of the great explorers, venturing to remote "Down Under"!'

Ngaire chuckled. 'I'm sure she found Kingsley Downs very different from what she expected. She seems like a very forthright woman!' she said, sipping her tea, a twinkle in her eye.

'That she is!' Cindy said with a laugh. 'Nobody gets anything past Alice.'

'I admire strong women,' said Ngaire. 'Tell me, are you a women's libber?'

Cindy smiled at the older woman, who obviously kept abreast of the times. 'My friend Jo likes to keep me up to date on the Women's Liberation movement. She lent me *The Female Eunuch*, which I've just finished. That gave me a lot to think about.'

Ngaire nodded. 'Indeed. I found it very stimulating too. Sometimes it takes a person like Germaine Greer to see things differently. When you live in a place, especially one that's steeped in tradition and resistant to change, you stop seeing, and some things really need to be reimagined. I think it is quite wrong that women are seen only as append-ages of their husbands, but then, I've never had a husband.'

'How do you stay switched on?' asked Cindy in amazement.

Ngaire passed the sandwich plate to Cindy. 'I'm a great reader and I tune in to the outside world through ABC radio. I'm not so fond of the television; I think it's more for entertainment than to inform. I like to hear other people's views. Even in Deniliquin, I've met a few people over the years who have quite remarkable ideas.'

Cindy swallowed the last of her crustless cucumber sandwich. 'I guess even in a small community like ours there are a few people thinking outside the box. Tell me, have you lived around here your whole life?'

'I don't think I've ever told you, but I did leave for a short time, and quickly learned that the city was not for me. After I came home and Alistair Campbell offered me the position in his office, I never felt any desire to leave again.'

Cindy glanced out at the garden. 'Well, I can see why you wanted to come back. There's no place like home, as they say. And you must have missed all your friends and relations. You surely know everyone in the district.'

'Not everyone, although of course I've known the Parnells for years,' said Ngaire, as she topped up Cindy's teacup. 'The family has been a client of our office for decades and I can even remember old Mr Parnell, Lawrence's father, and Rose of course.'

Cindy looked at Ngaire. No one ever seemed to volunteer any knowledge of Rose Parnell, except occasionally Mrs Flowers, who was tight-lipped on the subject at the best of times. Cindy knew she couldn't let this opportunity pass her by, no matter how nosy she sounded.

'It was hard on Murray not having his mother around while he was growing up,' said Cindy carefully. 'Over the years I have sometimes felt quite curious about what happened, but Mr Parnell never speaks about it, and neither does Murray.' Clasping her hands together, Cindy leaned forward. 'Ngaire, I hope I'm not asking you to break any confidences, but can you tell me what exactly happened to Mrs Parnell? I don't mean to pry, but she is my children's grandmother,' said Cindy.

Ngaire seemed to hesitate for a moment, but then she said, 'Yes, I can understand how you feel, and it's certainly not breaking any confidences to say that no one really knows exactly what happened to Rose, although at the time her sudden disappearance was the subject of intense speculation.'

'I'm not surprised – there must have been gossip around the town. What was Rose like?'

Ngaire sat back in her chair. 'Rose Parnell was a lovely woman, very quiet. I always found her to be thoughtful and considerate, although some people said she was secretive and difficult to know. It certainly rocked the community when Rose left. There was a lot of sympathy for Lawrence at the time and I suppose it's understandable that he won't talk about it. I think there was much loss of face for him. You have to remember that the Parnells are a long-established and respected family, so her leaving entailed not just shock and despair, but a level of embarrassment as well. Not good for a man with as much pride as Lawrence Parnell to be so publicly rejected.'

Ngaire paused for a moment to offer Cindy a piece of Madeira cake before she continued.

'The Floweres were away at a wedding and Murray was at boarding school. Lawrence had been away doing something with the war effort and on his way back, even though it was late, Lawrence decided to go to the pub in Yamboola. When he got home late that night, Rose and her car were gone. He rang the police straight away because he thought she'd been in a car accident. The police couldn't do much till morning and that's when they found her car on the Deniliquin road a couple of miles from the entrance to the property parked behind a clump of bushes. Lawrence wouldn't have seen it as he drove home on the Yamboola road on the opposite side of Kingsley Downs. Overnight Lawrence realised some of Rose's things were missing too. Since there was no sign of a struggle in the car and its keys had been left in it, the police concluded that Rose had rendezvoused with someone on the highway and had gone off with them. No one thought it was a local, or everyone would have known straight away. Many people thought that she must have gone off with an American serviceman.'

Cindy let out a breath she hadn't known she was holding. 'How would she have met him?'

'Rose was very involved with the Red Cross,' Ngaire said. 'They put on charity events and concerts for the war effort, that sort of thing, as well as the usual knitting and preparing food for passing troops. She used to go to Melbourne occasionally as part of her Red Cross work, too. I don't know what else she did there, but a rumour circulated that when she was in the city she spent some time with a soldier.'

Cindy shook her head in amazement. 'But it sounds such a risky thing to do,' she said, thinking of how Lawrence might have reacted if he'd found out.

'I must stress that I don't know if it was true. And you have to remember that those times were a bit chaotic. Lawrence was away quite a lot as part of the war effort and there were more than a million Yanks in the country at the time. A lot of men around here didn't like the Americans at all. They thought they had too much money and used it to take Australian women away from the locals. "Overpaid, oversexed and over here" was what they used to say about them. There was a lot of bitterness, and everyone had heard about the woman from Wagga Wagga who'd recently left her husband to go off with an American serviceman.' Ngaire took a bite of cake and chewed thoughtfully for a moment. 'I suppose that it was quite possible for Rose to have become involved with someone she'd met through the Red Cross, and in my opinion, she could just as easily have been involved with an Australian soldier. Either way, why she would want to do that I have no idea. Maybe she was sick of living in the country and wanted to get away? I sometimes got the impression that she didn't like it here, but I could have been wrong. As I said, she was not the sort of woman to say much. But, wherever she went, she covered her tracks very well. Evidently she didn't even contact her sister in Sydney. The police looked for her, but it was wartime and their resources were limited, and they couldn't find any clues as to where she went. The case was never closed and, as far as I am aware, she remains a missing person. Poor Lawrence. I remember how upset, angry and embarrassed he was. He demanded that their joint bank account be closed and he asked Alistair to stop the local news people writing about it.'

Cindy leaned back in her chair, taking it all in. 'So Rose really did disappear for good.' She tapped a finger against her chin. 'I'd forgotten that Murray had an aunt in Sydney. He mentioned her when we first met, but we haven't spoken about her since then,' she said, suddenly reminded of a conversation she'd had with Murray back in Palm Springs.

Ngaire nodded as she leaned forward and took the lid off the teapot, peering in.

'I think this tea has stewed. Would you like another cup?' she asked.

Cindy glanced at her watch. 'Thank you, Ngaire, but I had best get back to Murray and the kids. The twins will be home from school soon and I don't like to leave them too long by themselves. I never know what mischief they are likely to get up to,' Cindy said with a smile. The two women rose from the table and walked down the hall to the front door. 'I've had a lovely lunch and thank you for my plant cuttings and for telling me about Rose. How odd if she really did run off with an American. It would seem that the Parnells rather like them.' And that, Cindy thought privately, might explain why Lawrence did not.

Ngaire laughed as she walked her visitor to the car. 'So it would seem. I hope you will visit me again soon. It's nice to talk with someone who has progressive ideas.'

*

As soon as Cindy pulled up in the driveway of the big house, Russell came running to see her. She hugged him close and listened to his chatter as they went indoors about what he'd been up to while she was away. Cindy checked in on Mrs Flowers who was preparing the vegetables for dinner.

Glancing at the kitchen clock, she realised the twins would be waiting at the bus stop. Grabbing the car keys, she clattered down the steps and into the car to drive to where the school bus would let the twins off by the side of the Yamboola road.

Sally and Gordon were full of noisy questions and demands, and each had homework and chores to do, so that Cindy was kept occupied until she'd put the three children to bed. After dinner, Joanna rang and the two friends spoke for some time, sharing news and chatter. After she hung up, Cindy went and found Murray and Lawrence in the sitting room. Lawrence was buried behind *The Land* newspaper, while Murray was watching a show on television. Cindy took a seat on the armrest of her husband's armchair and waited for an ad break.

'What are your plans for the end of the month?' Cindy asked Murray a few moments later.

Murray stretched and yawned. 'We want to fertilise the north paddock, which means we'll have to move the sheep out of it. We need feed for next season. And while the sheep are out of the north paddock, I can see to the fences there. I think they might need some repairs. Dad is thinking of buying more stock while the wool price stays so good, so we'll have to go to the sales. Why?'

'Joanna is taking Sheree to Sydney to see her grandmother for her sixtieth birthday and will be going to the zoo and doing a few fun things like that. She's asked us all to go too, especially as Sheree and Russell get on so well.'

'Doubt I can make it, with all we've got planned. Why don't you and the children go? You'll have a much better time without me around anyway. I think I'd get in the way,' said Murray with a crooked smile.

Cindy patted his shoulder. 'That's not true, but it sounds like you've got a lot on your plate.' Cindy felt pleased. It was a shame Murray couldn't come, but it was a trip she was already looking forward to. 'Fancy a cup of tea?' she asked light-heartedly. 'Can I get you one, too?' she asked Lawrence.

Lawrence looked up from his newspaper and then carefully folded it.

'Thank you, no,' he said, rising to his feet. 'I'm getting an early night. Some of us need to get up at the crack of dawn because we have to work for a living, not take frivolous holidays.' With that, he stalked out of the room and made his way towards his bedroom.

'If that offer still stands, I'll have a cup of tea,' said Murray, looking at Cindy with a smile and a small shrug of his shoulders. 'I'll help you make it.'

They walked into the kitchen and put the kettle on.

'Honestly, Murray, I do my best with your father, but there is no pleasing him,' said Cindy in an exasperated voice. 'And it's not as though I spend my life being frivolous, I work hard around here, too.'

Murray held up a pacifying hand. 'I'll speak to him in the morning and tell him that you're entitled to take the kids to Sydney and that you are going to do just that. Easy for me to tell you to take no notice of what Dad says, but I know he can be difficult.' The kettle whistled and Cindy poured hot water into a waiting teapot. Murray took her hand reassuringly in his. 'Cindy, always remember that I'm on your side. Besides, it's not as though Dad does everything he should around here. He talks about working hard, but sometimes it's impossible to get him to do some of the things that really need to be taken care of.'

'Like what?' said Cindy, surprised. It was very unlike Murray to be critical of his father's work ethic.

'Well, I want to get rid of the blackberries that have

257

grown up around parts of the property. But Dad still hasn't got around to it.'

'I can't get close to that old peppercorn tree near the creek any more because the blackberries are so thick,' said Cindy, pouring the tea into two teacups and handing one to her husband, thinking sadly about the little memorial to her lost child that she had buried all those years ago. After sipping a mouthful of her tea, she asked, 'So you're fine if I take the kids off to Sydney?'

'Of course,' said Murray, blowing on his tea.

Cindy paused. 'Murray, I was thinking.' She took another sip of tea. 'When I was talking to Ngaire today, she mentioned your aunt in Sydney. You told me about her when we first met, but I'd forgotten all about her. Maybe I could look her up while I'm there,' said Cindy tentatively.

'Why would you want to do that?' asked Murray, looking at her sharply. 'I haven't thought about Aunt Marie in a long time.'

'I was thinking of the children. If they have a great-aunt living in Sydney, it would be nice for them to connect with her. They have so little family.' She put down her tea cup and reached over and touched his hand. 'They loved meeting their Aunt Alice, so I think it would be good for them if they could meet some of their relations here in Australia.'

'I suppose that's true,' said Murray slowly, as he processed the idea. 'How will you find her?'

'For a start, do you remember her surname?' asked Cindy.

'It's Williams but I have no idea where she lives. Somewhere in Sydney is all I know. I could ask Dad if he remembers it?'

Cindy pursed her lips. 'Don't bother. Maybe Ngaire might know. She seems to know everything else,' she suggested.

'What if Aunt Marie's moved? What if she doesn't want to see you?'

'For heaven's sake, Murray, I don't know, but it would be nice to at least *try* to find her,' said Cindy, rolling her eyes.

Murray nodded. 'You're right. See what you can do. It would be good for the kids to know that they have relatives closer than Palm Springs,' said Murray, smiling at his wife.

'Are we going to say anything to your father about trying to locate your aunt?' said Cindy.

'I don't think we need to stir up that hornet's nest, especially if nothing comes of it,' Murray said quickly, fidgeting.

'Yes, I agree. Best not to give him any more ammunition,' said Cindy. Murray was on her side, but he still became so uncomfortable at the thought of upsetting his father. 'And besides, like you say, she may have moved or might not want to be visited. I'll just see how I go.'

She patted his hand reassuringly and then took their empty tea cups over to the sink. Murray kissed her lightly and left the room to get ready for bed. As she rinsed the tea cups and patted them dry, Cindy smiled to herself. She had demurred for Murray's sake, but privately she vowed she would find Aunt Marie. How hard could it be?

*

Cindy was as thrilled as the three children when they arrived in Sydney. It had been a long and exhausting drive for the four of them. They checked into a new motel in the pleasant suburb of Chatswood, which was close to Jo's mother, Suzanne.

Suzanne Bright was as cheerful as her name. She welcomed them all for meals and offered to mind the children and to take them to the movies if Jo and Cindy wanted an outing to themselves.

The two friends tried to cram as much as they could into the two-week holiday. They visited Taronga Park Zoo, with its exotic animals and spectacular views of the harbour, which they crossed a few days later on the ferry to Manly. At Gordon's insistence, they visited Luna Park. Sheree and Russell were too young for a lot of the rides, but between the merry-go-round and dropping ping-pong balls into the gaping mouths of painted clown faces, they were well entertained. Sally was delighted when she won a small soft toy. They all shared great puffballs of fairy floss on sticks, as well as hot dogs. The twins insisted on going on the roller-coaster and so Cindy went along, too, all three of them screaming with fear and excitement, and everyone agreed they'd had the very best time.

They took the train over the Harbour Bridge to visit the newly opened Sydney Opera House. Both Cindy and Jo were impressed by the building's beautiful sails, which seemed to billow out over the water, their white tiles dazzling in the sunlight, while the four children raced up and down the long flight of stairs leading to the entrance. From the Opera House they walked around to the Botanic Gardens and had a picnic lunch before lying on the grass in the glorious sunshine.

Best of all, as far as Cindy was concerned, was the day they took the children to Freshwater Beach after a trip on the Manly ferry. Once they had overcome the challenge of the surf, the children could not get enough of jumping over the waves and trying to catch the foamy breakers.

'It's a bit different from a pool or swimming in a river, isn't it, guys?' said Cindy, laughing in delight. 'I haven't done anything like this since I left Santa Barbara. I'd nearly forgotten how much fun the beach can be.'

'I love the beach, too. You can't be a Sydney girl and not love the surf,' agreed Joanna. 'I miss it, living in the country.'

Mrs Bright's birthday bash, as Jo called her mother's sixtieth birthday, was as Suzanne had wanted: an afternoon barbecue in the backyard of her home. 'I'm so grateful that I'm still here to be able to enjoy this with good friends and family. I don't want anything more,' she said happily, and Cindy recalled the health scare Suzanne had had several years ago, which had temporarily brought Jo back to Sydney.

As the two friends sat side by side, watching their children run around the garden with the children of Jo's friends and relatives, Cindy said quietly to her friend, 'I'm so glad I came. My children have loved being here. They adore your mother. I wish they had a grandmother they could visit, too.'

'Have you thought more about finding Murray's aunt?' asked Jo.

Cindy drew a breath. 'I have her name and an old address which Ngaire managed to find. It's a street in Randwick. I looked up the number in the phone book and rang a couple of times to arrange a meeting, but there was no answer. It's a shame I haven't been able to see her and we've only got a day of our holiday left.'

'Well, we haven't got any plans tomorrow. We could always just drop in?' suggested Jo.

Cindy made a face. 'That's a bit rude, isn't it?' she said.

Jo shrugged.

'I'll try calling her one more time,' Cindy said, getting up and going to the phone in the main hallway. But once again the number rang out. Cindy returned to Jo shaking her head.

'Well, we haven't got any plans, why don't we just go to Randwick tomorrow?' said Jo enthusiastically.

Cindy nodded. 'I think that's our only shot at meeting her. What will we do with the children?'

'Do you want to bring all your kids or leave them with Mum? I'll leave Sheree with her and drive you over. I can hardly expect you to find Randwick on your own. It's right across town.'

'I might leave Russell with her, too, if you don't think she'll mind, but I think the twins should come in case we do manage to find her. She is their great-aunt, even if she has no idea Sally and Gordon exist. It's all quite exciting, isn't it?' Cindy said, with a laugh. 'Fingers crossed Marie is home tomorrow.'

*

The house in Randwick was a substantial red-brick home set behind a neat hedge. The house itself was well kept, although the windows were closed and the curtains drawn.

'There's no one there, can't we go?' sighed Gordon as the four of them stood on the street outside the gate.

'Dare you to knock on the door,' said Sally.

'All right, I will.' Gordon started up the path.

'Wait a minute,' said Cindy. She looked around. The street was quiet, and lined with mature trees and similar red-brick houses. Beside the gate and attached to the fence was an old letterbox. Cindy paused and opened it.

'Mummy, what are you doing?' asked Sally, horrified that her mother would look inside someone else's letterbox.

'It's all right, darling. I'm just checking something,' said Cindy reassuringly. She pulled out two letters. One looked to be some sort of circular, but the other had an address clearly printed on it.

'What's it say?' hissed Jo.

'Mrs M. Williams,' said Cindy triumphantly. 'It is the right place. You lot wait here a moment.'

Returning the mail to the letterbox, she hurried through the gate and along the path and up several steps to the front door, followed by Gordon. Jo and Sally stayed on the street by the car.

Cindy lifted the tarnished brass door knocker and banged it twice.

They waited, Gordon shifting his weight from foot to foot.

'See. No one's here, Mum,' he said.

'It's a big house, she could be hard of hearing,' said Cindy. 'Okay, I'll try once more, just in case.'

The knocker banged again. Gordon was just about to turn away in disappointment when they heard the rattle of the latch. He turned swiftly back in surprise as the door opened.

An attractive, well-dressed woman with bright eyes and an inquiring smile looked out at them.

'Oh, I thought you might be the new cleaning girl, but obviously you're not. Are you lost? How can I help?' She looked at Gordon. 'Oh, are you a Boy Scout looking for a job? Aren't you supposed to wear your uniform?'

'No, no, we're not any of those things,' said Cindy hastily, reaching to draw Gordon close beside her. 'I'm sorry to disturb you, but I'm looking for Mrs Marie Williams.'

To her astonishment, the woman beamed, spread her arms wide, and gave a small curtsy. 'That's me! I'm Marie Williams. And who are you, young man?' she asked Gordon.

Gordon was slightly taken aback but, remembering his manners, held out his hand. 'How do you do. I'm Gordon Parnell.'

The smile momentarily slipped from Marie Williams's face and her hand flew to her mouth. 'Parnell? From Yamboola?' She stared at Cindy, as fleeting expressions of shock, eagerness and hope skimmed across her face. 'Rose's Parnells?'

Cindy nodded. 'I'm sorry to just turn up like this, unannounced, but I did try to ring you and I really wanted to meet you before we go back home. My name is Cindy Parnell, I'm Murray Parnell's wife. This is his son, Gordon. Your great-nephew.'

Marie stared at her. 'Murray married and with children? Yes, I suppose he would be. And you . . . please, please come inside, off the doorstep. This is a shock, well, a lovely surprise. This way.'

'I have a friend and my daughter waiting outside, may they come in too?' asked Cindy.

'Good heavens, there's more!' said Marie, glancing over Gordon's shoulder towards the gate. 'How wonderful. Yes, yes. Young man, go and bring them inside. We'll put the kettle on.'

As Gordon hurried back down the steps, Marie and Cindy stared at each other for a moment.

'Come in, come in,' said Marie, inviting Cindy into the lobby.

'I thought it important for the children to meet their great-aunt,' said Cindy, stepping inside. 'I hope you don't mind this intrusion.'

Marie waved her hand. 'Tell me, how did you find me? It's been a long time since I've had any contact with the Parnells.'

'It was quite easy. I was given your address from years ago, but to tell you the truth, I didn't expect to find you still living here.'

'And how is Murray?' Marie asked excitedly.

'I've brought a photo of him,' said Cindy. She rummaged in her purse and handed Marie a photograph.

'Good heavens,' said Marie, looking at the picture in amazement. 'Murray looks so much like my son James, you would take them for brothers.'

Sally's voice called from behind her. 'Mum?'

Cindy turned as Jo appeared in the doorway, the children tumbling after her.

'Marie, this is my friend Joanna, and these are my twins, Sally and Gordon. Russell, their brother, is being minded by Jo's mother. Children, this is Mrs Williams, your great-aunt.'

Marie smiled, her eyes twinkling. 'Oh my, you are a good-looking pair. I am so pleased to meet you. I'm your Auntie Marie.' She leaned down and embraced them. Gordon submitted quietly to being hugged. Sally, however, returned the bear hug enthusiastically.

Marie laughed. 'Come through to the kitchen, everyone.' She led the way down a long hall to a large, messy but welcoming room out the back. Marie gestured to a small meals table in one corner of the bright room.

'You have a beautiful home,' Jo commented.

'Thank you, dear,' said Marie. 'My husband and I bought this house when we were first married, and I've never wanted to live anywhere else, and even though my husband died a few years back, and this place is really too large for one person to rattle around in, I still don't want to move. You see, my daughter and her brood live fairly close by, and my son, who is in Singapore at present, is moving back in a few months, thank goodness. He's getting married. We're so thrilled. And he wants to buy a house in the neighbourhood, too.' She went to the kitchen bench and poured steaming hot water from a kettle into a teapot. She turned to the children, beaming. 'Now, we grown-ups are having tea, so who wants cordial and who wants milk?'

'Are there biscuits?' asked Gordon.

'Gordon, don't be so rude,' said Cindy crossly. 'You should wait to be asked.'

'He's probably hungry, so it's a very good question,' said Marie kindly. 'Of course there are. Sally, they're in that tin on the sideboard. I'll give you a plate and you put out the biscuits. You can have two each.'

The children took the plate and scurried over to the tin, and Marie continued, 'We'll leave the tea to brew. Do come and sit down in the sunroom. I want to hear all about you.'

'I'll stay here with the children while they have their drink, and make the tea, if you like,' offered Joanna.

'Thank you, dear, that's most kind of you. You'll find cups in that cupboard. Come along, Cindy. You don't sound Australian, if you don't mind my saying,' Marie said, as she led the way to a cheerful sunroom.

'I'm American. I met Murray in California,' answered Cindy. 'Look, I hope I'm not holding you up. This is so kind of you . . . to be so welcoming out of the blue to virtual strangers,' she said, as Marie motioned her to a chair by the window.

'Nonsense. It's not every day you have family you don't know you had drop by.' Marie laughed. 'I'm so thrilled you found me. Murray wasn't all that much older than your twins when I last saw him. I can't believe that those children in the kitchen are his. I'd resigned myself to losing touch with my nephew. I used to send him letters and parcels for Christmas and his birthday for years, but they were always returned unopened. I thought it was such a pity.' She paused and Cindy saw a touch of sadness in her eyes, but then Marie seemed to shake herself. 'But here you are. It's just the best surprise.' She beamed happily at Cindy.

Cindy studied the elegant woman with the bubbly personality. Marie, she guessed, was in her sixties. Obviously, she had once been beautiful, for she was still a very attractive woman. Her eyes were a piercing blue, very similar to the colour of Murray's. Her fingers were graceful and surprisingly long. She sat in the chair beside Cindy, straight-backed, the carriage of her head erect on her slender neck. Cindy knew straight away that her dress was pure silk and a good label, and her low-heeled shoes were soft Italian leather. She wore vintage earrings set with what Cindy guessed were old diamonds. Marie's hair was smoothed back from her face in a sleek chignon. Cindy wished she could tame her unruly curls in such a fashionable way.

'And tell me, are you all living at Kingsley Downs?' Marie asked.

'Yes. Lawrence and Murray run the place together. Do you know it well?'

Marie shook her head. 'My husband and I went there once, not long after Rose and Lawrence were married. I found the place rather . . . remote. I'm not a country girl, I'm afraid, and I could never understand Rose giving up the life she had here to go and live in Yamboola. But of course, Lawrence was incredibly dashing – handsome, somewhat aloof, but also very charming at times, and the family were well off financially. And I was happy if my sister was happy.'

'It must have been very sad for you when Rose vanished,' said Cindy softly. She was not sure how Marie would react to such a statement, but she could hardly avoid acknowledging Rose's disappearance.

Marie cleared her throat. 'Yes, it was. We were quite close, so I felt her loss keenly for a long time. But to tell you the truth, as I look back, I remember that in our last few conversations, Rose seemed sad. I thought that was because Murray had gone away to school and she missed him, but my husband, Jim, who was very perceptive, had the feeling she wanted to unburden herself to us in some way. In those days, though, it was difficult to talk without the whole neighbourhood listening in on that old party line they had, so an opportunity didn't arise for us to speak together, in private. Then it was too late.' She drew a breath. 'I will never forget the morning the police arrived with the news she'd disappeared. I could offer them no help. I expected to hear from her, but wherever she went, she wasn't prepared to tell even me.'

'That must have been hard for you,' said Cindy sympathetically.

'It was. Still is in some ways. Time doesn't necessarily heal all wounds, though it does make them fade. But I can never get over the fact that I know Rose wanted to tell me something important, and she never got the chance. Maybe if she had, things would have turned out differently, especially for Murray.'

Cindy saw the sadness return to Marie's eyes.

'I know this probably sounds strange to you, but I've always felt rather like Rose and I are kindred spirits,' ventured Cindy. 'Because we were both city girls who ended up marrying country men and giving up the known for the unfamiliar. I met Murray while he was on holidays; how did Rose meet Lawrence?'

'They met in Sydney. I can't remember where. She worked such crazy hours. Classes during the day, shows at night . . .'

Cindy held up her hand. 'Whoa, what do you mean? What did your sister do?'

Marie looked at Cindy for a moment and then burst out laughing. 'You don't know the Pearson sisters? Of course you don't! Darling, we were *famous*!'

'You were one of the Pearson sisters!' exclaimed Jo as she came in with two cups of tea. 'Can you hang on for a minute before you start the story? I want to hear it all and I need to get my cuppa.'

'You'd better bring those twins in as well. Can't have my nephew and niece neglected now that we've found each other. I doubt if they'll ever hear the story from their grandfather, so they can hear it from me,' said Marie cheerfully.

Once everyone was together, Marie announced, 'Come with me, you lot. I've got some things I'd like you all to see.'

Marie ushered them into a large study. The room was taken up with a desk, two chairs, a lamp, and along one of the walls was a large bookcase. In one corner of the study stood a beautiful grand piano, its lid open and sheets of music scattered across the top. The room seemed to be smothered in photographs. Many of them seemed to be photos of playing children and holiday snaps, but there was also a picture of a ballerina, theatrically made up and wearing a classical ballet costume on a stage, holding a huge bouquet of flowers as she curtsied to the audience. There were other black and white photos of the same dancer, portraits taken in front of huge mirrors and at the barre of a ballet studio, as well as with various dancers. There were also photographs of a slim girl on a stage seated at a grand piano being applauded by a surrounding orchestra, and another of the same girl shaking hands with an obviously important dignitary.

Marie picked up the picture of the ballet dancer with the bouquet and showed it to the children.

'This was my sister, your grandmother, taken when she was just seventeen. She was such a wonderful dancer,' said Marie proudly.

'Oh my goodness!' said Cindy, looking at one of the pictures on the wall, quite stunned by what she saw. 'What a talented dancer!'

'Our parents thought so.' Marie smiled. 'Rose started dancing professionally with the Borovansky Ballet when she was quite young. She was performing with them when she met and married Lawrence.'

'And you were a concert pianist?' said Cindy.

'Indeed. But once I married and had my children I stopped performing. Too little time to practise, but I was very happy and busy with my own life.'

'I can hardly wait to tell Mum that I've met one of the famous Pearson sisters,' said Joanna. 'She's told me stories about how talented and glamorous you both were. She was a big fan.'

'Oh, it was a long time ago,' said Marie with a smile. 'Quite a different life, back then. Cindy, Murray never mentioned his mother was one of the Pearson sisters?'

'He doesn't talk about his mother much,' hedged Cindy. Cindy leaned over to the twins, holding a photo. 'What do you think about this picture?'

'She's really beautiful,' said Sally. 'I didn't even know we had a grandmother.'

'Me neither. Is she still a ballet dancer? Where is she now?' asked Gordon.

There was an awkward pause.

'We're not sure. Now, Sally and Gordon, do you like music and dancing?' asked Marie briskly.

Sally was thoughtful. 'Yes, I do. I'd love to learn the piano.'

'Sally!' said Cindy in a surprised voice. 'I had no idea you wanted to learn to play.'

'Do you still play?' Sally asked Marie.

'Yes. Not as well as I used to, but I still love it.'

'Can you play something, please, Auntie Marie?' asked Gordon.

'Oh, I'm sure Aunt Marie is busy right now—' began Cindy.

But Marie jumped up and clapped her hands. 'Of course I can. What's your favourite song, Gordon?'

'"Old Macdonald Had a Farm",' said Gordon immediately.

'That's a baby song,' said Sally scornfully.

Marie went to the piano. 'It's one of my favourites, too, especially if we make the animal noises very loudly.'

Marie sat down, ran her hands over the piano keys

270

and began to play the old tune with vigour, then she burst into song. Sally and Gordon sang with her, laughing as they tried out all the different animal noises.

After Marie had finished with 'Old Macdonald', she swung into a series of other popular songs. Sally sat beside her and watched Marie's hands as her fingers raced across the keyboard, and all of them sang along. As she finished with a long trilling crescendo, there was a burst of applause from the doorway. Cindy and Jo turned to see a smiling woman, maybe a year or two older than they were, come into the room, followed by a boy who looked to be Gordon and Sally's age and a girl of about ten.

'How come we weren't invited to this party?' She laughed as she went and kissed Marie. 'Hi, Mum.'

Marie clasped her hands together. 'Mon, you'll never guess! Now, this pretty girl is Sally and this is her twin, Gordon. This is their mother, Cindy, and her friend Joanna. Cindy, this is my daughter Monica and my grandchildren, Toby and Holly.'

'Lovely to meet you,' said Monica with a grin, seemingly unfazed by the impromptu gathering. 'Is there food? The kids are starving.'

'And that's not all, Mon,' said Marie, ignoring the question. 'Cindy's and the twins' last name is Parnell. They're your cousins!' she cried. 'Now, while you all get acquainted, let's go and make some cheese on toast.' Marie headed to the kitchen, followed by all the children.

Monica shrugged her shoulders and spread her arms wide, an amused smile on her face. 'Cousins? Where from? Did Mum drag you in here from the park?'

Jo and Cindy laughed. 'The twins are your Aunt Rose's grandchildren, and I'm married to your cousin Murray Parnell,' explained Cindy. 'We live at Kingsley Downs, in the Riverina.'

'This is just marvellous,' said Monica. 'I don't remember Mum having any contact with the Parnell side of the family for years. How did you track us down?'

Cindy explained what had happened.

Monica's smile faded momentarily. 'I'm afraid I don't remember Aunt Rose, or really Murray, for that matter. Oh, poor Aunt Rose. Mum keeps all the old photos of her,' she said, looking around the room.

'Yes, I've learned more in the last hour about Murray's mother than I've ever known. I'm not sure how much my husband knows about her, either. Your mother is an incredible woman, so generous, so warm.'

'Yes. She has a big heart, but I expect that she is also very excited to have you contact her. Heavens, come and tell me all about yourself and my long-lost cousin Murray. What a pity it's taken so long to meet you.'

Another hour flew by as the children finished their toasties, and Holly showed Sally what she could play on her grandmother's piano.

'We really must go,' said Cindy finally. 'I should be getting back to Jo's mother. I can't leave her looking after Russell for too much longer.'

'My goodness, bring him along next visit,' said Marie. 'When are you next coming to Sydney?'

'I'm not sure. But I'll call you when I get home. And I'm sure Murray would love to speak to you, too.'

'I'd love to see him again. Now we've found you, we must keep in touch. And any time you're in Sydney, feel free to stay here.'

Reluctantly Cindy, Jo and the twins made their way towards the front door.

'Come on, kids, say goodbye to Auntie Marie and thank her for a lovely afternoon,' said Cindy.

'Goodbye, and thank you for having us,' said Gordon, scampering like a freed rabbit through the door.

But Sally rushed forward and flung her arms around Marie's waist. 'Can you come to see us at Kingsley Downs?'

'What a sweet girl you are. I think a nice visit to Sydney to see me would be a lot more fun for you.' She smiled at Cindy. 'Perhaps a visit to the symphony or the ballet?'

Sally turned to Cindy, her eyes shining. 'Could we? Could we, please, Mum?'

Cindy's heart was touched by the excited expression on her daughter's face. 'We'll talk about it. Say goodbye, and go with the others.'

Marie leaned down and Sally kissed her cheek. 'Till we see you next time. And we'll arrange something special for us to do. Hang on a minute, I've got something I'd like to give you.' She dashed back to the study and returned a few seconds later with a large manila envelope, which she gave to Cindy.

'I've had these tucked away. This has been the loveliest surprise, hasn't it, Mon?' She hugged Cindy and Monica gave her a kiss.

'Welcome to our family, and please stay in touch!'

*

When they got back to Jo's mother's house, Cindy and Joanna went over the surprising details of their visit with Marie Williams.

'To be caught by surprise like that, yet she was so generous and immediately accepting,' said Joanna.

'I was a bit taken aback that Murray has never mentioned Rose was a dancer or that Marie was such an accomplished pianist,' said Cindy. 'Maybe Lawrence didn't tell him much about Rose at all. What a lot of news we have for him. Here, let's see what Marie's given us.'

Cindy opened the envelope and pulled out several photographs, as well as some newspaper and magazine cuttings. There was a copy of Marie's framed photograph of Rose on stage with the bouquet of flowers. There were several photos of them as young girls, Marie seated at the piano, and a school prizegiving with Rose holding an award. There were a few clippings from suburban newspapers, yellowed with age, about the two talented sisters, as well as a magazine article. There were assorted mentions over the years, more about Marie than Rose. There was no mention of Rose retiring, but in a clipping from the social pages of the *Sydney Morning Herald*, there was a wedding photo of Rose and Lawrence at the entrance of St Mark's Church at Darling Point.

Cindy studied the photograph.

'How beautiful she looked,' said Jo.

The photo showed Rose, slender and dark-haired, a small pearl tiara crowning her long veil. She wore a satin dress which clung to her slim, almost bony body. The dress had long sleeves and one of Rose's graceful arms was linked through Lawrence's, while the other held a bouquet of trailing roses. Rose was smiling softly, her huge eyes dominating her face. Lawrence looked very handsome in a dinner suit, his face beaming with a triumphant air.

'Lawrence looks like a movie star. You can see where Murray gets his good looks,' commented Joanna.

Cindy nodded in agreement. There was no doubt that Rose and Lawrence made a very handsome pair.

The caption gave their names: Lawrence Parnell, of Kingsley Downs via Yamboola, and the bride, formerly Miss Rose Pearson, the daughter of Mr and Mrs Henry Pearson, of Turramurra. And, it added, Mrs Parnell was the former ballerina Rose Pearson, lately of the Borovansky Ballet.

'I can see why Rose chose to marry Lawrence, but she must have found Kingsley Downs so remote and lonely after the exciting life she'd been used to, don't you think?' wondered Joanna.

'Yes, I can understand it if she did, but I don't think it lonely. Really it's not,' said Cindy. 'The landscape, the wildlife, the people always coming through. Even the solitude is comforting somehow. But of course that's just my opinion. I can't speak for Rose. Maybe she never found a good friend like I did.' She smiled at Jo.

'Or maybe you have a much nicer husband,' said Jo bleakly.

'Definitely,' said Cindy. 'Although I'm not sure how I'm going to explain to him about Sally's sudden passion to learn the piano. We might have to start sending her off to Mrs Henderson in Yamboola for lessons.'

*

Cindy wanted to share the news of finding Marie with Murray as soon as she could, so once the children were asleep in their motel room that night, she phoned him. Softly, trying to keep the excitement in her voice contained so as not to wake the children, she quickly summarised the visit to the house in Randwick. There was stunned silence for a moment at the other end of the phone.

'So you just walked in on her and Aunt Marie welcomed you with open arms! How extraordinary.'

'She was very gracious,' explained Cindy. 'And she wants you and Russell to visit as soon as possible. Sally was very taken with her. Did you know what a talented pair of sisters your mother and Marie were? They were quite famous. Suzanne was really impressed when Jo told her whom we'd met today. Oh, and the pictures of your mother! She was so beautiful. And did you know that Sally wants to learn to play the piano? She said she's always wanted to, but she's never mentioned it to me before. Strange.'

275

'First I've heard of all this, too. I vaguely remember my mother saying something about dancing,' said Murray, his voice somewhat cool. 'But after she left, music and dance didn't rate too highly in our all-male household. What else did Marie say about my mother?'

Cindy hesitated at his subdued tone. 'Marie told me a bit about your mother's career. She also said that they didn't see each other much after Rose married your father. She did mention that she wrote and sent you presents for years, but they were all returned to her, unopened.'

Murray was quiet for a moment. 'I see. Well, I'm glad the kids saw her. I've missed you. Have you had fun while you've been in Sydney?'

Cindy sensed his changing the subject meant he was uncomfortable talking any more about his mother. Cindy wondered if Lawrence was in earshot. 'We've had a ball. But I'll be glad to get home. Is everything all right?'

'Yes. It's still a bit dry. Hope we get rain soon.'

Cindy was now used to men on the land repeating the mantra of no rain or too much rain. She couldn't help but smile. 'Of course. See you tomorrow. I love you, Murray.'

'I love you, too,' he said as he hung up.

Cindy sighed as she replaced the handset in its cradle. It was like pulling teeth to get Murray to open up and tell her what he really felt about things. She had hoped he would want to connect with Marie immediately, but he had seemed somewhat noncommittal. At least she had the photographs and cuttings from Marie to show him. Maybe that would stir him into action so he might at least talk to his aunt.

*

The children were tired from their long trip home to Kingsley Downs, so they had a quick dinner before falling into bed and were asleep almost as soon as the lights went out.

Murray was alone on the verandah, sipping a beer, his feet stretched out on a calfskin stool. He went to get up as Cindy joined him, carrying the manila envelope.

'Stay there, darling. I've brought something to show you.' Sitting down in the chair next to him, Cindy opened the envelope and pulled out the photographs and cuttings, which she handed to Murray. She waited as he silently flipped through them.

'Aren't they lovely? Have you ever seen them before?' Cindy prodded. 'Rose was so beautiful. And Marie is such fun. Look, there are these newspaper and magazine articles, too. How fabulous your parents looked on their wedding day.'

Silently Murray studied the contents of the envelope.

Suddenly Lawrence loomed in front of them. 'Is there something I should know?' he demanded.

Murray was so startled that he fumbled as he tried to put everything back into the envelope, dropping a magazine cutting on the floor in his haste. Lawrence's eyes bulged as he caught sight of an image of Rose.

Cindy jumped to her feet, deciding to take the bull by the horns. Keeping her voice calm, she said, 'Lawrence, while I was in Sydney I tracked down Marie Williams, Murray's aunt, and she gave us a selection of photographs of Rose. She thought the children and Murray would be interested.'

Lawrence's face was like thunder. He went to snatch the envelope from his son, but Murray pulled it out of reach.

'That woman had no right interfering in our family. If I had known of your intentions in Sydney, Cynthia, I would have forbidden it!'

'Dad, please . . .' began Murray.

Lawrence glared at Cindy and said angrily, 'Why must you meddle all the time? Why are you so intent on raking over old coals? Just leave well enough alone.'

'I did it because I think our children should know their family,' snapped Cindy.

'We have no family, especially not those Pearsons!' He picked up the cutting that Murray had dropped and tore it in half, throwing the pieces onto the floor.

'Stop being so selfish,' hissed Cindy. 'I think the children should at least be able to see photos of their grandmother.'

'Well, I don't,' said Lawrence coldly. 'She forfeited that right many years ago.' He glared at Cindy, apparently about to say more, but then snapped his mouth closed and strode back inside.

'Cin . . . please, leave it,' said Murray. 'I know you thought it was the right thing to do to find Aunt Marie, but she's obviously someone Dad doesn't want back in our lives.'

'Marie isn't Rose! Can we have no contact with anyone else? Murray, why is he like this? What's his problem? Whatever happened between him and your mother all those years ago, he's got to let it go and stop punishing the rest of us for it,' said Cindy furiously.

'Maybe he can't.'

'What do you mean?'

'Nothing. Nothing.' Murray downed the last of his drink. 'I'm going to bed,' he said, and he stood up and took two steps towards the door.

'Both of you running off, unable to face whatever needs to be confronted. *Like father, like son*,' said Cindy hotly. She had been so excited about finding Marie and showing Murray the wonderful pictures, and now Lawrence had spoiled it, just as he spoiled so much else.

Murray spun on his heel and looked straight at Cindy.

His face was flushed, his eyes burning with anger, and he was breathing hard as if trying to restrain himself. He took two steps towards her and she backed away, bumping into the wall behind her. She looked at his contorted face, and saw that his body was rigid and shaking. For a moment she almost felt afraid of her husband. He took a step towards her, his hands balled in fists, and she closed her eyes and turned her face to the wall. A moment passed and nothing happened. She opened her eyes and saw that the anger had drained out of him, leaving him limp, his head hung low.

'I . . . I am nothing like my father,' he whispered, backing away from her.

'Murray . . .' Cindy started to say, stunned.

'Just leave it,' he said, holding his hands up. Quietly, he took the steps down into the garden and Cindy listened to his footsteps fading away into the darkness.

He didn't return for some time, but when he slipped into bed, he wrapped her in his arms and kissed her gently. They slept entwined and at peace.

*

The following morning, Lawrence took off for Melbourne without telling Murray anything about his plans. Cindy was relieved that he would be away from them for a while at least. The atmosphere about the house quickly became a lot more relaxed. The children ran and squealed and played hide and seek boisterously. Cindy told Mrs Flowers that she'd cook the dinner that evening, which they all ate together on the screened verandah. After dinner, they played board games and, as he'd never played them as a kid, Murray always managed to lose, to the delight of his children. After this pleasant family evening, and when the children were settled in bed, Cindy suggested the two of them have a quiet nightcap.

They sat close together on the sofa.

'I'm sorry for what I said last night,' she said. 'You're not like your father. And I'm sorry he got so upset when he found out about Marie and the photos.'

279

'I'm sorry, too,' said Murray, 'but let's not talk about it.'

'But why, darling?'

Murray put his glass down. 'Why do you Yanks have to chew through things, analyse everything?' He tried to sound jokey and light-hearted, but his tone had a rough edge.

Cindy was having none of it. 'It's called communication. And stop saying "Yank". Pushing things away and avoiding important discussions isn't healthy. Besides, the children are interested in their grandmother, Sally especially. I think she'll treasure those photos.' She paused, waiting for Murray to make a comment, but he was silent. 'Do you think your father kept pictures or letters from your mother somewhere in the house?'

'No.'

Cindy stared at Murray's pinched face, his tight expression. 'How do you know for sure?'

'Because I saw him burn a pile of her things years ago.' His voice was bitter. 'I asked you to leave things alone. I don't want to talk about this.'

'Murray, why are you like this? Why won't you at least talk about your mother with me? I'm your wife. Are you hurt because she left you? I can understand that –'

'No! You can't possibly understand!' he suddenly burst out.

Cindy jerked back in shock. 'Murray, I'm sure you're wrong and, if you tell me, I'll understand, I promise. Please share what you're feeling with me. You can't keep bottling up all this pain and . . . suffering –'

Murray jumped to his feet, his hands curled in fists, his knuckles white and his face contorted in pain. 'Please, Cindy, I can't talk about it. It hurts too much.'

She stood up and grabbed his arm, turning him to face her, but his head hung down and, to her shock, she saw tears squeeze from his tightly closed eyes.

'Murray, you know you can trust me. You have got to tell me whatever it is that you've hidden from me since we first met. I don't care how bad it is, you need to get it out. For God's sake, share it with me, or one of us will go crazy.' She spoke urgently, in a low voice, guiding him back down onto the sofa. She was hugely relieved when he allowed her to lead him, though when he sat down he dropped his face into his hands and his shoulders slumped.

He was crying. Cindy rested her arm across his shoulders. 'Start at the beginning,' she said softly. She heard the slight tremor in her voice. She knew she might not like what was to come, but she said soothingly, 'It doesn't matter how bad it is, Murray. I'm your wife and I love you and I'm here for you, always.'

His shoulders shook and in a small broken voice he said, 'I was just a kid. A little kid. I didn't know what to do . . .'

'Do about what, darling?' she said encouragingly.

Murray took a deep breath and put his hands together between his knees, and started to speak.

'I don't know how long or how many times it happened. I should have noticed, but she never said anything. Some days she stayed in bed all day, curtains drawn so it was dark. Dad said she was sick, but now I think she was just very unhappy.' He paused and Cindy waited, hardly daring to draw breath. 'She was always so quiet. At times she would keep me at arm's length and I thought she didn't love me, but at other times she hugged me so hard it hurt.'

'And your father? What did he say?' asked Cindy, trying to keep her voice calm.

'He just said not to worry about her. But one night I heard them arguing, and she was shouting. I'd never heard her raise her voice before, so I got out of bed and tiptoed towards them and I heard her saying, "Lawrence, I can't

281

live like this." And then Dad said, "You're here now, so just get used to it. It's about time you did."' Murray wiped a hand across his eyes. 'I was scared, and I ran back to bed and hid under the covers. I'd never heard them arguing like that before. I heard Mum come into the room and she stood by my bed and rested her hand on me. I pretended to be asleep. I wished I could say something, but I didn't know what to say.'

He was struggling and Cindy knew there was more to come. 'You poor little boy,' she whispered.

'Another time I was home on holidays and, early one morning when it was barely dawn, I heard them arguing again. It was a Sunday, so the Flowerses weren't around and I thought Dad would be getting ready for church. I always went with him. Then I heard Mum cry out and I ran to see what was going on.' He stopped. Murray lifted his head and stared into the distance, and then spoke so calmly that Cindy was frightened of what would come next.

'She was sitting on the floor of the bathroom, leaning against the tub, holding her face. What I remember most was the blood; she was bleeding from her nose and mouth. My father was standing over her, holding her arm, trying to pull her to her feet. I ran to him and grabbed his arm, shouting for him to stop. He just flicked me away, and got my mother to stand. She had one hand on her mouth and the other was holding on to the door. My father grabbed me and said, "Your mother fell and hit her head on the bathtub. Help her clean herself up. I have to go to church." And he left. My mother just repeated what my father had said, but in a flat voice. So I got a towel and she began to wipe her face. When she'd stopped bleeding and had cleaned herself up, she went back to bed.' Murray took a breath. 'I stayed and I scrubbed and scrubbed the bathroom, trying to get rid of all the blood. Have you any idea how much there is from a bleeding nose and mouth? I thought I'd wear through the floor. Mum stayed in bed and when I finished she said I was a good boy. A big help. She was going to rest, please don't say anything to anyone and worry them. She'd be fine, it was just a silly accident. But I knew it wasn't an accident, because when I'd looked through the partly opened bathroom door, I had seen my father hit her, more than once.'

Murray stopped.

Cindy gasped. She was stunned. So this was the secret that Murray had kept hidden all these years.

'Cindy, Mum was so unhappy, and I knew Dad hit her and I couldn't help her. I could do nothing, so that's why she ran away. If I could have made her happy, she would have stayed. I was useless to her. That's why I don't want to talk about it. If I'd been stronger, if I'd stood up to him, she would have stayed, I just know it.' His voice broke.

Cindy hugged Murray tight. 'Murray, Murray darling, you were a little boy. Of course you couldn't do anything. It was not your fault that your mother left. If she was being beaten by your father, you would have been the only thing keeping her here. I'm sure she didn't blame you for anything. Why would she? Your father was the one who drove her away, not you.'

Cindy was aghast that her husband had been carrying this unnecessary guilt around with him all these years. It was tragic.

Murray shook his head violently from side to side, as if trying to shake the memory from his head. 'I don't know, I don't know. There was so much blood. I hated seeing my beautiful mother like that. I felt so helpless. So . . . inadequate.' He drew a shaky breath. 'I went back to school as soon as the holidays were over, but I hated not knowing what was happening to her back home.'

283

Cindy watched as he got up and paced around the room. 'Did she come and see you at school?'

'Yes. Once. With Dad. That was the last time I saw her. She left before I came back home again.'

'I don't suppose you ever discussed this with your father?'

Murray looked at her, his face a picture of horror.

'No! Of course not. My father was so distraught, so upset when she left, that I actually felt sorry for him. He put his arms around me for the first and only time I can remember, saying over and over, "You're all I've got. Don't ever leave me, son. Your mother didn't love either of us enough, but I won't ever run out on you like she did." So there was just us after that for years, until I found you.'

'Oh, my poor darling. You've carried all this around with you for all these years . . .' Cindy tightened her arms around her husband, who wept unashamedly on her shoulder.

Suddenly the door opened, and Gordon stood there, frowning.

'Mum, what's going on?'

'It's all right, honey. Your dad is upset. I showed him the photos of his mom, your grandmother, and he's feeling sad.'

Gordon looked bewildered. He'd never seen his father be anything other than strong. 'Will Grandfather be sad, too, when he sees them?'

Cindy held out an arm. 'I don't know. Why don't you come and give your dad a hug.'

Gordon ran to them and wrapped his arms around them both. Seeing Murray's face, he gave Cindy a worried look. 'Daddy is crying.'

'Yes, he is,' said Cindy gently. 'And that's okay. It's good. It shows how much he loved his mom.'

Murray straightened up and hugged Gordon to him. 'I love you, my big boy.'

Gordon nodded and held on to his father until Cindy kissed her son and took him back to bed.

When she returned, Murray was composed, sipping a glass of water and looking thoughtful.

'Thank you for listening,' he said, with a crooked smile. 'I never thought I'd tell anyone about my mother. I've wanted to tell you for years, but I thought you would think I had let her down, too.'

'Oh, for heaven's sake, Murray, can't you see that it was your father who let her down? It wasn't you. Your father has spent most of your life emotionally abusing you. Things need to change.'

'Maybe,' replied Murray doubtfully. 'Is Gordy okay?'

Cindy kissed him. 'He was a little worried about you. But Murray, this does change things. We need to get away from your father. I can't stay here in this house now, with my children, knowing that he was so violent towards your mother.'

'He wouldn't be violent towards you and the children, I'm sure,' replied Murray hastily.

'There was that time that he shook Russell, after he got lost. We can't be sure Lawrence won't do it again. He has a problem. A temper he can barely keep reined in much of the time. Murray, we need to put our children first. We have to have our own home. Maybe on Kingsley Downs, but I want our children well away from your father's reach.'

'But . . .' began Murray, seemingly at a loss for words.

'My darling, it's time to stop tiptoeing around your messed-up father! He has to deal with his own demons in his own way. I want a house of our own, to raise our children our way, a place where we can all feel secure and safe and loved. You have to put us first. *We* have to put us first.'

There was silence for a long moment, and Cindy's heart thudded in her chest as she watched her husband. But then Murray straightened and nodded. 'You're right. Changes will have to be made.' He gently touched her cheek before standing and leaving the room.

Cindy started to shake. It was heartbreaking to see how wounded her husband was. She silently cursed Lawrence, and her heart went out to her unknown mother-in-law, a damaged, frightened yet proud woman who simply couldn't cope any more with the shocking violence perpetrated against her. What a terrible decision she'd had to make. Cindy thought hard and tried to put herself in Rose's place. If Rose had tried to tell people the truth, who would have believed her? Lawrence was too highly respected, too wealthy, too powerful. He would have destroyed her. To run and take Murray with her would have had profound consequences for the boy, and Lawrence would not have let his son go freely. He would have tracked them down and taken back what he saw as rightfully his. And how could Rose have taken Murray from Kingsley Downs anyway? He was as much a part of the station as the big house itself, the old pepper-corn tree, the weathered fences with their leaning posts, the woolshed and the flocks of Merinos, the very land on which they had come to rest. It was his past and his future. What could Rose have given him instead? A loving mother, yes, but also insecurity, a furious father, endless fights, and separation from all he loved.

No, Rose had had no choice.

9

CINDY DREW A DEEP breath of pleasure, smiling at the magnificent display of roses in front of her. *What perfect timing*, she thought. The massed flowers were glorious, the shady trees had been hung with lights, and on the lawns were tables and chairs and a portable dance floor beside a formidable sound system awaiting the arrival of a local band. The bar and long tables for the food were in place along the verandah. Supervising and checking everything was one of the guests of honour, Sally.

Cindy watched her tall, beautiful, grown-up daughter conferring with Mrs Flowers. The housekeeper's now grey hair was pulled back in a tight little knot and she moved more slowly these days, but she was determined to be part of the evening. Sally then turned to Joanna and thanked her for helping with the flowers, as well as lending some extra vases to accommodate the magnificent arrangements. Sally looked again at her list of things needing to be done. Such an organised person, thought Cindy, in spite of the fact that she had never lost her rebel streak, her competitiveness with her twin, and the occasional delightful burst of tomboy fun she shared with her younger brother.

Joanna joined Cindy on the edge of the verandah. 'This garden is a dream. You've done wonders with this place over the last fifteen or so years. It's a credit to you. We're going to have a gorgeous evening.'

'I hope so,' said Cindy. 'Gosh, it's hard to believe we're celebrating Sally's engagement party. Where have the years gone? Still, she's older than I was when I ran away to marry Murray.' Cindy shook her head at the memory. 'I was so naïve. I arrived in Australia completely unprepared for life at Kingsley Downs. I was certainly in for a few surprises.'

Joanna squeezed her arm affectionately. 'Right, I'm off back home, if there's nothing more you want me to do. Donald and I will be back later. I'm so looking forward to the party. This evening will be quite a milestone for the Parnells.'

Cindy waved her friend off, but instead of going back into the house she started to wander through the garden, reflecting on all that had happened leading up to tonight's celebrations.

How the years had flown by. She could look back now with a better perspective. The best thing that had happened had been the change in Murray. After he'd unburdened himself to Cindy of his guilt about Rose, Murray had finally confronted his father about it. He'd told Cindy that his father denied ever hitting Rose, saying that Murray must have imagined it. But Murray had stuck to his guns and said that he knew what he had seen. After their conversation, Murray had continued to work with his father, and the two were always respectful to each other, but their previous close relationship had been irreparably fractured.

Whether Murray had entirely excised his demon shadows, Cindy wasn't sure, but she felt it best to leave things as they now were, especially when Murray would sometimes hold her and murmur, 'I'm so damned lucky to have you and the kids.'

It wasn't Cindy's way of dealing with issues – she'd always preferred to talk them through frankly – but Murray's attitude was to let sleeping dogs lie. However, he had certainly come a long way toward being more open in the last fifteen years.

Initially, after learning of Lawrence's violence towards Rose, Cindy had wanted to pack up and leave Kingsley Downs. Lawrence's actions repulsed her. But such a move, she knew, would break her husband's heart. She understood that the property was Murray's life's work, and his children's inheritance, and he couldn't just walk away from it without a great deal of regret. She hadn't wanted to force such a heartbreaking decision on him.

Eventually they'd settled on a compromise, deciding that a house must be built for them several kilometres away from the big house. Cindy would rarely have to meet Lawrence, but Murray could continue to help in the development of Kingsley Downs while Lawrence was at the helm.

Cindy had loathed the six months she'd had to spend still living with Lawrence while their new house was being built, but thankfully her father-in-law was away frequently during that time, as he'd been appointed to the Wool Corporation Board as a regional representative and took his role in the flourishing wool industry very seriously.

When at last the day had come when the whole family could move into their own house, Cindy had felt nothing but joy. The house was situated near the unseen, overgrown rubble of the old house, and was closer to Yamboola. Here, finally, Cindy had been able to create the home she had always wanted; a place that was light and airy, full of family photos and things she cherished. Her treasures included handmade gifts from the children, like the wobbly cup and saucer Sally had made when she'd tried potting, and the slightly more practical coffee-mug tree that Russell had made in his woodworking class. She loved the painting over the fireplace, a picture she had admired in a gallery in Melbourne, and which had turned up unexpectedly under the Christmas tree six months later. And on the mantelpiece was a little pile of shells, a reminder of a wonderful family holiday in Queensland. Cindy had turned the new house into a welcoming and happy home filled with laughter and love, and had found in it a deep contentment that she'd never felt in the big house.

Sally had taken piano lessons, although after a few years she'd lost enthusiasm, especially after she started school in Melbourne and a whole new world of interests and friends opened up to her. Russell, however, had learned to play the piano as well as the guitar. Cindy loved hearing music in the house. It made the place seem so alive.

Lawrence, now silver-haired and looking distin-guished and dignified, only visited Cindy and Murray's home on rare occasions. He was more polite these days, but he still ruled the big house in his autocratic way. When the children came home for school holidays, they were still obliged to attend at least one stiff and uncomfortable dinner at the big house with Lawrence at the head of the table. Mrs Flowers continued to look after him and the household, and Tom was the quiet, indispensable pres-ence he'd always been, although Cindy knew his health was no longer quite so robust.

Cindy smiled to herself as she thought with pride of her children. They had grown into fine young adults. Gordon, who had been away at agricultural college, was working as a jackaroo on a property in South Australia, but had come home for his sister's engagement. Gordon was as passionate about working on their land as his father and grandfather.

Russell, now in his final year at school, was studying hard, determined to do well enough to get into veterinary science at university. He had always loved working with animals and wanted to put that love to a practical use.

Sally had been thinking she might like to be a journalist. Then she'd met Ashley Broad. He had just qualified as a pharmacist and was working in a pharmacy in an outer suburb of Melbourne. The two of them had scraped together the deposit for a house in a newly developed suburb and were working towards having a pharmacy of their own one day.

Over the years, Cindy and Murray had grown closer together. More than friends and lovers, they were a team, prepared to face the world together no matter what was flung at them. Cindy was pleased when she noticed how, in time, Murray occasionally referred to his mother, so that Rose became an acknowledged presence in their lives. Cindy had displayed the photos Marie had given them alongside their family photos, and they looked at them often. Murray had also written to Marie soon after the Sydney holiday, and Marie had written a long, warm letter back, and bit by bit the family had become quite close again. As the children had grown, Mon and Marie had visited Cindy and Murray once or twice, and the grandchildren had enjoyed country holidays at Kingsley Downs. In return, Gordon, Sally and Russell had stayed at Marie's house when in Sydney. Sadly, Marie had died unexpectedly a year ago, and they all missed her.

Life at Kingsley Downs was dictated not just by the personal relationships, or by its smooth functioning, the care of the animals, feed and maintenance, but most importantly, by the weather. And as Cindy reflected on her life, inevitably she thought of the horror drought which had been one of the hardest things she'd experienced at Kingsley Downs.

As she looked around her lush garden now, she remembered with pain a time, not so long ago, when the big dry was into its fourth year with next to no rain and the garden had been little better than a desert.

Day after day, the sun had shone down from eternally cloudless skies as the paddocks shrivelled to grey-brown, rancorous dust. Lawrence and Murray had sold off much of the stock at painfully low prices, keeping only the best breeding rams and ewes. Sometimes transporting the sheep to the saleyards had cost more than the price they'd got for them at auction. Yet, even with the depleted flock, there had not been enough fodder, and the Parnells had been reduced to hand-feeding. Moreover, their straitened circumstances had forced them to supplement the expensive grain with the local hardy saltbush. Despite all their efforts, the scrawny lambs frequently became too weak to forage in the dry stalks and sticks of bushes.

Lawrence sent some of the stock they had left out on the long paddock. He had wanted to keep the best of the breeding stock so that, when the infernal drought ended, they would still have enough good-quality bloodlines to start over. He hired a drover from near Hay to walk them to a property outside Wilcannia for agistment. He said they had spent too many years breeding up the progeny to lose the line now. A couple of weeks later, a drover on horseback and a couple of dogs had begun the long walk to Wilcannia, taking several thousand of the Parnells' sheep along the old stock routes which were reserved for such a contingency.

'I don't know, Cindy,' Murray had said quietly. 'I sometimes think it's never going to rain. God knows when we'll see those sheep again, but the only hope we have in saving them is the grass along those tracks. I guess we're lucky that Dad found a place to agist them. Some mobs stay on the move for months, just looking for feed. Who'd bloody want to be on the land? It's a mug's game.'

He had turned away from Cindy, his face full of frustration, and picked up his hat and jammed it on his head. Cindy was silently relieved the children were away at school and didn't have to witness their father under such strain.

Neighbours had supported each other as best they could. Joanna and Donald were also struggling through the drought. It was a pitiless time.

The memories were still painful. It had been very traumatic going out to help Murray hand-feed the sheep and seeing the scrawny beasts struggling to reach the grain, or simply lying down in the dust, too weak to stand, resigned to their fate as eagles circled overhead.

The drought had seemed endless. Lawrence and Murray eventually faced the painful task of shooting the stock which were too weak to survive on the little feed left in the paddocks or the scarce water in the dams.

Cindy remembered the day she'd been walking through the big house, looking for Mrs Flowers, assuming that Lawrence was away, and had passed by his study. Lawrence had been standing beside his desk holding his rifle.

'What do you want?' he'd snapped when he saw her staring at him. He looked dishevelled, and his moleskin pants were caked in dust and blood.

'I didn't know you were here,' Cindy had stammered. 'I was looking for Mrs Flowers.'

Lawrence slammed the bolt of his rifle shut and ignored her.

'Is everything all right?' she'd asked.

'No. I'm shooting my bloody sheep. What do you think?' His face had twisted, his eyes burning bright, his mouth tight in a grimace.

'I'm sorry, Lawrence.' She'd jumped backwards as Lawrence grabbed the box of ammunition and pushed roughly past her.

Still shaking from that encounter, Cindy had found Mrs Flowers restocking the storeroom.

'Terrible thing,' Mrs Flowers had said. 'Mr Parnell has spent years breeding those sheep. Best in the district. Now he has to shoot them. I'm not surprised that he looked so grim. He can take things to heart more than you'd think.'

'It's just so awful. I know Murray will be upset. I wish I could help, but I just can't bear seeing the poor creatures struggle,' Cindy replied.

'I know. But we've been through this before, and when the other sheep come back from agistment, they'll be able to build the flock up again. At least Tom says the price for wool is holding,' Mrs Flowers had said, trying to look for a bright side.

'That's good for the growers who aren't in this drought, so let's hope the prices stay that way when we finally get some rain. I don't see how they can keep paying top dollar to the producers while stockpiling so much of the wool clip. It seems like a very big gamble,' Cindy had confided. She would never have voiced this to Lawrence, and Murray always brushed her concerns aside.

'Mr Parnell is very confident that there won't be any problem selling it all, and he should know, seeing as he's on the board,' Mrs Flowers had replied with some pride.

Cindy hadn't felt she could share Mrs Flowers's confidence. Things had just seemed too desperate, and the drought all-pervasive. She'd hated seeing the looks on the children's faces when they came home for holidays and saw the state of the place. She knew that drought was just another part of country life, but she fervently hoped she would never see a drought like it ever again. A lot of graziers had done it really tough, feeding their stock before their families, almost. And the number of suicides had been tragic. Some men had just got overwhelmed and hadn't been able to see a way through it. Cindy blamed the banks as much as the weather: they seemed to move in as soon as a man got into trouble and tried to take his property away. The landholders had faced an impossible choice: pay up, or get out.

It hadn't just been Lawrence shooting the stock. Murray had joined him in the terrible task. It had been late when Murray had finally returned home that awful night. He was too tired for supper and had just poured himself a whisky, then stripped off his filthy clothes and had had a shower.

When he'd finally slid into bed, Cindy had reached for him and curled beside him, her arm across his chest and her head on his shoulder. He lay on his back, one arm under his head.

'I'm sorry you had to do that today,' she'd murmured.

'It's horrible. I hate it. It's like a war, an invasion. Killing the weak and maimed. It's their eyes, Cin. They look at you, wanting help, or just pleading for you to put them out of their misery. These animals trusted us and we let them down . . .' He stopped and rubbed his eyes, as though blotting out the awful memories of that day.

Cindy had stroked his hair, now grey at the temples. 'Go to sleep, darling,' she said. 'It'll be okay. At least, it will when it rains.'

And at last it had rained. She would never forget that day. The clouds had gathered and what had started as a gentle, gauzy sheen over the paddocks had soon become solid sheets of water, tumbling from the sky as though it would never stop. It had rained all day, and the next, and the next. In days, the dams filled and soon green shoots began to push through the softened soil.

In a few weeks, the horror of the drought had been replaced by new pastures and the agisted sheep had returned to begin building up the Kingsley Downs flock all over again. Wool prices continued to climb and the property had become prosperous once more.

But for Cindy that drought was seared into her memory.

It had given her an insight into the vicissitudes of life on the land, and an admiration for those who hung in there: the small farmers, the big holdings, the old families, those with a passion for life on the land in spite of the heartbreak the drought had wrought. Cindy was proud that she was part of a culture, a way of life, that city people had little inkling about, and she realised that it was a way of life that had also claimed her soul.

The next few years had seen good and regular rain, and the flocks had flourished with the addition of the best ewes and rams Lawrence had been able to find.

Lawrence had continued to revel in his involvement in the Wool Corporation. He talked about the lavish wool promotions which he attended. He mixed socially with the other big-name boardroom players as well as the overseas buyers, whom he talked about later with arrogance rather than respect.

To Cindy's astonishment and annoyance, Lawrence had begun to spend money as he never had before. He upgraded his satellite dish so he could receive better television, radio and phone reception. He handed the old Daimler over to Murray and bought himself a top-of-the-range Jaguar. He'd also bought a light plane, carved out a runway and hangar in a western paddock and both he and Murray learned to fly. Lawrence loved his single-engine plane. He frequently flew off visiting other properties around the country and attending field days, as well as flying down to Melbourne for board meetings. Times had certainly changed since Cindy had first come to Kingsley Downs.

With a slight jolt, Cindy returned to the moment as Sally nudged her from her musings.

'Mum, the guests will be here soon, and you haven't even changed. What have you been doing?'

'Just thinking about us, and wondering where all the years have gone,' Cindy replied, giving her daughter a hug. Her daughter returned Cindy's embrace and then shooed her towards the house. Cindy smiled as she walked indoors. So many things had changed, but some things were still the same.

*

By sunset all the guests for Sally's engagement party had arrived. The band was tuning up, a group of Ashley's mates were gathered around the keg of beer, Sally and her girlfriends were watching them from the verandah, and Cindy and Joanna circulated with plates of food, enjoying exchanging banter with the young people. Murray, his grey hair now slightly thinning, his face more weathered but his frame firm and lean, stood with his contemporaries, drinks in hand, discussing the latest wool prices and ram sales.

It was lovely to have so many of their friends there to share Sally and Ashley's party, Cindy thought. She was happy that Marie's grandchildren, Toby and Holly, were able to be there, too, though she missed Marie's exuberant presence.

Lawrence arrived in time for the toasts. He said a few words, gave Sally a kiss and handed her an envelope with a cheque in it which would more than cover the honeymoon. He spent some time circulating, being charming, but quietly left once the music and dancing started.

After a couple of dances with Murray and then with Donald, Cindy finally collapsed in a chair beside Joanna.

'I can't remember the last time I danced like a mad thing,' she said breathlessly, laughing.

Jo grinned at her friend. 'Terrific party, Cin. Everyone is having a great time. Looks like Lawrence was splashing his money around on Sally and Ashley.'

Cindy rolled her eyes. 'Yes, he's spending like it's going out of fashion these days. Not like when Murray and I were first married. Then we couldn't get a penny out of him. But then, he's always been generous with the kids. Sometimes I think he tries to buy their affection.'

Joanna shook her head. 'Your kids are too sensible to be taken in by that. Mind you, I've noticed that he's always rather polite to you these days.'

Cindy nodded in agreement. 'Yes, he mightn't like me, but I think he respects me.' Before she could say anything else, Murray and Donald wandered over and sat down beside them.

'Great night, Cin,' said Donald. 'I can't believe Sally's getting married. Look at them all on the dance floor, having the time of their lives, and yet it doesn't seem all that long ago that all of them were just young kids together.'

'I was thinking much the same thing myself earlier this evening,' said Cindy with a smile. 'Are you two driving home, or staying in one of our bedrooms? Most of the kids are bunking down in the shearers' quarters. There's a big barbecue recovery breakfast planned.'

'Ha, reminds me of those B&S balls! I think we'd better stay. We've had a bit too much partying to be able to drive home safely,' said Jo. 'Not that we'll get a lot of sleep with all this noise going on.'

As the four friends settled contentedly into their chairs, they were entertained by Sally's friends belting out

'Girls Just Wanna Have Fun' as they danced wildly on the little dance floor. Life, Cindy thought, couldn't get much better than this.

*

But a few days later, things changed when Cindy received a phone call from Alice. As soon as she heard Alice's voice, she knew something was wrong, for Alice never phoned.

'It's Babs,' Alice said without preamble. 'She's sick. She's got breast cancer. She's a fighter, but I thought you'd want to know. She told me not to tell you, of course.'

'Oh, no! Oh, Alice, that's terrible.' Cindy felt her heart constrict and tears sprang to her eyes. 'I'll come immediately.'

'You don't have to rush to her bedside, she's not at death's door – yet,' said Alice ominously. 'But the prognosis, long-term, is not looking so good. Of course, we both know Babs can be a drama queen at times.'

Cindy bit her tongue. She knew that Babs was not the drama queen in the family. She had never been one to exaggerate, which made Cindy feel even more alarmed.

'What about Joey? Has she told him?'

'Yes. I persuaded her. He's a grown man with a family, for goodness sake.' Alice sniffed. 'Babs still indulges him, but he had to know the truth. Babs will be very happy if you give her a call, now that you know.'

'I call her quite often, and she's said nothing to me,' said Cindy. She felt a dreadful twinge of guilt. 'I should have brought her out here, taken the kids there, and now . . .' Suddenly, she couldn't speak.

'No point in going into the ifs and buts now,' said Alice briskly. 'I just thought you should know. She doesn't expect you to come, she knows that you have a very busy life and Sally's wedding coming up and all.'

'Thank you, Alice, I'm glad you told me. I'll tell Murray right away. Take care and give our love to Spencer,' said Cindy, putting down the phone. She felt she might burst into tears.

Murray simply held her tightly. There was little he could say to comfort her except to agree that she had to leave for Palm Springs as soon as possible. 'Of course you must go. I'm only sorry we couldn't have gone sooner so Babs could meet the kids.'

Cindy nodded. 'I wish she could too, but they're so busy with their own lives at the moment. Murray, I feel so guilty that I didn't find the time to see Babs before this. There just always seemed to be something going on. Something else to spend the money on. The years just seem to have slipped away and I owe Babs such a lot, I should have made time for her. And poor Joey. I know he has a wonderful partner in Kelly and children of his own, but it will be terrible for him to lose his mother.' She stopped.

Murray must have known what she was thinking, because he said gently, 'You're right. We've both lost our mothers, so we can understand how he must be feeling.' He stroked her hand. 'What about your father, Cindy? Will you find time to visit him while you're away?'

She gave a wan smile. 'Yes. I was thinking I'd see my dad, of course. He's not getting any younger. Oh, Murray, it feels rather like I'm saying goodbye to everyone . . .' She buried her face in Murray's chest and cried.

*

Cindy felt small and fragile as she hunkered down in her seat in the aircraft.

People were talking and laughing all around her, stowing bags, getting settled with magazines and books and blankets. She turned her face towards the window, hoping no one chatty sat beside her and asked her questions; *Off on holiday, then? Seeing family? Where are you headed?* She just craved solitude so she could be alone with her thoughts.

Murray had driven her to Melbourne and the children had all come to the airport to see her off. How she wished Babs could see how well the children had turned out. She was so proud of them, making choices for their futures, deciding on their careers.

Occasionally Cindy had wondered what sort of career she would have had if she hadn't met Murray, but now she struggled to remember what her dreams had been. Palm Springs had been unlike any place she'd ever imagined and Alice and Babs had opened her eyes to so many different ideas and experiences. College life had been fun, and that world had seemed a place filled with the promise of opportunities. But over the years she had gradually lost contact with the friends she'd known there, and occasionally she wondered what had happened to them. Had they led richly busy and fulfilled lives, striding the world stage as successful achievers, or had some failed at life, never meeting their yearbook hopes and predictions? And where did she fit in? What would they think of Cindy's life, contained as it mostly was within the small world of Kingsley Downs?

But her life, in spite of all its dramas and ups and downs, had been a success. Cindy only had to look at her children to know that. And now she wanted, very much, to be able to tell Babs this was so, and reassure her that her impulsive marriage all those years ago had turned out for the best.

Cindy was tired when she finally landed in Los Angeles, but she hired a car and headed off on the two-hour drive down Interstate 10 to Palm Springs. She could hardly wait to see her American family again. She knew from Babs that Joey had fallen madly in love and had moved in with a young girl called Kelly, and that babies had come along and suddenly he was a family man, although he and Kelly had never bothered to marry. Babs had been thrilled to see her son happily settled, although she had also told Cindy that Alice was scandalised by their actions. She'd told Joey bluntly they shouldn't be 'living in sin, but must formalise their relationship for the sake of the children'.

Cindy had laughed and she was now looking forward to meeting Joey's little family.

When she turned off onto the highway, she started to smile and, although the areas she drove through had changed a lot, she was soon back in familiar territory. And while the desert might have blossomed with more lavish condos, gated communities and golf courses, when she pulled up outside Babs's house she saw that it was just the same as she remembered it, with its well-established desert plants in the front garden and the same white-walled fence. It was dark now, but lights glowed from within the house and the light over the front door was welcoming. Cindy hesitated on the doorstep and rang the bell.

Babs opened the door, smiling. 'Why are you ringing the bell? This is your home!'

'Oh, Babs.' Cindy opened her arms and they held each other. The years they'd been apart seemed to dissolve in their embrace and Cindy felt as though she had never been away. Cindy was shocked by how old and tired Babs looked. Hugging her, Cindy felt how thin she had become. However, Babs's voice was still the same; bright, comforting, caring.

'Honey, you didn't have to come, but I'm so happy you're here,' Babs murmured as tears ran down Cindy's cheeks. 'Now, now, let me look at you.' Babs stepped back, holding Cindy's hands. 'What a beautiful woman you are. Come on in, come in.'

It was a homecoming. As she looked around, Cindy saw that everything was more or less as it had been when

she'd left. Her room was made up, and Babs had resur-
rected some of her college photos and an old teddy, and
her favourite cushions lay on the bed.

'Babs, I can't believe that you kept those things of mine,'
Cindy said delightedly. The familiarity of those objects,
worn with memories, was comforting and reassuring.

'You didn't want them shipped to you, but I couldn't
bring myself to throw them away, so I kept them, waiting
for the day when I could bring them out again. Now the
day has come, and here you are,' said Babs. She had a
hesitancy about her that gave the impression of frailty, but
she sparkled with joy.

Once they were settled at the table and eating their
supper, Cindy took a breath.

'Now, Babs, lay it on the line. How do you feel, how
is your treatment going?'

A shadow momentarily crossed her aunt's face, but
then Babs smiled forcefully. 'As well as can be expected,
as they say. I'm in remission, but the cancer could come
back. Still, I am optimistic.'

'It's the 1980s, Babs. Medical science is making so
many breakthroughs, advancing so much . . . You're
going to be just fine,' said Cindy firmly.

'We'll see. Whatever happens, happens.' Babs clasped
Cindy's hand across the table. 'I've missed you, Cindy. It's
so good to see you.'

'Babs, I'm so sorry that I've not come before to visit
you, but I want you to get strong and we'll fly you out to
Kingsley Downs. How about next summer? Your summer,
not ours. Or spring? When all the lambs are dropping?'

Babs waved a hand as though to brush away such
suggestions. 'We'll see, let's just enjoy having you here
now. Alice and Spencer are looking forward to seeing you.
Joey can't wait to see you. As I told you in my letters,
he's only about an hour away in San Bernardino, so he'll

come and see you as soon as he can.' She began to clear the table, and Cindy jumped up to help. 'You must be tired. Jet-lagged. Why don't you go to bed and see if you can sleep through till morning.' Babs sighed contentedly as she moved about the kitchen. 'I can't believe you're here, back in your room. It's like all the years have just telescoped and it was only yesterday you were playing with Joey in the pool at the old apartment with dear old Sol and Deidre.' Babs paused as she stacked their plates. 'I still miss those two so very much, although it's been years since they died. They were about the kindest people I've ever met. And you, Cindy. Look at the long journey your life has taken. Are you happy, Cin? No regrets?'

Cindy shook her head. 'No regrets. I know marrying Murray the way I did was impulsive, and I was young, but it was the best thing I ever did.'

Babs nodded. 'I'm glad. Alice always said you were strong and you'd make the most of whatever came along. Dear Alice, she and Spencer have been so kind and helpful. Alice is just the same. She never ages, she is constantly into some new thing, she has so much energy, although in the last few years, I think she has made some dubious decisions. I've tried to say so, but as you know, you can never tell Alice a thing. I'm so glad she has Spencer. He's very sensible.'

'And how is Spencer?' asked Cindy, helping her aunt load their dishes into the dishwasher.

Babs rubbed her back. 'Getting older, like we all are. Wakes up every day with a new pain, according to Alice. Sometimes he's like a fussy kid, but he still plays golf and goes to the club, so he does okay. He's driven me to the doctor and the hospital many times. Says it gives him something to do since he's retired and Alice is so busy with the shop. She threatens to sell it, but I can't imagine her doing that. And now of course she has a second boutique in Palm Desert on El Paseo – did I tell you about that?'

Cindy nodded. She'd heard this news before, but it was just so nice to hear it in person.

Wiping her hands on a tea towel, Babs said, 'Now, Spencer will come by and collect us whenever you're ready tomorrow and the two of them will take us to lunch. They have somewhere really great in mind.'

Cindy yawned. 'Wonderful. And I'm sure Spencer doesn't drive you around because he has nothing else to do. He does it because he loves you, like we all do.' Cindy kissed Babs, holding her tight. Leaving her aunt in the kitchen, Cindy went to the bathroom and showered, the warm water seemingly melting her cares away. She fell into the bed in her old bedroom as though she had never been away.

*

The next morning, Alice arrived into Babs's house like a technicolour whirlwind on stilettos, a rush of pink and lime, flashing crystals, a new shade of colour in her hair and nails with glitter in the polish.

'Oh, Alice!' laughed Cindy, reaching to hug her. 'How marvellous you are.'

Spencer wandered into the house in the wake of his wife. He had indeed aged, but was smartly dressed in crisply pleated cream linen slacks and a lemon shirt, with a tangerine cashmere sweater over his shoulders. His hair had thinned and although he looked a bit wan and drawn, his smile was brilliant, showing dazzling teeth.

'Cindy, you are as lovely as always.' He hugged her and Alice leaned over for a small embrace and a kiss on the cheek, so as not to disturb her bouffant hairdo.

Alice eyed her niece. 'Cindy. You look exhausted. How many hours on that awful flight?'

'I'm fine, Alice,' Cindy said with a smile. 'Babs is looking after me.'

'How are you?' Alice turned to Babs like a school-teacher with an errant student.

'How would I be, now Cindy is here? Over the moon, of course. Come on now, let's go eat. Cin, you won't believe this fabulous new place.' Babs took Cindy's arm.

The lunch was delightful and Cindy was touched by the number of people who stopped at their table to greet her.

'You've spread the word, you two.' Cindy grinned at her aunts.

'You lived here, after all,' said Alice. 'And you are my niece.'

'Some of the best years of my life were spent here,' said Cindy. 'You're a marvel, Alice. So many projects on the go.'

'She doesn't know how to relax. You know what she's done at the second store, the one in Palm Desert?' said Spencer with pride.

Cindy shook her head. Spencer had never taken much interest in Alice's fashion business, but he was clearly dying to tell her something.

'She's put a hydroponic garden on the roof. It's just the latest thing,' Spencer announced.

'It was my idea. I sell the food to restaurants,' said Alice. 'The plants grow in long trays in water with nutrients in it. I had to put up some shade cloth for the summer, but the rest of the season things go nuts. Lettuces, tomatoes, greens, you name it. I worked out the formula to feed them with a pharmacist friend.'

Cindy was surprised. Since when had Alice had any interest in gardening? 'Good grief. How wonderful,' said Cindy. 'How did you discover such a thing?'

'My nutritionist. He's a wonder man. He was trained by Gayelord Hauser, you know. He preaches eating healthy food.'

Spencer and Babs interjected in unison, 'Five fruits and five vegetables every day!'

'It's my regime and it certainly works. I'm its best advertisement,' stated Alice loftily.

After lunch, they toured Palm Springs in Spencer's new Chevy so that Cindy could see all the changes that had occurred in the last twenty or so years. There were lots of new stores, restaurants and hotels, encircled by sprawling condominiums and golf course estates bordered by luxurious homes. The emerald lawns sharply delineated where the water supply stopped on one side of the road, while the desert stretched into the distance on the other.

It struck Cindy that amongst the tourists and extravagantly dressed locals, the residents of this popular desert community all seemed terribly old, and were dwarfed by their large cars, which they drove very slowly, hugging the wheel protectively.

As if reading her mind, Babs commented, 'This has become a popular place to retire, which is nice because there are people living here all year round now and not just visiting in winter.'

Spencer chuckled. 'Most people in Palm Springs don't buy green bananas any more, you know, Cindy.'

'Why not?' asked Cindy in a puzzled voice.

'They might not live long enough to see 'em ripen.' Spencer threw his head back and roared with laughter. Cindy guessed he'd told that joke many times before.

'You'd need money to settle here,' said Cindy.

'Not everyone who comes here has money, gosh no. There are some cheaper estates further out. Ugly towns have sprung up,' said Alice, pursing her lips. 'And Palm Springs is full of middle-aged divorcees all looking for a rich husband. They come into my shops. No dress sense. Mutton dressed as lamb. No idea. Fake jewels. I can spot them a mile away.'

'What about that woman, the one who offered to

help you with your business dealings? You certainly gave her a makeover,' said Babs pointedly.

'What do you mean?' asked Cindy.

Alice scowled. 'She was a sneak,' she sniffed. 'I gave her clothes at a discount, told her how to accessorise. I tried to introduce her to the best people.'

'But she took you out to lunch a lot,' said Spencer.

'It didn't cost her anything. Her brother owned the restaurant!' replied Alice indignantly.

'You told me that she was going to do your marketing. And didn't she talk you into one of these new computer things?' said Babs.

'What happened to her?' asked Cindy.

'She ran off with an ancient millionaire,' chortled Spencer.

'And some of my most expensive clothes!' snapped Alice.

'Oh dear, not a lot, I hope,' said Cindy. Babs was right, she thought. Alice did seem to have become more gullible and easily impressed by appearances these days.

'Worth every cent to see her gone and a lesson learned,' said Spencer. 'She could have done a lot more damage.'

'I've still got that silly box of a computer thing that I can't use cluttering up my desk. I've no idea why she thought it would be useful. Total waste of money,' said Alice crossly, and tried to change the subject. However, before she could launch into another story, Cindy realised that Babs was looking fatigued.

'Maybe I'm jet-lagged. I think an afternoon nap might be a good idea,' Cindy said tactfully. 'Would you mind if we called it a day?'

*

Cindy spent most of her visit with gentle Babs. They sat in the sun in the early morning before it got too hot, went for small walks, or an occasional drive. Special friends came by but didn't stay too long, as Babs tired easily.

Early one morning, while Spencer took Babs to a medical appointment, Cindy drove the rental car into Palm Springs to see Alice in her store. She also went to visit Babs's old shop, still in the same hotel foyer where it was now a desert icon. It looked much the same as she remembered it, and the children's clothes were beautiful, but they looked to be mass-produced, albeit perhaps in limited numbers. The fine hand-stitching that Babs had done was a lost art, thought Cindy.

At lunchtime, Cindy sat on the porch waiting for Babs to join her. Even the sound of Babs making sandwiches made Cindy smile. Some things just never changed. Babs made her way slowly outside and set two plates on the table. Cindy looked up at her face, pinched from the effort. She was about to say something when Babs asked, 'How have you found Palm Desert? There's been a lot of changes of late.'

Cindy nodded. 'Alice mentioned something about gangsters the other day! I wasn't sure what she meant?'

Babs waved her hand. 'There've always been gangsters here – they rented homes, gambled – but in the last few years there has been an influx of mafia leaders. One of them gave fifty thousand dollars to Cabazon Band of Mission Indians to start a casino on their land out near Indio in 1980.'

Cindy gasped. 'Oh my goodness! You never mentioned it in your letters.'

Babs demurred. 'Well, it's not like the wild mobster days of Chicago here. More the high-flyers who mix with celebrities and local rich businessmen. Spencer used to talk about the tycoons, tuxedos, clubs, beautiful women dripping in diamonds. Not a part of the desert we ever saw.' Babs smiled. 'It's been going on for twenty years. But using the Indians is not good.'

'Good heavens, how did that come about?' asked Cindy.

'The local Indians have declared their lands exempt from California gaming laws, so they've set up bingo halls and gambling places on their reservations. It's a smart way to fund their own community projects.' Babs took a sip of iced tea and coughed for a moment, holding a hankie over her mouth with a pale hand.

Cindy frowned at her, but Babs waved that she was okay. 'I suppose so,' Cindy said. 'I remember you mentioning some of these changes, but it didn't really register with me how big they were. And speaking of Indians, do you know what happened to Adsila, the Indian woman who used to work for Sol and Deidre?'

'I still see her from time to time. She and Francis are very involved in the American Indian Movement. They have a place in La Quinta, near Indio, where they run a gallery and shop. It's a picturesque village, you should visit one day. It's only about thirty minutes' drive away,' suggested Babs.

'Really? I'll do that! How wonderful. I might even go this afternoon, when you're having a rest,' replied Cindy.

*

Cindy thought La Quinta village was quaint, its main street filled with interesting and arty shops. She quickly spotted the modest gallery advertising Indian handicrafts.

Inside, a young woman was busy unpacking some items from a box, so Cindy walked around to admire the woven rugs and wall hangings, basketry, intricate carvings and other tribal artefacts. There were wonderful copies of old photographs of tribespeople and paintings of scenes that she remembered well from more than twenty years ago.

The pretty girl looked up. 'Can I help you with anything? I can explain what things are, which tribe or family made them. They are all from around here.'

'Yes, I can see that. Actually, I was looking for the owner of this gallery. Is she around? Adsila . . . ?'

'Yes, that's my mother. She's in the back. Shall I get her?' the girl asked curiously.

Cindy's eyes widened. 'You're Adsila's daughter? My goodness.' Cindy recalled the shy little girl who had to be coaxed to share a smile. 'I remember you. I visited your home a long time ago. Please tell your mother that Cindy, Babs's niece, is here. I hope she still remembers me.'

The young woman looked bemused and hurried out to summon her mother.

A few seconds later, Adsila, heavier, her glowing face a little more lined, came into the gallery. She was wearing a traditional Indian dress, elaborately beaded. Her hair was braided and wound up on her head, a silver and turquoise comb holding it in place, and on her feet were a pair of soft felt moccasins. She walked toward Cindy, arms outstretched.

'Cindy! My old friend. I am so happy to see you. It has been a very long time.'

They embraced and laughed together.

'It's wonderful to see you too, Adsila. You have such lovely special pieces in the shop. I so treasured the bowl you made and gave me,' said Cindy.

'You still have it?' asked Adsila.

'Not exactly, but I know where it is,' replied Cindy, and explained how she had buried it all those years ago under the peppercorn tree.

'That is very sad. You must take something to replace it. Please, Cindy, choose anything from in here as a gift from the Agua Caliente people,' said Adsila.

'Thank you, Adsila, I'll choose something small, maybe some jewellery for my daughter, but I would like to buy a few other items to take home as gifts. Who makes all these wonderful things? How did this all start?'

'Over the years Francis and I have been active in promoting our people and fighting for our rights, and this shop enables them to raise money through Indian craftwork.'

'What a wonderful thing to do. Please give Francis my best wishes.'

They talked about their children, and Adsila told Cindy proudly that she was a grandmother, and that her grandchildren were doing well and had had a good education.

'Much better than the one Francis and I received,' said Adsila. 'But we are doing well too, the family is around us and we are accepted as part of the history in the desert here now.'

After an hour, Cindy left with the gifts she'd bought in a small bag: a necklace for Sally, earrings for Joanna and belts with elaborate silver buckles studded with turquoise for Murray and the boys.

Cindy hurried excitedly back to Babs's house, keen to show her aunt the items she'd bought for her family at Adsila's. Entering the house, she found her aunt resting on the porch. Cindy put her handbag and car keys down on the hall stand and took a seat in the chair opposite Babs.

'Adsila seems so different. Not at all like the shy woman who used to iron for Deidre. She seems so full of confidence now,' Cindy said, pouring herself a glass of some of Babs's homemade iced tea from a jug on the table.

'I still remember how we chatted as she did Deidre's ironing when we first arrived. Joey really liked her,' said Babs.

'That was a long time ago,' sighed Cindy.

Babs leaned on her pale hand. 'Yes, a long time.'

Cindy paused. 'You were so brave, doing what you did, leaving Howard,' she said slowly. She was thoughtful a moment. 'I don't think I ever told you, Babs, but Murray's mother was also abused.'

Babs looked at Cindy in shock. 'Abused? By Lawrence?'

Cindy nodded. 'Yes. Murray told me that he saw his father hit his mother and leave her bleeding on the bathroom floor, and shortly after that incident Rose left. For many years, poor Murray felt that his mother had gone because he couldn't protect her.'

'That's terrible! He was just a little boy then, wasn't he?' said Babs indignantly.

Cindy nodded and took a sip of iced tea. 'I guess you can understand why Rose left, can't you, since you left Howard for the same reason,' said Cindy. 'But I still just can't imagine leaving my child.'

Babs pursed her lips. 'Cindy, it wasn't an easy decision for me to leave. Howard was violent and, although I felt I had no choice other than to go, I often felt guilty that I had deprived Joey of his father.'

'Does Joey know about the abuse?'

Babs nodded. 'We've spoken about it. He doesn't blame me for leaving. A lot of women can't leave. Many stay in violent and unhappy marriages because they think that staying is best for the family. Some women think it's their fault. And many women are just too frightened and haven't anywhere to go.'

'But you managed to leave,' said Cindy.

Babs shook her head. 'I did, but it's not always easy to be able to get out. Money is always an issue. Remember, it took me the best part of a year of planning before I went.' Babs's eyes were wet, her voice soft. 'I think Rose must have been very brave to leave, especially as she knew she was giving up her son, so she must have felt she had no other choice.'

Cindy was quiet for a moment. 'You're right,' she said finally.

313

Babs studied Cindy. 'How can you continue to associate with Lawrence? How can you trust your children to be around him when you know he can be violent?'

'I felt much better after we moved out of the big house,' said Cindy. 'And Lawrence has been somewhat different these past few years. Not warm or friendly, but not rude to me like he used to be. It's like he knows I have his number and have seen through the façade. He's done the best he can for Murray and I do believe deep down he loves his grandchildren.'

Babs nodded thoughtfully. 'Just the same, be careful of him, Cindy. Men like him . . .' She trailed off. 'Just be careful, that's all.'

Suddenly, Babs coughed hard and held a papery hand up to her face. Cindy noticed she was trembling.

'Are you all right, Babs?' Cindy asked, concerned. She reached over to Babs, but her aunt waved Cindy away.

'Just feeling a bit worn out. I think I'll take a nap.'

Cindy watched Babs's retreating back. Her aunt was sicker than she was admitting.

*

Joey and his family arrived the next day from San Bernardino, where he worked as a realtor. The cousins were overjoyed to see each other. Cindy was amazed to be confronted by a tall, handsome man and found it hard to believe this was the sweet little boy she'd shared Babs's house with all those years ago. Kelly, or as Joey called her, My Lovely Lady, was a pretty sylph with long blonde hair cascading down her back. She wore bold-patterned, flared bell-bottomed pants and a contrasting vest, and had silver and gold chains and big hoop earrings. Compared to the power suits, the punk look and the newest trend to wear exercise clothes around in public – a particular abhorrence of Alice's – Kelly looked comfortable and casual in a late hippy sort of way.

'Kids, say hi to Cousin Cindy,' said Joey to his two small children. The children stared shyly at Cindy, who gave them a quick embrace, as well as the two toy koalas she'd brought from Australia for them.

Joey kissed his mother gently, studying her, giving her a raised eyebrow and a questioning look. She flicked him away with a smile.

'I'm doing just fine, honey. It's so wonderful having Cindy here.'

They settled around the living room.

Kelly unpacked a basket of food she'd brought and Joey poured drinks as the children huddled around their grandmother, telling her their latest exploits and achievements at school.

Some time later, Joey and Cindy found themselves in the kitchen.

'Is life good?' asked Cindy.

'Yes. Except I worry about Mom. I know it means a lot to her that you came. I'm so glad you did.' He smiled. 'I try to visit her every week or so, but it's hard doing that, what with work and Kelly's Master in Environmental Science. Sometimes we have to do a lot of juggling.'

'I can understand that,' said Cindy. 'Goodness, I don't think I've ever heard of a degree in environmental science. What will Kelly do with it? Are there jobs in that field?'

'You bet. Sadly, in a way, it's a growing job market. Remember that huge oil spill off Santa Barbara?'

'Yes, of course. I read about it. The beach was unusable for ages. I had so many happy memories of that beach. It was a terrible thing,' Cindy replied.

'Kelly remembered it too, and Earth Day inspired her to work towards protecting the environment and not just exploiting it. She's quite passionate about it.'

'What about you, Joey? I would never have picked you to go into something like real estate.'

315

'Yeah, me either. But it pays the bills. I'm working on other things. I helped make a documentary that went around the festival circuit.'

'You did! How come Babs never told me?'

He shrugged. 'I was the third banana, so it was no big deal, but I learned a lot. You remember how much I loved the movies? I'm doing a cinema course, and I'm writing a film script. And Kelly and I are both involved in the local theatre group.'

Cindy playfully punched her cousin in the arm. 'Well, good for you, Joey! You sound very busy. I hope I'm invited to your big movie premiere one day.' Suddenly Cindy felt as though she was treading water. Here was Joey involved in exciting projects, and her life seemed monotonous and unexciting in comparison.

'You make me feel guilty. Lazy even. When I go back home I'll have to look for a more exciting interest than playing tennis and going to CWA meetings,' she told Joey.

'Talk to Kelly. I bet there are environmental issues happening in Australia right now. You should look into it.'

Cindy nodded. 'Okay, I will. It's a whole new area for me,' said Cindy. 'I feel like I missed the civil rights movement of the sixties and the Vietnam protests of the seventies entirely, so it would be good to get on the ground floor of something worthwhile.'

'Cin, you're too hard on yourself. From what Mom has told me over the years, you've raised a good family and worked hard with Murray on your property. So I think you've done very well.'

There was no doubting the truth of that, Cindy thought, but all the same, Joey had given her food for thought. It was about time she took up something new.

*

Cindy had decided to visit her father in Spokane for a couple of days, and then return to Palm Springs before heading back to Australia. Although the meeting with her elderly father and stepmother was brief, Cindy was glad she'd made the effort. She was pleased, too, that her father made time to take her to lunch alone, and although there were awkward pauses, they caught up on each other's news. Cindy was quietly delighted when she realised that her father was proud of her achievements. When Cindy extended an invitation for her father and stepmother to visit her in Australia, however, Lisa recoiled in horror at the thought of travelling so far from Spokane. Cindy's father had seemed only marginally more interested.

Cindy did, however, muster the courage to ask if he could pass on to her any small items which had belonged to her mother to give to Sally, and her father had found a small brooch to give to his granddaughter.

When Cindy returned to Palm Springs, she thought Babs seemed a bit weaker.

'Nonsense,' said Babs. 'Your imagination is running away with you. I'm just fine. You know how good this climate is for your health.'

On the final day of her holiday, Cindy had lunch with Alice and Spencer. Babs declined the invitation, saying that she could catch up with her sister any time.

Spencer took them to one of Palm Springs's hot new restaurants, and as Cindy looked around at the stylish and trendy décor before choosing her meal from the extensive menu, she momentarily yearned for places like this closer to her home.

'It would be nice to be able to come to a place like this whenever you wanted to,' she said wistfully.

'You're very unfortunate in that regard,' said Spencer. 'Living in a place as remote as Kingsley Downs does have

317

its drawbacks. Beer, steak, eggs and chips, as you call them, had Alice in a state.' He laughed at the memory.

'All the same, you made the right choice. It could all have been very different. In fact, I think you've been very lucky,' said Alice, with a sideways glance at Spencer. He shook his head.

'Of course I did. Why would you think otherwise?' asked Cindy, looking from one to the other, confused.

Spencer and Alice exchanged another glance and Spencer rolled his eyes and waved his hand indicating for Alice to speak.

'Remember Robbie Wilson?' she said. 'Turned into a first-class lawyer, working out of San Francisco. Well, he died quite recently.' She paused dramatically. 'And from what Spencer has heard, it was from that disease that *homosexuals* get. AIDS, I think it's called.'

Cindy gaped, looking from Alice to Spencer in shock as the truth sank in. Spencer nodded without meeting her eye. She didn't know what to say. Poor Robbie, dead at such a comparatively young age. Someone she'd thought so wonderful, and who, for a brief time, had broken her heart. She was filled with confusion. If Robbie Wilson had been gay, as they called it now, how had she fitted into his life?

As if to answer that question, Alice said indignantly, 'I always thought there was something odd about that boy. You were fortunate to get away from him. I just don't understand people like that. There is obviously something very wrong with them. How could you have got mixed up with such a person? I think his type is quite disgusting.' She sniffed and wiped the table in front of her with her napkin, as if she suddenly felt unclean.

'Alice, you really liked him! He was a good man. It doesn't matter who he loved – man or woman,' Cindy said sharply. 'And he left me, not the other way around.'

318

'Well, I think it's just not *normal*,' said Alice vehemently.

Suddenly Cindy understood. Robbie had dated her because he needed to appear to be a part of 'normal' society. Perhaps he had even been trying to convince himself. But in the end, he must have accepted who he really was and so he had walked away from her. It would have taken courage to do that. There was also the fact that had Robbie not dropped her in the manner he did, she might never have fallen in love with Murray.

She was aware that Alice was staring at her. She gave a small shrug. 'I'm very sorry to hear that. It's a terrible way to die. He was a lovely person.'

Alice looked as though she was about to answer back when Spencer lifted his menu. 'Anyway, let's order,' he said, clearly wanting to move on from the uncomfortable topic.

In the car on the way home, Cindy found herself thinking of Robbie again. She hoped he had found someone who'd also taken the brave step of admitting who they really were and whom they loved. She hoped he'd been happy.

*

Babs and Cindy spent a last quiet night together. Cindy made a simple salad and poached chicken breasts. Babs didn't seem to enjoy eating anything too complicated. As they had dinner, Cindy told her aunt what she had just learned about Robbie.

'How very sad,' said Babs. 'You were so upset when he dropped you, but at least now you can understand why.'

'And then along came Murray,' said Cindy, with a smile.

'Yes, indeed,' said Babs quietly. 'He was handsome and charming. I was surprised he'd never been married before. And once he saw you, I knew he was totally smitten. Someone like me didn't stand a chance!' Babs chuckled quietly.

'Babs! What do you mean?'

'Oh, nothing at all, now. But I remember at the time that I was rather impressed by him. Of course, I had no desire to race off to Australia, so it was no more than a passing interest.' She gave a wan smile. 'I'm so pleased you had the courage to marry him and take off to the other side of the world! I doubt I would have.'

'It was a pretty reckless decision,' Cindy said.

'But it turned out to be the right one,' Babs said, patting her hand.

The next day, Cindy found it difficult to say goodbye to her aunt. Babs was firm and strong, though what it cost her Cindy wasn't sure.

Babs took Cindy by the shoulders and looked deep into her eyes. 'Remember, you have a family, and they are the lucky ones. There's too many who aren't so fortunate. I love you, and I hope you hurry back to see me again. I know you and Joey will always be close, just the way we have been. Now, I want you to just drive away, like you did when you were heading back to college, always happy, never looking back.'

'Babs . . . I . . .' Cindy was close to tears as she held Babs's thin, weightless hands.

'None of that, my girl. I'll be here waiting for you next time you visit.' And, with surprising strength, Babs nudged her towards the door. Cindy picked up her bag, opened the door and stepped outside. Babs gently closed the door behind her.

Cindy quickly drove away, knowing Babs would be watching, but around the corner she stopped, pulled over and, resting her head on the steering wheel, wept.

*

As Murray drove her home from the airport, he kept reaching out to touch her.

'I missed you. Are you glad you went?'

Cindy was glad to see her husband again too. 'I am, I really am. Babs assures me that she is in remission, but I don't know how long it will last. She puts on a brave face, but she seems to be getting weaker and weaker.'

Swiftly, Cindy sank back into her normal life, back to conversations about lamb sales, the price of the wool clip and the latest tales from the Wool Board. Lawrence always seemed to be going somewhere on business in his plane. There was a feeling of heightened energy about Kingsley Downs, as though the pace of life had suddenly been notched up a gear.

The seasons passed. One day, Cindy was sitting outside with her mid-morning coffee, soaking up the warmth of the sun and admiring her roses, now in full bloom. At quiet times like this, she often thought about Babs. Her cancer had returned and, although she was staying positive, Cindy couldn't help but worry.

The phone rang and she put down her cup and hurried inside. There was an echo on the line as she answered, and suddenly she went cold. It was an international call.

'Cin, it's Joey . . .' Her cousin's voice faltered.

'Oh, Joey. No. No . . . it's Babs . . . isn't it?'

'Yes, she died an hour ago. Peacefully at home. Kelly and I were with her.'

Cindy's throat constricted and she choked on the words. 'Oh, Joey . . . I'm so sorry. Are you okay?'

'I'm . . .' His voice broke. 'She loved you very much.'

Cindy felt the tears running down her face. 'I know. I loved her too. Is Alice all right? I should come over for the funeral . . .'

'No, Alice told me to tell you not to. Mom left instructions to keep things simple. She was a no-fuss person, as you know.'

'I feel so empty,' said Cindy. 'Joey, we must see more of each other. Bring the children out to visit. We'd so love to have you.'

'We'll talk about it, Cin. Kelly and the children send their love.'

There was little more to say. Cindy hung up the phone and walked back outside.

But it seemed now that the roses had faded and the sun had lost its warmth.

10

THE SMALL WHITE DOT slowly enlarged and grew into the angular shape of Lawrence's plane. The indistinct buzz of the engine grew louder.

'Here they come,' sighed Mrs Flowers, her forehead dusted with flour, looking from her kitchen window across the paddocks towards the property's little airstrip. 'I do hope everything is to his liking. I've never known Mr Parnell to fuss so much about what I serve for morning tea!'

Cindy nodded and then peered out the window to the driveway, looking for the two or three visitors who were coming by car. They'd flown into Deniliquin that morning because they couldn't land their plane on Lawrence's rough strip. Murray was anxious that this visit should go off without a hitch, hence Cindy's presence at the big house.

Over the last few years, Cindy had felt less hostility than she once had when she was in Lawrence's house or in his presence. Although she could not forget – or forgive – the behaviour that must have driven Rose from the house, Cindy recognised that, over time, Lawrence had mellowed. While there would never be real warmth between them, she had to acknowledge that he loved his grandchildren. He was generous towards them, and always seemed to enjoy their company, especially that of the boys, and he'd been the proud grandfather at Sally's wedding the previous year.

Cindy spied a flurry of dust in the distance. 'Looks like our guests are right on time.'

Murray had told Cindy that the head of the Wool Corporation Board, the man whom Lawrence always referred to as the Emperor, was bringing some investors whom he described as 'novices in the wool game', to show them a well-regarded sheep station and get a few pointers before they headed off to some big sheep sales.

'Though it's their financial advisers who make all the decisions,' Murray had added.

In the past few years, wool had really boomed. Industry prices were at near record levels, helped by the bank and government guarantees. It seemed everyone wanted to get in on the act. Prices for top-quality breeding lines were going through the roof. In South Australia, a champion ram had been bought by an entrepreneur for close to a million dollars. Both Murray and Cindy had thought the price crazy.

Now Murray hurried into the kitchen, dressed in his best wool jacket and tie, his boots shining, the crease in his pants sharp. 'All set? Dad will drive his passengers up to the house and the car from Deni is coming up the drive.'

'So is it tea and scones first, or after the shearing demonstration and the wool classer?' asked Mrs Flowers, clearly flustered as she reorganised the scones yet again. 'These visitors must be very important for Mr Parnell to go to the expense of hiring shearers and bringing in a wool classer for a couple of hours.'

'I believe the morning tea will be after they've seen the woolshed demo. We'll play it by ear, Mrs F. Keep the scones warm. My father is keen to make a good impression with these businessmen,' said Murray as he hurried out.

'I'd better be on the welcoming committee with him,' said Cindy with a smile. She smoothed her skirt and her hair, adjusted her pearls and followed her husband outside, where a car was just pulling up in front of the house.

A driver in a dark suit opened the car doors and three men stepped from the vehicle. Murray moved forward and shook hands, introducing himself and then Cindy.

'Mr Packer, Mr Elliot, and Mr Price, this is my wife, Cindy.'

Cindy smiled a greeting at the men and assumed her role as hostess. 'Would you care to freshen up inside, gentlemen? There's tea, coffee, or a cold drink,' she said.

'My father's plane has just landed and he's driving over to the house now with our other guests,' added Murray.

'Take us over to the woolshed. We can meet them there and just get on with things,' said the large man in dark glasses, moleskin pants and an expensive jumper.

The other visitors also wore graziers' outfits similar to Murray's, but their hats were new and their boots stiff and uncreased, their manner similarly brusque and businesslike.

'Of course,' said Murray. 'Hop in the ute and we'll head over there.'

As they drove away, Cindy turned to the driver standing by the car. 'Would you like a cup of tea? They'll be ages at the shed.'

The driver nodded gratefully.

'Yes, thanks,' he said and he followed Cindy onto the verandah where the elaborate morning tea had been set out.

At least the driver has manners, Cindy thought ruefully, as she poured out some tea.

*

Less than two hours later, the visitors left, leaving Mrs Flowers's cakes and scones untouched.

Three of the men returned to Deniliquin airport, while Lawrence planned to fly on to Bathurst with the other two.

'How did all that go?' Cindy asked Murray, as they drove back to their house later that day.

'All right, I guess. They were just businessmen. They aren't interested in life on the land and how hard we have to work to achieve our successes. They're interested in the quickest way to make money out of wool and are only prepared to invest in projects they think will bring them a fast return.' He sighed. 'I suppose it's true that we're on the land to make money, too, but somehow they seemed so nakedly mercenary about their motives that it made me feel uncomfortable. And it's a shame about Mrs Flowers's morning tea! She went to so much trouble.'

'I know. Never mind, darling,' said Cindy sympathetically. 'We probably won't ever meet them again, unless we run into them when we go down to Sydney in January for the Bicentenary celebrations.'

That afternoon, Shirley Jackson happened to drop in, no doubt curious about their important visitors.

Dressed in her tweed skirt and hand-knitted jumper, she was a bit more rotund than when Cindy had first met her, but she remained a kind and reliable neighbour. The photos she had once loved to show Cindy of her children, house and property had now been replaced by a Grandma's brag book, which she produced at every possible opportunity.

'I've got eight grandchildren now, and they're all just as cute as can be. Have I shown you the latest pictures of little Karen?' she asked, producing her book right on cue as Cindy offered her a cup of tea. Without waiting for an answer, Shirley whipped out the book and flipped to the end. 'That's her in the bath. Hasn't she got a lovely smile? I think it's just like her mother's. I've got a new photo of Sean, too. He's a lovely little chap. No idea where his red hair came from, but it does make him look cheeky, don't you think?'

As Cindy waited for the kettle to boil, Shirley prattled on, turning the pages of her little photo album.

Cindy passed her a piece of cake and a scone. Shirley chewed gratefully, still managing to highlight her grandchildren's achievements while downing the sweets.

'Mrs Flowers overdid the hospitality. I'll pack up a few more cakes for you to take home to Percy,' Cindy explained.

Shirley wiped her mouth with a napkin. 'Oh, thanks for that. Perce does like Mrs F's cakes. So, were these men just visiting, or here on business?' Shirley asked bluntly. 'We heard you had shearers and a wool classer here. Perce would have been happy to come and help.'

'It was fine, thanks,' said Cindy, happy to satisfy Shirley's curiosity. She explained that the men had come to get a general idea of how a sheep station was run. 'Really, they had no idea how the wool gets from a sheep to a suit.'

Shirley clicked her tongue. 'I'm not surprised. Lot of those types around these days, but that's good to know,' said Shirley, sounding relieved. 'Frankly, we were afraid Mr Parnell might have been selling up!'

'Gosh, no! I couldn't imagine Lawrence ever selling Kingsley Downs. I think he'd rather cut off his right arm,' said Cindy emphatically.

Shirley pursed her lips and reached for another scone. 'Well, land values are going up. Been a few properties around here that have gone for very good prices, as you know. My Perce says that he thinks it would be a good time to get off the land, if one had a mind to. He reckons that things can't keep rising like this.'

Cindy cocked her head. 'A lot of people think they will. Those men who were here today are really important people. They're in businesses like newspapers, cattle, minerals and goodness knows what else, but they're now diversifying into wool. They wouldn't be putting money into sheep if they didn't think it would make them money,' said Cindy.

Shirley didn't look impressed. 'Good for them, but my Perce is comfortable with how we're getting along, now that we're running some cattle as well as our sheep. We're nothing as big and fancy as Kingsley Downs, but we've been doing good enough. Mind you, Perce will be pleased when I tell him that Lawrence won't be selling up. Don't like seeing too much change around here.'

*

It was almost a week before Lawrence returned from Bathurst. Murray commented that his father seemed pleased with himself and had obviously enjoyed mixing with the movers and shakers from the big end of town. But Cindy was surprised when Murray mentioned the following day that the bank manager had been out to Kingsley Downs.

'Why do you think the bank manager was visiting?' she asked.

'Phil Watson and Dad get on well. It's not the first time he's been out to see Dad. It probably means nothing,' replied Murray, somewhat tersely.

He made no further comment, but Cindy sensed

Murray was worried. And later that evening she found him in his office, looking through some papers.

'Paperwork? At this hour?' she exclaimed.

'Ah, just catching up.'

Cindy sat down by his desk. 'What do you think he's planning now?'

'Who? Oh, you mean Dad . . . Well, I'm not privy to everything he does, Cin. He keeps telling me we're in fine shape. Which we are. Last season we had our best year ever.'

Cindy looked at her husband. 'But . . . ?'

He leaned back and gave her a small smile. 'Read me like a book, huh?' But then he looked concerned. 'It's the outlays. He's pretty keen about extending our investment here. Expanding the size of the place if suitable land becomes available, increasing the flock.'

Cindy frowned. 'Golly. Does Kingsley Downs have the capacity to carry more sheep?'

'I guess so, provided the weather stays good and we don't get another drought. My concern is that we're in this game for the long term, and those high-flying executive types he's mixing with are investors, looking for the quick buck. They know bugger-all about wool. They might be advised that wool is the hot thing to be in for the moment, but I think Dad is just flattered by their interest,' said Murray ruefully.

'So when do they get out?'

'Hopefully before the wool stockpile blows up. There must be millions of bales of wool stashed in various places around the country.'

Cindy was stunned. 'Millions of bales! How are they ever going to sell it off?'

'They're hanging on to it, building up an artificially high price. Greed, basically. Dad says they're hoping to get to a thousand cents a kilo. You know, Cin, Australian wool producers supply more than eighty per cent of the world's apparel wool, so where else are the overseas processors going to buy such suitable wool if they don't buy ours? Eventually they'll have to come around and pay the price the Wool Corp is asking. They haven't a lot of choice.'

Cindy stood up. 'That's madness! Pure greed. Oh dear. Well, I hope your father doesn't do anything silly. Try to talk to him, Murray.'

He looked at his hands. 'I can ask questions, but that's about it. He still holds the reins.'

'Yes, and you're doing all the work!' said Cindy in frustration. She crossed her arms. 'He rushes about in that plane big-noting himself. It's so unlike him. He's always been so particular about every tiny thing around Kingsley Downs. I guess it shows he trusts you to keep on top of it.'

'He's almost eighty years old. I don't begrudge him enjoying himself a bit, Cin.'

'*Hmph*. I think there's more to it. I think he's up to something with these businesspeople; he's not the playboy type,' said Cindy, her eyes narrowed.

Murray leaned back in his chair, rubbing his eyes. 'Anyway, enough of Dad. What arrangements have you made for our holiday in January for the Bicentennial celebrations? I'm really looking forward to it.' He reached forward and pulled Cindy into his lap.

Cindy grinned. 'I've found a big apartment in Neutral Bay which will comfortably fit us all, and it has great views of Sydney Harbour. So we can have all the family together to watch the celebrations. It'll be a once in a lifetime event.'

Murray kissed her neck gently. 'Yep. It's going to be huge. I guess Australia only gets a two-hundredth birthday once,' he said, releasing Cindy.

Cindy stood up and smoothed her hair. 'I've been reading that the Aboriginals don't see it that way, and I can't blame them for being outraged. After all, the arrival of the First Fleet was the beginning of the end for their civilisation,' she commented. 'My American Indian friends from Palm Springs view the coming of the Europeans in exactly the same way.'

'Well, at least the PM has quashed the idea of a re-enactment. I think that the replacement idea of having a fleet of tall ships sail up the coast and then enter the harbour sounds spectacular.' Murray paused, frowning. 'I have to say, though, a lot of blacks do get a raw deal and their living standards in some places are terrible, but I'm not sure about giving them their own land, at least not mine. As far as I'm concerned, no one has any right to this land but us Parnells. We've worked for years to develop this property, and I don't want anyone taking it away from us,' Murray said with some heat.

Cindy took her husband's hand.

'Darling, I am sure that would never happen.'

*

Two weeks later, Cindy and Murray were having morning tea in the kitchen when the phone rang. Cindy heard Murray talking to his father.

'Yeah, righto, yes, I can hear you. Where are you? What do you mean? Ah. I see . . . Okay, I'll meet you at the hayshed. What've you bought? Right . . . okay. So how long . . . ? See ya.'

'What was all that about?' Cindy broke open a warm scone.

Murray walked back in, a dumbfounded expression on his face. 'That was Dad on the phone.'

'I gathered that.'

'From his damn car!'

Cindy nearly spat out her tea. 'What?'

'He now has a portable phone in the Jag! Said he went to the sales and he's bought a ram.'

'Did you know he was getting another ram? When is it coming?' Lawrence's behaviour was getting more and more erratic.

Murray shook his head. 'No. I didn't. He's bringing it in now. Wants to acclimatise the thing in the barn. He must have someone with him who's followed him up with it.'

'Was it a spur-of-the-moment buy? Why does he want to put it out in the shed?' asked Cindy. Without waiting for answers, she continued, 'Well, you said he wanted to improve the bloodlines of Kingsley Downs, and I expect this ram is part of that.'

'We generally do this sort of thing together,' grumbled Murray, as he glanced at his watch. 'He's twenty minutes away. A car phone. What bloody next?'

*

As Murray swung into the old truck, Cindy followed him.

'I'm coming too. I want to see this new animal. And the car phone. I bet both have cost a fortune.'

They drove past the woolshed and over to the large tin shed where hay and grain were stored. Lawrence's Jaguar was parked to one side and he was standing beside it, looking impatient. The jackaroo roared up on his motorbike to join him.

Murray parked as Lawrence signalled to him.

'Give us a hand,' he called.

'What's up? Where's the truck?'

'I wasn't leaving this fellow to some carrier.' Lawrence started gesticulating to the jackaroo.

'What the hell . . . ?' Murray stopped as Cindy joined him.

'What's going on?' she asked.

'Look,' said Murray, as he moved forward to help the jackaroo.

'Good heavens,' gasped Cindy.

Lawrence had removed part of the back seat of the Jag, and sitting on a blanket on the leather was a huge disgruntled ram.

'Look at the size of the thing!' Cindy had never seen such a huge sheep.

'Careful with those ties I've had to use to strap him in. Didn't want him to move around,' said Lawrence by way of explanation. 'Now, go easy getting him out of the Jag. Easier if I'd taken the ute to the sales, but I didn't know I'd be buying this champion. He's far too valuable to leave for anyone else to transport, so I brought him home myself.'

'Did you drive straight through? I thought you were staying the night in Wagga,' said Murray, as he and the jackaroo eased the ram out of the elegant car.

'Oh, I did,' replied Lawrence with a rare grin. 'I asked the girl at the motel where I could stable my car. She looked at the Jag and said, "I see why you'd want that car under cover." And I said, "It's not the car that I'm concerned about. It's the passenger in the back."' And to Cindy's amazement, Lawrence actually laughed.

As the superb ram got to its feet and shook itself indignantly, Murray ran his hand over its head, parting the wool along its back. He straightened up and looked at his father.

'He's a good 'un, isn't he?' said Lawrence, obviously pleased with himself.

'How much did you pay for this animal?' Murray asked.

Lawrence watched the jackaroo lead the ram into the shed. 'Put him into the pen we use to treat any sick sheep,' he called after him. 'Put up the rails and tether him there. Give him a feed and water and let him settle down.' He glanced at Cindy and then at Murray.

As Cindy went over to look at the ram, she heard Lawrence say, 'You'll probably read about it in *The Land*, so I'll tell you. I paid $160,000 for that ram. He's called

Hercules Two and he's from a good old line. Very docile. His progeny will return us money in no time.'

'Bit of an impulsive buy, wasn't it?' remarked Murray drily.

'Maybe, son, but I know what I'm doing.'

*

That night Murray poured himself a stiff Scotch and sat down opposite Cindy.

'I hope that ram is nice and snug,' said Cindy.

'Yes. Might be a bit cold tonight.' Murray looked at her and they both burst out laughing.

'Still, it's an awful lot of money,' said Cindy. 'Is he worth it?'

'It's a pretty famous bloodline. Linked right back to the Peppins. But to make it worthwhile, you've got to see a lot of bang for your buck . . . so to speak.' Murray took a sip of his drink. 'I'm not sure if Dad has a plan; I think this was just an impulsive purchase, and that's unusual for Dad. He's always taken time to think things through in the past.' Murray frowned. 'I have to say this wool boom has really gripped him. But I don't think Dad would ever do anything to put Kingsley Downs at risk.'

'I know that some of the other landowners around here are diversifying, even the Jacksons. Running a few cattle and such. Do you think Lawrence would do that?' Cindy asked.

'Dad's a wool man through and through. I don't think he'd want to change. But he's heading off somewhere again tomorrow. I'm babysitting Hercules. Talk about a fortune on four legs. I hope the ewes are as impressed with him as Dad was.'

'Oh dear, what if they want nothing to do with him?' Cindy giggled, but Murray didn't laugh.

*

That year, Russell was the only one of the children to come home for Christmas. Sally and Ashley were spending it with Ashley's parents and Gordon was unable to get the time off from the cattle station where he was working, so it was a relatively quiet time.

However, Cindy's Christmas present from Lawrence was a stunning surprise. When they all went over to Lawrence's place for Christmas dinner, there under the traditional Christmas tree was an envelope marked 'Cynthia', and in it were two tickets to the huge Bicentennial Fashion Extravaganza at the Sydney Opera House, to be hosted by the Chairman of the Wool Corporation and whose guests of honour were Prince Charles and Princess Diana.

'Good heavens!' Cindy exclaimed, and she read the invitation out to Murray. '*Presented by the Wool Corporation and the International Wool Secretariat to showcase Australia's ultrafine Merino wool in an haute couture show featuring collections from the world's top nine fashion designers on the same runway.* Murray! Princess Diana. Think of it! What will I wear? Did you know about this?'

Murray shook his head. 'Well, I knew about the show, and I mentioned it to Dad, because of his being on the board, and asked if it would be possible to get tickets. He said they were scarce and expensive, but he obviously managed to get some.'

'Well, it's certainly a lovely surprise, so thanks for planting the seed. It's so nice of your father. Oh goodness, wait till I tell Alice! She will be pea green with envy.'

*

Indeed, the trip to Sydney and the Bicentennial celebrations was a time Cindy would never forget. The gala evening was a particular standout. Cindy let her head go and bought a very expensive gown from one of Sydney's most fashionable boutiques. She didn't care if she'd never have the opportunity to wear the dress again, but she was gratified when Murray gave a very appreciative whistle when she put it on.

'You look very handsome yourself,' she said to Murray, who was in his evening suit. 'We might have been married for more than twenty-five years, but I think you still look pretty good when you get dressed up, too.'

The Opera House had been beautifully decorated for the occasion and was swarming with the press. Cindy was thrilled to see the couture clothes from some of the biggest names in the fashion world: Versace, Donna Karan, Jean Muir and Oscar de la Renta. But it was Princess Diana who stole the show. To Cindy she looked more beautiful in person than she was in her photos, and she seemed to enjoy herself immensely. Cindy admired her midnight-blue ballerina-length dress and two-toned shoes decorated with little pink polka dots. 'How absolutely perfect,' Cindy whispered to Murray.

As the evening wore on and Cindy watched Princess Diana chatting with designer Jean Muir, she couldn't help but remember Alice's pool-side fashion parades in Palm Springs. She had thought those so thrilling, but they paled in comparison with this evening. She would have loved to hear Alice's commentary on this avant-garde show.

*

Before she knew it, summer was waning. Cindy clung to every moment of those fading days where the heat cooled at sundown and the light softly lingered.

The seasons were so different from those of her childhood in Spokane, where fall and spring were definite events with a personality and time frame. There, days lengthened and shortened, gardens wilted, filled with gold and russet, or turned from bare and stark to soft hazy green. Spring and fall were a brief interlude to prepare for the coming heat or chill. Here, it seemed to Cindy, one morning was overpoweringly hot, while the next brought a looming frost.

Just as Rose had created a small sitting room in the big house, which gave a serene view across the paddocks towards the setting sun, so Cindy had enclosed a section of the verandah she called the Sundowner Room in her new house. Here she and Murray, family and friends, could gather to watch the sunset. In the height of summer, they could lower the slotted bamboo blinds, turn on the fans and pretend they were in Asia.

On one late summer evening, as the last rays of the sun faded, Cindy put her needlepoint to one side, picked up her gin and tonic and let the dying light of the day soothe her.

'Hey, Mum, can I join you?' a familiar voice called to her.

Cindy looked up to see her son approaching her. 'Gordon! What a lovely surprise, of course you may. Have you got an early mark?'

'Dad and I got through the job faster than we thought. I'm about to get stuck into some work on my computer. I'm not disturbing you, am I?'

'Not at all,' said Cindy gladly. She was delighted that Gordon was back home fulltime now, learning the ropes from his father and grandfather and staking his own claim to Kingsley Downs. 'Why don't you stay and have a quick sundowner? How's the work going on that breeding program? I must say, while it seems a bit complicated, your spreadsheets and charts are a lot more comprehensive than the coloured pins in the chart behind your father's office door,' said Cindy with a smile.

'Computer programs are the way of the future,' said Gordon, pouring himself a beer. 'Ewes are pretty reliable

337

at giving birth, but it helps if you can put in the variables, like unpredictable weather, pasture growth, fecundity, and so on. It's easier to keep track of them in a computer that flags things. I'm also making sure the younger ewes are with some of the older ones to learn the ropes, as it were. Plus we're thinking of putting up special shelters for the ewes, in case the coming winter is a harsh one.'

They chatted quietly before Murray came in and joined them. Listening to father and son discuss plans, probabilities and possibilities, the old dog and the young pup wanting to try out new ideas, Cindy felt a rush of contentment.

Later, when Gordon had gone to finish his work on his computer, she asked Murray, 'When you were Gordon's age, did you have as many new ideas and plans as he does?'

Murray shook his head. 'Not really. As far as I was concerned, Dad's way, like his father's, was tried and true, but once someone else started doing something different and it worked, everyone copied it.'

'I don't think shearing will ever change. Do you? There's no way a machine or chemicals could get a fleece off a sheep better than those brawny men in their navy singlets with those sweeping, steady hands,' said Cindy. 'It still fascinates me. It's like a ballet; pull the beast out of the pen, onto the stand, buzz up the belly and in two minutes the whole fleece comes off in one piece and the animal is down the chute naked and stunned. And the fleece is floating onto the classing table.'

Murray smiled. 'Listen to you. I never thought you'd take such an interest. Gordon is proving to be good with the wool classing. Jack Turner, who comes with the contractor and gun shearers most years, is pretty pleased with him. Takes a lot to impress a wool expert like him.'

'Just the same, Gordon does have a few ideas of his

own. I hope you and Lawrence hear him out. Your father is very set in his ways.'

'Yeah, but I don't think it helps that Gordon keeps talking about running some cattle on Kingsley Downs,' said Murray. 'I'm not opposed to it – could be the right way to diversify – but well, you know Dad.'

*

Cindy was in her vegetable garden deciding what she'd plant for the coming season. She noticed the wire on the chook run had parted company with the frame and made a mental note to get Gordon or Murray to fix it.

Then she heard Murray calling her, and felt surprised that he had come back to the house so early, as lunch was still a long way off.

'What's up?' she said as she hurried to meet him.

'I've got news.' Murray was flushed. 'Come inside. I need a strong coffee. It's Dad. You're not going to believe what he's done. I'm in shock.'

'Try me,' said Cindy, following Murray into the kitchen and measuring out the coffee into the coffee pot.

'He's bought a wool property outside Bathurst!' Murray paced about the kitchen, his hands flying as he spoke. 'He looked at it when he flew those businessmen up there three months ago. Evidently one of them showed an interest in it, but the sale fell through and it came back onto the market. Now Dad's gone and bought it. It's craziness.'

Cindy's mouth dropped open. 'Why? Who's going to run it?'

'It has a manager of some sort already, apparently. Anyway, Dad says he's taking advantage of the wool price, and there's no suitable land going around here, so he's buying in Bathurst.'

'Is that wise?' asked Cindy worriedly.

Murray paused his pacing and put his hands on his head. 'I don't know. Dad isn't stupid, and Bathurst has a wonderful reputation for fine Merino wool, but Dad's always been hands-on. I'm not at all happy about leaving someone else to run a place we own,' said Murray, his voice stretched with anxiety. 'I bet it wasn't cheap and the one thing I did find out from Dad was that he has borrowed the money for the purchase in Swiss francs.'

Cindy blinked. 'You're joking. Why would he do that?'

'Because the interest rates for Swiss francs are way lower than the rate here. Evidently, Phil Watson told him that everyone was doing it. You can borrow more money because the repayments will be less than they would be in Australian dollars,' explained Murray.

Cindy shook her head. 'Well, I wouldn't know about that, but you said the bank manager was a long-time friend, so he's unlikely to lead your father astray.'

Murray crossed his arms. 'Cindy, I'm getting a bad feeling about all of this. I don't know how much debt Dad has put us in and I don't know what the place is really like. I'm pretty surprised that he didn't even mention it to me before going ahead. Maybe he thought I'd argue with him over borrowing foreign currency. But you know what? I'm going to drive up to Bathurst and check it out.' Hands on hips, Murray let out a long, aggrieved breath.

'Take Gordon with you, and you can share the driving. It'll save time,' Cindy suggested. 'I wouldn't mind coming, either.'

'Good idea. Maybe once we've seen the property, we can calm down.'

*

There was a tilted, faded sign reading *Mirooball Station* hanging on the fencepost beside a bleached sheep's skull.

The sign had been used for target practice and was studded with bullet holes. Murray turned into the station and drove along the rutted track that wound between neglected paddocks.

'Fences are crook,' commented Gordon.

They spotted two figures on horseback riding towards them, so Murray pulled over and got out.

An older man and a teenager reined in their horses.

'G'day.' The man leaned down and said sullenly, 'What are you doing here? This is private property.'

'My father has just bought this place, so we thought we'd come and have a look around. Are you Roger Fenton?' asked Murray.

'Nah. He's up at the shed. I'm just visiting. You plan on staying here?' the man asked.

'Depends,' said Murray.

The man gave a nod towards Cindy. 'The missus might find the accommodation a bit basic. Nigel let the place go. Hasn't been a woman on this place in years. Well, one that stayed.' He touched the brim of his hat. 'We'll be off then.' He nodded, kicked his horse and the two of them trotted away.

Murray drove on further, following the track uphill.

'Expansive views, but pretty exposed land,' said Cindy.

'Yes, totally open to the weather I'd say, gale-force winds and snow in winter, and hot enough in summer,' said Murray.

As they came over the crest of a ridge, the paddocks of the property stretched before them.

'Ah, civilisation,' commented Murray sardonically, surveying rusting car wrecks, old machinery and a wasteland of old sheep-dipping trenches where the grass had been poisoned from chemicals years before. There was a leaning corrugated-iron shed, its sun-cracked, slatted wooden door resting on a single hinge and blue-grey paint peeling off it in large scabs.

'Basic is putting it mildly,' said Cindy weakly. 'I hope Lawrence got a bargain with this place, because it certainly needs work.'

They drove further in silence. At the wooden, hand-hewn woolshed, which had seen better days, they got out and followed the sound of hammering until they came across a bearded man in an oilskin coat, with a greying ponytail.

'You must be Roger Fenton?' said Murray and, at a nod from the other man, Murray introduced himself. 'This is my wife, Cindy, and my son, Gordon.'

'Yeah, g'day.' Fenton put down the hammer and held out his hand. 'Come to check the place out, eh? Be good to see someone take this on properly. Plenty to do.'

'So, how many sheep is this place carrying?' asked Murray.

'Only a couple thousand, nowhere near what it could.'

'Seems a waste,' said Gordon.

'Lost a few lambs this season,' Fenton replied.

'Fences need fixing up, I see,' said Murray.

'It can be done. But the last few years were a battle for Nigel – the previous owner. You want me to run you round in the ute and fill yer in? How long yer stayin'? The main house is in that gully, bit more sheltered, like.'

Murray glanced at his watch. He looked at Cindy. 'Do you want to stay overnight?'

Cindy could tell Murray wanted to spend more time investigating the place. 'If there's somewhere to put our heads down and some food, I don't mind staying.'

'Yeah, but it's not fancy,' warned Fenton. 'When I said that I'd stay till the new people moved in, Nigel left the place as soon as it was sold. Walked off with hardly a word. Hard for him after all these years to see this place

342

go to someone else, not that he put a lot of work into it lately.'

'Why was that?' asked Murray.

Fenton pulled a tin out of his pocket and swiftly rolled a cigarette, talking as he did so. 'He had two sons. One didn't want to know about working. Used to hang around here with his mates, drinking and doing drugs. The other kid went to the city. Reckon between them, they cleaned the boss out of his money.' He lit his cigarette and inhaled deeply. 'Nigel's been here since he was a kid, but when his sons went feral, he sort of lost interest in the place. Started drinking himself, and that's when his missus left.'

'That's a sad story,' said Cindy.

'Don't get me wrong. Nigel Kelly worked damned hard, once. But at the end he just figured he wasn't relevant anymore, I guess.'

'I see,' said Murray. 'I suppose that explains quite a bit. Maybe we'll head over to the main house before we look at the rest of the place, and a cup of tea wouldn't go astray.'

'Righto. Follow me.'

*

The house was a sad sight. It was made of local stone and mud bricks, but the wooden door and window frames had splintered and the corrugated-iron roof over the verandah was rusting and rattling. Faded chintz-covered chairs sagged along the verandah, no doubt sheltering mice or rats. A discarded fleece, studded with burrs, had been tossed in a corner.

The building crouched defensively against the landscape. Perhaps it had once been warm and welcoming inside, but in its current state Cindy found that hard to imagine. As if to accentuate its decrepitude, an unseen dog gave a desultory bark.

They waited for Fenton, who clumped up the steps and went indoors, shrugging off his coat.

'Kitchen's in there,' he said to Cindy, pointing. 'You'll find all yer need. No fresh milk, but there's tinned or long life. Now, there's a bit of an office down here. There's breeding records and such kept there.'

'Do you want a hand, Mum?' whispered Gordon.

She gave him a thumbs up. 'I can manage tea and there'll be a tin of biscuits for sure. But tell Dad that I've just looked in one of the bedrooms and there's no way I'm spending the night here. It's filthy beyond belief, and the sheets, if there are any, might walk off with me!'

Gordon nodded in agreement, giving her a wink and a smile.

*

As the sun began to go down, Murray announced they would head on into town for the night. He'd spent two hours going through the breeding records and had made notes. Now he tucked his notebook into his top pocket and headed for the car. A lone cricket gave a half-hearted chirp in the gathering gloom.

Fenton appeared and they thanked him.

'Can't say I blame you chaps for staying in town. I'm here for as long as yers want. The clearing sale is next Saturday. I believe your father organised it. Anything you saw you want kept?'

They shook their heads. The machinery was old and obsolete and there was nothing in the house of any value.

'I guess the stock are the main asset,' said Murray. 'Any wild dogs around?'

'Some. And blasted feral cats. Big as dogs, some of them. You see them yellow eyes at night, gives me the creeps.'

'Shoot them. Or set baits. Keep them away from the sheep. And fix the bloody fences.'

Cindy asked about a toilet.

'Ah, the indoor plumbing isn't crash hot. Use the dunny out the back,' advised Fenton.

Cindy headed around the back to find that the outdoor toilet had a magnificent view across the open expanse of paddocks, because its door was lying on the yellowed grass. She tiptoed past, thinking it could well be sheltering a large snake. She paused as she spied a peppercorn tree with an old refrigerator on its side beneath it. Cartons and boxes of rubbish that had never been taken away lay scattered about. She shook her head sadly.

'Dad, the place is a mess. What'd Grandfather pay for it?' asked Gordon, as they drove away from Mirooball Station.

'Damned if I know, but with a lot of hard work, the place could be made to pay. I think it certainly has the potential to give us a good return . . . eventually,' said Murray wearily. 'I'm ready for a beer and a meat pie.'

'Me too,' chorused Cindy and Gordon.

*

In the following weeks, Murray became resigned to the fact that a lot of work was needed to fix up Mirooball. He and Lawrence decided to let Fenton go and they dispatched Gordon to start getting the place sorted. Murray was loath to spend much money on the property initially, but he did want Gordon to make repairs to the fences and clean up the old house so that it was habitable.

Gordon checked in with his parents regularly, and admitted he was a bit lonely.

'It snows here in winter, so I'm thinking of planting a wind-break around a couple of the home paddocks, but that will take years to grow. I might get a decent horse. Easier to get round this rugged country on a horse than a bike.'

'Why don't you take a break and come home to see us?' asked Cindy. 'Russell and Sally and Ashley are coming for the long weekend.'

'I'm tempted, but frankly I don't like leaving the place. Mirooball has a bit of a reputation for parties, music raves and camping here with drugs and so on, thanks to the previous owner. I don't think he cared much what went on, but I do.'

'Well, we miss you. Come when you can.'

Cindy was used to being without her children now, and over time had become involved in many causes. Just recently she had heard about some people in Victoria who called themselves Landcare and who were working to stop land degradation in their area. After her conversation about the environment with Kelly in Palm Springs, Cindy made herself known to these Victorians and was impressed by their work in restoring waterways, stopping soil erosion and halting soil salinity. She had decided to set up a similar group in her own catchment area. Her ambition entailed a lot of meetings, persuasion and time.

She was sitting at her little desk just off the kitchen one morning, looking at her diary to plan the coming week's meetings, when the phone rang and her daughter's voice greeted her.

'Sal! How lovely to hear from you. How are you both?'

'The usual – busy! Ashley sends his love.'

They chatted for a few minutes, then Sally said, 'Mum, actually, the reason I'm ringing is that I have some news for you. I wanted to save the big announcement till I saw you and Dad in person, but I just can't wait . . . I'm pregnant!'

Cindy shrieked and jumped up and down, happy tears springing into her eyes. 'Oh, Sal, how wonderful! How long have you known?'

Sally laughed. 'I've been dying to tell you for ages, but I thought I'd just be sure everything is okay, and it is.

Ashley is going to tell his parents . . . but I wanted you to know first. You're going to be a grandmother!'

'Sally, darling . . . I don't know what to think. I'm so thrilled. When's the baby due? Oh Sally, oh my, a baby, a grandchild.' Cindy brushed the tears of joy from her face. 'Oh, I wish Babs was here. I'll tell Jo as soon as I've hung up and I'll have to ring Aunt Alice.'

'Tell Alice what? What are you hatching now?' asked Murray, coming into the kitchen.

'Here, here! Murray, take the phone. Talk to Sally. Sal, I'm putting your father on, tell him, darling . . .'

Murray looked puzzled as he took the phone from Cindy, who put her arm around him as he started to speak to his daughter.

Then Murray's expression changed. He gave out a huge whoop and then rubbed his eyes with the back of his hand. 'My darling girl . . . that's such wonderful news! When is it due? Are you all right? I can't wait to see you.'

As Sally chatted to her father, Cindy poured two mugs of tea. As soon as Murray had finished speaking and hung up the phone, the two of them raised their mugs and gently clinked them.

'Grandparents, huh?' Murray leaned over and kissed his wife. 'You're the most beautiful grandmother I've ever seen.'

'I just can't wait to hold that baby. I am so excited. But it's so weird. I still feel twenty years old, although a little wiser, and yet I'm about to become a grandmother. Where has the time gone, Murray?' she said wistfully.

Murray shook his head. 'No idea. But they've been special years. Good and bad.' He looked at Cindy, still slim, a few strands of silver in her auburn curls, the lines in her face reflecting all the laughter and funny expressions he knew so well. 'You've stuck it out with me, Cin. Through everything. I wouldn't have made it without you,' he added in a husky voice. 'Things were so tough sometimes, I wouldn't have blamed you if you'd gone back home.'

'Murray, *this* is my home. Our home, our children's home.' She touched his face. 'I wouldn't change anything.'

Murray sipped his tea. 'You know what this means. Dad's going to be a great-grandfather. I wonder how he'll feel about that!'

'We should tell him. Let's go over tonight and take a bottle of the good port he likes, and you can tell him the news then,' suggested Cindy, suddenly flushed with goodwill.

*

In the car that evening, Murray reached for Cindy's hand.

'You know Dad isn't the effusive type, so don't expect a lot of hurrahs.'

'You don't have to tell me that. I know he's never been one to heap praise on you, but he is proud of his grandchildren in his own way,' admitted Cindy.

Lawrence greeted them politely, shaking Murray's hand and nodding at Cindy with an almost gracious, 'Good evening, Cynthia.' He was dressed in immaculately creased slacks and a cashmere sweater over the R.M. Williams shirt.

He led the way into the small sitting room he favoured, where crystal glasses and a decanter were set out. Murray handed him the bottle of good port.

'I brought over the special edition.'

Lawrence raised an eyebrow. 'This is the Christmas bottle. Are we celebrating something?'

'Well, actually, yes we are.' Murray put his hand on his father's shoulder and said with a smile, 'Dad, you're going to be a great-grandfather.'

'Sally is pregnant,' added Cindy.

Lawrence's eyes closed for a second and his mouth twitched in a suppressed smile. The fleeting expression on his face caught Cindy by surprise. *It seems that Sally's news has really pleased him*, she thought. Then Lawrence clapped Murray on the back, and pumped his hand.

'Well, that is wonderful news indeed, son. Quite a pleasant surprise. I hadn't considered that I would ever reach this status. Of course, it means you'll be a grandfather – how do you feel about that?'

Murray smiled broadly. 'Just amazing. Cindy and I were just saying we still feel as young as ever. You too, Dad. You're damned fit for your age.'

Lawrence began pouring the port. 'Age is immaterial. It's what you do with your time that counts. Are we likely to see Sally anytime soon?'

'She and Ashley are coming home for the long weekend, so you'll see her then. Russell is coming home for a few days, too.'

'And Gordon?'

'He says not,' said Cindy firmly, before Lawrence could mutter about him leaving the new station. 'He's been very conscientious about looking after Mirooball.'

'Cold place, Bathurst. Snows in winter. Might need coats for the sheep,' said Lawrence calmly. 'And boots.'

'Coats and boots?' said Cindy incredulously.

Murray laughed. 'It's been a bit of a fad in some areas to stick blue plasticised fabric on the sheep to keep the fleeces cleaner.'

The men chatted a bit longer about business and wool matters. Cindy listened out of politeness and sipped her port. Expensive it might be, but she found it rather sickly. She glanced around the room, which hadn't changed since the day she'd first arrived at Kingsley Downs as a bride. She thought fleetingly of Rose, the forgotten person in the celebrations.

Murray drained his glass. 'Well, we'd better get back, Dad. We just wanted to share the good news with you right away.'

They all got to their feet and Lawrence shook Murray's hand.

'Kind of you, son. Congratulations all round. I hope things progress well. I'll have to have a think about some appropriate gift when the time comes. Good night, Cynthia.'

*

As the weeks passed, everyone slipped back into their usual routines.

Cindy kept in regular touch with Sally, asking about her progress, monitoring every checkup and twinge and offering suggestions for morning sickness, although her daughter had none, as well as ideas for decorating the nursery.

Finally Murray suggested that Cindy should drive down to Melbourne and spend some time with her daughter. The trip meant a lot to Cindy. She'd never forget the moment when her daughter reached for her mother's hand and placed it on her belly. Cindy could feel the fluttering movements of her first grandchild. It was the most joyous of moments.

'Would you rather a boy or a girl?' she asked.

'I don't care, Mum,' said Sally. 'I just want to have a healthy, happy baby. What comes, comes. Ash will be with me at the birth. I'm doing the Lamaze technique, so he can help me with the breathing while I'm in labour and keep me comfortable. I want to have as natural a birth as possible. And hopefully I'll be able to breastfeed for a year.'

Cindy shook her head in wonder. 'It's all very different from what your Dad and I went through. Your father wasn't allowed anywhere near me when I was giving birth. He wasn't even allowed to hold you until I left hospital.'

'That's barbaric,' exclaimed Sally. 'Especially after you miscarried in that bushfire.'

Cindy bit her lip. 'I sometimes still think of that little soul and it comforts me to feel that its spirit is still here at Kingsley Downs, with tokens of its birth still resting under the peppercorn tree in Adsila's bowl.' Cindy leaned over and kissed her daughter. 'But, darling, have no fear, you'll have a healthy, happy baby, I know it.'

Sally had decided to decorate the nursery in a circus theme and the two women spent days shopping for baby items. Even after Cindy returned home, there were frequent phone calls and long discussions over what type of stroller, carry basket, cot and bath should be bought.

Murray was amused by it all.

'Cin, if you ask me, the way you're going on about this baby, you'll end up like Shirley Jackson. Are you going to have a Grandma's brag book as well?' he asked one evening over dinner.

Cindy laughed. 'Probably, although I promise I won't stop and show it to everyone I meet in the street,' she said. 'But I'm not as excited as Sally is. She rang me this morning while you were out checking the fences in the north paddock and asked if I could look around and find that lucky charm she wore when she was a little girl.'

'That gold teddy bear you bought for her one Christmas?'

'That's it. She bought a teddy for the nursery and that's when she thought of it. She wants to have her lucky charm for her baby.'

'Sentimental, isn't she? You've already sent down her stuffed toys and dolls,' Murray said with a grin.

'The trouble is that I can't find the charm anywhere. I've looked all through our house and it's nowhere to be found, and you know what, I'm not sure that I've seen it for years. I think it must have been left behind when we moved out of your father's house. I'll have to go over there and go through the drawers in Sally's old room. I'd better tell your father I'm coming to rummage around.'

Murray put his knife and fork down as he finished his meal. 'Dad's not around. He's taken off again. Literally. I think he's getting a bit old for flying these days, but he won't listen to me, of course. Mrs Flowers is there, you can get her to help. But it'll be a bit like looking for a needle in a haystack, if you ask me.'

The next day, Murray and Cindy drove over to the big house. 'No point in taking two cars. I'll only be about half an hour, so I can collect you on the way back,' Murray said. 'I won't come in, but say hi to Mrs F for me.'

Cindy walked through the front garden, where everything was unchanged, although the roses needed pruning. She went through the front door, calling out to Mrs Flowers, who came bustling down the hallway.

'Hi, Mrs F. I'm on a mission for Sally.' Cindy explained about the gold bear.

'Oh yes, I remember that little bear,' replied Mrs Flowers. 'Tom was planning on driving me into Yamboola. I need to pick up a few things. But if you want me to stay and help, I don't mind. Tom can drive me later,' Mrs Flowers replied.

'Not at all.' Cindy felt a rush of affection for the warm-hearted housekeeper. 'You do what you planned. I'll be fine. I probably won't find it, anyway.'

The back door banged as Mrs Flowers left, and Cindy went down the dim hallway. How dark this house was. She opened the door to Sally's old room. It was funny, she thought, that they still all called it Sally's room even though her daughter had vacated it when she was nearly eight when they'd moved to their new house. Originally, according to Mrs Flowers, Rose had used it as a day room to sew and a place to take a quiet rest.

Cindy opened the empty wardrobe, which had once held all the pretty dresses that Babs had lovingly made for Sally. Cindy looked at the empty shelves where Sally had stored her old schoolbooks and workbooks. There was nothing there now.

She closed the wardrobe and went into the small, very old-fashioned ensuite. The washbasin on the sink had drawers on either side. Cindy pulled them open one by one. In one, Cindy was astonished to find an old plastic comb, a little mirror and plastic jewellery for Sally's dolls. In another drawer was a Mason Pearson child's hairbrush, and some little ornaments.

Heavens, Cindy thought. *Fancy leaving all this here.* They must have forgotten it when they'd moved, she concluded. Sally hadn't been all that keen on dolls and that sort of thing, so she probably hadn't noticed or cared that the items were missing.

Cindy kept opening the drawers, but found nothing until she reached one of the bottom drawers. In it, there were a few little boxes containing things that must have once been precious to Sally: shells, stones, dried flowers. Cindy rummaged around and then she saw a little round pill box she recognised. She opened it and inside was tucked a tiny, fat gold teddy bear pendant with a loop at the back of its neck that had once held a chain.

'Hello, lucky Teddy! You're being called back into service.' Pleased with what she'd found, Cindy put the little box in her jeans pocket and tried to push the drawer shut with her foot, but it wouldn't close. She gave it a gentle shove.

Now, why won't the drawer close? she wondered. She jiggled it and pushed it again, and then realised that something had fallen down behind it, preventing it from closing. She yanked the drawer out altogether, so that she could find whatever it was that was causing the problem. Reaching through to the back and up behind the other drawers, Cindy felt something and dragged it out.

It was a small wallet. *Where on earth did Sally find this?* she thought. Cindy had never seen it before. Curious, she opened the little purse.

The first thing she saw was a card with the name *Mrs Rose Parnell* printed on it. There was also something that she quickly guessed was a petrol ration card, as well as a driver's licence, a few pound notes and a chequebook with Rose's name printed on it. There was also a tiny address book.

Cindy started to tremble with excitement as she realised that this was Rose's wallet, which had obviously slipped down behind the drawers and been resting there, undisturbed, all these years.

She held the old red leather wallet to her cheek.

'Oh my,' she breathed. Her fingers shook slightly as she began to flip through the address book, looking at the entries written in Rose's neat cursive writing.

Before she could examine it further, she heard Murray outside, blowing the car horn, so she hurried out, waving the wallet. 'You'll never guess what I found!' Cindy ran to the car and scrambled into the front seat.

'So you found it then!'

'The teddy? Yes. But look . . . your mother's wallet!'

Murray blanched and bit his lip as he took the purse from Cindy. 'You found this? That's amazing, after all these years. I think I remember it.' He opened the purse and took out the chequebook and looked at it intently, as though it might supply him with answers.

'And Murray, I found your mother's address book, too,' said Cindy, excitedly holding up the little book.

'Maybe there might be someone listed in the book who is still around and might know where your mother went.'

'Have you had a chance to look inside it?' he asked.

'Not really. You turned up before I could have a proper look.' She opened it and started reading out names. 'Any of these ring a bell?'

Murray shook his head.

'Ooh look, here's Marie's name and address. Isn't this exciting?'

'Yes, I guess it is. But I don't know any of the other names. I could ask my father if he knew who they were, but I'm not sure I really want to have another confrontation with him over my mother.' Murray sounded bitter. 'Cindy, the reality is that my mother left here more than forty years ago. How could we ever track down the people in this address book after all that time? I don't think it would be feasible.'

'No, I suppose not,' said Cindy with a sigh. She thought for a moment, and then said brightly, 'But Murray, the police have much better resources these days. I mean, they have computers and that sort of thing. I think we should take the wallet with the address book in it and hand it over to them, let them have a go at finding the people whose names she's written down. There aren't very many, so it won't be a big ask. Murray, this is the first clue we've found that might lead us to your mother. I think we should definitely give it to the police.'

Murray thought for a minute, tapping his fingers on the steering wheel. 'The missing persons file was never closed, as far as I know,' he mused. 'Yes, I think you're right, let's take it to the police. How about we drive into Deniliquin now and see what the cops have to say?'

Cindy nodded her agreement, and Murray turned the car around and headed towards Deniliquin.

In the police station they were treated politely, but the

detective they spoke to didn't seem very optimistic about getting any results from the address book, pointing out all the difficulties entailed in reviewing a case that was more than forty years old. However, he kept everything and promised to do his best to track down the people whom Rose had listed in the address book. He added that he'd also check missing persons records. He laboriously wrote a receipt, listing all the contents.

Murray and Cindy drove back home. Their conversation swung between optimism and apprehension until in the end they stopped speaking, each becoming engrossed in their own thoughts, one remembering, one trying to imagine.

*

As soon as she arrived back home, Cindy phoned Sally to say that she'd found the little bear. She mentioned finding Rose's purse, but Sally didn't seem particularly interested. 'Let's see what the police say first, Mum. No point in getting excited till then.' So Cindy phoned Joanna to tell her what had happened, hoping that her friend would think the discovery as thrilling as she did.

'Can you believe it! Just finding the wallet like that. And with the address book in it. I wonder how many people in it are still living at the same address or are even alive, let alone able to tell us where Rose went? The police have said that they'll do their best to find out, so we've left everything at the police station. Not that they sounded very confident. Still, you never know,' Cindy told her friend.

'That's amazing. How does Murray feel about it?'

'We're both quite excited . . . It's a tangible clue that might lead us to Rose. Of course, after all this time, the whole thing might come to nothing, but one can hope. So many unanswered questions.'

Joanna was quiet a moment. 'Cindy, you're right, this is exciting, I guess,' she said finally. 'It's amazing that you found the purse at all.'

'I know. If I hadn't been looking for Sally's charm, it could have stayed there forever. It was just luck,' said Cindy.

'Cin!' Joanna's voice rose in exasperation. 'That's not what I meant. Think . . . What woman runs away from home and leaves behind her personal effects? Her *wallet,* of all things! With money, her driver's licence, her cheque-book, her petrol ration card in it. Why would she do that? It's just too strange.'

Cindy was silent a moment, struggling to think of an answer. She heard a loud buzzer go off at Jo's end of the line.

'Cin, I've got to go. My cake's ready and Donald's family is due over here any moment,' said Jo hurriedly. 'Let's catch up soon.' And with that, she rang off.

Cindy slowly hung up the phone.

But deep inside, she felt a seed of doubt bloom. It was indeed very strange.

11

CINDY DROPPED THE BOOK she was reading, sensing movement in the quiet scene she could see from her chair in the Sundowner Room. There were only a few weeks until Christmas when all the family would be home to celebrate. She loved the holiday time, especially sharing it now with her eighteen-month-old granddaughter, Emily. Cindy smiled as she thought about the toddler, running around the house after Murray, squealing with delight, the centre of the family's attention.

Kingsley Downs had never looked so good. Fat ewes foraged in fresh green pasture after the recent rain. The creek was flowing strongly and there was not a breath of wind to ripple its surface. Breaking the stillness were two distant figures walking along the fence line, engaged in animated conversation.

Lawrence was gesticulating, while Murray had his hands clasped behind his back. Cindy had the impression of a king touring his domain while the prince in waiting was obediently attentive.

It had been a good season. Hercules Two had earned his high price, and Kingsley Downs had produced its highest-ever wool clips, but Murray worried these extraordinary times could not last and that Kingsley Downs would not be able to repay the debts they'd run up in expanding the operation. Lawrence, however, had dismissed his son's concerns.

*

That evening, after they had finished dinner, Murray shared his fears with Cindy.

'I've always trusted Dad's judgement, but I'm not sure that Mirooball was such a smart buy. Maybe over the long term. Gordon has done an amazing job, but at present the returns from Mirooball aren't great,' said Murray.

'Won't it come good?' Cindy asked.

'I'm not sure we have time to wait and see. I question the tactics of the Wool Corp. The board keeps raising the price of the wool clip, they say as a show of confidence, but no one is buying at those prices. At the same time, they're raising the wool levy on the woolgrowers to cover the Wool Corp's costs, which means that the price of running this place is also rising. And all these loans Dad has taken out could be crippling us because the Australian dollar has dropped. So those Swiss francs loans are now damned expensive to pay back, as the interest rate is much higher and our income is less,' grumbled Murray. 'I can't see how it can go on.'

Cindy nodded worriedly. 'Jo said Donald was questioning what the Wool Board is doing – that the board is too high-handed – and he's not the only one thinking that way. Maybe you and Donald should call a meeting of the local woolgrowers so people can voice their concerns.'

'Dad won't like that.' Murray pinched the bridge of his nose.

'I'm sure he won't, but perhaps if some pressure is put on the Wool Corp the board might reconsider its approach. Something should be done.'

Murray sighed and looked up at his wife. 'Maybe you're right. People need to be able to say what they think, though I doubt the Wool Corp will listen. I'll ring Donald and see what he says.'

*

Over the next few days, Cindy, Murray, Jo and Donald began to ring around the district and sound out other graziers, and found that most shared their anxieties. They also spoke to the local newspaper and radio station, and both agreed to send a representative along to any meeting that was arranged.

One young reporter got back to Cindy and said he'd do some digging to see what facts and figures he could find about the state of the wool trade and bring them along, too.

A meeting was arranged in the School of Arts hall in Yamboola. Cindy and Joanna helped set up the hall and arranged for tea and coffee to be served afterwards. As several graziers wanted to speak, it was agreed that Donald should introduce them and run a question time after that. Murray had declined to do this job out of loyalty to his father. He knew Lawrence was very unhappy about the whole meeting idea.

'It could be a bit awkward for you to be there, Dad,' Murray had explained. 'Seeing as you're a member of the Wool Corp Board.'

'Why am I suddenly the bad guy?' demanded Lawrence. 'Everyone has made a damned lot of money from their wool because of the Corporation's guaranteed price.'

'Agreed. But it's gone on too long; it can't last. And the board isn't making any effort to sort things out sensibly. There's too much greed, arrogance, ignorance and duplicity. You watch, the blame game will start soon enough, human nature being what it is.'

'Cynthia should never have butted into this. It's men's business,' Lawrence exploded. 'I'd better come and set the record straight.'

Lawrence was as good as his word, and attended the overflowing meeting. He arrived after everyone else and strode to the front row, where a seat was hastily made available for him.

Brett Jones, the young reporter from the local paper, asked Donald if he could read a short statement on the research he'd done on the wool industry, which he thought people might find interesting.

To the crackling noise of the sound system, Donald stepped forward, welcomed everyone and thanked them for coming.

'This meeting has been called tonight because many of us believe we're not being listened to by the Wool Corporation. We question its tactics and believe it's heading in the wrong direction and that if it keeps to its present path, the future of wool in this country could be severely damaged.'

This brought a smattering of angry mutters, some in agreement, some not.

'We are all in this together,' Donald added. 'So we want to hear your views and ideas. But first we'll hear from our guest speakers. First up is Brett Jones, who, as some of you might know, is a journalist with *The Regional Times*.'

Brett moved to the podium, opened his notebook, tapped the microphone and began speaking.

'Good evening, everyone. I've been covering local news in this area for five years, but I am also a grazier's son. I approached Mrs Parnell to say that I was prepared to look into the Wool Corporation and their proposals for the future direction of our wool industry and present my findings this evening. I think some of you may find these facts surprising.'

Brett baldly detailed the growing wool stockpile, the lack of buyers and the rising costs being sheeted back to the woolgrower. 'It's calculated that the Wool Corp's borrowings to cover this have passed two billion dollars.'

There was a gasp and murmurs at this outrageous sum. Brett continued, 'It appears the Wool Corp thinks the world will be forced to buy our wool and the stockpile will fall and everything will be all right.'

He paused to take a sip of water. Cindy looked around the packed hall. There was barely a sound as the audience took in what he was saying.

'To my way of thinking, the Wool Corporation is just digging itself into an ever-deepening black hole. It assumes that the government and the Australian taxpayer will continue to pay for their folly of maintaining a high wool price. But what will happen when the government is forced to pull the plug?'

Brett raised his voice in his dramatic conclusion. 'It is my belief that when the government no longer supports the Wool Corp, the entire wool industry will go into freefall.'

There was a loud reaction to this remark from the audience.

Brett continued, 'There is a plan, I'm told off the record, to reduce wool production by up to 350 million kilos. Farmers will be paid to shoot old or surplus sheep and taxpayers will foot the compensation bill.'

As shouts of, 'No way! Outrageous!' rumbled around the room, Brett raised his voice one more time.

'I have interviewed a lot of local woolgrowers who are placing the blame at the feet of the politicians. But in light of my investigations, I believe the leaders of the wool industry should be held accountable. And the question remains: what next for woolgrowers? Thank you.'

Cindy was shocked by what Brett had said and she stared at Lawrence. She could tell he was livid.

A well-known grazier rose, obviously upset by Brett's report, and began to speak. 'Even if only half of what this young bloke has to say is true, it spells disaster for us,' he said. 'It sounds like we need to get our industry out of the hands of those greedy mugs on the Wool Board. We need our industry to be unencumbered by debt and self-indulgence, so we can operate in a free market environment. But first, I call for a Royal Commission into how we bloody got to this state of affairs!' He shook his fist as applause and a few 'hear, hears' broke out.

Donald asked the other official speakers to make further comments, and it quickly became evident that they, too, queried the direction in which the Wool Corp was taking the industry. When they had finished having their say, Donald called for comments from the floor.

Lawrence rose to his feet. The room hushed, waiting to hear what the well-regarded grazier, a member of the Wool Corp Board, had to say. Lawrence began to speak in his usual calm, polite way, determined to allay the worries of the audience.

'The people who question the wool industry and where it's going are doom and gloom merchants with no real knowledge of the workings of the wool industry. Don't believe the alarm bells you've heard from this young man from the press. Wool's always been Australia's golden fleece. The world wants it. Remember, in World

War One we sold the entire wool clip to Britain, and in World War Two, it was the same thing. The fifties were a boom time, too, when wool sold for a pound a pound during the Korean War. Wool has made us rich. Wool has been the backbone of the Australian economy for two hundred years. Nothing will ever replace wool, not cotton, not synthetics, nothing.'

He paused and looked around the room. Some of the audience, people who had known Lawrence for years, seemed calmed by his positive words, but others looked hostile and one or two muttered angry remarks under their breath. Lawrence glared at them, and to Cindy's shock and dismay, he suddenly lost his temper.

'Some of you people in the room are ingrates, questioning the actions of the Wool Board,' he roared. 'We know what we're doing. There is nothing that you need to panic about, take my word for that.' Lawrence looked around the room, as though defying anyone to contradict him. 'Wool will always be king,' he thundered, and turned and strode from the hall.

After Lawrence's speech, it was impossible for Donald to bring the room to order, as everyone broke into conversation with their neighbours, so Donald closed the meeting. Many of the audience left right away, but others stayed for a cup of tea and concerned conversation.

Brett was surrounded and the photographer was busy recording it all as Joanna hugged Cindy.

'Look what we've started,' Jo whispered. 'Poor Lawrence, he was furious.'

'Do you really believe it will get to the stage of shooting our sheep, like Brett said they were doing in Western Australia?' asked Cindy.

'I really don't know. Let's hope not,' sighed Joanna. 'But I think we're facing dire straits.'

As Cindy sipped her tea, she cursed Lawrence's extravagances and worried about just what would become of Kingsley Downs if Brett's dramatic predictions came true.

*

The day after the hostile meeting, Lawrence flew his plane to Melbourne. Both Cindy and Murray thought he was getting too old to fly, and had tried to dissuade him, but he took little notice.

Shortly after lunch, the phone rang. Cindy thought it would be Joanna, calling to discuss the extraordinary meeting the night before. But as the caller identified himself, she realised it was the call she had long hoped for, though she'd almost given up thinking anyone from the police would ever contact her.

'It's Senior Constable Fielding here, Mrs Parnell. We're very sorry, but our inquiries regarding the information you gave us about that missing person have drawn a total blank. We went through Mrs Parnell's address book, but we could find no one at all who was mentioned in it. We did manage to make contact with the children of one or two of the entries, but they could tell us nothing. I'm afraid they'd never heard of Mrs Rose Parnell. We've checked all possible databases and her name never comes up.'

Cindy sighed. 'I see. That is disappointing, of course. But it was a long time ago and so it was a long shot to believe that you'd get a result,' she said. 'Well, thank you for your help. I'll call in to collect the purse in a day or so, if that's all right.'

Cindy was disappointed but not surprised. When she told Murray, he agreed with her. It was, after all, a long time ago.

*

Lawrence returned safely from Melbourne and a meeting of the Wool Corp Board, still angry over what he saw as Murray and Cindy's disloyalty in arranging the community meeting.

'Did he tell the board what the graziers felt in this district about the way it was handling things? What did he tell you?' asked Cindy, after Murray had spoken to his father.

Murray shrugged. 'Total intransigence as far as the board goes. Its members are sticking to their guns.'

'I see,' said Cindy, annoyed. 'I just hope they start to listen soon, before it's too late, and that includes your father, or we'll all be in a sinking ship.'

Needing to distract herself, Cindy glanced at the kitchen clock and calculated what time it would be in Palm Springs. Early evening, so Alice would still be up watching television. She hadn't spoken to Alice for some time and she felt a pang of guilt. Since Spencer had died the previous year from a heart attack, she'd been checking in on Alice more regularly than she used to, but somehow the weeks had slipped by without her making contact.

After Spencer's death, her aunt had sold the store in Palm Springs and installed a manager in the boutique in Palm Desert. Cindy hoped that Alice was still keeping close tabs on the paperwork, the way Spencer had for so many years.

The phone rang several times before Alice finally picked up. 'It's damned late. Who is this?' she demanded.

'Sorry, Alice. It's me, Cindy. I thought you'd be watching TV. How are you?'

'Oh it's you, Cindy. I'm watching Andy Rooney. Apart from him and *Jeopardy*, I tell you, there's nothing but rubbish on television.'

'Why don't you read a good book, then?' Cindy asked.

'I only read biographies of people I admire or I can learn something from. Not many of those left, now.'

Cindy suppressed a sigh. Alice was getting grouchier with age. 'How is everything? I hope you're not still having a problem with that girl, Sandra, who's running the store?'

'Good grief. Don't mention that terrible woman to me. She's caused me so much trouble. My lawyer is still dealing with it.'

'Why on earth do you need a lawyer? What has she done?' asked Cindy in alarm.

'The girl set herself up as more than just a shop manager. In the beginning, she was so helpful and polite. Said she was a business expert and a former accountant and she knew her way around taxation and deductions and how to save me money. So I let her do my book-keeping and pay my accounts and so on.'

'Alice! I can't believe you did that. What happened to the accountant Spencer always used for your business?'

'He's getting doddery. Sandra said there were better ways to do things. It all seemed fine. She's so charming, you know. The shop had been doing well. But I suddenly got a tax demand from the IRS. I mean, how embarrassing.'

'You owed the IRS money?'

'Apparently. And I think she said the store is facing receivership, whatever that is.'

'Alice! How? You own that store outright, it's been making money . . . What has Sandra done?'

'I seem to owe money to fashion houses. Sandra was buying a lot of stock, and she used the boutique as collateral for some idea she ran past me about a marketing program her friend set up. It seemed to be a good idea, and I signed some papers to get a loan for it. It didn't come off. Cindy, I think Sandra and her friend, Clarice, are in cahoots,' said Alice indignantly. 'Spencer's valuable coin collection has disappeared from his desk, too. I keep my jewellery locked away. But really, Cindy, it's all beyond me.'

'I can see why you've gone to a lawyer,' said Cindy, shocked by what Alice was telling her. Babs had always said Alice was gullible to suggestions about easy money, but with the faithful Spencer around, Alice had been protected from avaricious so-called friends. Now, without Spencer, it was a different story.

'Apart from going to a lawyer, are you doing anything else to get to the bottom of it all?' asked Cindy.

'Of course I'm trying to get someone to sort it out,' replied Alice crossly. 'I have two guys, two gay people, who have offered to help me. They say they want to run the shop. They said Sandra has been robbing me blind.'

'Good lord, Alice, how well do you know these men? How do you know they won't rob you blind as well? You must get reliable advice. Go to Spencer's old firm, for goodness sake. You need proper legal advice. I think Sandra should be reported to the authorities. She probably makes a business out of swindling people like you.'

'There's nothing wrong with my business acumen, Cindy. I'm just too trusting,' said Alice, bristling. 'Anyway, as a matter of fact I have a new career.'

'Alice, what on earth do you mean?' Cindy's heart sank.

Cindy could visualise Alice settling in to tell her about her latest venture, crossing her long legs, immaculately mani-cured feet in high-heeled sandals. In a fleeting aside, Cindy realised she had never, ever, seen Alice anything but perfectly groomed; nails, hairdo, clothes, accessories, the lot.

'You know what a retirement haven this place is for all the movie stars and the great doyens of show business. We won't see their like again. Hollywood, show business, Broadway, has lost the old glamour, the razzamatazz, the talent, but those who had it are all here.'

'I agree, Alice. But they're all *old*,' said Cindy affectionately.

'That might well be true, but real talent never dies. I'm talking *show business* . . . Ginger Rogers, Fred Astaire, the big musicals. It's all coming back.'

'Alice! Whatever do you mean?' said Cindy, leaning her head on her hand in exasperation.

'Y'know how the Plaza Theatre's been closed for years?'

'Yes, Joey and I loved going there to the movies.'

'This very clever guy came up with an idea for a show, and it's taken forever to convince the mayor to re-open the Plaza for a season each year. But he has finally agreed, and we're going to be putting on a show there,' said Alice proudly.

'What sort of a show, exactly?'

'It's an extravaganza! It's going to be called "The Fabulous Palm Springs Follies"! I'll read you what we're doing from our advertising flyer.' She paused, cleared her throat with a theatrical cough and started to read, '*A Legendary Line-Up of Long-Legged Lovelies, our internationally acclaimed guest stars, classic variety acts, present the music and dance of the 40s, 50s, 60s and 70s, all performed by a cast old enough to have lived it!*'

'Ah, well, and just what is your role?' asked Cindy cautiously.

'I'm assisting the wonderful costume designer. We had the first lot of auditions and over four hundred turned up . . . all former Vegas showgirls, Radio City Music Hall Rockettes, performers from Paris's Folies Bergère, and Broadway veterans. I couldn't believe it. And the rule is they must be over fifty-five!'

'I'm a bit stunned,' admitted Cindy. 'I didn't think feathers and sequins was your style.'

'Oh, the designs are bigger and better than any show you've seen. I tell you, when it's up and going it will put Palm Springs on the map just like the canyons and the tramway!'

'It does sound amazing. I just hadn't thought it your sort of thing. Please tell me you haven't invested in the show?' asked Cindy, feeling quite helpless.

'Not a cent. I can't spare a dime these days, anyway. This show is class, Cindy. Style, showbiz and stars. It's an inspiration. Eighty-year-old, high-kicking glamour girls! You gotta hand it to them,' said Alice.

'Well, I'm pleased you've found something to keep you occupied,' said Cindy, rather bemused.

'I have so many admirers now,' Alice boasted. 'I think I was a bit lonely after Spencer died, but now everybody wants to be my friend. You know how popular I've always been, not that I ever dreamed anyone would take advantage of me. But Cindy, do you know what they said in the write-up about the Follies? They called me a legend of the desert. They're right, of course, but it's nice to be recognised.'

'It certainly is, and you are a legend, Alice,' said Cindy, laughing. 'Send me some photos of the showgirls.'

*

Christmas was a happy time. Even Lawrence did his best to join in the festivities with the rest of the family, although Cindy knew he was still annoyed over the Yamboola graziers' meeting.

The only thing that marred Christmas Day was the Flowerses announcement that they had decided to retire in the new year.

Cindy felt devastated. Mrs Flowers had been her ally and companion for nearly thirty years, and she wondered how she would manage without the friendship of the kind housekeeper.

'It won't ever really be the same again,' said Cindy sadly when the two of them were alone in the kitchen, and Mrs Flowers shifted her feet and wrung her hands on her apron.

'That's how I feel. And well, I – Tom and me – we thought that maybe the time had come. He's not as fit as he used to be. I don't want to leave you in the lurch, Mrs P, but we thought this might be the time to buy a little place on the coast and retire.'

'Oh, we will miss you both dreadfully. It's your decision, of course.'

'Don't you worry about Mr Parnell. I've made arrangements with him for someone to come in three times a week. She's a most reliable person who'll do the cleaning and laundry and make sure Mr Parnell has plenty of food. She'll do a bit of cooking, too.'

'We're going to miss you so much,' said Cindy. 'We've been through quite a bit together, haven't we?'

'We have got on well. I'll miss all of you, but we'll keep in touch,' Mrs Flowers promised, her eyes glistening with tears.

*

The new year had usually been a happy time for Cindy, but 1991 turned into a disaster when, in February, the government finally made the decision to stop guaranteeing the Wool Corporation's financial borrowings. This decision created the worst business collapse Australia had ever seen, sending the corporation into a freefalling spiral which ended in the morass of a twelve-billion-dollar loss for the wool industry.

Even though Cindy and Murray had suspected that a disaster was looming, they were still devastated when it finally happened. Cindy was in shock when they heard the news on television.

'What will that mean for us? Does this mean that wool prices will collapse? Will we be able to keep this place going? Oh Murray, I couldn't bear to lose Kingsley Downs. Or our home.'

'I really don't know, Cindy. Everything will be up in the air. I'll have to speak to Dad, so we can devise a plan. I can't do it without him, because he controls our finances, but I can tell you one thing for sure: there'll be no replacement for Tom. A station manager on Kingsley Downs is a luxury we can no longer afford,' said Murray grimly.

But Lawrence was reclusive, refusing to talk to them, remaining in his study with the door closed.

'He's in total denial,' Cindy said to Murray. 'We're going to have to do something. And quickly.'

'Yes, I know. But it's really hard to talk to him at present. It's as though he refuses to acknowledge the truth about what has happened to him.'

'And to us as well! Murray, we must have a serious talk with him. The three of us. Everyone is trying to get out and salvage something and we don't even know what the debt is on this place and Mirooball. How can we make rational decisions about the future if we don't know the true state of affairs?'

'You're right, but he won't agree to anything if he thinks we're pushing him into a corner,' said Murray.

'We're on the edge of a precipice, not a corner. Your father can't just ignore the situation. Why don't we go over this evening, have a civilised drink and ask a few hard questions?'

Murray bit his lip. 'We can try.'

'You'll just have to take control. That's the end of it,' said Cindy firmly. 'Thank goodness Russell got that job offer, even if the veterinary practice is in Inverell, and the job doesn't actually start for a while. But it's kind of him to agree to stay with us and help out in the meantime. You can certainly use his help right now.'

*

As arranged with Murray, late that afternoon Cindy walked into Lawrence's sitting room, unannounced and uninvited. Lawrence looked up from his conversation with Murray and frowned.

'Did you want something, Cynthia?'

She sat down. 'Yes, both of us do. Murray, could I have a glass of wine, please?'

Lawrence half rose out of his seat, then sat back down as Murray poured her a glass of wine. Lawrence frowned as Murray handed Cindy her drink.

'Dad, I asked Cin to come over and join us, as the three of us need to have an urgent talk. Cindy and I are extremely worried about the situation here since the collapse of the wool industry. I know you've always kept the finances of the property to yourself, but circumstances have now most definitely changed, and Cindy and I think we have a right to know exactly where we stand, financially. What actions do we need to take to make sure that Kingsley Downs is secure?' Murray looked anxiously at his father.

'We'll be fine, son,' Lawrence answered somewhat airily. 'No need for you to be concerned.'

'But Dad, we should all be concerned. And unless you take Cindy and me into your confidence and let us look at the finances, I can't be sure we have a secure financial plan to keep our heads above water,' said Murray desperately.

'It's only fair to the children that we take constructive action now,' said Cindy impatiently. It seemed ridiculous to her that, in this time of crisis, Lawrence would refuse to be frank with them. 'Kingsley Downs is important to them, too. I think it only right that you let us know exactly where we all stand.'

Lawrence glared at her. 'How dare you dictate to me?' he snapped. 'I'm in charge here. What would you know about the running of this property? You're an interfering woman who doesn't know her place.'

'If you're so confident that everything is fine, then show your son the books. Just what is our debt?' said Cindy, unperturbed by his insult and determined to get Lawrence to agree. 'I know there are many places around here in trouble. I've heard that the banks are querying the viability of properties we always thought were successful. We just want to make sure Kingsley Downs isn't in the same boat.'

'Bloody banks,' said Lawrence angrily. 'When they think they can make money from you, they can't lend you enough, but then, at the first hint you're in trouble, they pounce like the scavengers they are.'

'What've they said to you?' asked Murray warily.

'They send me letters, and I've had the odd phone call, but as I tell them, I've been with their organisation for more than fifty years, so I expect to be treated with a bit of loyalty and respect,' Lawrence replied haughtily. 'They can come and see me.'

'Dad,' said Murray, now deeply alarmed by his father's disclosures, 'the banks are pushing landowners to sell their properties if they think they can't meet their obligations; and if they won't or can't do that, then the banks will move to a mortgagee sale. We need to see the books so we can work something out fast, to make sure that a mortgagee sale doesn't happen to us.'

'Rubbish,' protested Lawrence.

'Then let us see what we owe and how we can cope with the debts,' said Cindy, now completely exasperated. 'The longer you leave it, the worse it will be. We need to plan some strategy to get us out of this nightmare.'

'We! Listen to her!' exclaimed Lawrence, his voice rising. 'You're not part of Kingsley Downs. I don't see that you have any right to examine my affairs. No right at all.'

'Dad . . .'

'It's all right, Murray,' snapped Cindy, dropping any pretence of politeness now, thoroughly angered by

Lawrence's stubbornness. She pointed at her father-in-law. 'You are a selfish man! Your son has worked all his life for you and Kingsley Downs –'

'Just as I did,' interrupted Lawrence. 'He has to wait his turn, just like I did! You're the pushy, greedy one here.'

'If we wait, there won't be anything for your son and your grandchildren to inherit! Don't be so stubborn and irrational. I will not stand by and see my children's future ruined because of your selfishness! Just let us look at the accounts before it's too damned late!' Her voice rose in anger as Cindy slammed down her glass. She jumped to her feet. 'Murray, I am going to wait in the car. You are going to take your father into his office and get the account ledgers. It's now or never, because if we can't work out a way to save this place, then we'll walk away from here with nothing and your father can see out his days in a nursing home by himself.'

Ashen-faced, she stomped past Murray, who looked at his wife in a mixture of amazement and admiration as she went outside, drawing deep breaths in the warm twilight before shakily getting into the car. She had stood up to Lawrence before, but never like this, and she thought that their fragile relationship might now be shattered forever.

*

To Cindy's surprise and relief, it didn't take long for Murray to appear with an armful of manila folders and ledgers.

Murray dumped them on the back seat of the car. 'I don't believe it. We've finally got hold of the accounts.'

'What did your father say?'

'Absolutely nothing. Maybe your standing up to him did the trick, or maybe he's relieved to share the burden. Or perhaps he thinks we won't be able to fathom the accounts at all.'

'You forget I was a bright maths student. I'm sure we'll work them out,' said Cindy firmly.

It took her two days of hard work, poring over the figures, checking them again, until she emerged, grim-faced, to confront Murray with her findings. She made them both a cup of coffee and they sat at the kitchen table to face how extensive the debt over Kingsley Downs really was.

'Murray, I can't believe this. It's far worse than I ever dreamed. Your father has borrowed way over his head. I think we're going to have to do something drastic if we're going to save this place. See what you think.'

Cindy quickly showed Murray a summary of the financial situation.

Murray gave a long whistle. 'I can't believe what a precarious state we're in, Cindy,' he said, clearly horrified by his wife's conclusions. 'We'll need to come up with a few options quickly, just to be able to make the repayments on the loans, and then we'll need to look at some more permanent solutions, if we're to salvage anything from this mess.'

In the end, they decided that instead of selling Mirooball, they'd lease it for the time being, until land prices stabilised.

'Good fat lamb country. Someone could make a go of raising lambs on it, I'm sure,' said Murray. 'And a lease would give us a definite revenue stream.'

'Maybe whoever leases it could use Gordon on the place. Of course, he could come back here to work, now that Tom's gone, but we wouldn't be able to pay him much,' said Cindy.

'I'm also thinking we might have to divide up Kingsley Downs and sell part of it,' said Murray softly.

They sat in silence for a moment as the terrible words hung in the air. Cindy could see that Murray's eyes were wet. She reached across and took his hand.

'Murray, I've been hoping that there'd be some way we could avoid that,' said Cindy sadly.

Murray shook his head. 'Darling, I might not be able to add up as quickly as you can, but I do understand the bottom line. If we can't sell part of the place, then we'll have no place at all,' said Murray.

'That's a very brave decision, but it's the right one,' admitted Cindy. 'It means you'll have to go over your father's head.'

'I know, and I can't do that, because everything is in his name. I'll just have to make him see reason. I'm not entirely sure that he understands the terrible position he's got us into,' said Murray. 'But yes, for the moment, I'm going to take charge. I'll run this place in such a way that when we have to put some of it up for sale, it will look the best it possibly can. We need to get top dollar.'

'I don't think Kingsley Downs will need all that much sprucing up,' said Cindy. 'You and Tom have always kept everything well maintained, but I suppose you could get rid of those terrible noxious weeds and blackberry bushes that have spread. Remember when the kids were little and we used to go for picnics at the creek? Can't get close these days, the bushes have grown so. I haven't been able to get to that lovely peppercorn tree in years.'

'Yes, good idea. Not a good look to have noxious weeds making it difficult for the stock to access the water-ways,' said Murray in agreement. 'I'll get someone to bring in some equipment to get rid of them quickly. In the meantime, Russell and I can do some maintenance around the sheds and check on all the fences and the windmills. But the most valuable thing here is the name Kingsley Downs,' said Murray with a sigh. 'I can't believe it's come to this. What would my grandfather say?'

Cindy went and put her arms around him. 'You've done your best. What's happened to us is your father's fault.

All we can do is try to salvage what we can, sell what we have to, and try to hang on in the hope that we'll eventually be able to build it back up again,' she comforted him.

Murray and Cindy held each other for a long moment. After everything they'd been through, neither could believe that they might be facing the end of Kingsley Downs. It was a nightmare come to pass.

*

Once they'd made the decision to act, events quickly rolled forward.

Murray made an appointment to see the bank manager. Cindy was not sure how he did it, but he also managed to drag his father into the bank with him.

Murray, still quite shaken by their dire financial situation, told Cindy later how Lawrence had sat in the manager's office, stony-faced, as the full horror of their debt was revealed. The bank manager was sympathetic, but told them that head office was demanding their debt be brought under control immediately. He agreed that selling off a parcel of the Kingsley Downs land, leasing Mirooball, if possible, and diversifying into cattle, would be the best way to go. Extravagances like Lawrence's beloved plane would have to go.

After that, Cindy and Murray didn't see much of Lawrence, as he kept to himself at the big house. Russell went over to see him, but said Lawrence made it clear he didn't want company. Sometimes they spotted him at the woolshed, or riding slowly beside the fences; a solitary figure.

'Is selling the big house part of your plan?' asked Russell.

'Not at present. An undeveloped block might prove to be more attractive, but it will really depend on what we're offered by interested buyers,' Murray told him. 'I'm going over to see your grandfather later today and run a few things past him, so I'll have a word with him. There's still a bit we have to sign off on. Dad and I should have sorted this out years ago,' admitted Murray.

'If we can't save the place, there won't be much to spread around for you or anyone else,' Cindy said grimly to her son.

'Don't worry about me,' said Russell. 'I don't think you have to worry about Sally, either. Neither of us really wants to end up on Kingsley Downs. But Gordon does, so it would be nice if there was something left for him.'

'Then, let's do it for your father and Gordon,' said Cindy, sounding more cheerful than she actually felt.

'When I take this paperwork back to Dad, do you want to come with me?' Murray asked Cindy. 'You stand up to him and you really understand what's happening.'

*

Lawrence did not offer either of them anything to drink, or even suggest that they all sit down together around the dining room table, so that they could discuss things more comfortably. Instead, he busied himself behind his desk in his study, as Murray sat in the chair opposite and Cindy hovered in the doorway. Lawrence didn't bother to greet her, turning his attention straight to his son. Murray made no comment about his father's rude behaviour, but stood up, gave Cindy his seat and went and found himself another chair.

Murray was businesslike and, pulling his notebook from his top pocket, he ran through some figures and projections.

'So, Dad, we could try to sell the north-eastern paddocks near the creek. Here are the papers that need to be signed so we can go ahead and put it in the hands of an agent. Of course, we might have to sell other parts of Kingsley Downs as well. And I reckon if we get a couple of hundred head of good beef cattle, that might give us an income stream, but I can discuss that idea further when I get back.'

'Back from where?' Lawrence asked.

'I have a buyer for the plane, Dad. Of course, I'll need to get the ownership papers from you before I can finish the transaction –'

Lawrence's head shot up. 'Is it necessary to sell my plane? Have you been through my wardrobe and picked out my boots, hats and coats to sell as well?'

'Dad . . . please.'

Cindy spoke. 'We need cash to pay the crew coming to clean up. No one will buy a place full of weeds. Besides, if we're trying to salvage this place, you can hardly keep an extravagance like the plane. If we don't sell it, then the Jag might have to go instead,' she said firmly. *Really*, she thought, *Lawrence is in such denial about everything*.

Trying to avoid any more fireworks, Murray hurried on. 'The buyer is offering a good price. He lives in north Queensland, so I'm flying the plane up and, if he likes it, I'll leave it with him and then get a commercial flight back.'

Lawrence didn't answer, but went to his safe and found the papers for the plane. Then he signed the other documents Murray had placed on the desk before pushing them across to his son. He stood up.

'If you'll both excuse me. I do have other commitments.'

Cindy rose from her chair and went into the hallway, while Murray said quietly, 'It's all for the best, Dad. For us, for all the family. We'll be okay.'

'Whatever you say, Murray.' Lawrence sounded bitter, almost as though he was about to add, 'You're the boss, son.' But Cindy was sure that Lawrence was not yet ready to relinquish the reins of Kingsley Downs entirely.

*

'How's Grandfather taking the thought of selling part of Kingsley Downs?' asked Sally in a phone conversation with her mother.

'He was really upset, and I suppose I can understand how he feels, but we just can't afford to be sentimental in times like these.'

'He must feel the world he's always known is crashing down around him. Not that it's all that easy for Dad and you, either. When will Dad fly to Queensland?'

'Tomorrow. I think he's looking forward to it, even if it's for the last time.'

*

Early next morning, Cindy drove Murray to their little airstrip. She kissed him goodbye and watched as he took off and the small dot that was the plane disappeared to the north.

Later that day, two workers arrived with heavy equipment and started ripping into the weeds and undergrowth along the creek. Cindy was sitting at her desk doing the household accounts when the phone shrilled, making her jump.

'Hello?'

'Mrs Parnell? Marcus Swift here, I'm looking to buy that plane of yours. I understood Mr Parnell was bringing it up today? I expected him to be here by now. Is there a hold-up?'

Cindy felt her heart thud in her chest. 'What! He left here early this morning. He must be there by now. How's the weather where you are? Could that be a problem?' White-faced, Cindy looked at Russell as he came into the kitchen. She put her hand over the receiver to tell him that his father's plane was missing.

Russell grasped the phone from her and quickly asked several questions.

'So you'll report that it's missing to the authorities in Queensland? We'll do the same at this end.' Russell hung up and looked at his mother grimly.

'Russell, I can't believe this. If anything happens to your father, I don't know how I'll cope,' said Cindy, choking back her tears.

'I'm sure he'll be fine, Mum,' said Russell, trying to comfort his mother. 'We can't panic yet. Mr Swift said the weather isn't great; let's just hope Dad put down somewhere to wait it out. I'll ring the civil aviation authorities; they'll know what to do.'

Cindy sat still, numbed by the thought that something might have happened to Murray.

'I'll ring Sally and Gordon and tell them what's happening, too, and I'd better tell Grandfather,' suggested Russell.

'We'll have to wait for him to get home. I saw him drive off this morning. Thanks for offering to ring Sally and Gordon, but maybe we should wait a little while and just see if . . . if your father shows up. I wouldn't want to worry them unnecessarily.'

Russell nodded, and reached for his mother's hand.

*

After Russell had made his calls, Cindy tried to ring Jo a couple of times, needing her support and reassurance, but there was no answer. Eventually, as time passed without any news, Cindy decided it was time to ring her children. They were hard calls to make, but she tried to sound positive as she broke the news to Gordon and Sally that Murray's plane was missing in Queensland. She told them to stay put till she had more news.

As the sun began to sink in the late afternoon, Cindy straightened up. 'I'm going to the big house to see your grandfather. I can't tell him that Murray is missing over the phone. That's not right. If he's not there, I'll wait until he comes.'

'Do you want me to come with you?' asked Russell.

'No, darling. One of us has to stay by the phone, in case we get a call. You can ring me at the big house if there's any news.'

In the gathering twilight, Cindy drove to the big house along the track she knew so intimately. The grand old home came into view. There were no lights on yet, and she couldn't see Lawrence's car parked out the front.

The door was unlocked, so she went inside and walked slowly through the house, unchanged since the first time she'd set foot on Kingsley Downs.

Without Mrs Flowers's presence, there was no smell of food cooking, of furniture polish or a winter fire, or the perfume of summer roses that Cindy recalled. The house was a shell, where Lawrence merely existed, living with his ghosts and memories, thought Cindy with a shiver.

She went through the house and sat on the front verandah, where they'd gathered for drinks in those early years, where Lawrence had stiffly held sway.

Had Lawrence always been like that, or was his imperious attitude an armour against his feelings, his secrets? Had he ever known, or shown, softness, pain, or guilt? Was the image he presented to the world very different from the person he truly was? wondered Cindy. No, she concluded. He was an enigma. She thought of all the years her husband had had to put up with his callous father. *My poor darling Murray. Please come home to me safely.* She closed her eyes and prayed, tears burning beneath her lids.

Suddenly a hand fell on her shoulder. Lawrence stood beside her.

'Cynthia? May I ask why you're here?' he asked coldly.

Cindy brushed her eyes, stepped away from him. 'I have to speak to you.'

'Is it necessary to invade my home? What is so important? What more do you want to harass me about?'

'Lawrence, please turn on a light.'

He moved to the lamp on the small table, his straight back outlined against the flyscreen shielding the night sky. As the small pool of yellow light flicked on, Cindy let out her breath.

'It's Murray. The plane hasn't turned up, he's overdue. There's been bad weather, so we're hoping he's put down somewhere on someone's strip or –'

Lawrence sucked in his breath. 'There's a search organised?' His voice sounded faintly strangled.

'Yes, all the authorities have been notified. We're all praying he'll turn up safe and sound.'

Lawrence jabbed an accusatory finger at Cindy. His faced was screwed up with hatred. 'This is your fault, Cynthia. He would never have been trying to sell the plane without your influence. You have pushed him into doing things against our better judgement.'

'Rubbish, Lawrence. We wouldn't be in this position if you hadn't been so damned arrogant,' snapped Cindy. She was furious. Instead of sympathy, Lawrence was laying blame.

'How dare you speak to me in that manner? I rue the day my poor son ever clapped eyes on you.' He took a step towards her. 'Why didn't you go back? Why don't you go back now! You have never fitted in here. You've caused nothing but trouble. I never wanted you here,' he shouted at her.

Rage burning through her, Cindy opened her mouth to shout back at him when the phone in the corner of the room rang. Lawrence stalked over and picked up the receiver.

'What?' he barked. He paused a moment and then looked at Cindy, his eyes narrowed. 'It's for you.'

Cindy snatched the receiver from him, desperately hoping for news of Murray.

'Mrs Parnell, I'm ringing from your place,' came the shaky voice of one of the men who had been clearing the weeds. 'We were just packing up and we've . . . we've found something. A body, well, you know, remains . . . been there some time.'

'A body?' said Cindy, frowning. 'Like a swaggie, or an old blackfellow?'

'We think it's a woman. We found a gold watch and a wedding ring.'

Cindy felt her heart hammer and a roaring started in her ears.

'Call the police,' she said, her eyes swivelling to Lawrence. 'Call them right now. Tell them to go to the big house. Tell them they need to speak to Lawrence Parnell. That a skeleton has been found.'

For a second, everything around Cindy seemed to happen in slow motion . . . Lawrence's expression, the phone falling from her hand . . .

But then, as Lawrence let out an animal noise and suddenly lunged towards her, Cindy snapped to life, lurching forward, skidding on the floor as she slid from his reach. She heard a crash behind her as she sprinted from the verandah into the darkening garden.

Stumbling, she reached the car, flinging herself inside.

She drove wildly home, sobbing, glancing frantically in her rear-vision mirror, but there was no sign of any car following her.

*

At the house, Russell was waiting for her by the front door.

'Mum! What's happened? Why get the police so urgently?' asked Russell, looking concerned as he hurried down the steps to meet her.

Cindy grabbed him, trying to get her breath. She held his arm tightly as they went into the kitchen, where the workers were drinking tea. They both jumped to their feet.

'Sorry this has happened,' said the older man. 'It gave us a fright. Thought it was an old Aboriginal, until my mate saw these. We thought we'd better let you know.' He fished in his pocket and placed a ring and a watch on the kitchen table.

Shakily, Cindy picked up the watch. It was caked in dirt and, as she started to rub it off, she caught her breath and silently handed it to Russell.

He stared at it and then slowly read aloud the words engraved on its back, '*To Rose, every minute with you is precious.*'

Russell caught his breath and put his arms around his mother. 'So now we know . . .'

Cindy slowly nodded her head.

*

Cindy sat at the table listening quietly to Russell and the two workers while they waited for the police. She tried not to think about Murray and Rose, as her emotions threatened to overwhelm her.

Finally, red and blue lights flashed up the drive. Cindy and Russell walked to the front door.

'Mrs Parnell?' The tall officer removed his hat.

'Come in.' Cindy led them to the side verandah and sat stiffly in one of the wicker chairs, Russell standing behind her, his hand on her shoulder. 'Have you had word about my husband?'

'Your husband? No. We've been over to the other house, looking for Mr Lawrence Parnell. We went through the house, but we couldn't find him in there. My constable did a bit of a search.' He cleared his throat, 'Mrs Parnell,

I am sorry to have to tell you, but unfortunately we found Lawrence Parnell dead by one of the trees in a paddock near the house,' said the police officer gravely. 'He took his own life.'

Cindy exhaled and gripped Russell's hand. She didn't know how to feel. Relieved? Angry? Shaken?

'He shot himself. Definite suicide,' said the policeman quietly. 'He left a note of sorts,' he added, shifting uncomfortably.

'What did it say?' asked Cindy.

'*It was an accident*,' the officer replied, frowning.

'Thank you,' said Cindy quietly.

The police asked her some questions and took notes, as Cindy tried to answer them calmly, but all she could think of was Murray. Was he alive? How would she tell him about Rose? About Lawrence?

The police finally finished and bid Cindy and Russell good night. Then they asked the workmen to show them where they had found Rose's body. Further investigations would begin in the morning, the police added.

'I hope your husband is okay,' they added as they left.

Cindy sat still, holding Russell's hand. Gently, she told him what she knew about Lawrence and Rose.

'I guess the truth finally came out,' said Russell in a shocked tone.

'And it was no accident, Russell,' said Cindy bitterly. 'Lawrence had been mistreating and abusing Rose for a long time. Whether he intended for her die or not, a man who's violent and abuses his wife for years is guilty of her death in my book.'

She was quiet a moment.

'We'll have to call Gordon and Sally,' said Russell finally.

'Let's wait. It's late. Maybe we'll have news in the morning,' Cindy managed to say.

*

The night hours glued together with agonising slowness. Cindy curled in a chair, the phone close by, while Russell slept fitfully in the next room.

The call came an hour after first light. Cindy flung herself onto the telephone. Russell sat beside her as Cindy listened, tears beginning to stream down her face.

'Thank you. Yes. I understand . . .'

'Mum . . . ?' Russell's face was suddenly that of a frightened little boy.

She took his hand. 'Dad's alive. They found the plane. He crash-landed in a paddock near Charters Towers. He's got a broken leg, they think, but he'll be okay. He's being driven to hospital. I have to ring Sally and Gordon right away.'

'You do that, Mum. I'll make us both a cup of tea.' Russell gave her a quick hug and went to the kitchen.

Cindy slumped back in her chair and burst into tears, the emotion of the past twenty-four hours flooding over her. Murray was alive. That was all that mattered now.

*

Cindy sat quietly in the Sundowner Room, gazing out at her favourite scene, though now the dark shapes of cattle had started to replace the grey smudges of the Merinos.

In the far reaches of the house, she could hear the subdued voices of her family. Cindy was so pleased that Marie's family had remained close, though it had been a while since they'd come to Kingsley Downs.

Shortly after Lawrence's death, there had been a quiet, private service for him and his ashes had been scattered over Kingsley Downs.

Now that Murray alone controlled the property's finances, he and Cindy had quickly begun to put things in order to try to salvage what they could. It was decided that, since fat lambs could be successfully raised on Mirooball

Station, Gordon would stay on there and see if he could make a go of it, rather than leasing the place straight away. Murray had to admit that his father's investment might not have been such a poor one after all. Gordon had also told his parents that he'd met a nice Bathurst girl, and was in no hurry to return home.

Kingsley Downs was to be divided up and, to Murray's surprise, they were offered an impressive sum for the block which included the big house, because it was an historic home. Cindy was relieved, not just because the sale would reduce their debt, but because she could never see herself, or Murray, living in a house with such a sad history. On their section, the beef cattle which had replaced the Merinos were profitable and were proving to be less trouble.

She heard a footfall and without turning Cindy gathered her handbag and pashmina. She wore a slim black dress, but had added a gold brooch which pinned a fresh yellow rosebud to her shoulder, plucked from Rose's garden.

'Do I pass muster?'

'Always.'

Murray, leaning on a cane to support his mending leg, smiled. 'You're a very beautiful woman. Inside and out. I love you, Cin.'

She went to him and kissed him lightly. 'I'm the lucky one. Are you ready for this?'

'I'm ready.'

She took his arm. 'Lean on me.'

*

The Anglican Church in Yamboola had been one of the first buildings Cindy had noticed when she'd arrived in the small town. It had seemed quaint and old-fashioned, although it met the needs of its country congregation. It was a small white wooden building with a green tin roof where good people worshipped, prayed for rain and shared the vicissitudes of a rural existence, facing the universal joys and sadness of birth, marriage and death.

They had expected a modest gathering for Rose's funeral service, but to Murray's surprise the church was overflowing.

'So many people! Most didn't know her,' he exclaimed softly to Cindy as they entered the little church.

'They're here for you, darling. To show their respect and support.'

It was a gathering of ordinary people: resilient, brave, humble and practical. These were people who weathered the storms of life with humour and stoicism, who often kept to themselves, but were always first to help family, friend, or neighbour.

As Murray made his way into the church, he was slowed by warm greetings from people he had known most of his life. Mrs Flowers put her arms around Murray and held him for a long moment. The Flowerses had been shocked and shaken by the revelations about their long-time employers. Moving away from Mrs F, Murray nodded his head as he passed row after row of friends and well-wishers. Neighbours like the Jacksons, friends like Jo and Donald, business and professional people who'd dealt with the Parnells over the years, old school friends, football teammates and their families surrounded him.

For a moment, Murray gazed about the church at those who'd come to pay their respects to his mother, Rose Parnell. Then he sat beside his wife and the minister began the service.

Cindy listened to his comforting words, but couldn't help reflecting on what Lawrence had done.

The site where Rose's remains had been found had been meticulously cleared and a small suitcase filled with a few of Rose's clothes and an empty handbag had been found buried there as well. Cindy remained puzzled as to how Rose's car had been left on the Deniliquin Road.

Murray thought about it and said, 'He must have come home early and then gone to the pub later on. And really, the car was only about six or seven miles from the house. Dad could have driven it up there, abandoned it and walked back home in the dark.'

After the service, Murray and Cindy stood at the church door with the Reverend Peters, thanking each person as they left and headed towards the morning tea set out in the School of Arts hall.

Reverend Peters excused himself to change and join them at the morning tea.

'Can you walk up the road okay?' Cindy asked her husband.

'Let's just sit a minute,' suggested Murray, pointing to the wooden bench beneath the jacaranda tree at the side of the little church.

He sat stiffly, rested his cane against the bench and put his arm around Cindy's shoulders.

They were silent a moment.

'What're you thinking?' prompted Cindy.

'That you were just a girl when I found you in Palm Springs. As fresh and bubbly and sweet as springwater.'

He looked into her face and Cindy caught her breath at the tender expression in his eyes. 'Did you ever have regrets? Did you ever want to change things?' he asked her quietly.

'Never. Ever,' she said firmly. 'Not ever.'

His expression changed and he looked away from Cindy. He closed his eyes and a tear slid down his cheek.

Cindy took his hand, and finally Murray said the words she knew would eventually heal his heart.

'She never left. She never left me, Cin. She stayed. Because of me. I know it.'

Cindy reached for him and held her husband while he wept. He cried for the years he'd lived without his mother. The years of hurt thinking she'd left him because she didn't love him enough. Knowing now that his life had been filled with lies, told by his father.

'It's over, darling.'

It was a wound that would heal, Cindy thought. *I'll make sure of that*. But there'd always be a scar. Cindy sighed inwardly. Gently, she wiped away Murray's tears and she kissed him.

Cindy held her husband's arm as they walked slowly through the shady trees that divided the main street; friendly faces smiled as they passed. The open-hearted landscape stretched into the distance no longer feeling strange or small or different. The journey she'd started, what seemed so long ago, and so far away, had come to end where she knew she was meant to be. Her home.